WARRIOR, WAYFARER

ROBERT P MILLER

ISBN: 1456579614
ISBN-13: 9781456579616
Library of Congress Control Number: 2011901832

ACKNOWLEDGEMENTS

Adrenaline locks important events in the memory, while details of the distant past slip away. Two former Army officers were especially helpful in sorting out the frenetic activity of Engineer Officer Candidate School in 1969.

COL William D. Ridgely AUS Ret., a contemporary of mine in training and in Vietnam, offered valuable suggestions in his critique of my manuscript.

Mr. Gustav J. Person, Installation Historian, Fort Belvoir, Virginia, provided documents and timely responses to my requests.

My gratitude goes to them for their assistance and kind encouragement. I am also indebted to COL Charles R. Houston USAR Ret., and Mr. Edward N. Johnson for their review and support of my original manuscript.

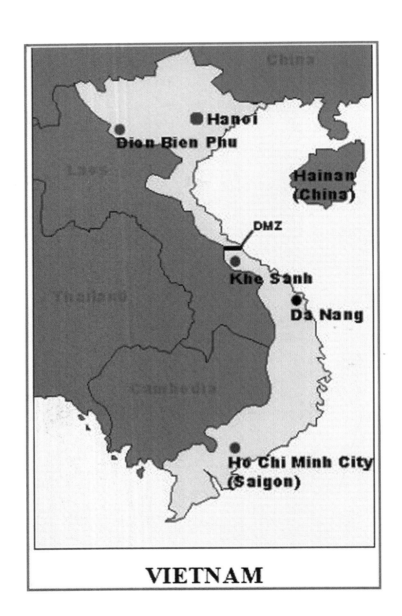

VIETNAM

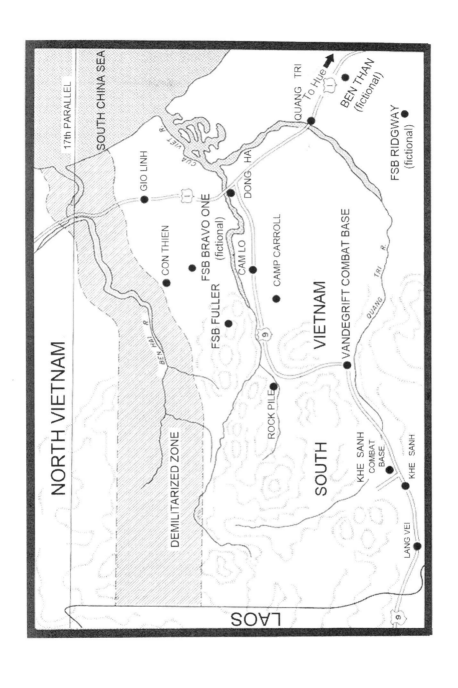

FOREWORD

What was the war in Vietnam really like for the Americans engaged in it? Award-winning films exemplified by *Apocalypse Now* and *The Deer Hunter* shaped the popular image of the war. The former was all about Joseph Conrad's *Heart of Darkness*, not Vietnam, and the latter revealed a psychological truth but little about Vietnam. After seeing *Platoon*, Bob Hope remarked that he had no idea that the war had been that terrible. Hope had been to Vietnam many times to entertain the troops, and he had been right before he saw the movie. The overwhelming majority of servicemen in the war were support troops performing necessary jobs in sealed-off base camps. War for them was far more boring than terrible.

What, then, was it like for the grunts in the field? It was humping, filling sandbags, stringing wire, humping, fighting to stay awake on guard duty, cleaning weapons, humping, fatigue, abject terror, living like pigs, being rotated out of the field and into monotony. It is the "abject terror" part that plays in movie houses and predominates in novels. That is not to compare the two. The best fiction is far more expansive and authentic than the best films. Yet even the finest narratives on the experience of war are glimpses in space and time. For the war was fought by Americans in force from 1965 to 1972 and in terrain ranging from the uninhabited, triple-canopy jungle of the Annamite Mountains of the far north to the highly populated south, the water courses of the Mekong Delta. Besides the military occupational specialty (MOS) and the when and where, a serviceperson's experience was influenced by the quality of the chain of command. So no narrative and certainly no movie can answer the question of what the war was really like. It had too much flux and too many faces.

Warrior, Wayfarer is historical fiction. The title suggests the making of a spiritual journey entwined and directed by war. It arrives there leisurely, through five months of training, a brief stateside assignment, and the pursuit of a woman. Adhering to the historical claim of the novel, most of the events in Officer Candidate School and in Vietnam actually occurred, many exactly as described. Fire base names and unit designations have been changed with some exceptions—Khe Sanh and the 101st Division, most conspicuously. The characters are either fictional or composites with the exception of Brig. Gen. Arthur Sweeney, who is correctly identified and accurately portrayed. In two words he distilled the essence of command.

The use of profanity in the military has a long tradition. Herman Wouk, in his classic novel *The Caine Mutiny*, chose to omit it, writing that "...billingsgate is largely monotonous and not significant, mere verbal punctuation of a sort," adding that it was annoying to some readers. Mores have fundamentally changed during succeeding generations, and most war novels of late include profanity as a voice of realism. Servicemen in Vietnam were so obscenity-proficient that they often spliced together the syllables of everyday words with it. In *Warrior, Wayfarer* it appears sparingly, lest it choke the dialogue, dull the reader's ear, and bloat the page count.

A second difference is that this work does not focus on the major combat arms—the hunters and the hunted. *Warrior, Wayfarer* follows a member of the Combat Engineers—the builders and the destroyers, and the hunted. The roads that infantry units rarely tread on were constructed and maintained by engineers. To give some perspective on casualty rates, from August 1970 through July 1971, my platoon suffered 7.7% killed in action—seven times higher than the KIA rate for the average in-country troop level for 1970-71. Many infantry platoons suffered more grievous losses, but not on average.

So a seldom seen face of war appears in the following pages. It often wears the same look of fear as its larger brothers: sometimes palpable, sometimes gnawing, sometimes imperceptible.

Note: Abbreviations and acronyms thrive in the military. Abbreviations appear in capital letters without periods (e.g., OD—olive drab, and a euphemism for the Army); acronyms appear in italicized capitals (e.g., *ARVN*—Army of the Republic of Vietnam).

For the combat engineers who built, fought, and died in the Vietnam War.

One of the many parts of Dewey Canyon II and Lam Son 719 [Feb. – Apr. 1971] which I continue to recall with professional pride and admiration was the performance of the 45th Engineer Group with its two battalions…there is probably no [other] person who participated in the operation who can really appreciate the contribution of those engineers. It was the most outstanding performance that I observed in my thirty-four years of service.

Lt. Gen. James Sutherland Jr.
CG, XXIV Corps

A seeker of purpose may light on
a foot soldier in a parsonage,
an itinerant at a way station,
a wayfarer in the wilderness.
Anonymous

PART ONE
APRIL 1969

"Gentlemen, charge your glasses and quaff a brew for the white knight of the olive drab, the guidon of the military-industrial complex, the savior of the western world—well, our asses anyway—drink!—to a year of guarding Atomic Demolitions Munitions...Christ, that's hard to say after a few beers—and oh, let's not forget to drink to the poet laureate of guard duty, John Milton, whose immortal words, 'They also serve who only stand and wait' gave worth to three centuries of CYAs—drink!—you too, Piloski, even though your ass won't be covered when you get to Nam."

Press Patrick was holding forth in the Enlisted Men's Club at Fort Leonard Wood, Missouri. He and nine of the soldiers at the table had been in their last week of training when their first sergeant asked if any of the college graduates in the company was interested in guarding nuclear land mines in West Germany for the remainder of his hitch in the Army. All had signed on with the exuberance of penning discharge papers. Now, four days following graduation from Advanced Individual Training—and four evenings of drinking canned 3.2 beer to excess—they were mired in a holding company awaiting orders.

"Just think, Piloski, had you finished your last year of college, you'd be going to Germany instead of Nam next month," said one of the ADM volunteers.

Piloski smirked and shot back: "Shit, man, you'll be freezing your ass off next winter walking circles around nuke mines. I'll be in a headquarters company in Saigon listening to the clattering of palm fronds—know why?" He raised both hands and wiggled his fingers. "Thirty-eight words per minute. These golden, nimble digits will peck their way into a desk job."

"More likely it'll be thirty-eight steps in a rice paddy, a peck from a Bouncing Betty, and that nimble digit in your mouth will be singing soprano," another volunteer offered.

1

Aware that he could not compete against the odds, Piloski changed the subject. "What do we have, two, maybe three days left until we get our orders? There must be some way getting out of pulling detail."

"Sick call?" a voice offered lamely.

"Nah, it's got to be daring," Press declared. "It's got to be something that hasn't been tried and won't raise suspicion, at least not enough to bother about." A general discussion ensued for a few minutes but was cut off abruptly by the sound of Press's fist engaging the tabletop. "God, that's it, that's it—"

"What is?" asked Wilson, a private with a knobby facial topography.

"Don't rush me, Rushmore. It's the most powerful of garrison weapons, an instrument that gives generals pause and coaxes supply sergeants into distributing rather than hoarding. It's a veritable—"

"Cut the bullshit and just tell us," Wilson demanded.

"You haven't guessed yet, Rushmore? Let me just say that this article is the cause of bed wetting in recruits and early menopause in *WACS*, it—"

"Jesus, Patrick, spare us the snake oil treatment and say it in one word or less," Wilson broke in. "And don't call me 'Rushmore.'"

"Okay, in one word or less, gentlemen—the unsung hero of military bureaucracy and the sidearm of the stateside army: The *Clipboard*."

For several seconds the soldiers looked at each other with puzzled expressions. Piloski ended the silence. "You know, it might work. Sergeant Salway wasn't at formation this morning. If some of us showed up with clipboards at formation tomorrow, he might get sucked into thinking that we have a carryover detail."

Deep fissures embedded Wilson's brow. "Maybe, but Salway's a T-crosser—does everything by the book. One other thing—getting caught would probably mean being kicked out of the ADM program."

"Not if we work it right and leave some wiggle room," Press countered. "Besides, the OD has been sticking it to us for almost five months; we're in need of a little morale booster, a return tweak. What better way is there to test the power of the clipboard while having a little fun for a change. So, who's in?" Press leaned back in his chair and scrutinized the faces of the soldiers at the table. While most at least essayed the merits, Wilson's features were fractured in disapproval. "Ah, the anticlines of rejection," he blurted out to Wilson's immediate "You're full of shit, Patrick." Then he gazed at Piloski. Registered on his pudgy face were folds of assent.

"What the hell, so what if it goes bust—what are they going to do, send me to Nam?" Piloski quipped.

2

"FALL IN!" The command was crisp, almost clipped, like two quick whacks of a pile driver, its deep flat tone originating closer to the bowels than the throat. Press had anticipated the command and was moving smartly to form the third rank on his left. He was six feet tall, with tawny hair that should have been crewcut length by now but was much shorter, courtesy of a sadistic drill sergeant. He dropped his left arm after the line was dressed and stood at attention. His straight stance belied his character, for inside was a zigzag of competing directions: cold reasoning and warm sentiment, a latent seriousness and active lightheartedness, the theory of morality and the practice of deceit. His eyes, fastened on the man in front, were his most distinctive feature, a luminous blue that seemed to radiate light. They gave away nothing as soldiers in the 159th Holding Company stood ready to take on some of the most unsavory details on post.

Press and Piloski knew something about the sergeant standing before them. Cardboard-starched fatigues, spit-slavered boots, and batter-post bearing hinted at the lack of gray in Sergeant First Class Edwin R. Salway's world.

"Answer up when I call your name," boomed Sfc. Salway. Forty-six names followed, most pronounced correctly. When Press's and Piloski's opportunity came to answer up, both barked "Here, Sergeant!" as if they had been honor graduates of drill sergeant school. Their responses, a half octave lower than most, induced an appreciative flicker in Salway's normally stony eyes.

Salway began to apportion men methodically, rank by rank; first, to the sorting of field jackets and fatigues at the Reception Center; next, to the *edible* garbage pig farm detail—garbage was separated at the mess hall into 1) inedible, which went to the landfill, and 2) edible, which was sold to area pig farms—Night Infiltration Range raking, and Enlisted Men's Club cleanup. Press and Piloski were next, standing stiffly erect, clipboards grasped tightly in left hand, mid-thigh level. Were there a regulation for proper placement of clipboard while at attention, the two civilians camouflaged as soldiers intuitively conformed to it.

The critical juncture now arrived. As Salway finished the paperwork on the last detail, he lifted his gaze from the clipboard cradled in the crook of his left arm and enveloped the clipboards in the third rank. His crystalline-structured mind accepted the symmetry of the moment.

"What detail you men on?"

"Inventory, Sergeant," replied Press.

"Where?"

"Post headquarters, Sergeant. Sergeant Williams told us he'd pick us up at 0800."

Press knew that the credibility quotient rose when lies were laced with specifics. And he knew from the phone book that there were four sergeants on post named "Williams." He also counted on an observation made often during his twenty-three years: the supremacy of style. And this morning, with boots, brass, and bearing, he and Piloski reflected striking images of Sfc. Salway. No twinge of uncertainty stalled Salway's conclusion: *STRAC* soldiers could not be slackers.

Press flashed an engaging grin as formation broke, and he and Piloski, who seemed to smile with every breath, lost themselves in the glut of soldiers and vehicles. "I told you we could do it. Salway may be an English name, but he's got to have some Prussian blood."

Piloski nodded his head slowly. "I admit that was easy, but were you serious about what you suggested last night—taking on post headquarters? Seems a tad risky; why not just take the day off?"

"No challenge in it. The reason it'll work is because it's too outlandish—it's the big lie. It's worked like a charm throughout history, even in our own country. Take Senator McCarthy—Joe, not Gene—for example. He held up a piece of paper and said it was a list of fifty-seven commies in the State Department. His bluff wasn't called, partly because it was just too preposterous to think of such a prominent official lying his ass off. Of course, he had another thing going for him"—Press paused for emphasis—"the critical mass of the bluff or the lie: repetition coupled with conviction. McCarthy didn't equivocate or go about it meekly. He went on the attack at every opportunity. Look at Goebbels, who told the big lie so often and with such conviction that millions believed him. Hell, I've got an uncle who still believes half that bullshit."

"That's what makes you think we can pull it off?"

Press grinned and looked at him. Piloski was nondescript—average build, common blue eyes, an almost colorless shade of light hair, semi-attractive features—a person you might see three or four times a day and notice only because of his laminated smile. "No, it's this," Press said, holding up his clipboard. "This is the magic weapon, our list of names."

It was unseasonably warm for early April. After a bleak winter of training, the two were in high spirits as they started on their mile walk to post headquarters. Skirting a field where a company of recruits was taking bayonet training, they stopped to listen to a sergeant first class introduce the last of the instructors.

"And this is Sergeant Cummings. Sergeant Cummings may look young, but he's a decorated combat veteran with twelve confirmed kills in Vietnam. Listen to Sergeant Cummings; he can teach you how to stay alive."

"Ah, the floodgates of my memory are opening wide," Press said. "Four months ago I sharpened my bayonet skills on the same field. The Army must assign all their top VC killers to bayonet training. The instructors we had were all in double digits. Certainly they'd never bullshit about something like that."

The platoons formed into three discrete circles and began to practice. "What's the spirit of the bayonet?" a drill sergeant shouted. "*To kill*," chorused the trainees.

"I can't hear you!"

"*TO KILL!*" the trainees bellowed.

The ensuing back and forth resembled the reciprocation of a motorcycle engine: gusts of obscenity stoked the intake/compression; the trainees' roar poured out of the power/exhaust stroke. Even from a distance of thirty yards, Press could see the bulging and pulsing of a blood vessel in the sergeant's neck. "Seems to like his line of work," he said, pointing his clipboard at the sergeant.

"I know this is fun for you, but while you stroll down memory lane, I'm going to stroll out of here," Piloski whispered. "Ol' Sarge is giving us the once over."

"Wait a second. That trainee over there can't quite seem to evoke the spirit of the bayonet—could be morally unfit."

"You can stay here—I'm going down the street." As Piloski moved away, two drill sergeants moved in on the silent trainee.

"Look a little menacing, trainee, your 'on guard' is attracting crows," yelled the junior sergeant.

"What's the spirit of the bayonet, trainee?" asked the senior sergeant at the top of his lungs.

"I'm sorry, sir, I—"

"Don't call me *sir*, fart brain. You call officers *sir*. Do I look that goddamn dumb?"

"No, sir—I mean sergeant."

The junior sergeant, green in the art of intimidation, chortled and grinned inanely. "Stand tall!" he snorted from behind the trainee. The older drill sergeant nudged the brim of his Smokey the Bear hat upward and thrust his sneering face within two inches of the trainee's. "Now suppose you tell me, fish breath, why you can't get the spirit?"

5

"Because I don't think I can kill anybody, Sergeant. Not like that, anyway."

"Let me tell you something, peppercock. If you don't kill the enemy, he's gonna kill you and maybe your buddies. If everybody lived in your dream world, we'd lose the war."

The sergeant first class began walking toward the trainee when he changed direction and approached Press.

"What you doing here, soldier?" he asked.

"Detail, Sergeant," said Press.

"What kind of detail?" the sergeant asked, eyeing the clipboard.

"Don't know, Sergeant."

Exasperation spread over the sergeant's face. "I know we're scrapping the bottom of the barrel in recruiting, but your brain is at half-mast."

"Haven't reported yet, Sergeant. But he knows, if you want to ask him," Press said, and pointed to Piloski, who was still moving away at something short of a run.

"Beat it," the sergeant ordered, shaking his head.

Like most early-forties construction, the post headquarters' building was solid, but squat and drab, army generic. Inside the main office, six clerks labored behind manual typewriters, thumping keys at the route step of thirty-five words per minute, mostly on forms in quintuplet, thickened with carbon paper, requiring a heavy hand to produce an intelligible fifth copy.

Press and Piloski entered headquarters in long strides and swept past the row of clerk typists, stopping at the desk of Specialist Fifth Class Mason.

"Good morning, Specialist," said Press, affecting military bearing.

"Morning, men, what can I do for you?" Mason's tone was sincere and his face so devoid of bureaucratic misanthropy that, for an instant, Press felt a pang of guilt.

"Apparently QM isn't satisfied with the current replacement schedule on typewriters and has asked S-4 to conduct surveys covering a cross section of uses. We've been selected for that detail. Private Piloski here is a mechanical engineer—specialized in office machines on the outside."

"What kind of a survey?"

"Well, it's simple; all we have to do is check key compression and carriage alignment," Piloski answered.

"Nobody told me anything about a survey, although these Royals are probably as old as the post."

"Sergeant Williams told us to be here at zero eight-thirty. We thought it was all arranged. We can set up another time if that's more convenient," said Press.

"No, no, go ahead—just wait till they finish a page before you interrupt them."

Press heard a hiss, followed by a low, long expletive and looked to see Spec 4 Odoms pull out a sheaf of paper for a re-do. Before he could reload his typewriter, Press eased him out of his swivel chair, stuffed a letterhead into the carriage, and pecked the underline key across the page. After removing and rotating the page ninety degrees, he repeated the process, the second line made perpendicular to the first.

"What are you doing that for?" inquired the incredulous clerk.

"Linear progression analysis," Press answered, holding up the specimen for a cursory inspection before clamping it to his clipboard. "The test is probably some by-product of a joint government-university project."

"Why are you using a letterhead?" another clerk asked Piloski.

"Weight—the test requires standard letterhead weight."

After they completed their bogus tests, Press told one of the clerks that he would be receiving a new typewriter in two weeks, one of the latest electric models. He and Piloski then walked to Mason's desk. "As long as I'm here, I might as well check on the status of my orders," Press said. "I'm scheduled for atomic demolitions duty in Germany."

"So you're part of that ADM group," Mason said. "You're lucky as hell— most guys are going straight to Nam. I can tell you that your orders haven't been cut—in fact, Major Dedson has the files for your group. He should be back any minute, and he may want to see you; just have a seat."

"I'm going to the next office," Piloski said, retreating to a door.

"You won't have to wait after all, Patrick; that's Major Dedson coming in."

Press turned to see an officer of medium height enter the office. He had carbon black hair, gray-flecked around the ears, which were small and close against the sides of his head. Lacking a single coarse feature, he projected an urbane and aristocratic image. Had he been clad in charcoal gray rather than army green, most people would assume that he belonged to a profession more benign and lucrative. Yet the row of combat ribbons trussed on his chest belied his image. As the major approached, his most pronounced feature came into focus. His eyes were a grave, smoky gray and seemed to convey a hypnotic power.

"This man is in the ADM contingent, sir, Mason offered. While he was here on a detail, he inquired about his orders."

Major Dedson smiled broadly, but his eyes, unalloyed with the warmth of his expression, fastened on Press with a disturbing penetration. Standing at an uncomfortable attention, subconsciously sealing his thoughts from encroachment, and still callow in military etiquette, Press wondered if the circumstance called for a salute. He did nothing.

"Private Patrick," the major read from his nametag. "Step into my office. I'll be in directly." Three uncomfortable minutes for Press later, he entered his office and said, "I'm glad you came in. I was going to summon you this afternoon." Scanning some files, he quickly drew one. After perusing it briefly, he pursed his lips and gestured toward a chair. "You probably feel fortunate with your ADM assignment and, incidentally, you should have your orders Thursday, but for the life of me, I don't understand why we select college graduates, especially those with a master's degree, to pull eighteen months of guard duty. We should be tapping soldiers who will concentrate on the task at hand. Your mind will be wandering all over the place, Patrick."

Press's antennae picked up a disconcerting signal as Major Dedson continued. "Your 201 file shows excellent test scores, high aptitude and a bent for leadership. You passed the OCS exam with superior grades." He leaned forward and said with obvious sincerity, "More than ever before we need junior officers with the suppleness of mind to react quickly—to break, sometimes, with rigid military orthodoxy, especially in Vietnam. You see, Vietnam is a company and platoon-level war. The platoon leader has more responsibility and more decision-making capability than perhaps any time in our history. Your record shows that you possess the native ability for making the decisions expected of first-rate officers. I can offer you that opportunity. Because of the meningitis outbreak at Fort Polk, I've been given several additional selections for classes at the Officer Candidate School at Fort Belvoir, Virginia. How do you feel about becoming an officer?" The major sat back and waited impassively through a long silence.

Press, his tongue no longer spry, finally spoke. "Well, sir, I feel that this is one helluva decision, and I would like to think about it."

"In combat, Private Patrick, life and death decisions are often made instantaneously—most, viscerally. Some decisions, as important as this one, just seem right or wrong, and months of thinking about it won't change the initial instinctive reaction."

"The part you said about life and death decisions, sir, that's what concerns me—what if it's death?"

"Of course, if you go to Vietnam, there's a chance you could get killed, but it's a dead certainty that boredom will kill you every day you're on guard duty in Germany."

"That may be true, sir, but getting killed by boredom is a little less permanent than getting killed by gunfire," Press said, regaining his composure.

The major smiled and after a pause his expression changed. "I can assure you of this much: if you go on guard duty in Germany, you'll hate the tedium and will return with the debris of squandered time; if you go to OCS and on to Vietnam, the experience will unlock you."

Press was struck by the sincerity in the major's voice and discomfited by his gaze.

An instant later Dedson was back to business. "I have to fill the openings by Thursday morning, and although I've plenty of applicants, I want to select the most qualified personnel. Tell you what—think about it for a day—I'm sure they don't have anything too taxing for you to do. Come in no later than tomorrow morning if you decide on OCS."

Press and Piloski spoke little as they walked to the PX for a snack. They sat outside so they could warm themselves in the sun. Press was very much a person of place. His spirits rose with the thermometer. An ideal day was eighty degrees, a few puffs of clouds to lend contrast to an expanse of blue, and a breeze that lolled amiably, spreading the mixed fragrances of early spring.

He pointed to a manila folder in Piloski's hand. "Looks like you picked up some reading material at headquarters."

"Oh, these," Piloski said, displaying his pneumatic smile. "I told one of the paper pushers that I would like to have a job like his when I got to Nam. You know, I think he was flattered, and he told me that if I became familiar with some of the more frequently used forms, I'd have it knocked. He fixed me up with about fifteen of them, so that when I get to Nam I'll rattle off a string of numbers and tell them that I worked with the forms while on details at post headquarters." While Press grinned in admiration, Piloski inquired if he was interested in Dedson's offer.

"No way," said Press. "But he had a penetrating look, and I can't help but feel that he sniffed out our phony detail. Anyway, he probably thought that since I took the OCS test, he had me in the bag."

"Why did you take it?"

"It was between the test and the likelihood of an outside detail in cold rain. Besides, I was curious and wanted to see how I would do. If I were as bright as Dedson says, I would've beat the draft in the first place."

"Did you try?"

Press thought for a moment. "I procrastinated, I guess. I didn't try the guard or reserves until three months before finishing grad school, and by then Illinois had a waiting list. I got my draft notice just as Humphrey was closing the gap on Nixon. I could see that glimmer of light at the end of Westmoreland's tunnel. We'd be released at the end of the war, which, by my calculation, would be about six months from now. Nixon's been in office over two months and do you think we'd hear something about his secret plan to end the war? Come to think of it, *he* certainly lied with conviction."

No other event keeps the cadence of army life quite like the morning formation. The ritual is bedrock for discipline, accountability, and communication. Salway eyed the two privates standing at field manual attention in the third rank. They had been on a special inventory detail yesterday, carrying clipboards. They were carrying clipboards this morning. He needed no syllogism to make up his mind. The three core conditions were met; there was no need for questions.

Formation broke. The excitement of performing a phony detail had waned, so Press and Piloski decided to spend the day reading magazines at the post library. In the evening they went to the EM Club and drank a fair quantity of Carling's Black Label beer. Press learned that Wilson and Ortiz, two other ADM bound privates, had been offered a chance to attend Officer Candidate School. Like Press, they had turned down Major Dedson's offer.

Early next morning Press woke with a dull pain in the back of his head, yet he was comforted by the thought that it was Thursday, and he would receive his orders soon. On his way to formation, he watched as a basic combat training company marched along an adjacent street. A sergeant was keeping cadence:

A little bird...with a yellow bill
Sat upon...my window sill
I coaxed him in...with a piece of bread
And then I crushed his...fucking head
Sound Off
[Chorus]: One, two
Sound off
[Chorus]: Three, four
Bring it on down

[Chorus]: One, two, three, four…one, two…three, four!

Arriving for formation, he thought of what he wanted to see in Germany, until his concentration was snapped by the cold rap of Salway's terse command: "FALL IN!" Standing tall as soldiers formed in the customary calibration of Army life, Salway's fatigues had the stiffness of sheet metal, his brass the brilliance of sunburst, his boots the sheen of obsidian. Salway exuded *command presence.*

Hoisting his clipboard gut level, he began reading the roster in basso profundo. The troops provided contrapuntal, often in much higher register. Press stood in a semi-slouch, usually the position of the hour-long, character building attention-stand: one knee bent, listing alternately front and rear, right and left. Far from *STRAC,* he sported scuffed boots, smudged brass, and wrinkled fatigues.

"Oliviera, Samuel."

"Here, Sergeant."

"Preston, Patrick."

"That's Patrick, Preston, Sergeant," corrected Press for the first time in six roll calls.

Salway sent a chilling look Press's way and continued the roll call. He then began parceling off soldiers to the usual duties. The pig farm detail was generously stocked, thanks to Wednesday's nutritional menu, highlighted by cream chipped beef and the monthly appearance of stewed prunes. Salway dismissed the soldiers with assignments and told the ADM group to step forward. He began to pass out orders with almost deliberate slowness. After six soldiers were given orders, Press could see that only one remained in Salway's hand. He felt an uneasiness in his stomach as the seventh order was doled out. He, Wilson, and Ortiz remained.

A smirk appeared on Salway's normally impassive face as he addressed the three privates. "DOD revised the ADM allocation yesterday. The new allocation is for seven. Your asses are going to Nam." His smirk began to curdle and almost as an aside, he continued: "There's a note here from Major Dedson. It says that if any of the three of you want to see him about anything, come to his office before 1000 hours."

"But Sergeant, that's not fair," Press blurted out.

"You got a personal problem? See a chaplain," Salway said, and he turned and walked off.

2

It was one-thirty on Friday afternoon when Press stepped off the plane at Washington National Airport. Normally, he was not one to question his judgment, but since Thursday morning he had thought of nothing other than his decision to attend OCS. All three had opted for it, despite assurances from several Vietnam returnees at Fort Leonard Wood that college graduates serving in Vietnam invariably landed administrative jobs. The winning argument was that that if you kept extending your departure date, the war would end before your turn came.

Limousine service to Fort Belvoir was not direct, but Press did not mind. The limo wove down the George Washington Parkway to Alexandria, where it deposited a couple at the Old Colony Inn, a brown brick colonial-style building. The limo's route took him past Mt. Vernon, where he had visited when he was eleven years old. With no memory of the Potomac River valley having such serene beauty, seeing it as only a water course, he now looked on a body of history and was taken with its wide sprawl and stately pace south.

Fort Belvoir was an open post, split into halves by US Route 1. Press could see soldiers running in formation on an oval track as the limo turned off. He got out near an arch which had the inscription on its masthead: Through These Portals Pass the Leaders of Men. And below: Engineer Officer Candidate Regiment.

At the reception building, he was confirmed for the class beginning in ten days. "Tough draw," the clerk told him. "You got India Company—low crawlin' India. Here's a map with the building numbers. You'll be in number 1856 until your class starts. Indoctrination begins Monday. You got a pass till 1900 hours Sunday."

Press left headquarters and started along a gravel street, noting several printed exhortations to "Follow Me." The barracks were World II style—two story wood, painted white with maroon roofs. The narrow, mostly traffic-less streets were tree-lined, and the whole presented an agreeable view: on the upper tier the contrasting colors of leafs and shingles; on the lower the whites of limestone and wood. The only feature to mar the pleasant setting was an occasional dumpster. Press stopped to watch a garbage truck equipped with large forks jutting out of the front attack one of the blue bins at his corner. As the truck's engine and hydraulic system screamed, the dumpster was thrust high in the air, lids flopping, and then waving, the last a signal of surrender, and its contents fell to the truck's belly. In seconds the dumpster was back down, holding its ground at the intersection. Just after the truck moved off, two platoons of candidates marched by, singing "California Dreamin'." The second platoon sung a stanza behind the first, and Press marveled at their harmony and coordination. He whistled the tune as he walked to his barracks, trying to free himself of the sound of moments earlier. After selecting a bunk, he changed into civilian clothes, stored his gear in a footlocker, and left to catch a bus for Washington, DC.

Before leaving Ft. Leonard Wood, he had phoned a college friend, Roger Schwartz, who lived in Rockville, Maryland. Roger invited him to dinner on Saturday and gave him the address of his girlfriend's apartment in Arlington, Virginia. He assured Press that they had planned to have dinner there and one more person would not be a problem.

The view as he crossed into Washington was splendid. Press had heard that the Cherry Blossom Festival was in progress, and he spent what remained of the afternoon walking around the Tidal Basin, feeling for a change the full magnitude of freedom his surroundings embodied. He walked for a few minutes with a tour group and learned that the more than 3,000 cherry trees began with 500 saplings presented by Japan in 1912 as a symbol of peace. Many of the original trees were still in blossom, exceeding a life expectancy of forty-seven years, and were now presiding over their fourth war.

At six he took a bus to Georgetown. He had heard of a popular night spot called "1789," and was able to find it straight-off. As he walked downstairs, he encountered an outsized World War One era poster of Uncle Sam, finger pointing directly at him, captioned: "I WANT YOU."

"You got me," Press said to the poster.

After eating a cheeseburger, sans onions, which he loved but gave up in order to improve prospects, he placed himself strategically at the bar next to three young women, two comely and one large-boned and plain. They looked to be his age. They were discussing a movie that he had seen, and within minutes he joined their conversation with what he thought was an astute observation on the plot.

The large-boned one listened for a few seconds, then said, "Butt out, Marine," and gave him a wanton flounce of her hips.

"Marine? You cut me to the quick."

"Soldier, sailor, whatever, butt out."

"My only connection with the military is that I'm a direct descendent of Oliver Cromwell."

"Oliver who?" asked another.

"Let me introduce myself. I'm Press Patrick, private citizen."

"If you're not in the military, why's your hair so short?" asked the third, a tall brunette with a voluptuous figure.

"Oh, training—training for the world swimming championship next month in Brussels. It'll be my last competition of course. Most guys are washed up by their early twenties."

The brunette needed reassurance. "You sure you're a swimmer?" she asked.

"You probably don't recall the picture of Don Schollander on the cover of *Life Magazine* during the sixty-four Olympics. I was slightly out-of-focus in the group photo on page forty-three. Can I buy you ladies a drink? And some stuffed mushrooms—I hear they're very good here."

"I'm Allison, Allison Parker," said the brunette. "Sheila and Ellen," she said, pointing to the others sequentially.

With the drinks and mushrooms came tacit acceptance. Soon, Press and Allison began to exclude the others from their conversation. He learned that she was a secretary in a Georgetown law firm and that she loved to dance. The band started playing at nine o'clock and for the next four hours they rocked, boogied, and danced slowly. During the first several slow numbers, they kept a respectable interval; the next few brought occasional closeness. The issue of proximity was settled by midnight. Press and Allison clung to each other, each straining to find a few more square inches of contact. He had not been with a girl since Christmas leave and tried to think of a successful way of asking to spend the night with her.

The awkward moment came at closing. "Are you driving?" Press asked.

"Yes."

"What about the others?"

"Ellen has a car."

"Can I see you to your apartment?"

She hesitated for a respectable five seconds, and then took his hand.

Her apartment was an efficiency, the smallest he had ever been in. It was on the second floor of an old building and although tastefully decorated, was almost too neat for Press's comfort.

They stood for some moments face to face and then, as if neither had means of support, reached for each other. They kissed like duelers and explorers, as fierce bird-like pecks and jostling gave way to a roaming of their tongues. When they broke off Press began to unfasten the buttons on the back of her blouse.

"You've done this before," she said.

"Buttons are a piece of cake. It's the one hand bra unhooking, especially these three-prong jobs, that gives me trouble."

"You're in a position to use two hands."

"Yes, the first of many, I hope," said Press, as he brought his other hand around to facilitate matters.

Allison let her blouse and bra fall to the floor.

He held her breasts in his hands and stroked them against his stomach. "I hope I can last, but I'm horny as hell and these are perfection."

Their lovemaking was gradual and graceful as they caressed each other with hands and mouths. Ten minutes elapsed before they began in earnest. It was not long before they changed positions, Allison getting on top. Press was surprised by the sudden change of rhythm—from a sustainable pace to lusty abandon. He cupped her breasts in his hands and tried thinking of other things, but her moves were too arousing for him to wait for her. Laying there afterwards, vaguely aware of her snuggling up beside him, stroking his forearm, tenderly kissing his chest and inching up to his shoulder, he slid into sleep.

Press opened one eye and fixed it on the clock on the bedside table. Eight-thirty. He raised his sight and saw Allison, clad in a terrycloth bathrobe, making coffee. He brushed aside the covers and struggled out of bed.

"Good morning. If you get into the shower now, breakfast should be ready by the time you finish."

"This is a full-service establishment," he said after he kissed the tip of her nose and made for the bathroom. After showering, he borrowed her razor, lathered his face with soap, and shaved. He then dressed and sat at the table.

"I had a wonderful evening," she said as she scraped a skillet full of scrambled eggs on his plate.

Press looked up and smiled engagingly. "It could not have, in any measure, surpassed the time I had."

"If you don't have any plans—if you don't have to train for your swimming today, I could take you on a tour of Washington."

Press was silent for a moment and then looked Allison directly in the eyes. "I've got a confession to make. I did tell you a half-truth last night—well, not even a half-truth."

"My *perfect* breasts?"

"No, that's true. It's what I told you about being a swimmer. I'm not a swimmer, at least in competition. And I'm not a private citizen. I'm a private in the Army. My haircut is standard military issue."

A look of incomprehension, which quickly became rage, spread across Allison's face. "You bastard. Oh, my God. Get out, you bastard. Get out! Get out! My God, you're nothing but a liar, and I thought you were *somebody*."

"Look, Allison, I'm very sorry, but everything else I told you was the truth. I had no intention of lying to you for the long term. It was just a matter of expediency. We couldn't meet on normal terms. Had I told you I was in the Army, our relationship would have gone nowhere."

"That's just where it's going—nowhere."

"But Allison—"

"Get out this instant, *now*, you bastard!"

"Before I go let me ask you—am I being kicked out because I lied or because I'm in the Army?"

"Both!" she exclaimed.

Press walked to the door and turned. "I'm sorry for the lie, but I couldn't do anything about the Army. Goodbye, Allison." After he closed the door he heard sobbing on the other side. "Damn," he said, and descended the staircase slowly.

Press spent the later morning hours at the National Gallery of Art. The French Impressionists appealed to him most with their unfettered rhythmic strokes seemingly splashed on a prism rather than a canvass, faces brushed *con brio*, landscapes vibrant with flung paint, an agreeable compromise between the orthodoxy of realism and the anarchy of abstraction. He dawdled through eight rooms and became hungry. Just before leaving he took ten dollars from his wallet and purchased a reprint of Monet and one of Pissarro.

It was a little after one when he arrived at a hot dog kiosk at 4th and Constitution and bought a chili dog. As he took his first bite, he noticed a middle-aged black man with no legs sitting in a wheelchair near a fence, selling thick, octagonal, foot-long souvenir pencils. After taking a second bite, he strolled over to the man and in a characteristically brash manner asked him how he had lost his legs.

"Korea. Fifty-one. Anti-personnel mine."

"How long had you been there?"

"A year. Went in on the Inchon landing."

"What was your specialty?"

"Combat infantryman."

"You want a hot dog?"

"Already had lunch."

"I could use a couple of pencils," Press said, giving the man two dollars.

The man gave Press the pencils and then asked, "Which service you in?"

"Does it show?"

"Basic training cut."

Press rubbed the stubble on his head. "Army, stationed at Belvoir."

"You're lucky, best post in the States."

"I start OCS the week after next."

"Okay, you're not so lucky."

Press laughed and was about to walk away when he noticed five military decorations stitched onto the man's jacket, which was folded over the right arm of his wheelchair. He recognized the good conduct ribbon and assumed the others were commendation and Korean campaign ribbons. What he did not see piqued his interest. Lingering for a few moments, he let his curiosity overcome his sense of propriety. "I couldn't help but notice your ribbons, and I was wondering why the Purple Heart is not among them?"

The man, who would have been handsome were not for a pockmarked complexion, began to shake his head. He said nothing.

"I'm sorry; I had no right to ask." Press turned to go.

The man held up his hand. "I almost talked myself into believin' it. Truth is I went through the war without a scratch, and I earned these medals—all of 'em. When I got out I got a job as a trolley car operator here in DC. One night in fifty-five I had three teenage boys in the car, ridin' for the fun of it. When we got to the end of the line, I went out behind the car to take a leak. One of the boys started playin' with the controls and threw it in reverse. Damn car ran over me. Happened two years after I got out of the service. I shoulda lost 'em in Korea."

Press nodded. "Look, I'm going to be taking a lot of notes in the next few months, so I might as well stockpile some pencils," he said, taking a five dollar bill from his wallet and giving it to the man. "A few more ought to see me through."

As he started to walk away, the veteran said, "Imagine gettin' it from a trolley car while takin' a whiz. It shoulda been a mine."

Press hopped out of the taxi in Arlington, checked again that the address he had written down matched the number on the apartment building, and paid the driver. He was a few minutes early and rather than risk upsetting Roger's girlfriend, decided to stroll along the tree-lined street for a few minutes. Despite the demoralizing rejection in the morning, his mood was upbeat. The memories of confinement and petty harassment of the past few months receded in the present reality of freedom in a pleasant place. Sure, he would soon be confined again and the hazing would be far worse, but it would also keep him stateside for more than a year.

He entered the three-story brick building promptly at six o'clock and climbed the steps to the third floor. A few seconds after he knocked, the door was opened by a lanky, good-looking young man with longish, wavy dark hair.

"Press!" he exclaimed. "Welcome! Com'on in. How military of you—on time for the first time since I've known you."

"Good to see you, Roger. It's been way too long," Press said as he handed him a bottle of wine. "I can see you've had no hand in decorating the apartment; it looks great."

"Quite true, my friend. Come into the kitchen and meet Lynn. She shares the apartment with another student. As I recall, you could knock down heaps of Lasagna. Lynn, here's our guest—another reprobate from Chi-town."

Roger introduced them. Lynn was a first-year George Washington University law student from Iowa. Press soon learned that she had an easy manner and could with alacrity carry on a conversation while preparing a meal. While her features at rest were attractive, her expressions were kinetic, elfin, appealing.

After fifteen minutes of free-for-all conversation, Press said, "You're going to make a very good trial lawyer, Lynn."

"What makes you think I want to be a trial lawyer?"

"Because of comparative advantage: when you're presenting your case, the judge and jury won't succumb to distractions or be subjected to boredom."

"Here, here," affirmed Roger. "I've been telling you that for eight months."

"You both exaggerate," Lynn scolded.

"Not I," Press said. "You have more faces than Mr. Potato Head and all are alluring."

"Thank you for the second part. My nickname in grade school was Red, after Red Skelton—not flattering, and I've none of his comedic genius."

Roger went over to her and kissed her on the cheek, while Press wandered into the living room and stood at the bay window looking out. In a voice loud enough to carry to the kitchen, he said, "I've never seen so many trees crowded into one city block. You've got the best of both worlds: shade in the summer and sunshine in the winter."

"And hundreds of autumn leaves that blow into your car when you open the door."

Press turned quickly on hearing this new voice. Nearly always ready with a rejoinder, he was silent, caught in an optical double-take, as he looked at her. Never had he seen anyone so appealing. He was taken straightaway with her large, gleaming, chestnut-colored eyes—eyes embossed with intelligence, able, he was sure, to espy hidden thoughts. Only slightly less alluring was shoulder-length hair the shade of milk chocolate, and skin so clear and lustrous that he imagined it buffed by a jeweler's cloth.

"Have you ever seen such ogling before?" Roger joked, standing next to the kitchen doorway.

"He does look a little frisky," Lynn agreed from just inside the kitchen.

"I'm sorry—I was taken by surprise. I'm Press Patrick."

"Celia Halley, Lynn's roommate."

Lynn slid past Roger and said, "Why Press, I believe you're blushing."

"It's the klieg lights I'm under...okay, I'll confess: I always blush in the presence of beautiful women. And Roger didn't warn me—never let on that the apartment housed *two* very attractive females."

"I can see why you and Roger are friends," Celia said.

"Press and I went to college together, but as you can see from his haircut, he's fallen on hard times and now works for Uncle Sam." Turning to Press Roger continued, "Celia is a first year grad student at GW. You two ought to get on well together, both being poly-sci mongers."

"Is that like in *fish* mongers, Roger?" Celia asked.

"Oh, no, no. I would be the last to equate an honorable trade with the study of politics."

"Roger hasn't changed at all. If he can't quantify it— that means divisible by a whole number—it's no good," said Press.

"That's because of those required liberal arts courses taught by speciously brilliant professors," Roger countered.

Celia's nose made a slight zigzag. "Okay, I'll bite. *Speciously* brilliant?"

"Yeah. Their lectures sound great to a cursory ear, but on reflection you can't find a damn thing to grab hold of."

"When's Jim picking you up?" Lynn asked Celia from the kitchen.

"He's not. The dean has a touch of the flu, so he's filling in for him in Houston."

"Sorry to hear it, but we can salvage some of the evening. I'll set another place."

"Please don't bother. I can fend for myself."

"No bother at all. And I'm sure Press won't mind."

"Mind? I insist on it—with your permission, Lynn."

"Now that that's settled—Roger, why don't you open Press's thoughtful gift and we'll toast to his eventual reemergence as a civilian."

After the bottle was uncorked and the toast given, Lynn motioned Roger with her eyes to join her in the kitchen.

Celia had appeared a little uneasy during Lynn's toast, and Press wondered if she harbored hostile feelings about the military. He decided to probe for her feelings on the subject.

"How did you become interested in political science?" he asked.

"My dad was on the school board in Seattle when I was in grade school and my mother was—still is—a volunteer for any project that came her way, so the talk at the dinner table centered around politics. I guess it became second nature. How did you get taken in?"

"Like you, it was at the dinner table. My dad teaches economics, a disciple of Friedman, and we had a constant parade of people through the house— faculty and grad students mostly. I'm an only child, and my parents wove me into the give and take of adult discourse early. You wouldn't believe how economists can haggle. I remember one hypothetical argument about the economies of scale in a world where people had an average height of two feet. It went on for two hours, an hour per foot. They argued about politics as much as economics, entwined as they are, although always deriding politics as a less exact discipline, and an inferior one. Are you non-partisan or do you lean one way or another?"

"I have no affiliation. I'm independent to the bone."

"Not necessarily a party affiliation, but on issues. For example, most everybody remotely connected with a university is against the war."

Celia's face hardened. "I hate the war."

"I'm not very fond of it, either."

"I'd say you're in the wrong line of work."

He reddened. "I'm a draftee." Then with some aplomb, added: "*Pressed into service, you might say.*"

She rolled her eyes at his pun. "Are you stationed here?"

"I'll be at Fort Belvoir for the next five months attending Officer Candidate School." He read Celia's expression as saying, *you hypocrite.* "I know what you're thinking, but if I hadn't signed up for OCS, I'd be on the plane to Vietnam in a few weeks, and as a private I'd have little control over myself. It would be imposed by others. And by going to OCS there's an excellent chance of realizing my one animating goal in life—outlasting the war."

"What makes you think that?"

"I believe what Curtis LeMay said about war is true: 'You've got to kill people, and when you kill enough, they stop fighting.' Well, they've just about killed enough of us."

A deeply pained look spread over her face. "So now somebody else is going instead of you," she said finally.

"Sounds like we're getting into slash-and-burn repartee."

"You strike me as the sparring type."

He nodded. "I've been known to enjoy it. Tell me, do you believe in the self-determination of countries?"

"Of course. And I can see where you're taking it: the same should be true for individuals."

"Exactly," he said, and immediately changed the subject.

They conversed for a few minutes about her courses, Press learning that she was taking a light load of classes while working part-time for US Senator Henry Jackson, a Democrat from Washington.

Celia excused herself a few minutes later, saying she wanted to change for dinner, and Press joined Lynn and Roger in the kitchen. "Is this fellow Jim a casual date for Celia, or is there something more serious to it?" he asked Lynn.

"I thought you'd want to know that. My guess is more casual. He's an associate law professor and almost thirty I'd say. Nice guy, but a little too, too... reserved. Of course there is safety in reserve but little attraction."

"She certainly is vehement about the war."

"With good reason," Lynn said. "Her brother was killed at Khe Sanh last year. He was a Marine lieutenant, and they were very close—her only sibling."

"That's terrible. She didn't say; she just let me make an ass of myself. I've never been known for a fixed footing, but right now it's fixed in my mouth."

Celia returned minutes later, wearing wheat jeans and a sleeveless blouse, which accentuated her figure. She had pulled her hair back, and Press was struck again by her radiant good looks.

"Lynn just told me about your brother. I was very sorry to hear it. What I said about avoiding the war and quoting LeMay must have sounded obscene to you—at the very least cavalier. I regret it very much."

He had never been more sincere, and Celia must have sensed it, for she looked at him with a gentle expression and said, "I don't blame you. What I find obscene are body counts and body bags. Life is much too precious to be squandered so promiscuously."

Press was thankful that Lynn and Roger came in at that moment with the dinner. When they sat down to eat, the conversation turned light and humorous, and the two friends from Chicago began telling stories about one another.

"The first time we met was in a freshman history class," Roger recounted. "I didn't take much notice until the professor asked Press what the biggest difference was between people at the turn of the century and the present. After about five seconds of deliberation, he answered: 'Back then everybody wore hats; now, practically nobody does.' That broke up the class and embarrassed the professor. I knew that I had to get to know him."

"Let me give you an example of Roger in class," said Press. "We also took an astronomy course together, and one of the students was really obnoxious—a guy with a huge posterior. One day the professor was writing down something about a star's right ascension on the board, and Baby Huey stood up—right in front of Roger—and copied it in his notebook. Before he erased it, the professor asked if everyone had gotten it. 'No,' says Roger. 'What's the matter?' asked the professor, 'can't decipher my writing?' 'I can't even see your writing,' says Roger. 'It's been eclipsed—a total...lunar...eclipse.'"

They all laughed, and Roger glowed with reminiscence. The banter went on for more than an hour.

After dessert Press followed Lynn into the kitchen, ostensibly to fill his coffee cup. "This is a bit embarrassing," he began, "but I'm going to ask Celia out next week, and if Roger listens in and she tells me to fly a kite, I'd just as soon not have him rassing me about it for the next five years."

"Do you want the good news first or the bad?"

"The good—the bad will be fighting an uphill battle."

"You're getting too used to the Army. Okay, the good. It's obvious that Celia is attracted to you."

"It may be obvious to you, but not to me."

"Men are stupid that way. Some things that women discern intuitively, men can get only with a Mack truck."

"So what's the bad news?"

"I don't believe she would risk becoming emotionally involved with someone in the military."

"You don't think she would chance one date?"

"I don't think so. I saw sparks between you two at the table, and she'll not take the chance of getting electrocuted."

"Well, I've already got my finger in the socket."

Lynn made a face which epitomized his plight. "Don't worry about Roger; in fifteen minutes we'll be out for a stroll."

"Thanks, Lynn," he said with sincerity.

It was a long fifteen minutes for Press, who silently rehearsed how he would ask Celia for a date. Just as the door closed and they were gone, he turned to her. "I'm sure it's obvious to you that I put Lynn up to dragging Roger out for a walk. I didn't want him around guffawing or harrumphing when I asked you out for dinner next Saturday."

"I'm sorry, Press, I've got a date for Saturday."

"Is there a possibility that you can break it? My schedule is anything but flexible."

"Sorry, I can't."

"Think of it this way: Our lives from this moment can be divergence or intersecting—there's promise in the latter but no future in the former. Now may be our only chance."

"*Our* only chance?"

"Okay, if you insist on a singular pronoun—*my* only chance. But if *I* don't ask and *you* don't accept, then *we* may never see each other again."

"Oh, don't *you* believe in fate?"

"No, *I* believe that one date is worth a thousand fates."

Celia released the clasp on the beret holding her hair in place, wrinkled her small, straight nose and laughed.

Press changed tactics. "I know what it is: you don't like my short hair. I probably look ugly to you."

"Let's just say your hair is not a selling point."

"Think back a decade, when butches and flattops were in style."

"You mean those pushbrooms? They were the male equivalent of bangs."

"It's not a permanent condition, you know. It won't prevent me from picking up the check at some expensive DC restaurant—the kind with roving minstrels. Besides, as we get to know each other, my appearance can only improve, at least after the first half of OCS."

"The answer's still *no*."

"Of course! I'll be off Sunday afternoon. We could have a picnic. I know the perfect place, near Mount Vernon."

She hesitated for a moment before answering. "I don't think so."

"One thing that you should know about me, Celia, is that I don't give up; I'm irre*press*ible."

"You probably use that bad pun weekly."

"I'll tell you what: if you take me up on my picnic offer, and that's the last time you want to see me, I'll promise not to ask again. It's in your hands. We can sparkle like a star or melt like a snowflake."

She shook her head in disbelief and then threw her head back in an attempt to regroup the hair that had cascaded over her eyes. A mischievous grin appeared. A smile then tiptoed across her face. Press, enchanted, shuddered perceptively.

"Okay," she finally said. "A week from tomorrow at one."

3

Indoctrination week was the most enjoyable Press had spent in the Army. The seventy member class was bused all over the post for a myriad of activities, from briefings conducted in stately red brick buildings to inoculations in the old, nearly vacant dilapidated hospital. Built during World War I, the hospital was a single story grid—no body, just interconnecting wings, each sealed from the next by double doors. Hundreds had died in the sealed wards during the flu pandemic of 1918. They also went to the Post Exchange, where they each purchased two pairs of Corcoran combat boots, which, along with stitched name tags for their fatigue shirts, were considered essential accessories of an officer candidate's wardrobe.

Buck sergeant Reg Ague became the de facto leader of the OCS class. Being prior service, he lent his expertise to others on matters great and small, from the psychological mastery of OCS to the proper way of breaking in their new boots. He was never without an opinion. Often when the class rode a bus to various briefings, Ague would pick up the mike, turn the speaker system to its loudest setting, and begin a commentary on the next event. Wilson complained to Press that he was beginning to develop a monologue ear.

On Thursday afternoon Press met with Captain Arnold at battalion headquarters. It was Arnold's responsibility to choose the branch of service in which Press would receive his commission.

"Your 201 file gives a pretty clear picture of your interests and aptitude. You've had little math and no engineering in college, so I would rule out the Corps of Engineers. Everything here points to Military Intelligence."

"What kind of duty could I expect, sir?"

"Well, your first assignment would be stateside—probably background investigations like the one that would be conducted on you. Your overseas duty would most likely involve gathering and analyzing data or interrogating POWs."

"That sounds fine to me, sir," said Press.

"It's done then. The background investigation will take a minimum of seven weeks. Good luck, soldier."

By Friday enough information had permeated through the unofficial network to give the class a sobering view of what to expect on Monday. The class would be broken down into two platoons, housed in separate barracks, each administered by two tactical officers who were recent OCS graduates. They would be assisted by select members of India Company's junior class. The first eight weeks were the most abusive. Normally, candidates wishing to quit the program had to stick it out for the first seven weeks. Those judged unfit to become officers were culled from the platoon during the last half of the program, either by being first recycled to another company or by outright dismissal. The remainder would be commissioned on 26 September.

On Sunday Press caught a late morning bus to Arlington. He shopped at a deli Roger had recommended then took a cab to Celia's apartment building. When she opened the door, he said without a hint of exaggeration: "You look fantastic. I'm glad you didn't forget."

"How could I; you must have asked Lynn to remind me every few hours this weekend."

They loaded her Volkswagen Beetle and started off toward Mt. Vernon. When they were nearly two miles away, he said, "Pull over to the left about a hundred yards up."

"But there's no place to park."

"Just pull off on the shoulder."

"It's not even a park—just a long strip of grass next to the river."

"Let's call it a field expedient: park-like and certainly not crowded. In fact, it's so much like a park that no doubt someday it will be. We're merely ahead of our time."

Dubious but willing, Celia pulled off the road. They spread a blanket on the riverbank and covered one corner with French bread, assorted meats and cheeses, coleslaw, potato salad, and a bottle of Rothschild Bordeaux, which he acquired at Central Liquors in DC on Saturday.

"I had only coffee this morning in preparation," said Press.

"You must have some kind of appetite if you expect to eat even a quarter of this."

"I do. My metabolism runs like a freight train engine—I've got to keep the boiler stoked. Right now I'm starved. What would you like on your sandwich?"

"A little of everything."

"Mayo or mustard?"

"Mayo."

"Between bites, why don't you tell me more about yourself—free time stuff, like sports, for example." Press smiled in his most disarming manner.

"I play a little tennis, and I love to swim—" she paused on seeing a grin on his face, then continued, "anything wrong with that?"

"Of course not. They're two of my favorites."

"I really haven't had much time for anything in the last few years, except for study and part-time work. You haven't said much about yourself."

"I'm from a middle class enclave in Chicago: Hyde Park. I've told you that my dad is an economics professor; Mother is a violinist with the Chicago Symphony and does some guest solo playing in smaller Midwest cities. I don't remember when music didn't fill the house: either my mother practicing or Beethoven or Mozart, or someone on the phonograph. Anyway, I'm the product of an economist and a musician. Can you imagine the mismatching of my genes?"

"Music by the numbers." she said, and they laughed. "Please, continue."

"There wasn't much to do in Hyde Park, so I spent a lot of time in the college library, courtesy of my dad's employment. I'm probably one of the few people who has read *Bartlett's Familiar Quotations* cover-to-cover."

"So that's where you get your lines."

"We lived a few blocks from the Museum of Science and Industry—Chicago has great museums—and I visited so often the staff knew me."

"You didn't grow tired of it?"

"Not at all. The word 'museum' doesn't imply change, but the rest of the name does, and new exhibits and modifications appeared frequently."

Press watched Celia as she bit into her sandwich. She was wearing a maroon blouse and navy shorts. Her hair fell freely and framed her face in a manner that made Press think he had never seen anything so beautiful.

"To the important things in my life," he continued. "I'll wolf down a peanut butter and jelly sandwich at the slightest provocation, and I'll chase it with a quart of bean soup. A couple of my most endearing qualities are that I'm steadfast and rarely exaggerate."

"Do you smile all the time?" Celia asked.

"What makes you think so?"

"Your face is so smooth except for two creases that start at the corners of your mouth and reach for the sky; and two smaller ones at the corners of your eyes that crinkle when you smile—like now."

"Thank you. That wasn't just a line to keep me interested, was it?"

"You're impossible."

They laughed and he poured some wine, tasted it, and passed a cup to Celia. They drank and talked about frivolous subjects, until she asked him if he thought that the US was really winning the war and how long would it go on.

He bit his lip in a pensive manner and after a while said: "The war reminds me of something I witnessed a couple of years ago. I drove my mother to a shopping mall in Oak Brook, a Chicago suburb. I don't care for shopping, so I went to a library nearby. I had to visit the men's room and while standing there, I noticed a centipede struggling in a spider's web off to my right. The centipede was about an inch and a half long. I expected to see some giant attack spider trundle out and was shocked when a tiny one— one-hundredth of the weight of the centipede—poked his head out of a hiding place. Instead of retreating into the crack in the wall, the feisty little thing attacks. The centipede maneuvers a little and almost gets hold of the spider. But the spider is quick on his web and dances away only to return to the attack, which he does again and again along the centipede's exposed flank. The centipede constantly curls his huge body in an attempt to get at the spider and maybe to shred the web, but the effort's wearing him down. The spider backs away. I think it's a standoff, so I leave. The librarian is at her desk just outside the bathroom and she looks at me as I close the door. After a few minutes of browsing, curiosity pulls me back to the men's room. The centipede is a little farther along in the web. The spider makes another attack. The centipede is clearly tired and can hardly turn. The spider withdraws and nothing happens for a couple of minutes, so I leave for a second time. The librarian looks up again. We're the only two in the adult section. Of course after a couple of minutes I've got to return. The web is torn near the edge where the centipede is now struggling to get out. But the spider is determined and attacks once more. This time the centipede, unimpeded— sorry—whips around on the loose strands and bites the spider. The spider goes limp, crushed in the centipede's jaws. The centipede nibbles for a while and then slowly makes his way out of the web. I make my way out of the bathroom. By this time the librarian is obviously convinced that I'm a pervert. She opens her mouth to speak but I say: 'It was a great fight—a unanimous decision for the centipede.' Her jaw goes slack, thinking now that I'm crazy as well as perverted, and I steal away to the periodical room."

"That's an interesting story, but what you're saying is that we'll eventually prevail in Vietnam."

"Well, that's the conventional thinking. But remember, the centipede stumbled into the web and his heart was obviously not in the fight—not until he found himself in a struggle to the death. It's not that way for us. We stumbled into the web but can declare victory and disentangle ourselves. When we decide to leave, and we will, the North will not make the mistake of the spider, but will sit in that jungle web and wait us out. Then it will strike a much smaller and weaker victim."

"You'd think with all the sophisticated equipment the military's got, they'd be able to find them anywhere."

"It's like what Marcellus says in *Hamlet*, when a ghost appears: 'We do it wrong, being so majestical / To offer it a show of violence / For it is as the air, invulnerable / And our vain blows malicious mockery.'"

"So now you're quoting Shakespeare. What do you think the chances are of you being sent there?"

"Negligible. When I graduate from OCS, I'll have a choice of either taking what they give me or volunteering indefinitely and getting my choice of assignments or locations. It's not actually indefinite—only one year added. If I choose vol-indef, it would be two and a half years before I could be sent there. Surely the war would be over by then."

Celia said nothing, and Press was certain that she was contemplating their future or, as he feared, lack of one.

"Will you see me again?" he asked.

"You're not supposed to ask until we arrive back at my door."

"So if you decline, the joint embarrassment will be short-lived and I would give you a peck on the cheek and never see you again. I promised that if you said *no*, I would not ask you again, and I'll keep my promise." He smiled and continued, "I'm hoping that if you consider saying *no* now, the welter of embarrassment would be so great that you at the very least would hedge."

"I don't know that I'd call it a *welter* of embarrassment—a tinge perhaps," she responded.

"Oh, no, no. Seismic."

"Minuscule."

"Mountainous."

"Granular."

"Spring-tide."

"Trickle"

"Spate."

"Dollop."

"Acre-foot."

"Tuft."

Press and Celia continued to barter words: they were spontaneous, deliberative, poetic and silly; they laughed, shouted, pointed, and pondered. When they finished he smiled. It was a smile of several shadings, in equal measure buoyant and meditative, a smile reflecting the surge of emotion inside and the acceptance of feelings that had long been quiescently stowed—no, stockpiled—away. When he finally spoke, he said, "'Stay, moment, stay. You are so fair.'"

"Shakespeare again?"

"No, not Shakespeare."

She studied him for a time. "Probably something with a double meaning."

"You might say that."

"Something you're not going to tell me."

"Right again," he said with a grin. "Another time, perhaps."

"That's assuming there is another time."

"If there isn't, you'll never know the other meaning."

"Curiosity may prove to be a weak incentive."

"There's no slight, sensing, attaching allure on your part?"

"There might be some interest, but I'd like to know what you see in me that you want to see again?"

"You compose the eye, for one; I like the sound of your voice, and the way you string your words together—the turn of your mind."

She giggled. "That's all?"

"Suiting the eye and the ear is a pretty good start." On impulse he leaned forward, until their faces were inches away. He inhaled slowly and deeply then touched her cheek. "That does it," he said, withdrawing. "You please four of the senses. I'm much too shy to try for the fifth; besides, you'd knock my head off."

"I don't believe for a minute that you're shy about anything, but you're right about that."

He smiled and raised his glass to her. "To sum it up in two words or less: I'm besotted. Will you see me again?"

She lowered her eyes fractionally and said, "Yes, I would like to see you again."

Press was elated. "I can't leave Belvoir for probably eight weeks, but we have a couple of hours off for Sunday morning services. You probably haven't been asked out on many dates to go to church. Would you go to church with me—are you religious?"

"I don't go as often as I used to, but yes, I am."

"What faith?"

"Catholic."

"Catholic services are held in the big chapel, adjacent to a large parking lot. The Episcopal chapel fronts a field of green that stretches as far as the eye can reasonably see. It has a courtyard with lots of azaleas and flowers, a birdbath instead of asphalt, frosted panes of glass in huge casings, flag draped wooden tresses—all and all the type of place brides see themselves being married in." Celia blushed and Press smiled and continued: "I understand that they serve coffee and cookies following the service. As far as it being Episcopal, didn't Pope John soften the hard line about attending competing Christian services—some encyclical or papal bull or something?"

"Ecumenical Council—Vatican Two, and don't worry, I won't go to hell for going to an Episcopal service. Your approach to religion sounds a little on the self-serving side."

"Maybe, but it's a good opportunity for recruitment."

"You don't belong to a church, then?"

"I hold to what Seneca said long ago: 'Religion is regarded by the common people as true; by the wise as false, and by rulers as useful.'"

"Did you knowingly insult me, or are you obtuse?" she asked.

"I'm sorry. I spouted it out before I realized the implication."

"Don't you think it's just a little hypocritical going to church for the express purpose of a date?"

"Well, I guess I look at it as a field expedient. I would like to see you again and we've got nowhere to go except to church, and you never know, some of it might rub off on me. Let's have another glass of wine and dangle our feet in the water."

4

Monday, 21 April, was more than a transitional day for the members of OCS Class 69-39. The mental and physical assault would relegate basic training memories to a pleasant pastime. During the ceremony the new candidates pinned OCS brass onto their collars, were divided into two platoons, and met their tactical officers. Press's senior tac officer was 2nd Lt. John Holt. His platoon's junior tac officer was 2nd Lt. Brad Hausser. After the ceremony, Lt. Holt ordered the 2nd platoon outside. He drew a roster sheet from a folder and read the first name: "Candidate Ague, take command of the platoon."

"Yes, sir," Ague said and stepped to the front.

"Drop," Holt commanded. "Push out twenty." Ague fell to the ground and counted out twenty pushups. Speaking to the platoon, Holt said: "When addressing officers, senior and junior candidates, the first three words out of your mouths are, 'Sir, Candidate and your name.' Before you ask a question or make a statement, you must first ask permission." Holt looked toward the bottom of the roster: "Yoder, front and center."

"Sir, Candidate Yoder, yes, sir."

"Recover, Ague. You're the platoon leader. Yoder, you're the platoon sergeant. You will assist the platoon leader and take charge in his absence." Holt turned to the platoon: "Whenever you are in the OCS area, you will be in one of two modes of locomotion: double-time or low crawl. I prefer low crawl, but sometimes I bow to expediency. Ague, double-time the platoon back to the company area."

Ague started the platoon in double-time. Before a minute elapsed six India Company junior candidates swarmed over the platoon. Two came upon Ague, one on each side, shouting in stereo. Junior Candidate Young castigated Ague for lack of military bearing, his mouth coming indecently close to Ague's face. Junior Candidate Lansing made use of his considerable lung power while accusing Ague of having a canine ancestry. Six inches shorter than Ague, Lansing jumped with the rapidity and tenacity of a Dingo in pursuit of larger game, timing his leaps so that his most abusive barks reverberated in Ague's ear.

Ague had failed to note the route they had taken to the ceremony. He received no guidance on the return. Each time he missed a "column right" or "column left," one of the tac officers would drop him for twenty push-ups. Yoder would then take charge, and when he missed a turn and was dropped, one of the platoon members would take over until Ague or Yoder returned. The platoon could not be left leaderless.

With less than a half mile to go, Ague was dropped for a fourth infraction. As he caught up with the platoon, one of the tac officers and two junior candidates encircled him. Their medley of questions, commands, and imprecations caused his face to knead with fear. Simultaneously Ague was asked if he had mastered carry-over arithmetic, told he was too stupid to count cadence, ordered to keep his eyeballs screwed to the front, and close his mouth and breathe through his nose. Winded to the extreme, he was sorely pressed to remain abreast of the platoon.

They finally arrived in the company area, in front of their new barracks, and Holt told Ague to dismiss the platoon. Ague executed the order but not everyone took the mandated two steps to the rear. "Drop," Holt commanded. The platoon went down in the front lean and rest position. Although there is merit in the "front lean" description, the "and rest" is a cruel misnomer. It is the position of the pushup in the raised position. What is so pernicious is its interminable duration. While the order for pushups is normally accompanied with a specified number to perform, the participant in the front lean and rest has no idea of *when* he would be told to recover, there being little linkage between the offense and the punishment.

After five minutes Press began to shift weight alternately from one arm to the other. Resting one arm did little for the pain, but it relieved the stiffness. Soon he began to lower a knee, moving the fulcrum of his body to a more forgiving position as it made contact with the ground. Junior candidates prowled the ranks. Little more than ventriloquists for the tac officers, the sight of a swayed back or a bent knee sent their tonsils wailing.

They were fifteen minutes into their ordeal when Holt spoke. "I'll give you some advice. The only way to succeed in OCS is to become a team. There is no room for the individual. Understand this: cooperate and graduate...on your feet!"

The platoon recovered slowly, most candidates nursing sore joints. "Drop—not fast enough," Holt ordered. Two minutes later he gave the command to recover. Despite their soreness the candidates snapped to attention. They were dismissed, and they entered the barracks to locate their bunks. Press found that he had an upper bunk on the second floor. His bunk mate was Bill King, a twenty-four-year-old from Cleveland who gone through AIT with him at Fort Leonard Wood.

"I feel like I've been hit by a hammer," King said. "How about you?"

"Holt made a strong first impression. We'll have hell to pay if he keeps this pace for long. I hate to think of putting in twenty-three weeks of this so we can learn to cooperate."

"I think Ague is going to crack. You could see it in his eyes. He looked like he just got off the bus in the wrong city."

"He'll be AWOL before midnight," Press agreed. "I'm just glad my name doesn't start with an 'A.'"

Their conversation was cut short by a curt order to form outside. "Move! Move! Move! Move!" six junior candidates screamed, flush with authority. The platoon formed, leaderless. Ague, his face visible through the glass of the barrack's door, his expression impassive, refused to join the ranks. Holt, his inner dialogue audible with the pursing of his lips, his finger stroking a pen, waited on the company street. Press, his interest piqued by the unfolding decision, his breath now normal, flicked his eyes in Holt's direction. Hausser, his attention harnessed on eye movement, his jaw tight, spotted the tangential glance. "Drop, Candidate, push out twenty-five," he ordered.

A minute passed before Holt started to read the roll, making certain that apart from Ague all were present. When he reached "Patrick," he asked Press if the roster was correct, that his last name was Patrick and his first name was Preston.

"Sir, Candidate Patrick, yes, sir, that's correct."

Hausser broke in. "Do you want to tell us why your name's ass backward, Patrick?"

"Sir, Candidate Patrick, I was a breach birth, sir." Press regretted that he had said it before the other candidates laughed and Hausser, red-faced, dropped them all.

"OCS isn't for wise guys, Patrick. We'll see how long you last, how long the platoon will tolerate you getting them in trouble. Everybody push out twenty-five. Fifty for you, wise guy." Hausser stepped back and crossed his arms. He had thin lips and a wide, lopsided mouth, but it was the fervency in his eyes that alarmed Press.

As he did his push-ups, he looked up at the door to the barracks and saw Ague's face still framed by a square window pane. Lt. Holt's lips were no longer pursed, and Press was convinced that the tactical officer would not intercede. Ague would wash out. What would he feel? Relief, embarrassment, humiliation? Would he be able to convince himself that his action was of little moment or would he be subjecting himself to periods of self-recrimination?

"Candidate Barker, you're the new platoon leader. Take the platoon to your old barracks and pick up your gear," Holt ordered.

The platoon double-timed to their former barracks and picked up their duffel bags. Most weighed fifty pounds or more, prompting King to say to Press: "I hope they don't expect us to double-time with these."

The candidates had only seconds to secure their gear before Hausser screamed, "Out, out, out!" and decanted them from the barracks. Thirty seconds later they formed in the street. Holt walked to the front and commanded: "Drop. Low crawl to your new home."

What the hell did I get myself into, Press said to himself as he crawled along the gravel road, dragging his duffel bag, stones digging into his forearms, elbows, and knees, his lungs clawing for air to sustain his rock-ribbed rendition of a breast stroke. The platoon lacked any semblance of a formation, but the tac officers harassed only the stragglers. Press was near the middle. He looked back occasionally to see where Hausser was. The realization that Hausser would have a field day if he fell back propelled him forward. He had rarely perspired in his life, but now he was drenched. Sweat lubricated his hand and he found it increasingly difficult to maintain a grip on the strap of his duffel bag. His hunger became acute and he felt himself losing strength. The thought that Holt would certainly stop this madness at the mid-point kept him moving. A sharp stone penetrated the crazy bone of his right elbow, and he swore savagely. The inside of his left knee throbbed with pain, and when he glanced at it, he saw a spreading red stain. The platoon reached mid-point with no reprieve. Press wanted desperately to get up and walk off. Only the stigma of labeling himself a quitter made him go on. He was going to finish the low crawl, and he was going to finish OCS.

The platoon reached its barracks after twenty minutes of low crawling. The arms, legs, and underbellies of the candidates' fatigues were limestone-white. They wavered at attention, but Barker was able to dismiss them without further misfortune.

They unpacked and changed fatigues and were given minute instructions by the juniors on how to fold and place clothing in their footlockers. At noon they formed for mess. Holt explained meal etiquette before they broke formation. Press was famished as he entered the cavernous mess hall and picked up a tray. When he sat down, he sat at attention: arms and shoulders folded back with hands joined at the small of the back, contact between the buttocks and the chair confined to the first two inches of the seat. When he and two others were joined by Junior Candidate Lansing, they requested permission to eat.

The square meal is an apt description of the eating motions candidates practice during their first eight weeks of OCS. Every movement is executed at right angles, except for the eyes, which must remain focused on imaginary cross hairs straight ahead, leaving food to be cut and consumed using peripheral vision. While chewing, hands must be placed in the lap. Besides enforcing strict discipline, the square meal serves to restrict caloric intake, for candidates are given less than ten minutes at the table and invariably leave with a portion of the meal remaining on their trays.

"Give me an interesting fact, Patrick," Lansing ordered.

Press was on his seventh bite and time was running low. He had to think quickly, but methodically. War. Something about war. Military history class. Anecdotes. "Sir, Candidate Patrick. The highest ranking American killed in World War Two was Lieutenant General Lesley McNair."

"Not interesting enough, beanhead."

"Sir, Candidate Patrick. He was killed by the US Army Air Corps."

"Eat, Patrick."

Press left the mess hall almost as hungry as when he arrived. His mind was on food, on how he could obtain it surreptitiously at the hospital or at other vending machines outside of the OCS area. He was not alone. Wilson and King talked of nothing else before they formed again at one o'clock.

Holt knew what was on the candidates' minds and issued another of the innumerable rules that governed life at OCS. "Pogey bait is strictly forbidden," he began. "In case you haven't yet heard, pogey bait is anything edible that isn't served in the mess hall at mealtime. Each of you will have KP duty twice during OCS. You will be on your honor not to eat except at mealtimes. Don't attempt to rathole pogey bait in the barracks; there isn't one square inch of area in the barracks that isn't known to Lieutenant Hausser or me or to your junior candidate supervisors. Barker, double-time the platoon to the barbershop."

The OCS haircut is not so much a cut as it is a shave. Press had for some time pondered the military's need for the standard training cut and concluded that its purpose was to quash individuality, instill discipline and obedience, and facilitate the development of a group consciousness. As the cold clipper skidded across his scalp and his meager fluff floated to the floor, he considered canceling his date with Celia, and that he wanted more than anything. All he could see in the mirror was the clash of his tanned face and white head.

Wilson was standing in line at attention as Press climbed down from the chair. Noting the glum expression on his face, Wilson motioned him closer with his eyes. Press came near and Wilson whispered out of the corner of his mouth: "You are truly ugly."

Press smiled and was immediately taken to task by a junior candidate with an oil drum chest and a large head with spike-like hair. His name was Boruff. "What are you smiling for, beanhead? Do think this is a place where you can smoke, joke, and hang around? In case the notion hasn't permeated that Neanderthal skull of yours, you can be assured that OCS is deadly serious. Do you understand that, beanhead?"

"Sir, Candidate Patrick, yes sir."

The next stop for those with fresh haircuts was the small PX next door. They were told to buy paste wax for the barracks's wood floors, cosmoline and wire brushes for their M-14 Assault Rifles, notebooks, typing paper, and any toiletries or boot polish they might need. Two juniors were monitoring the purchases, one at the cash register and one roaming the isles. Press picked out the items he needed and a tube of toothpaste. He then went to the aisle where the candy was, next to the checkout. Neither junior was looking in his direction. He knelt down as if to tie his boot laces, but instead quickly took two candy bars from a shelf and stuffed them under his bloused pants. Standing, he felt the candy secure above the elastic cord encircling his leg at mid-calf. He paid for the items under the cocked eye of Lansing. When Lansing turned for a moment, he removed the toothpaste from the bag and placed it back on the counter.

The woman at the register said, "Candidate, your toothpaste."

To her bewilderment, he said, "It's not mine."

Press joined the partial formation with his spirits slightly higher than at their nadir in the barber chair. *Control*, he thought, I've got to regain some control. I'll play their silly game, but not solely by their rules. Now, if I could only get to those candy bars—pogey bait!—God, what a place.

When the platoon entered the barracks, Press's hunger was so acute that he decided to risk eating the candy in the shadows of two juniors patrolling the second floor. He saw his chance when Junior Candidate Boruff, four bunks down, embarked on a vitriolic lashing of Wilson for failing to come to attention the instant he asked him a question. His voice boomed like a salvo from a siege gun, and it soon became obvious he enjoyed pounding candidates into submission with it. He had an impressive vocabulary, brutal and theatrical. As he railed on, candidates looked for a grin or smirk, some slight gesture to suggest that his boffo performance was part of the game. No—he took himself seriously.

Although entertained, Press had been busy eating. At the outset of Boruff's diatribe, he opened his footlocker and knelt beside it. Removing the candy from his pants leg, he tore the wrappers off and shoved a bar into his mouth. While he chewed feverishly, he flattened the wrappers and slid them into a sock, which he placed at the bottom of the stack. Keeping low and with an eye on the other junior, he crammed the second bar into his mouth. He almost spat it out a moment later when Boruff, his head only inches from Wilson's, said, "No wonder you're slow; you've got a rock formation on your shoulders. Maybe I should go easy on you—I mean, what the hell could the IQ be of a pile of conglomerate? Porous conglomerate," he added, as if his insult had been too tepid. Press now smiled as he considered a similarity between himself and Boruff: surely at this moment they had the two most occupied mouths in OCS.

A few minutes later Holt called an inspection. Hausser took the second floor. Inspections were a way of life since basic training, but none were a match for the OCS inspection. Hausser flipped a quarter onto the first bunk. No bounce. He retrieved the quarter and yanked the blanket and both sheets to the end of the bunk. By the time he stood in front of Press, Hausser's path was strewn with sheets and blankets and the contents from the top insert of King's footlocker.

"Your belt buckle is scratched, candidate."

No shit, you idiot, Press thought. "Sir, Candidate Patrick, yes, sir," he said.

"Why Patrick—*why* is it scratched?"

"Sir, Candidate Patrick, low crawling, sir."

"You idiot, Patrick. I know what caused the scratches; what I'm asking is why are there scratches *now*?"

"Sir, Candidate Patrick, no excuse, sir."

"Drop, Patrick, give me twenty...listen up, all of you. I don't ever want to hear you say 'no excuse.' Low crawling is SOP until you're junior candidates. Frequent applications of the Blitz Cloth will keep your brass in excellent condition." Hausser did not bother to toss his coin on Press's bunk. He shoved the mattress off the bunk and went on to inspect Press's footlocker. "What's this, Patrick?"

Press looked around and saw Hausser reach for his bottom sock. Holding it up by the toe, he repeated his question. The color drained from Press's face. Lying or equivocating were grounds for dismissal. How was he to answer?

Hausser grew impatient. "Your mind obviously lacks the materials for thought, Patrick, so I'll tell you. Your sock was almost a half inch out of line." He dropped the sock, picked up the insert, turned it over and followed suit with the footlocker. Hausser went on to strip every bunk on the second floor.

The candidates were given twenty minutes to clean up and then were called to formation. Physical training was an integral part of OCS, but if India Company's reputation was deserved, PT was the mission. The streets and straight rows of the battalion's buildings abutted the PT field, which on Wednesday afternoons became the parade ground. The quarter mile square was bordered on the far side by US Route 1. In the center was an oval track. India Company eschewed the track and ran on softer ground at the periphery of the field. As the second platoon ran onto the field, Press knew that they were in for yet another form of torture.

The platoon stayed in formation for the first lap. During the second a frail looking candidate named Whitworth, running next to Press, began to fall back. The formation deteriorated rapidly during the third lap. Press's lungs heaved; his legs ached from cumulative exertion. He slowed his pace and found himself running alone, listening to the leaden thuds of his combat boots on the giving ground. He glanced back. Half the platoon was behind him, but he was losing ground to those in front. Holt and Hausser looked as if they were gliding along, for the first time leading by example. Soon, Press's boots became too heavy and his lungs too torpid for him to continue. He slowed to a wobbly walk, then fell to his knees and vomited. Again, he thought: what the hell am I doing here?

Evening chow was a duplication of noon mess. Still hungry, the platoon returned to the barracks, where the juniors took over from the tac officers. Amid harassment the candidates were each assigned an M-14 and learned the sundry housekeeping duties. Lights out came at 2200, and the candidates were warned that anyone found out of his bunk between 2200 and 0530 would be punished. But many minor activities, polishing boots and brass for example, and some more important ones, such as writing military letters, could be accomplished only after taps had sounded. The certainty of being punished overcame the mere possibility of it, and thus another contradiction was institutionalized: Do it, but don't get caught.

Press lay awake at 2300, his boots and brass polished, and though exhausted, unable to sleep. For the past fifteen minutes his leg muscles had throbbed in a palsied rhythm, like reverberating sound waves. Now, they contracted into gnarled cores and he experienced the most acute pain of his life. His moans woke King.

"What's the problem up there?" he asked.

"Legs."

"Charley horse?"

"In both legs."

King got up and pushed his finger tips against Press's thigh. "Christ," he said, "they're like bricks. Whitworth, wake up—help with the other leg."

Although Whitworth slept in the next bunk, King had to kick his mattress to wake him. "Coming," he said in a voice full of sleep. He began to knead the other thigh while Press writhed in agony.

Wilson came over a few minutes later and gave King a tube of Ben Gay. "Here, just don't rub it on his balls."

"Glad to see you still have a sense of humor after Boruff raked you over the *rocks*," Press said between his teeth. "He's the only guy I know who has a majority of the molecules in his body massed at the mouth."

"I'd say your nemesis is far worse."

"Oh, kid Hausser—yeah, he's gonna be a problem," Press agreed.

"They're loosening up," King said, applying the Ben Gay.

"Thanks. I can take over now," Press said, and he began to rub the ointment on his calves, avoiding the gash on his knee. As the pain began to subside, hunger became his chief assailant. Vietnam couldn't be this bad, he thought as he lay back, now overcome by exhaustion. Thirty seconds later he was asleep.

5

Brilliant Sunday morning sunshine crowded the shadows cast by the maple tree Press was standing under as he waited for Celia. He saw the red Volkswagen Beetle turn the corner, and he walked into the sunlight and waved. Celia stopped the car, and Press opened her door. He stood immobile as she stepped out. She was wearing a white dress with matching gloves and her dark hair swirled on her shoulders as she turned and smiled in her effervescent way.

"If you're not the most beautiful creature I've ever seen, I'll garnish the roof of this old bug and eat it in front of the battalion," he said.

Celia stood on the toes of her shoes, leaned forward and brushed her lips against his cheek. "Thank you," she whispered.

"Since we've got some time till service starts, let me give you a walking tour of our playground here at Fort Belvoir—from the outside. Inside the OCS compound I'm free game for the jackals wearing white or red tabs on their lapels. They're the junior and senior candidates who help the tactical officers whip us into shape."

"Tell me about your week; was it as bad as you expected? And your hair— let me see the top."

Press hesitated.

"You'll have to take your hat off in church, in front of the whole congregation," she teased.

He lifted his cap.

"My God, what did the barber use, hair remover?"

"Very funny—remember, this isn't permanent."

"What was it like—were the big boys mean to you?" she asked, laughing, and took his arm.

"The first day was terrible and I thought it couldn't get any worse. I was right, but not by much. It didn't get any better, either—day after day of hazing, running, and low crawling. One of the tactical officers has it in for me. He's insecure as hell, and immature. It's hard to fathom how the Army put him in a job like this. He's remarked a couple of times that he's street smart, which implies that he's a little short on time in the classroom. While that shouldn't mean much—George Washington didn't have formal schooling past fifth grade—I think it bothers Hausser, and he'll be striking out at people because of it.

"If what I've seen so far is any indication, this is not a school that develops leadership. It's a mere culling process, a Darwinian 'survival of the fittest' in the physical sense and a search for the Hemingway-type hero in the mental. If you show grace under pressure with three or four guys yelling at you at the decibel level of a race car engine, you're rewarded with a gold bar in your twenty-third week."

"Maybe the Army feels that you're less likely to crack in combat if you can stand up to the pressure in OCS," Celia reasoned.

"There's that, and probably the assumption that the obedience training will stick and you'll obey the order to take that hill. But here's the rub: some guys might graduate thinking that this is the way to run a platoon." He stopped himself from adding that many of the fragging incidences in Vietnam were sparked by poor leadership; instead, he took both of her hands. "I'm sorry. I didn't intend to be so serious. Let's talk about you—how did your week go?"

"Pretty dull on the school side. Have you ever analyzed proportional representation systems in post-war Europe? You don't have to answer. It was livelier in Senator Jackson's office. I've been doing some fact-checking with the Pentagon on that huge cost overrun on the C5A transport plane. You know that the Senator is an ardent supporter of the military, but he's livid over this."

"I remember reading about it during orientation week, when we could read newspapers and listen to radios. Anything of interest happen this week?"

"On Wednesday Howard University closed down after students occupied eight buildings."

"That's pretty close to home."

"True, but it's getting to be commonplace now, and everybody is taking it in stride."

"So, tell me, how is ol' Homer?"

"Homer?"

"The fellow you've been seeing."

"His name's Jim, as I'm sure you're aware. And he's fine."

"It was impolitic for me to ask, wasn't it?"

"As a matter of fact, it did take my mind off you."

Press laughed, and said, "Com'on, let's go to church."

They parked in a small lot and walked slowly to the chapel, which was set in a grove of oak trees. A narrow walk on the left led to a flower-lined courtyard flush with the variegated colors of spring. Strolling slowly along the approach, Celia said, "You were right—it's beautiful and so serene."

They entered the chapel and took seats near the rear. A shaft of sunlight shone through one of the few non-frosted panes of glass, bringing a blush to the cheek of a parishioner in the front row. Flags hung from the stout rafters overhead. At ten o'clock a priest clad in a simple white surplice and purple sash began the service. He looked to be no older than thirty-five, and he was atypical of the chaplains Press had seen in his brief stay in the Army. His sermon was based on tolerance of ideas, and, at one point, he alluded to the student demonstrators opposing the war.

Apart from weddings and an occasional funeral, Press had not been in church for seven years. He was comfortable now and at peace after a week of turmoil. Attendance was sparse at the service, at most fifty people, he guessed. Few were in uniform and most were older women. He often glanced out the corner of his eye at Celia. She knew of course, and he would see a hint of a smile cross her lips.

Following the service they joined the others in the courtyard. Two linen-covered tables were set, one with a coffee urn, the other with assorted cookies. They met and chatted with several members of the congregation. Two older ladies, gussied in their Sunday finest, gushed with pleasure at meeting them. After Mrs. Whiting introduced herself and her friend, Mrs. Raymond, both widows, she said: "You're such a handsome couple; how long have you been married?"

"Two years and we're still very much in love."

Celia laughed. "He's exaggerating on both counts. We've known each other for two weeks. This is Press Patrick. I'm Celia Halley."

"I'm terribly embarrassed," said Mrs. Whiting. "Most of the candidates who attend services are married, and I mistakenly assumed you were too. Have you only just arrived at Fort Belvoir?"

"I've just started training," said Press. "Miss Halley is a grad student at George Washington."

"I've never seen such a beautiful mix of spring flowers, and the bouquet is wonderful," Celia said. "The congregation must have some committed gardeners."

When the ladies beamed unabashedly, Press said, "I think we've got two of them here."

"It's a collective effort by the Officers' Wives Garden Club," Mrs. Raymond said, unselfishly.

"It keeps us out of trouble," Mrs. Whiting joked.

"Have you met our pastor, Reverend Browne?" asked Mrs. Raymond.

"No, but it looks as though the opportunity is about to present itself," Press replied, as Rev. Browne, having filled his coffee cup, approached.

"Oh, Reverend Browne, may I present Miss Halley and Candidate Patrick," said Mrs. Raymond.

"Welcome to Fairfax Chapel," said Rev. Browne.

"Thank you," said Celia. "We enjoyed the service very much, and what a lovely chapel."

"Are you a chaplain, Reverend Browne?" asked Press.

"I am, going on ten years. As you can see, most of our modest attendance consists of permanent residents. I wish we had more active duty participants."

"It's too bad more didn't hear your sermon; it was very good—topical as well," said Press.

"Thank you. Some people, even in the military, mistakenly feel that because the Army is monolithic in structure, it is in thought."

"Can we borrow Miss Halley for a few minutes?" asked Mrs. Whiting. "We'd like to show her some of the nasturtiums we planted some time ago."

"Only if you promise to bring her back," said Press.

After they left, he turned to the pastor. "The chaplains I've met so far have been gung-ho. One who talked to us in basic training cussed like a trooper and ached for the chance to machine-gun commies. Another in advanced training warned us that we would go straight to hell if we faltered in combat. 'In combat,' he said, 'the Fifth Commandment reads: Thou shalt kill.'"

"I've met a few like that, but most of the chaplains here are pretty much the standard stock preacher," Rev. Browne assured him. "You look like you're a recent arrival—"

"Oh, the haircut. I've got two more months before they let it grow out a little. I've been here two weeks."

"How long have you known Miss, ah—"

"Halley. I met Celia shortly after my arrival."

"Are you both Episcopalian, or just one?"

"Neither. Celia is Catholic and I don't belong to a church."

A puzzled expression appeared on Rev. Browne's face. "Why did you choose our service?"

"Sanctuary, I suppose. The only way I can leave the OCS area is for Sunday morning services and with Fairfax Chapel's setting, not to mention the amenities, you had no serious rival."

Rev. Browne laughed. "You're honest about it, anyway. Who knows, if you make a habit of it, perhaps you'll join the fold."

"I think if I were to join any church, it would be yours."

"Would you like some more coffee and cookies?"

"Thanks," said Press, turning toward the urn, "coffee only—I think having more than eight cookies in public is not socially acceptable."

Rev. Browne smiled. "I understand that you candidates don't get much to eat in your first weeks here."

"It's the price of leadership. God knows—excuse me—that you can't have officers who aren't made of stern stuff."

"And are *you* made of stern stuff?"

"I've never been tested, that is, till now. In a way, though, I think I am. When they pull something nonsensical or have a policy that I have no truck with, like our starvation diet, I feel a need to fight back."

Rev. Browne smiled. "Does that mean you're going to do battle with your superiors?"

"It's the only way I'll survive. It won't be a set-piece battle—more like guerrilla warfare, excursions behind the lines, feints, that sort of thing."

"I think it will be an interesting contest. I'd like to know how you fare. You'll keep me posted?"

Celia rejoined them in time to hear Rev. Browne's last words. "Keep you posted on what, Reverend Browne—some harebrain scheme Press has cooked up in the past few minutes?"

"Let's take a stroll, and I'll tell you all about it," Press suggested. After excusing themselves, they walked toward a lilac bush near the gray stone wall, and he began: "I have a plan to establish a fuller diet. I'll give you some money, and you go to a specialty shop and buy one of those books that's not a book at all—the kind that people put valuables or keepsakes in—make it a large one. The more it looks like a Bible, the better. Then buy as many packages of peanut butter and cheese crackers as the case will hold. Also buy a magazine, an army magazine. Don't look at me like I've gone off the deep end—it's a great idea. Put a heavy rubber band around the book; the magazine should be loose. Wrap them in plain brown paper and on the return address corner use a bold pen to mark it from Reverend Timothy Patrick. Except for today, mail it on Sunday afternoon. I'll return it to you every Sunday morning."

"Is there a Reverend Timothy Patrick?"

"There could be, somewhere."

"What makes you think I'll see you every Sunday?" Celia said in a tone which he could not interpret.

"I was hoping for a *fait accompli*, acceptance that we've established a fine tradition here—church services, conversations with the sweet old ladies and Rev. Browne."

"You know that I'm dating someone else."

"Is it serious?"

"No, but I think he wants it to be."

"I shouldn't have asked you. Sunday morning is the only time we can see each other, and I'd rather starve during the week and see you than be stuffed as a Christmas goose and not see you."

"I want to see you again, but why all this subterfuge? Why don't we just go to the PX and you can take some food back with you?"

"The white tabs—the juniors—will be lying in wait. I probably wouldn't get a hundred yards into the compound if I'm carrying anything. They even checked my bloused fatigues yesterday on the way back from the PX."

"What makes you think your plan will succeed?"

"Mail call is after noon mess. After we fall out, either Holt or Hausser stands at the barracks steps and looks at the contents of each package."

"Won't they become suspicious if you bring in a Bible every week."

"But I won't be. Here's what happens: first, if last week is SOP, when a package is received the candidate unwraps it and throws the paper into the dumpster behind the platoon. Your package should arrive in the Tuesday mail. As I walk back to the dumpster with it, I'll pull a string out of my pocket, one end already secured to a large paper clip, the other to a ring, and I'll attach the paper clip to the rubber band on the big book. At one of the upper corners of the dumpster there's a two or three millimeter crack about two inches long. I'll drop the case and the wrapping paper into the dumpster with one hand, while placing the string through the crack with the other. The ring will catch and the package will stop three feet deep in the dumpster and hang there until I retrieve it at night."

"Why, if you're going to throw the package into the dumpster, do you want it to look like a Bible?"

"Because if one of the juniors is sniffing around during mail call and watches me unwrap what he supposes is a Bible, he probably won't inspect it. To finish the scenario, once I let the case drop, I keep the magazine in my hand and return to the ranks. When we're dismissed and I enter the barracks, all the tac officer will see is the magazine. Of course I'll have to be careful to remove the case the night before the garbage truck comes. But that's easy. All I have to do is hide it under dumpster. There's about five inches of clearance between the bottom of the dumpster and the ground."

"How long did it take you to concoct this outrageous scheme?"

"When your stomach is in constant want of food, inspiration is the means of survival."

Press and Celia were among the last churchgoers in the courtyard. Press glanced at his watch and said, "The time god must have it in for us—I've got to return to the compound."

"What will you do this afternoon?" she asked.

"We have a special parade at 1400—two o'clock. I also get to clean my weapon—make sure there's no rust—and basically do whatever I'm told to do by the juniors. What about you?"

"I've got some research to do for Senator Jackson."

They walked to the car and Press opened the door for Celia. He got in and they drove to the OCS area.

"Here's the money for my *CARE* package. I'm rolling in it now that I've jumped three pay grades—we draw E-5 pay, a whole 226.20 per month." '

"I knew there was something I liked about you—you're rich." She kissed him on his cheek and said, "See you next Sunday—good luck this week."

Press got out of the car, watched Celia drive off, drew a deep breath, and walked back to his barracks.

6

The first weeks of OCS combined instruction in the simpler, more easily grasped arts and sciences of war with frequent doses of physical training. Press scored well on subjects such as cover and concealment, field fortifications, and map reading. He performed less well during PT. A new junior candidate came on the scene during the second week in the person of Cal Whitehurst. His sole responsibility was to lead the platoon in its perimeter run of the parade field. Rodin could not have improved on his physique. Underneath the olive drab fatigues moved countless layers of muscle; his massive lungs pumped like air compressors; his stout legs reciprocated like locomotive pistons. He could run for miles without tiring. The platoon quickly dubbed him "Mr. Universe."

Press dreaded the great parade field run. Although his muscles were no longer sore, he lacked stamina for the long run. Generally, during the third lap, the formation would disintegrate, Press invariably somewhere in the middle, running more on competitive spirit than physiological endowment. By the fifth lap, Mr. Universe would catch the rear echelon of the platoon. His look of disdain would cause a momentary spurt of speed among the laggards. Press refused to let Whitehurst lap him. Rarely did the platoon run more than four miles in one PT session during the first weeks. Although the heat and humidity would not approach the oppressive levels of July and August, Fort Belvoir experienced occasional temperature spikes in the eighties. Often during the parade field run, two or three candidates would suffer heat exhaustion, Whitworth usually among them. During one run Press, on the verge of lapping Whitworth, glanced at him to say a word of encouragement; instead, he took him by the arm and said, "You've got to stop." Whitworth saw the earnest look on his face, and they walked a few yards to a shade tree. Rather than being soaked with perspiration like the others, Whitworth's skin was clammy and etiolated; his eyes had lost focus, and his legs were wobbly. Half collapsing, half assisted by Press, he went down under the tree. Holt came up a minute later, dispensed a salt tablet, and told Press to watch for the signs of heatstroke. Heat prostration was considered necessary during the early training—after all, there was as much variance among the candidates physically as there was mentally, and the tac officers could not take the measure of superior athletes without wreaking havoc with the weaker members of the platoon. Heat stroke, however, could cause death, and a death would most likely lead to a tac officer being relieved from command.

Also, early in its training, the platoon was introduced to the field training exercise (FTX). Ft. Belvoir's hinterland was laced with miles of tactical roads—mean dirt traces cut through swamps and forests. Much of the terrain was hilly. On a day in early May at seven in the evening, the candidates formed outside the barracks, each equipped with M-14 Assault Rifle, steel pot, gas mask, entrenching tool, and full pack. John Byer, a candidate from Fresno, was the platoon leader. Seth Wagner was the platoon sergeant. The evening's assignment entailed locating two field sites using azimuths and coordinates—the practical application of their course in map reading. Byer double-timed the platoon to the field, where he received the first problem.

"Listen up," he addressed the platoon. "We're going to split into squads. Wilson will lead the first squad, I'll take the second, and Carter will take the third. Here's the coordinates for each squad's intermediate objective. Shoot an azimuth from your start point." He passed out note cards to the two leaders. "And this is your azimuth from your intermediate to the final objective, which is a point along a tactical road." Byer gave maps to Carter and Wilson. "First squad starts at the southern end of the clearing, second squad starts here, and third squad starts at the northern end. Each squad should be separated by 200 meters. When you reach the intermediate objective, shoot your second azimuth for the final objective. Cool Jack"—Holt's new nickname—"said that we should all meet there around dark. Any questions?...Good, let's synchronize our watches—I have 1921. First and third squads move out."

Press, in the first squad, wondered why Byer wanted to synchronize watches. Too many war movies he thought, as Wilson double-timed the squad to the start point.

"Listen up," Wilson said, pulling out his Lensatic compass. "Okay, let's see what direction we'll be going." He found the coordinates and penciled an "X" on the map at the crest of a hill. With a gesture of "follow me" he indicated a clump of trees in the distance and said, "Those trees are our first landmark; they're dead on our azimuth, and we've—"

"Wait," said Press. "That's through pretty rough terrain. Why not just shoot an azimuth on the map from the coordinates of the intermediate objective to the first tactical road?" Snatching the map from Wilson's hand, he continued: "The azimuth from the intermediate to the final objective is 137 degrees. We'll draw a line from the intermediate to the road and then shoot a back azimuth on the map to our coordinates here. There are only two tactical roads, and the second is so close to the first, that if the second is the final objective, we'll only be off by a hundred meters or so. Nothing to it."

"That's not the purpose of the exercise," said Wilson testily. "We're supposed to practice what we learned in the classroom, not make it easy for ourselves."

"Surely you've learned about field expedients. There's a swamp between our intermediate objective and the first tactical road." He drew a line on the map tracing the swamp. "You know what that is? It's the perfect thalweg."

"What the hell is a thalweg?" Wilson asked, a look of concern crossing his corrugated face.

Press shook his head in disbelief. "My God, Rushmore, how in the world did you get past grammar school without knowing about thalwegs? Whitworth, do you know what a thalweg is?"

"What do you take me for, an ignoramus? I've known since fifth grade geography."

Fault lines spread over Wilson's Brow. "All right, damn it, what the hell is a thalweg?"

In the tone of an impatient teacher Press said, "It's a line connecting the lowest points of a valley. If we get bogged down and are the last to reach the road, guess who gets no rest for the run back to the barracks? It'll be one heart-thumping romp through the woods. Let's take a vote on the route—"

Wilson sucked in his breath and stood as a desert monument. "This is the Army—not a goddamn democracy," he spat out. "When you're in charge, we'll do it your way, which of course will be the easy way. Besides, we have our orders." He glanced at his watch. "Let's move out."

The squad wended its way single file through the dense woods, negotiating downed trees, thickets, gullies and ravines. They advanced from landmark to landmark, never straying far from their straight-line course. They reached the intermediate objective after thirty-five minutes, took a compass reading, and set out for a line-of-sight landmark on the way to their final objective.

The downhill trek took only fifteen minutes. After five minutes on level ground, Press could feel the squish of a liquid cushion under his boots. Farther on the suction noises became louder with each tug of a foot from black oozing muck. The squad slowed its pace appreciably in the energy-sapping swamp, and as they began sloshing through knee-deep water, gaseous bubbles rose to the surface and popped, releasing the stench of rotted vegetation. When they reached midpoint, the water was almost waist-high, causing them to unsling their M-14s and hold them at high port arms.

"I guess we're in the middle of the thalweg," Whitworth said in his reedy voice, coming abreast of Press. "Did you make it up, or is that a real word?"

"I came upon it in map reading class this afternoon. I was paging through the glossary when it caught my eye, and I said to myself there is a term I would never use."

Whitworth stumbled on a branch and grasped Press's forearm for support. "Suppose there's anything in here other than us?" he asked.

"The only poisonous snake Holt told us to watch out for was the diamondback. Remember those World War Two movies—the Americans wading through jungle streams on Guadalcanal or Burma or some faraway place when you were ten years old and you thought how neat?"

"Yeah, I wanted to be an airborne ranger," said Whitworth.

"Only trouble was, sitting on your ass in a movie theater, your body didn't slog through this stuff, you were only big eyes and imagination, you didn't run out of breath—your nose didn't have to smell this shit, either."

"Think of it this way, Patrick. What would you be doing in the outside world right now—most likely something boring, like finishing the steak dinner your girlfriend prepared. She, scantily clad—"

"Shut-up, Whitworth."

"Just trying to make conversation—take your mind away from unpleasant circumstances."

"Well, change the subject, then."

"Rumor has it that you're an atheist. Anything to it?"

"That sure as hell is a change of subject."

"Are you or aren't you?"

"I am."

"I don't think I've ever met one before, at least not an avowed atheist."

"You make 'atheist' sound like communist."

Whitworth ignored the rebuke and continued. "You believe, then, that life is pointless?"

"From the metaphysical standpoint, yes. In the purely physical world the point is to procreate, and I believe it's such a worthy goal that since I was a sophomore in high school, I've been practicing as much as I can."

Whitworth shook his head and whispered inaudibly, "God help you."

Minutes later, the squad emerged from the swamp and once more encountered a forest mosaic of fallen limbs, branches, and trees. The soldiers had to slide down steep banks of streams and once across, kick footholds in the soft soil to scale the far banks.

Considerable good-natured ribbing from the second and third squads greeted the first squad, as its mud-caked and bedraggled members trudged the last few yards to the objective. The others were well rested after having arrived more than twenty minutes earlier. Holt critiqued the evening's problem, noting that all three squads had no difficulty shooting azimuths and finding the objectives. "The first squad drew the most difficult terrain, as you may have gathered from this exercise," he said. "In past exercises some squads have chosen to go *around* the swamp. Byer, form the platoon."

Press walked past Wilson and said, "Thanks, Rushmore. With only five minutes of rest we're going to suffer on the way back."

"Gut it out," Wilson replied. "And don't call me 'Rushmore.'"

"Fine, horst head."

"Horse head? You can't even be consistent in your put-downs."

"Not horse—*horst*. It's a great block of rock that sticks out of two level tracts of earth."

"Asshole."

Although they had been forewarned, the candidates were to learn first-hand the importance of securing their gear tightly for the boonie run. Loose gear flopped about, interfering with the rhythm of their bodies; mess kits and ponchos slapped against arms and elbows as packs bounced on candidates' backs. It was like running a race in coveralls rather than shorts. And they kicked up a racket: a thousand muffled, tinny clinks from inside the mess kits blended with the flounce of entrenching tools and the swish of canvass against fatigue shirts. Holt ordered the platoon to sing. Unlike some of the companies in OCS, India sung none of the popular tunes of the day. The second platoon had developed a crude chant, which was shouted, not sung.

We're on the move
We're in the groove
Incomin' India
Always low crawlin'

Always high ballin'
Ironmen India
We're *FEBA* bound
We're fury and sound
Intrepid India

They had learned the acronym *FEBA*—forward edge of the battle area—early in their training. While more verses would be added, that is all they had in early May. Breathless and off key, with ill-felt gusto, the candidates repeated the refrain ad nauseam, until Holt dropped them for fifty meters of low crawling.

Most military training posts have a Heartbreak Hill. Belvoir's was a long, ten-degree incline which came at the end of the run and transformed the already-heavy components of the infantryman into millstones. The rasping and heaving of lungs approached the noise level of the equipment. After reaching the summit, the quarter mile run to the barracks was a mixture of pain and pleasure: pain because they were still running, pleasure because they were near the end and the demand for oxygen was less on the level than on the rise. They filled the night air with a fresh refrain of "Incomin' India," shouted now with volume and swagger.

They were welcomed back to the barracks after taps by the juniors. "Move! Move! Move! Move!" they shouted, as the candidates poured through the doors. "You've got ten minutes," Boruff roared, standing like a traffic cop just inside the barracks.

Press undressed quickly, stuffing his muddy fatigues in his laundry bag and wrapping a towel around his waist. "We're going to have another jam in the shower," he said to King.

"Some evening I'd love to linger in the shower," King responded. "Five minutes. A mere five minutes under hot water." He shook his head. "But no, they won't allow us even a small pleasure."

Press grabbed his boots and toilet kit, put on his shower tongs, and went downstairs. Boruff and Lansing were expediting clean-up and bowel movements. "Eyeball the clock, beanheads, you got one minute in the shower," Lansing shouted.

Press joined the line in the latrine, which consisted of a wash basin for boots and gear, four sinks, four open commodes, a long horizontal urinal, and a shower pit with six heads. After hosing the mud off of his boots and visiting the urinal, he entered the showers and washed himself as best he could in two minutes. He found an open sink, where he brushed his teeth. On the way out he picked up his boots and rushed past Boruff.

Boruff was in prime form: "Get your ass off the shitter, Perini; you've been sitten' there for a full minute...Whitworth, you better put meat on that skeleton or you'll get sucked down a flushing toilet—*as you pass by.*" He laughed heartily at his joke. "Isn't that right, Whitworth?"

"Sir, Candidate Whitworth, yes sir."

"Speak from your gut, Whitworth, only a dog can hear you."

Lights were soon turned out and stray candidates herded into bed. Press hoisted himself onto the top bunk and began to polish his belt buckle. By this time, candidates had learned to twist their buckles around while low crawling, thus avoiding scratches and late night applications of the Blitz Cloth. Press quickly finished and held his buckle up for inspection. Instead of the gleam of moonlight, he saw the glint of a grin and turned to face Boruff.

"Real fine, Patrick, just subvert the rules of OCS. Why do you think we took such great pains to get you beanheads into bed as soon as possible after taps? It sure as hell wasn't to polish your brass."

Press was looking into Boruff's face, less than a foot away. The great orifice opened, and Boruff began a general harangue about rules violations and the sanctity of taps. He went on for minutes without noticeably taking a breath. He never groped for words; his only pauses were for effect. Press was held in awe, convinced that he was listening to the quintessential mouth.

When he finished he pointed to Press's belt buckle and said, "Let's see how it will stand up to an impromptu inspection." Press gave him the buckle and Boruff, without looking at it, gouged its face against the top of the bed post. He held it up to the moonlight and said, "Eyeball your brass. How do you account for this scratch, Patrick?"

"Sir, Candidate Patrick. Negligence, sir."

"Whose negligence, beanhead?" Boruff said in an ominous tone.

"Sir, Candidate Patrick. Mine, sir."

"Lock and load this, Patrick: we're watching you. Real close." Boruff dropped the buckle on Press's bed and walked to the stairs. Absolute silence followed him down the steps and when the outside door closed, the second floor became a whisper- gallery as the candidates again took up their after-taps chores and a few minutes for casual conversation.

As Press began to polish his boots, he watched a candidate two bunks down, Jim Petras, unscrew the top of a toothpaste tube and hold it above his mouth. He squeezed the tube and a ribbon of toothpaste coated his tongue.

Press put his boots on his footlocker and walked over to Petras' bunk. "Are you *that* hungry, Petras?"

"Can't stand it anymore; I'm starved."

Press lowered his voice. "Can you wait a few minutes? I may be able to help."

"You got some pogey bait ratholed?" Petras whispered.

"I know where I can get hold of some peanut butter and cheese crackers. But give me fifteen minutes."

"I'll be in your debt forever," Petras said.

Press went back to his footlocker, finished his boots, put on his shower tongs, and slowly descended the stairs. The moon bathed the outside with enough light that he could be seen from a distance. Deciding to risk it, he went out the door and quickly down the steps. He slowed his pace on the gravel, stepping as lightly as possible. He was halfway to the dumpster, when he heard footfalls coming from around the corner of the barracks. He dashed to the dumpster and crouched in its shadow. A guard came into view, a candidate like himself, and Press wondered what action the guard would take if he were to see him. Press had pulled guard duty the week before and had watched a candidate's wife deliver a sack from Arby's to her husband, who was waiting at the edge of the OCS compound. He had let him pass unchallenged.

Without looking toward the dumpster, the guard made a left turn and walked in the opposite direction. Press reached for the string on the inside of the dumpster and pulled the case up. He was now adept at retrieving the crackers, and it took him only a few seconds to extract two packages. Instead of putting the case back in the dumpster, he placed it under the dumpster. Garbage collection was scheduled for the next day. On previous collections, the garbage truck driver had been oblivious to the stone-blending gray case. Press quickly returned to the barracks, smiling, and went to Petras' bunk. "Shhhhh, don't mention this to anyone."

"I won't, I won't. Thanks a million, Patrick," Petras said as he ripped away the wrapper and started to cram several crackers into his mouth.

"Don't," Press whispered. "Chew slowly—savor them."

The former mess hall in the row of India Company buildings was used as a study hall. Except for the evenings on which field training exercises were conducted, the candidates would file into the building for two hours of supervised study. All other activities were strictly forbidden.

The evening before the communications' course test, the candidates were ensconced in the study hall, sitting in wooden folding chairs, four to a table. Press sat between King and O'Malley, a candidate he did not know well. He was reading a letter from Piloski with his direct vision, while Boruff stalked the room in his periphery. "Piloski landed a job as a company clerk in the headquarters company of an engineer battalion in a place called Chu Lai," he whispered to King. "He says he spent his leave practicing on the type-writer and memorizing forms." King nodded and smiled, and Press folded and shoved the letter under the last page of his tablet. He was skimming a page on commo wire and did not sense the presence of Boruff behind him until his mind was reeled in by words spoken in a deep bass: "What are you doing, beanhead?"

Press turned slowly and gazed up at him.

"Eyeball me, beanhead!" he barked, standing behind Press with splayed feet and arms folded over his chest.

O'Malley said, "Sir, Candidate O'Malley, I *am* looking at you."

"What were you reading, beanhead?"

O'Malley pointed to the page facing him. "Sir, Candidate O'Malley. Do you mean presently or sometime in the past?"

"Just answer the question."

"Sir, Candidate O'Malley. In the last few minutes I was reading my commo book, sir. Radio telephone procedures."

"Well, you won't mind me relieving you of this, then, will you, O'Malley," Boruff said, as he removed a magazine from under the communications' book. He folded his arms and stood still for a few seconds, glaring at several tables of candidates and nodding his head fatuously in the manner of Mussolini.

When Press saw O'Malley the next day, he looked distressed.

"Why so glum?" Press inquired.

"I was told this morning that I would have to appear before the Honor Board."

"Hell, you didn't lie to Boruff. You put that magazine away a good five minutes before he confronted you."

"The charge isn't for lying. It's for quibbling."

"Quibbling?"

"That's right. They think I was being evasive. I'm wondering if he didn't set me up, knowing that if he caught me reading it at the time, that I would admit it."

"What are you going to tell the Honor Council?"

"The truth. That I had been reading the magazine, but had put it away long before Boruff approached."

"Good luck, O'Malley," Press said. "I think you'll be okay."

7

During the weekend the homogeneity of the platoon was disrupted by the arrival from other companies of five former junior candidates whose leadership skills or academics were deemed insufficient for graduation. They were now "retreads" in India Company. One of them, a hapless candidate named Anders, wilted under the strain of India. The next week Anders received permission to quit the program as soon as his orders could be cut.

Shortly after taps two days before Anders' scheduled departure, Boruff, now a senior candidate, began prowling the barracks. He heard a sniffle and nosed around till he found the source of the sound that undoubtedly offended his meaning of manhood.

"Are you *crying*, Anders?"

Between taps and reveille, candidates did not leave their bunks when being addressed by superiors. Anders pulled the sheet up to his chin and confessed feebly that he was indeed crying.

"*Why* are you crying, Anders?"

"Sir, Candidate Anders, I can't take it anymore, sir."

"*I can't take it anymore*," Boruff mocked in a child's tone. "Well, that's just too goddamn bad, Anders. You're going to be with us a couple more days, and until then you're just going to have to grow a backbone."

Boruff's castigation caused a slight rise in Ander's whimpers. This infuriated Boruff and he pushed his face further into Ander's body zone. "You're a disgrace to your uniform. Don't you have any pride, you gutless sniveling lizard? You're as useless as dung in the desert— hell, you're worse; at least you can build a fire with turds!" Boruff was fully engaged now. Almost in angry cobra motion, tongue coiled, he would rear back and then spit out an insult while lunging forward. This whipsaw-like thrashing became almost self-energizing. They had both lost control—in opposite directions. In less than two minutes Anders had become a sobbing, jellied mass.

Sitting up in his bunk, Press could not believe what he was hearing. He tried to screw up his courage and reason with Boruff. He hesitated, caught up in an internal debate as Boruff continued.

"You can't do anything right, can you, you slime ball. What have you got to say for yourself, coward?...Speak!...Speak!" A few unintelligible words slid out of Anders, mercifully cut short by a voice in the darkness.

"Don't you think he's had enough? He's quitting the program."

Before the first sentence was completed a sense of shame gripped Press. Why didn't I do it? he thought.

Boruff turned slowly and words banged out of his mouth single action: "WHITWORTH!...YOU...DARE...TO...QUESTION...ME!" Recovering from the effects of unbridled insubordination, his words began to ring out rapid fire: "You just made the biggest mistake of your life. You're history, Whitworth."

Press thought frantically as Boruff continued his barrage. In slightly louder than a whisper, he spoke to King below. "He certainly has command presence."

Boruff's head snapped toward Press's bunk. "Who's talking?" After several moments of silence, he repeated the question in a more menacing tone.

"Sir, Candidate Patrick. I just made an observation to Candidate King, sir."

"And just exactly what was it, Patrick?"

"Sir, Candidate Patrick. You were framed in the moonlight and I complimented you on your military bearing, sir."

Boruff did not get an opportunity to rebuke Press. The senior candidate leader, Richards, having heard enough from the first floor, appeared at the top of the steps and said, "Let's let them get some sleep, Mike."

Boruff knew that a protest would be futile, but he stopped at Press's bunk on his way out and whispered, "You've stepped in deep shit, Patrick."

Press waited until he was out of earshot and then said aloud: "If a prize fighter's hands are considered a lethal weapon, so should Boruff's blow torch mouth."

As Boruff and Richards walked on the street, they could not have missed a peel of laughter coming from the barracks.

Following classes the next afternoon, Holt accompanied the platoon to the parade field for physical training. Field manual PT in the Army is as exact and undemanding as close order drill. The junior candidates could now do PT mechanically and for hours without tiring appreciably. After rotating exercise leaders four times, Holt told the platoon to continue exercising for thirty minutes before returning to the barracks. Press watched him start back to his office as King mounted the platform for a turn.

With fifteen minutes remaining, Press was called on to lead the next exercise. He leaped onto the platform and began. "The next exercise is the finger curl, a four-count exercise. The starting position is with both arms at your sides, hands flat against your flanks. On the first count move your index fingers two inches out; on the second count curl your fingers, on the third count move them back to the first count position; and on the fourth return them back to the starting position. We'll do twenty repetitions."

Press began the exercise, and the candidates counted repetitions with the volume and swagger normally reserved for the *FEBA* chant. When they reached number fifteen, Press noticed that Boruff, Lansing, and two other senior candidates were watching from the perimeter of the field, about 100 yards away. Inexplicably, Boruff kept his larynx in check and merely shook his head. The group turned and walked away.

Petras had charge of quarters duty that day and called Press over to the headquarters shack after evening mess. "Whitworth's been put back four weeks to Delta Company—Cool Jack just signed the paperwork."

Press felt a deep anger building. "He's not going to make it," was all he said.

"That's not all. Look in Hausser's in-basket."

Press reached in and withdrew a handwritten note from Boruff reporting his unauthorized physical training exercise. "This will probably make me a retread," he stated.

"Only if he receives it," Petras said, a sly look on his face. "I have to go outside for a minute. Watch things here, will you?"

Press looked at the message again and crumpled it. I'd rather risk it all than become a retread, he said to himself. When Petras returned, he thanked him, walked out into the dusk and dropped the note into the dumpster.

8

"...and while Christianity does not have a monopoly on morality, we, as Christians, must reach out to those who reject Christ as Savior. We must also reach out to those wayward adventurers who rely not on God's word in defining morality, but solely on their own experience, on their own insights, on their own prejudices. They define morality on their own terms and live in a world where faith is no safeguard, nor is truth. They live in a gray twilight— neither feeling God's love nor seeking it. And when darkness closes in on their lives, they will stand before Him, silent...but not soulless."

Celia lifted an eye, leaned against Press and whispered, "He's talking about you."

Rev. Browne finished his sermon and, in short order, the service. Celia took Press's arm as they walked from the chapel to the courtyard. He squeezed her hand as they stood a discreet fifteen feet from the cookies and coffee and said, "It's the end of an era, my sweet, there'll be no more lunging at the cookie tray. In fact, I may have none at all."

"But you'll disappoint the parishioners. What will they talk about if there's no display of after-service gluttony?"

"They can say that you've transformed me into a model of rectitude."

Celia wrinkled her nose at him. Press bowed his head until their lips were four inches apart. "Maybe I'll get a pass next Sunday and we'll go someplace where I can kiss you a thousand times."

The widows Whiting and Raymond twittered at the looks Celia and Press were giving each other. "Have you ever seen two people so much in love?" Mrs. Whiting asked, within earshot of the pair.

"They were made for each other," Mrs. Raymond concurred. The ladies were inching up on the couple, as they did every Sunday after services. "Go ahead, Press, have a cookie or two," urged Mrs. Raymond as they approached them.

"Not for a few more minutes, Mrs. Raymond; I'm trying to reform myself."

"Don't tell us—you have full mess hall privileges," said Mrs. Whiting.

"As of yesterday. Tomorrow we start a week of training in the field."

"Mr. Anderson told me that he saw a group of candidates practicing riot control on the parade ground," Mrs. Raymond said.

"I think most of the battalion has been practicing. We spent two hours late Thursday afternoon on riot control. Then we got to low crawl around the track. The rumor mill has it that there will be more demonstrations at the Pentagon. If we can't handle the demonstrators, we're well trained to skulk away on our hands and knees."

"Do you think there will be demonstrations?" asked Mrs. Whiting.

"I've no idea. Except for what Celia tells me on Sunday morning, I haven't heard or seen a thing—not one word on the radio, not a line of newsprint. OCS is an insular world. That should change this week—at least for one candidate."

"What do you mean?" asked Celia.

"Holt will ask for volunteers for various duties—one being command information. The fortunate fellow gets to read the paper, clip items of interest, and pin the clippings to the bulletin board."

"And who will this information czar be?" asked Rev. Browne, who had joined the group while Press was talking.

"You can bet Press will be waving his hand in the air like a third grader with the right answer," said Celia.

"No doubt he'll go straight to the cooking section and clip recipes," Rev. Browne said with a laugh.

"True, and Celia has sent her last *CARE* package."

"That's too bad, I'll miss your conveyor-belt appetite," Rev. Browne joked.

They all laughed and Press good-naturedly let the ensemble poke fun at him for a few minutes before stepping up to the table. After a half-hour of socializing, he drew Celia aside. They had a routine now of walking slowly around the edge of the courtyard. He would pluck a flower and put the blossom in her hair and tell her how beautiful she looked.

They strolled for a minute in silence before he spoke. "Have you seen Homer lately?"

"His name's Jim and the answer is no."

"Why not? He didn't throw you over for a younger woman, did he?"

"Don't be silly. I explained to him that I was seeing you."

"Did he ask if you were serious?"

"Yes."

"Well, what did you say?"

"What did you think I said?"

"You said, 'I'm madly in love with him; his image rises with the sun and sets only when my dreams give way to the deepest slumber. And when I wake I cry to dream again.' You said—"

"Don't flatter yourself, Preston."

"Does that mean you don't love me?"

"Oh, so now we make the leap from not seeing Jim to being in love with you?"

"Are you denying it?"

"Sorry, that won't work. I will admit to one thing, though."

"What's that?"

"You scare me a little."

"How so?"

"You remind me of a leading man in the movies—dashing and terribly good looking—"

"My hair hasn't even grown out yet."

"Let me finish. You're flip. You fling one-liners like the star of a romantic comedy. You might pass an ethical frisking, but I'm not sure about your values. They seem sometimes as variable as a wind sock. That's what I like about Jim. He's steady and rocklike. You're more celluloid—I feel I only know the surface you...have you ever taken a hard look at yourself?"

"My eye is too near to me."

"Your image is too dear to you. And that's precisely what I mean by being flip. This is a serious discussion."

"Whew."

"What are you whewing for?"

"I've decided to postpone singing Rudolfo's love aria to Mimi."

"There you go again. You...you...oh, it's my own damn fault; I can't help the way I'm attracted to you."

"I can't help it, either. I've loved you from the time of our picnic on the Potomac. I've loved you while low crawling around the parade field, on boonie runs, dozing in the classroom and, especially, at night in the top bunk, where I'd hug my pillow and wish it were you. I'm very glad you're no longer seeing Homer—sorry, a relapse—Jim. Maybe my morals aren't quite as fixed as his: he sails steadfastly on Polaris and I occasionally on Jupiter. Maybe it's my skepticism. Maybe it's the uncertainty of life. One thing that I believe—and it might be taken for a lack of values—is that in the broad and diverse history of humanity there are many truths—or no truths; the world is far more gray than black and white."

"Say that again."

"Say what again?"

"That you love me."

"I love you, Celia Halley."

She looked at him with ever-widening eyes, as if they could hear his words as they searched his face—misty brown eyes that shimmered with the discovery of what was once imagined was now reality.

"You love me, too," he said.

"You know I'm crazy about you."

He glanced at his watch. "We've got forty-five minutes. Let's bid farewell to Reverend Browne and the ladies and park in a remote corner of the boonies."

She took his hand and they set off in search of Rev. Browne. They found him near the road, saying goodbye to a colonel and his wife. He turned toward the two and smiled discerningly.

"Your sermon was very interesting this morning, Reverend. I'd like to discuss it with you sometime."

"It would certainly be my pleasure, Press."

"I thought it was a great sermon, Rev. Browne. Maybe some of it penetrated this thick head," Celia said, her hand tugging at Press's garrison cap.

After leaving the chapel grounds, they got into her Volkswagen and drove to Ft. Belvoir's outback. Within seconds of coming to a stop on an isolated tactical road, Press put his arm around her shoulders and drew her close to him. They kissed slowly, luxuriously, electrically. They could not get enough of each other and smothered each other until finally they had to pull away to breathe.

"I've never felt this way," Press said between breaths. "One part passion and one part love brew a magic potion."

He put his hand under her breast and lowered his head, kissing the folds of dress covering her breast. Seconds later he raised his head and said, "I prefer skin to cotton—can I unzip you?"

Celia nodded and he reached behind her and pulled the zipper down. He then grasped the clips of her bra, undoing them with a practiced hand.

"You're experienced in this," she said.

"Experienced enough to wish we were in a Nash rather than a Volkswagen." He let her dress slip off her shoulders and then put a finger from each hand under her bra straps and pulled the bra away. "You're beautiful," he said as he lowered his head.

She inhaled sharply as Press drew her to his mouth. He began alternating between kissing her lips and her breasts.

"Celia, let's—"

"Not like this—not for my first time."

He stopped and looked at her. "You're a virgin?"

"I know it sounds old-fashioned, but I was going to save myself for marriage. I'm not so sure now."

"You have no idea how much I want you."

"Not anymore than I want you. My feeling for you is so strong, so overwhelming, but as I said at the chapel, it's not yet the *right* feeling. And this is not the right place."

He understood the paradox. He was in love for the first time in his life, but he was also in wonderment, for prior to this new sensation he behaved as if all phenomena conformed to the exactness of physical science or the logical vagaries of human nature.

When Celia dropped him off at the OCS compound, he walked to the Day Room instead of returning to the barracks. Married candidates would often meet their wives there, before going to the guest house for an hour. Adjacent to the compound, the guest house was a subdivided barracks whose tiny rooms and board walls seemed to conduct sound rather than adsorb it. The "*shack* shack" was often full on Sunday afternoons, and a passerby could conjure a herd of wildebeests inside during the height of mating season. Upon leaving, most of the wives would slink out; most of the husbands would strut.

Press opened the door to the Day Room and looked around. Bill King was standing in the far corner of the room, holding his three-year-old daughter. King's wife, who was strikingly attractive, dabbed a handkerchief at the sleeve of the girl's dress.

"Greetings," Press said, approaching them. "Hello, Ginny. I'm Uncle Press," he introduced himself to the little girl.

"I'm Anne," Mrs. King said. "I feel I know you from what all Bill has told me about OCS."

"You're not my uncle," Ginny stated matter-of-factly.

"I'm your pretend uncle, and I'll be staying with you for a little while this afternoon."

Ginny executed a toddler's stranglehold on her dad's neck and looked betrayed. He kissed her on her forehead and said, "Mommy and I won't be gone long, Buttercup."

"Have you ever played Ginger Bread Man?" Press asked.

Ginny looked intrigued.

"See that long rug over there?" Press continued. "I'll get on my hands and knees in the middle, and you stand at the beginning. If you can catch me before I get to the end, you win the game."

Two minutes later Press was shouting behind him, "Run, run, as fast as you can; you can't catch me, I'm the Ginger Bread Man!"

King and his wife left unnoticed as Ginny, howling in delight, caught Press a foot away from the finish. When they returned fifty-five minutes later, Press and Ginny were sitting on a sofa—he gesticulating, she listening with big-eyed attention.

"Mommy, Daddy!" she cried. "Uncle Press told me the story about the 'Two Little Pigs.'"

"That's the '*Three* Little Pigs,' honey," her mother corrected.

"No, Mommy. Hausser the Pig was too dumb to build a house and the wolf ate him before the story began."

King laughed, and Press asked how long would Anne and Ginny remain in the area.

"They're staying at the Old Colony Inn in Alexandria tonight and going back to Cleveland in the morning," King stated.

"When you come back for another visit, I'll be glad to spend some time with Ginny," Press offered.

"Thank you," Anne said. "But it won't be until Bill gets an overnight pass."

Press smiled, Anne blushed, King shrugged his shoulders—a sheepish expression on his face—and Ginny broke the silence with, "Tell me another story, Uncle Press."

9

The next day the class boarded buses bound for Camp A.P. Hill and five days of infantry tactical training. It was a week designed to heighten *espirit de corps* and unit cohesion, as well as for practicing the art and science of war. He felt a little silly wearing an Australian bush hat, but it was OCS tradition that candidates deck themselves out with theatrical head gear. The trip took just over an hour, the last minutes of which were devoted to morale building shouts of *FEBA* and other acronyms of the infantry lexicon.

The candidates threw themselves into the week. Although the heat was oppressive, the tactical problems were interesting, if not difficult. Everything was preparatory, however, to the escape and evasion course of the final night. The class was bused to a starting point near US 301. A local road ran parallel to the US route about a half mile away. Between the two highways was dense overgrowth. The candidates would start out individually or in small groups at midnight. They were expected to traverse five miles of the difficult terrain by first light while remaining between the two roads. Although it would be a laborious undertaking, a far greater risk lie ahead. Volunteer NCOs would form an irregular line somewhere between the starting point and the objective. Those who did not succeed in evading the "enemy" would be subjected to hostile treatment: hours of interrogation, being stripped to skivvies and forced to sit in a hole occupied by several large non-poisonous snakes or being partially hung from a tree like a side of beef.

None of the prospects appealed to Press. He sat at the start point, thinking. It was almost midnight when Wilson approached him.

"You got a plan yet to evade the course, Patrick?" he said with some sarcasm.

"I think so. Call King over here, will you? I'll get Ortiz and Petras."

A few minutes later, the group was huddled together, and Press began. "Here's my idea. When we came in on the bus, I noticed a couple of tents, company size, about a quarter mile back. Why not reconnoiter and see who's there. Maybe they'll let us sack out until three or so."

"Are you crazy—you want to wait till three to start?" Wilson asked, amazed.

"I don't think he's finished," King offered.

"Thanks," Press said. "The next part is actually the nub of it. When we leave the tent, we'll make our way to the road on our western border and walk along the tree line until we get back. Of course they may anticipate somebody taking that route, but if we wait to leave until a couple of hours before dawn, our potential captors will probably have already slaked their thirst on guys captured at one or two o'clock or on booze."

"What do you mean on booze?" Wilson asked, incredulous.

"Do you think these guys are going to sit out all night in a bug-infested area and stay sober?" asked Ortiz.

"Always the easy way, huh Patrick?" said Wilson.

"You know what the chances are of any of us having to do this for real if we go to Vietnam?" Press countered. "You guys will be engineers and ride everywhere you go. I'll be MI, probably at some huge base. Besides, this is the ultimate field expedient."

"Nobody said we couldn't do it," King added.

"Count me out," Wilson said. "I'm going to do it right."

"Yeah, and if they catch you, Rushmore, you'll come out *scree*."

"I don't know what the hell you're talking about, Patrick, but I suggest you grow up. And stop calling me 'Rushmore.'"

As soon as Wilson left, the others hiked to the campground and found it to be occupied by a unit from the Maryland National Guard. Half the bunks were unused and the sergeant in charge told the candidates to make themselves at home. A poker game was going on under a Coleman lantern. One of the players asked if any of the candidates wanted to make it six so that they could play high-low and other split-the-pot games. Press volunteered to play for an hour, won twelve dollars, and threw a five dollar bill into the beer kitty before finding an empty bunk.

The four candidates got up at three fifteen and assembled outside the tent.

"It's less likely that they think anyone would sneak up Highway 301. How about it?" Press suggested.

King, Ortiz, and Petras agreed and they started off. For all they knew, the "enemy" was just as likely to stake out sections adjacent to the roads as to occupy intercepting sites deep in the woods, so they stole up the right-of-way along US 301 as silently as possible. They could be seen, but they would not be heard. Whenever a car passed by, they shrank into the woods until blackness again enshrouded the landscape. Their trek was rapid and uneventful, and they arrived at their camp site just before dawn. After taking hot showers, they got into their cots and slept until nine.

Wilson and five other "prisoners" arrived shortly after seven. Press sat next to Perini, one of the captured candidates, on the bus during the late Saturday morning ride back to Fort Belvoir.

"...and, you know, after an hour of interrogation, I no longer thought that it was simulated, that those guys were in our army," Perini was saying. "I couldn't tell them where anybody else was because I went alone, so they tied me down and dumped live cockroaches on me—some were the big ol' Palmetto kind. Jesus, here I was in my skivvies with those goddamn roaches crawling over me. I showered for forty minutes when I got back."

"I wonder what they did to Wilson?"

Perini shook his head. "He had it even worse than I did. I guess he hates snakes, because when they put him in the snake pit, he made up some story about four guys escaping along the road on the western border. When the two guys they sent came back at dawn empty-handed, they threw Wilson back into the snake pit. I thought he was going to go ballistic."

10

On Friday of Press's eleventh week, India's senior candidates were commissioned second lieutenants. Boruff was one of the first to haul his duffel bag from the barracks. A few minutes later Press entered the barracks and tacked a sheet of paper to the command information bulletin board. In typed letters it read:

> Senior-junior, giant-dwarf Boruff
> Regent of hate-rhymes, lord of folded arms,
> The anointed sovereign of sighs and groans,
> Liege of all loud mouths and run-amoks
>> Shakespeare Act 3 Scene 1
>> Love's Labour's Lost

Press had only slightly modified Shakespeare's passage and could not resist the parting shot.

At the end of the week Holt passed out white tabs, and the candidates ceremoniously placed them under their OCS brass and refastened them to their fatigue shirt collars. Among the privileges accorded to junior candidates were overnight passes on selected weekends, the gradual integration of team sports' activities, and the cessation of double-timing to class and mess, along with a decline in low crawling. Press was already reading the *Washington Post*, having been made command information officer. From the viewpoint of a soldier in a regular unit, the life of a junior candidate would seem austere and repressive, but from the shrunken nub of expectations of a first-term candidate, junior status was heady stuff. And besides being a watershed psychologically, the steady increase in body strength and endurance was remarkable.

Four days later Hausser was waiting for the candidates as they returned from the large consolidated mess hall where Press, still flush with an all-you-can-eat mentality, gorged himself unabashedly. The mail sack sat full on the barracks' steps. One package protruded from the sack, its thick brown wrapping paper torn at one corner—the end piece hanging limp, until a variable breeze made it wag. All eyes were drawn to it, for the words "pogey bait" were all but emblazoned under the cellophane skin. Newberg, the platoon sergeant, reached for the bag.

"This one last," said Hausser, pointing to the suspect package.

As Newberg passed out the mail, the face of each platoon member registered the same concern: *don't let it be mine*. Press had a sinking feeling. His mother often shopped at Marshall Field's and invariably brought home a box of Frango Mints. He now wished he had not gorged himself at lunch. His name was called twice, and he stepped up to receive cards. When it came time to read the name on the package, Newberg gave Press a wry look and shrugged his soldiers. "Patrick," he shouted. An audible sigh of relief escaped from the rest of the platoon. Every candidate had written home during the first week and informed his parents not to send anything edible.

"Sir, Candidate Patrick requests permission to speak."

"It had better be good, Patrick."

"Sir, Candidate Patrick. This package of pogey bait was sent to me by my mother against my express instructions, undoubtedly for my birthday tomorrow."

"Is this the first box of pogey bait you received in the mail, Patrick?"

"Sir, Candidate Patrick. Do I have to answer that, sir?"

"You're goddamn right you have to answer, and if you try to evade the question once more, I'll have you before the honor board for quibbling."

"Sir, Candidate Patrick. This is not the first."

"You're a college boy, Patrick, add 'em up. I want to know exactly how many."

"Sir, Candidate Patrick. I'm not sure...about seven, sir."

A collective gasp was followed by Hausser's rhetorical question: "Seven? *Seven?*" Obviously aware that most of those packages passed his screening, his face became scarlet. "Drop! Drop! On your back...on your stomach...on your feet...on your stomach...." So began the belly flop, the harshest form of physical punishment meted out by tac officers. After two minutes of continuous body movement, the offending candidate would be exhausted. Sometime in the fourth minute, Press began to vomit. Hausser looked in amazement at the quantity of regurgitated food on the gravel. "Bring me the pogey bait, Newberg," he ordered, then turned to Press, who was on his hands and knees, breathing deeply. "Write a military letter to Lieutenant Holt about your behavior, Patrick. Have it on his desk by 0800."

Addressing the platoon he continued: "You people don't deserve to be junior candidates. The way you botched the last two field problems made me retch"—the candidates almost laughed at his wording— "and this mockery of discipline by Patrick is the last straw. How many times were you told to work as a team? You're not a team—you're a mob. I thought you learned your lesson after that last OR." Hausser railed on, converting petty failures of the platoon into personal affronts. His vehemence gained momentum with every phrase, and even Press, still heaving on his hands and knees, sensed that Hausser's composure was at the vanishing point. Tears welled in his eyes and his voice cracked. He struggled with himself, seemingly wresting for control one moment, ranting the next. Unable to reconcile his emotions, he turned about and walked off. Forbes, the current platoon leader, dismissed the men, but the candidates milled around, dissecting Hausser's performance, some expressing disbelief, others contempt.

King and Wilson helped Press to his feet. "Geez, I've never seen a work-out like that," Wilson said.

"Which one, the one he did to me, or the one he did to himself?" Press quipped.

"Better get inside; you only have a few minutes to wash up and change before class," advised King.

"If Hausser's right, I'm already washed up," Press said, and started for the barracks.

He wrote the military letter after taps that evening and placed it in Holt's basket in the "tac shack" before morning chow. Late that afternoon, he was summoned to Holt's office, a closet-size cubicle in a clapboard building. After completing the requisite fifty push-ups, he stood at attention in front of the tac officer's desk.

"This is a serious offense, Patrick. Have you got anything to say in your defense?"

"Sir, Candidate Patrick. No, sir."

"In that case I'm placing you on leadership probation."

"Sir, Candidate Patrick requests permission to ask a question."

"What is it, Patrick?"

"Sir, Candidate Patrick. What are the implications of leadership probation, sir?"

Hausser had come into the office during his question and now stood next
to the desk, a wet, synthetic smile on his face. He answered before Holt could
speak. "It means, Patrick, that if you screw up again, you'll become a retread,
or if it's bad enough, you'll wind up like O'Malley—kicked out of the program. One thing's for sure"—he paused for effect—"you won't be getting laid
when it comes time for overnight passes. You won't be going off-post while
on probation." His gloat spread slowly over his face, till it almost touched
his ears, and Press watched in revulsion as saliva glistened on his articulated
mouth.

11

It was Saturday morning of a waning week fourteen. Holt stood at the head of the formation and unfolded a piece of paper. "This red slip is from your nuisance mining course instructor. Apparently several of you displayed an attitude which reflects poorly on India Company. Reform in five minutes with full gear."

Four-and-a-half minutes later, the platoon stood at attention, each man with backpack, canteen, entrenching tool, gas mask, steel pot and M-14 rifle. Hausser slithered through the ranks, checking to see if any candidate substituted paper for the mess kit and other accouterments in the back pack. One favorite ploy of candidates to lessen the load was to fill their canteens less than a quarter of capacity. During his random check, Hausser lifted Ortiz' canteen and found it nearly empty. "Drop Ortiz," he ordered. "Push out five zero." After Ortiz completed his pushups, but while still in the front lean and rest position, Holt asked him why he did not fill his canteen.

"Sir, Candidate Ortiz, no excuse, sir."

"I don't want an excuse, Ortiz. I want the reason your canteen is not full."

"Sir, Candidate Ortiz, I require less fluids than the average person, sir, the reduced weight helps me run, and the water here tastes like warm algae."

"Well, Ortiz, you're correct on two accounts; we'll see about the other... Recover."

Press rolled his eyes. The candidates knew that a boonie run was in the offing when Holt gave the order to form with full gear. They had hoped it would be an hour out and back. Now they were not so sure.

It started normally. The platoon double-timed to Section C. As the tac officers became winded, they ordered the platoon to low crawl. After an hour of running and crawling along dirt roads, the platoon veered off into the low lying terrain bordering Chicotink Creek. Their going was slowed appreciably by the unstable footing. Other than for a few birds, the only noises heard in the wilderness were the candidates' lungs gasping for air, the jostling of their equipment as it loosened from their bodies, and the sucking of air created from boots pulling out of the mud. Water quickly filled the holes, and as the candidates trudged along, their boots, socks, and bloused fatigue pants became saturated. When the platoon became strung out for more than a hundred yards, Holt ordered the lead element to halt. After the stragglers caught up, he ordered a ten-minute break. The temperature was climbing into the high eighties. Press wished that the humidity would drive the wet bulb into the red zone, where regulations stipulated that all physical training cease. During the third rest period he emptied his canteen and listened to the traffic coursing along US Route 1, now only a few hundreds yards away. He saw himself in a convertible, Celia next to him, on their way to a picnic along the banks of the Potomac, both with wind-sheared hair and gamboling spirits.

His reverie was cut short by Ortiz' sidling up next to him and asking if he had any water left. "Just emptied my canteen," Press answered. "Hold on for a half-hour, we have to be back for chow at noon."

"I'll ask around a little more. Damn that OR. We weren't that bad in nuisance mining—just a few jokes."

Press shook his head. "We become red tabs in two weeks, so this is probably our last physical test. I just hope that we can make it up Heartbreak Hill as a platoon, even sing a chorus or two of 'Incomin' India' on the way in. Maybe then we'll get the rest of the afternoon off."

Press had underestimated the severity of the "test." The platoon did make it up Heartbreak Hill more or less intact. Spirits soared as the candidates topped the crest, and soon the OCS area resonated with the by now familiar, and still insipid, chant.

Other platoons were marching or double timing to the mess hall, and in nonmilitary fashion, the candidates turned their heads to view India's entrance. Officer candidates uniformly viewed themselves in heroic proportions as they returned to the compound following a boonie run. But the spectacle of India's entry was far from the Roman Legions' tramp along the Appian Way into Rome. Even Respighi could not have rescued India from the snickers that greeted its approach. For the soldiers were dripping the leached-out, yellowish bottomland muck which all but impregnated their bodies and their gear. The squish of their footfalls on the stone-strewn streets mocked the bravado of their song.

They entered the barracks, lungs still working hard, showered, and changed into fresh fatigues. Holt had left word for the candidates to clean their weapons after the noon meal. They were assiduously performing that task when word came to form for weapons' inspection. A few more strokes of the ramrod or wire brush were hastily applied before the men poured out of the barracks. The inspection was cursory. After five minutes of peeping down M-14 barrels, Holt, in his normal laconic manner, said: "There's rust on your weapons. Form in five minutes with full gear." He turned to Hausser and told him that he would join the platoon in Section C. Before they broke formation, Hausser cautioned them to take salt tablets along.

Press was as incredulous as the others at the inevitability of another boonie run. So sure were the candidates that they would have the remainder of the day off, many had called their wives after lunch and arranged to meet them in the Day Room in mid-afternoon. Tightening his pack, Press looked over at Ron Gross, a retread from Charlie Company. "Better hurry up, Ron. If you're late for formation, you'll be knocking out fifty."

"I can't do it. I can't run anymore," said Gross, looking dazed.

Gross had the endurance of a vapor trial and could not cope with the physical rigors of OCS. Despite a significant gain in strength, his short legs carried pig iron-heavy hips and buttocks. No amount of PT could enable him to run stride for stride with his classmates. He had been told he would be released the next week. Press advised him to go on sick call for stomach cramps. Gross declined and stumbled out of the barracks after Press and Ortiz helped him with his gear.

The wet bulb was near the red zone, but the candidates knew that the temperature had peaked for the day. They became reconciled to their lot and started off with the hope that the run would only last an hour.

Gross dropped back before the platoon cleared the compound. Hausser halted the platoon.

"Can't take it, eh, Gross?" he taunted.

"Sir, Candidate Gross. I can't do it, sir."

"Would you like to sit it out, Gross?"

"Sir, Candidate Gross. I want to go on, but I don't have the strength, sir."

"Then you'll sit it out till we get back, and you'll sit it out there," said Hausser, pointing to a dumpster adjacent to Foxtrot Company.

"Sir, Candidate Gross. *In the dumpster*, sir?"

"That's right, Gross. Now move!"

Gross, who obviously had never heard such a demeaning and sadistic order issued, looked dumfounded.

"Get in there, you idiot!" Hausser screamed.

Gross ran to the dumpster, threw his M-14 over the side and pulled himself to the top. He lifted his right leg over the edge, lost his grip, and fell into the bin, his fall cushioned by nearly two days' accumulation of trash. Hausser told Gross not to leave until he returned.

Instead of a continual running and low crawling combination, which would have caused heat exhaustion in some, the tac officers introduced a new wrinkle to the exercise program. Holt joined the platoon in the bottomland and led it to a narrow but steep-banked stream, which was bisected by a rope strung between two trees. He ordered everyone to hit the ground and begin crossing the stream. The candidates were covered by a fresh coat of mud, and as they began to pull themselves across on the rope, it became increasingly slippery.

Press was fifth in line, his chest still heaving from running, when Hausser shouted at him: "What are you waiting for, Patrick, get your ass up there."

Press slung his M-14 over his shoulder and reached for the rope, losing his grip three times before jumping and catching it in the crook of his right arm, followed by a quick scissoring with his legs. The journey along the greasy fibers was slow and debilitating. He had inched himself halfway over the stream when he heard a hissing sound, followed by shouts of "Gas!" He saw candidates sprawled along the road donning gas masks, as Holt popped several CS grenades. There was no discernible movement of air, and Press calculated that he could cross before the spreading fog of tear gas reached him. He was wrong. The gas wafted over the stream while he hung suspended above the far bank. He fantasized that Holt had dropped dry ice into the water and that the gray cloud enveloping his body would be cool and refreshing. The fantasy was brief. The gas seeped along his flanks and penetrated every exposed pore, a thousand needle pricks puncturing his bare skin, propelling him in a furious but futile effort to advance, as it invaded and convulsed his lungs. Involuntarily loosening his hold on the rope, he dropped seven feet to the soft-sided bank, sliding on his backside into the stream. Arms and fingers palsied from being locked in place, eyes slammed shut, he fumbled for his gas mask, finally shoving it to his face. Soon the searing pain in his lungs subsided. Stumbling a few yards down the thigh-high stream to a gently sloping bank, he clawed his way to level ground. The gas lingered over the area for several more minutes and although it still seeped into the open pores on his arms, neck, and face, the pain paled in comparison with the recent explosion in his lungs.

For most candidates, especially those who had not inhaled the tear gas, the episode was preferable to running and low crawling. Press was able to regain his breath while the remaining candidates crossed the stream, yet he did not regain his strength, as was usual during respites.

"Form up and keep your masks on," Holt ordered a few minutes after the crossing.

"Oh shit," Press whispered into his mask. He and the others looked at one another through the smudged, plastic circles in their masks. They had done this before: running while wearing their masks. They started out in formation, but the less stalwart candidates began dropping back during the first quarter mile. Press began cursing silently as he tried to keep up with the main body. Goddamn it. What a damn fool I was to do this. Vietnam can't be worse than this goddamn hell hole. Leadership—bullshit. These bastards aren't developing leaders...they're seeing if we can take it. Big lungs and strong legs are the measures of leadership in this place. They should change that goddamn sign to read "through these portals pass men with small brains and big lungs"—oh, and command presence. Let's not forget that goddamn key ingredient.

Press was sucking in all the air that passed through the filter, but the restriction would not allow enough through to meet his needs. In one final spasm of cursing he lifted his mask and scooped enough air down to keep him in the main body.

A few minutes later Holt halted the thinned-out platoon. While the stragglers rejoined the main body under Hausser's fixed gaze, several candidates vomited along side the road, which earned them a minute of Hausser's invective.

The final hour was a repetition of the morning's run, except for the final few minutes. As platoon closed in on Heartbreak Hill, it was spread over a half mile of road. No one had enough left in him to introduce "Incomin' India," so when ordered to sing, the nucleus of the platoon began shouting the two syllable "*FEBA.*" In they came, dragging the first syllable: "*FEE-BA, FEE-BA, FEE-BA....*"

Either Holt did not approve of the chant or the manner of entry, or both, so he ordered everyone to low crawl back to the barracks. Press saw Gross lift his head out of the dumpster and watch the men scrape by on the hard packed gravel. A few other candidates walking nearby witnessed the platoon's less-than-heroic return, undoubtedly thankful that they did not draw India.

After the last of the platoon members crawled up the barracks's steps at 1630, Holt departed. A few minutes later Gross entered the barracks and approached Press and King.

"When Hausser came back he told me to keep my mouth shut about this, or they'd keep me here another six weeks. I'll tell you one thing, I never want to see another dumpster again," he said with conviction.

Press smiled. "Now Ron, don't be so hasty in your judgment. One person's prison could be another's salvation."

Gross shook his head before replying. "Patrick, they're kicking the wrong guy out of here."

12

The complexion of OCS changed during the final weeks. The senior candidate phase emphasized leadership and pride of accomplishment. The Army could not have possessors of the gold bar poised to drop at the merest infraction. Officers had to have the steely eyes of hunters, not the wary eyes of prey. Academics also changed. The senior candidates now carried slide rules as often as weapons. The course in timber trestle bridge construction required using trigonometry for the calculation of moment forces and other engineering applications. Demolition was the most interesting but required computing the amount and placement of explosives given the composition, density, and dimensions of the object to be demolished.

Press and a few others were assigned the task of felling a tree without completely severing it, and arranging for the trunk to come to rest perpendicular to an imaginary road as part of an abatis, or obstacle to tank travel. With senior status cockiness, they quickly calculated the problem on their slide rules, placed the requisite amount of C-4 plastic explosive on the tree, linked the charges with detonation cord, then implanted a blasting cap in the slab of explosive. After connecting the wire to the terminals of the blasting machine and shouting "fire in the hole" several times, King gave the handle a quick twist.

They expected to see the tree totter for a second before falling gracefully over the "road." The first syllable of "timber" played on Press's lips as the tree imitated one of the first unsuccessful launches of a Redstone rocket at Cape Canaveral. It separated cleanly from its stump and rose a few feet before crash landing parallel to the "road," affording the candidates a clear view up its hollow trunk.

The instructor strode up to the embarrassed group and said, "Fellows, you set a great charge for a fat, tropical hardwood. Next time you encounter a hollowed-out beech, why don't three of you just push it over and save the explosives."

Despite heavy emphasis on engineering subjects, the seniors still went out on field training exercises, mostly on Friday evenings. These included a night raid in assault boats, recon patrol, and combat patrol. Prior to each FTX Holt would generally send the platoon off with a terse statement. Press's favorite was issued as they formed for an ambush exercise. Holt stood before them, pursed his lips and said, "Execution trumps strategy every time. That's why in a moment of crisis, it is imperative to *act*. Even if it's wrong, it's almost always better to do *something*. You will be judged harsher for doing nothing."

Celia had to work on a paper the Sunday three weeks before graduation. Although for no identifiable reason, Press decided to go to Rev. Browne's service alone. He took a seat in the last pew, but instead of listening to the sermon, which was tenuously connected to an obscure biblical passage, his thoughts roamed. He wondered what posting he would receive—undoubtedly a military intelligence assignment, but how distant from Celia? Should he sign up for an additional year and secure a guaranteed tour in Maryland or Virginia? The idea of extending his term annoyed him. He thought of asking Celia to marry him but quickly discarded the notion. He was certain that she would reject him if he proposed prematurely. He would have to prove to her that he had become more serious, more committed. But could he become something he wasn't? Except for the military, life had been easy for him. He was well loved and had been pampered by his parents. Academics had been stimulating rather than stressful. Although he had spent a respectful number of hours in the university library, from his sophomore year he devoted more time to arguing politics and history with grad students in various Hyde Park bars, thanks to a phony identification card. Most of the courses he took were graded on class participation, term papers, and essay exams, where he excelled. OCS had been his only challenge, and he was not faring well. Leaving the chapel after mass, he decided that most people who knew him would say he was a finagler, but he would not say it of himself.

Press was chatting with the widows Whiting and Raymond in the courtyard when Rev. Browne approached. After exchanging pleasantries, he said, "I'm sorry Celia couldn't attend services today. You looked a little forlorn in the pew sitting alone. In fact, Press, I'm surprised that you came at all."

"Reverend Browne, the appeal of OCS can't compete with your eloquence in the pulpit."

Rev. Browne laughed and said, "You didn't hear a word of my sermon. But I'll let you make it up to me. Why don't you have dinner with us this afternoon. Joan would like to meet you, and it wouldn't be much to put an extra plate on the table."

"Thank you for the invitation. I would enjoy it very much."

"Good, I'll pick you up at the OCS entrance at four."

Rev. Browne was punctual, and it took only a few minutes to drive to his quarters, a brick duplex on Forney Loop. A girl of perhaps ten greeted them at the door.

"This is our daughter, Katherine. Oh, Joan," he said on seeing a shadow crossing the foyer, "here's half of the couple I've been telling you about."

Mrs. Browne came to the door and greeted Press. She was tall and attractive, but with features a little on the sharp side. "Welcome, Candidate Patrick. I'm always glad to meet someone who likes to listen to Grant's Sunday morning homilies."

"I wouldn't go that far, my dear. Press has confessed to an ulterior motive," Rev. Browne said with a chuckle.

"He means that I first came for sanctuary, but I've come to enjoy the experience."

The house was tastefully decorated, mostly with antiques and oriental rugs. When they were seated in the living room, Mrs. Browne asked Press what he thought of his training at Fort Belvoir.

"It's been difficult, and I'm sure I'll never have fond memories of it, but I'm a person of place, so I'm happy to be in a fort that lives up to its name."

"Have you had much experience with chaplains?"

"While I've never heard a chaplain other than your husband in church, most who lectured us in basic and advanced training seemed more interested in fighting communists than in matters of faith—altogether a very conservative lot."

"When are you getting married to your girlfriend?" Katherine asked impulsively.

"Katherine! That's impolite and none of your business," Mrs. Browne scolded.

"That's okay. I don't mind answering. But all I can tell you is that if it happens, I'd like it to happen here with your dad officiating and maybe you can be a flower girl."

"That's a very nice answer. Now, young lady, suppose you return to your homework." She addressed Press: "There's a comfortable chair in the study—actually a converted upstairs bedroom, but it's bright and friendly with a view of the woods. Dinner will be ready in an hour or so."

Rev. Browne showed him to the study, disappeared for a minute, and returned with two mugs of Pilsner beer. "Thank you," said Press, taking one. He sat in one of the two arm chairs. An oriental rug covered most of the hardwood floor; six bookcases stood against the interior wall, and an antique writing table and straight-back chair occupied the opposite side of the room. An eight by ten picture on the table showed Rev. Browne, clad in jungle gear, preaching on a fire base. Press looked closer. About fifty feet behind the chaplain's right shoulder, a puff of black smoke hung in the air, looking as if it came from nowhere. "Mrs. Browne was right, this is a pleasant room—certainly one that's conducive to writing Sunday sermons."

"Yes, this is a fine room, and writing in it is almost effortless."

"The picture of you on the table has piqued my curiosity. Where did the smoke come from?"

"A mortar detonated just as one of the men took the shot. Quite remarkable."

"It's so close, were you hit?"

"A small piece of shrapnel in the buttock. I was very fortunate."

"That would explain the grimace on your face."

"The sound of the explosion a moment later made it frightening, but no one else was hit, thank God."

Rev. Browne changed the subject to Press's likely assignment following graduation. After exhausting that, they drifted into the progress for peace in Vietnam under the Nixon administration. It was not until midway through the second beer than the conversation turned to Rev. Browne's favorite pursuit: the saving of souls.

"I know that you're, in a manner of speaking, beyond the penumbra of belief, and you're somewhat skeptical in your attitude toward life...if you don't mind telling me, I'm interested in how it came about. Have you a religious background?"

"What a great metaphor! 'Penumbra of belief' almost makes atheism palatable. But to answer your question, yes, my parents are Christians—Presbyterian, specifically. I went to church and Sunday school on a semi-regular basis and was, well, moderately religious."

"What influenced your change?"

"Reading. You'll probably think that reading has warped my soul, but my transformation started in high school, when I began reading about the genocide in the Second World War and watching those documentaries on TV showing bulldozers pushing naked, wasted bodies into mass graves. It had a profound effect on me. Those unspeakable horrors didn't occur in some Neolithic, backwater country, but in the land of Geothe, Beethoven, and Kant. One evening I went over to the rectory to discuss my feelings with our pastor. He was not what you would call receptive. The crux of our conversation was that I said I was confused and he asked what was I mad at. He told me that callow minds couldn't grapple with theological complexities, but, nevertheless, I should pray for guidance."

Rev. Browne grimaced.

"I didn't like his answer, obviously. But more than that, I believe the really important things in life are simple. It's the detail that's complicated."

"For example—"

"It's like comparing the relationship of energy and matter to some arcane changes in the supply of money. E equals MC square is universal and simple, whereas the money supply equation is strewn with exponents and a whole passel of Greek letters—runs a half-page and will soon be dated. To my reasoning there are three things to keep in mind when it comes to religious dogma: does it help people, does it have a neutral effect, or does it hurt people? The pastor wasn't interested in discussing any of that."

"What happened then?"

"I stopped going to services. I don't hold it against the pastor—it was in the evening, and he was helping his daughter with homework. I think she was a great joy to him, much as I'm sure Katherine is to you."

Rev. Browne smiled. "Yes, I have two great joys—my family and my ministry."

"In that order—family and work?" Press asked with a twinkle in his eye.

"You know I've never really thought about it, because they don't compete. I place a very great importance on serving the military community through my work in the Church, but instead of interfering with my family, it enhances my relationship with them." Rev. Browne smiled. "Saving souls—or making the effort—and enjoying family life are a source of great satisfaction."

"I don't doubt your devotion to the Church, but I hold to the passage I read in one of Forster's novels: 'Personal relationship is better than any institution.' This may shock you, and I may be feeling the beer—I haven't had much in the last five months—but I suspect that institutional religion has killed more people than it's saved. Granted, I have no idea of how many have been saved, but from my reading of history, religious conflict has taken tens of millions of lives."

"Even if the number is that high, you're talking about a weakness of man, not of religion and certainly not of faith in God."

"That may be, but what kind of God does organized religion purport to be the cause and the Creator of all things? I have trouble believing that a Creator who is all-powerful and one that you would willingly worship, would tolerate the extermination of ten million people and the killing of perhaps sixty or seventy million more in the wars of this century alone. Where were the great elucidators of morals while people were being slaughtered? They either kept a low profile or like Cardinal Spellman now—were supporters of one side or the other."

"That's a very cynical view of religion."

"Well, it's as Reverend William Sloane Coffin says of some of his non-believer acquaintances. They tell him they are too moral for religion. In any event, what am I supposed to do about it? My beliefs are based on my experience and reading and of course shaped by reasoning, which is essentially beyond my control."

Rev. Browne sighed. "Look, you can't depend on reason when it comes to accepting God. At our best we are a people of partial comprehensions—partial in both meanings of the word. And whether or not you channel a belief in God through a religious institution pales in comparison to the importance of accepting God, of having faith in Him. There's no way that I can prove to you His existence, compassion, and promise. It has to be a matter of faith."

"That's asking a lot for a person who believes in facts. It's a hell—heck of a leap from facts to faith."

Rev. Browne appeared saddened and said, "I don't believe that a life based on facts can be anything other than empty. Tolstoy put it stronger in *War and Peace*: 'If we admit that human life can be ruled by reason, the possibility of life is destroyed.'"

"I'm impressed; you didn't quote scripture. Hitler did almost everything by intuition. Had not the forces of reason prevailed, we'd be in a fine muddle today."

"Are you trying to equate depraved intuition and the evils of the world with faith?" Rev. Browne asked in a tone of exasperation.

"It may have sounded like it, but no—only that I side with reason. With David Hume. I also like what Locke, Voltaire, and Mill say when it comes to reason and tolerance, and what William James says about pluralism. And I'll admit that I'm a skeptic. This may shock you, but I believe that people are no damn good. I—"

"Wait," Rev. Browne interrupted. "You can't mean that."

"Let me explain. The people I'm talking about are those who will seek to gain at the expense of others, if there's no cost to them. Take a car in perfect condition to ten garages and see how many quotes you get for repairs. I don't know what percent are in this group, but it encompasses people who take more than give, who cause more pain than joy. If you could factor their lives into a human equation, they would run a deficit. Because of them and because of there being no satisfactory explanation as to what started everything and especially there being no knowledge of what comes after death and the fear that that generates, man invented God—all kinds of gods...man *needs* God, the more anthropomorphic the better—you know, a human body, like Jesus. Let's suppose God exists—a kind, merciful God of the New Testament. How much evil can He stomach before abandoning His hands-off policy? I mean, can He sit idly by and let Hitler and Stalin and others like them kill hundreds of millions of people and still be a kind, merciful God?"

"God created mankind with free will and—"

"Yet he interceded—Jesus did—if you believe that he performed miracles. He even brought Lazarus back from the dead. What does that tell you when a Supreme Being intercedes for an individual, but refuses to act as millions die ignominiously?"

"If you'll allow a quote from the Bible—from Psalms: 'The substance of Your word is truth. And every righteous judicial decision of Yours is to time indefinite.' We accept on faith God's infinite wisdom; that His actions have a purpose."

"My problem is that I don't have to experience an atrocity to be deeply offended by it. History has a face. I see the agony on the face of the Russian *kulak* as he and his family are being driven off their farm and marched to a labor camp, where they'll starve to death. If there is a God and that's a result of his purpose, I wouldn't want anything to do with Him."

Rev. Browne shook his head slowly. "So, you've read a lot but as a young man experienced little. It's like believing that because you've put your ear to the conch you know the sea."

Press did not give him time to continue. "If I can live my life on the whole in accordance with the moral precepts of the major religions—the way they're written, not practiced—then what does it matter? Spinoza may have been on to something when he wrote that we humans can achieve a spirituality on earth. The trick, he said, is to try to understand the evil, hatred, and persecution that surround us, and react to it equably—to transcend the hatred and leave life better than we found it. It's a large order, but that may be the way atheists find meaning. To me, tolerance is the key."

"You say tolerance, but could you mean *indifference?*"

Press turned scarlet. "Perhaps...I'm sure there are people who believe I belong in the *no damn good* group."

"That's where faith helps. If a person believes that there is a purpose to life, he will be more charitable to others. And what you said about the innocent suffering, all I can tell you is that life on earth, even a long one, is not an eye-blink in eternity. Do you really want to bet your moment on earth against eternity? You probably know of Pascal's wager: What is rational is to believe in God, because if you're right, there's great potential reward; if you're wrong, you've lost nothing."

"Yes, I've read it but found it a facile argument. Take redemption, for example. God will admit to heaven someone who lived a life of murder and mayhem, but who in his last hours on earth truly repents. That kind of justice turns my stomach. You just put your finger on my problem, though, with your comment on having a purpose to life. I lack the comfort of belief, the calm of purpose. I don't remember the poet's name, but I recall his lines: 'Seek the course on moldy pages / Span the girth of stormy ages / Plumb the future, ordain your life / Cleric solace, wayfarer strife.' You're the cleric, settled in your beliefs, and I'm the wayfarer, caught in history's slipstream."

"Up to now, knowing your fondness for expedience, I had a suspicion that it might extend to philosophy—depending on science and the rationalists for answers. And incidentally, some of them, just as James did, believed that humans should accept God. But back to my point. If it's true that you are a spiritual wayfarer, prospects are good that you'll eventually come around. You know, it takes a traumatic event for some to reach the threshold of faith, of finding a purpose. Perhaps if you go to Vietnam, you'll discover it there. You know the adage."

Press laughed. "Yeah, 'there are no atheists in foxholes.' I guess that would be the litmus test. It's funny though...most people accept the religion they're brought up with; some become ardent supporters and are so sure they're right that they will try to push their views down your throat. I've spent many hours going beyond the Bible—reading the *ancients,* the rationalists, the empiricists; almost all the philosophers. I even delved into Eastern religions. Yet *I'm* the one who is susceptible to instant inspiration in a foxhole."

"Don't discount it; I've seen it happen. Tell me though, just as a matter of interest, what do you find to be the major difference between Christianity and the eastern religions?"

Press reached for his beer and took a last swallow. "There are so many that it's hard to say. For one thing eastern religions go with the flow: life is difficult; there is suffering; there's no Supreme Deity, so in this impersonal world find spiritual fulfillment from within. Instead of heaven there's illumination. I guess I would say another major difference is that Christians have original sin. The 'Christ died for your sins' guilt complex...the legacy of St. Augustine: sex is dirty. To my knowledge eastern religions have none of that and would find that kind of thinking ridiculous."

"Have you discussed your beliefs with Celia?"

"Not in detail. It would put distance between us. She's unsure of our relationship as it is."

"Is that how you want to build a future with her?"

"No, it's not, but I know that she's right for me, and I think that with time I'll be right for her. The convergence theory of human affairs," Press said with a chuckle.

A second call for dinner was sounded. As they rose, Rev. Browne said, "I'm fond of you, Press, and of course of Celia. You've got a lot of potential. I hope you'll be honest with her, and it happens before your relationship develops much further." He walked to the door and then almost as an afterthought said, "I'm going to paraphrase Lincoln: You have a spiritual spot you cannot reach."

On the following Saturday India's seniors were given overnight passes. Press had been released from probation, and, after making dinner reservations in Washington and motel reservations in Alexandria, he packed his toilet kit and a change of clothes. While waiting for Celia to pick him up, he saw Whitworth place a duffel bag in the trunk of an airport limousine parked about thirty yards away. Their eyes caught as Whitworth stepped into the limo, and each raised his hand in recognition. Press wondered if Whitworth considered himself a failure and if so, it would be pure paradox, a cruel juxtaposition of truth and falsehood, even though, he conceded, one consistent with human nature and the triumph of style over substance. As the limo pulled away Press extended his hand to his cap in a farewell salute.

A few minutes later Celia picked him up, and they drove to the restaurant. As the maitre d' guided them to their table, they overheard one of the patrons say, "Must be one of those Special Forces types."

Press whispered to Celia: "People don't know what to make of the red tabs. Special Forces is the last thing I would be."

After sitting at their table, Celia spoke. "You know, you've never told me what you want to do after the Army."

"There's a good reason for that. I have no idea what I want to do. What does a person do with a master's degree in political science? I lack the patience for teaching, and I don't want to work for the government. I'll probably end up in business."

"Large company? Small company?"

"Small company, definitely."

The waiter approached their table and took their cocktail orders. When their drinks arrived Press touched Celia's glass with his and said, "You sparkle tonight. Whatever happens in our lives, how you look right now will be forever fixed in my memory, from the gleam in your eyes to that wayward strand of hair to your smile."

"Now that *your* hair is finally growing out, you don't look so bad, either. In fact, you're rather handsome—must be the uniform."

"I'll take the compliment any way I can get it."

They ordered dinner and Celia was telling Press of Senator Jackson's office lecture on how the domino theory was at work in Southeast Asia, when their waiter brought them two more drinks.

"From a gentleman who wishes to remain anonymous."

"Please thank him for us," said Press.

While he and Celia conversed, Press kept an eye on the waiter. A few minutes after he delivered their cocktails, the waiter stopped at a table and said a few words to a man who looked to be in his fifties, dining with one of the most elegant looking women Press had ever seen. The man smiled and nodded, and the waiter left.

Press turned to Celia and wondered if she would look elegant in middle age. No doubt, he concluded.

They ate slowly, and their conversation became intermittent. He knew that she was thinking the same thought. Press had been mulling over how to approach it and was a little afraid of Celia's response. He stabbed a piece of steak with his fork and slowly set it in his mouth. As he chewed and without taking his eyes from her, he decided on the approach he would use.

"Are you doing a *Tom Jones* on me?" she asked, a laugh in her eyes.

"I was thinking how to ask you, well, you know that I made a reservation at the Old Colony Inn. Will you stay with me tonight?"

"Just like that?"

"No, not quite like that. I love you and I want to make love to you—with you."

"If you put it that way, I guess I don't have any choice."

"Whew," Press exhaled. "I'll ask for the check."

"Let's finish dinner first."

"Just kidding."

"I know what 'Stay moment, stay; you are so fair' means," she said, smiling mischievously. "It's a passage from *Faust*."

"Clever girl. So tell me what you think it means."

"Faust would say those words only if he experienced complete contentment. I assume you were a very contented person when you said them. And near the end of the drama Faust did say the words. They were his redemption."

Press smiled. "Let's finish and go; the wait's driving me crazy."

As they were leaving, they went toward the table where their benefactors were seated. Press caught the man's eye and smiled and silently mouthed, *Thank you.* The man acknowledged the gesture, turned to his companion and said, "There's hope."

On their way to the car Press remarked, "Our patron has probably seen one too many protesters."

As Press filled in the obligatory form, falsely, the motel clerk leaned forward, looking for a ring on the young woman standing too close to the counter. Motels within minutes of military bases were subject to high levels of in-room copulation, and owners, eager to eradicate the for-hire, often curtailed the consensual. Press's easy manner swayed the clerk.

After entering their room, Celia turned to Press and said, "I'm unpracticed in this sort of thing. Is there a standard procedure?"

"Very funny. But I think it goes like this: after a decent interval of conversation, one of the parties goes to the bathroom. Then it's the other one's turn. What follows is more or less spontaneous."

"That sounds pretty good to me, except I'm too nervous to talk. You don't mind if I go first?"

Press waved his arm toward the bathroom. They rotated fifteen minutes later. When he returned Celia was in bed, covered by a sheet. He dimmed the light in the room and began to undress. "Are you okay?" he asked.

"Yes, honey. I'm okay, so far."

Press slid under the sheet, but did not close on her. He brought his hand to her face and ran his fingers through her hair. As he repeated the motions he said, "When we touched glasses at dinner, I thought how radiant you looked. You still shimmer."

"Will you promise to say that in the morning? I spent more than a few minutes with the make-up bottle. I might frighten you and you'll desert me in the light of day."

"Fat chance. There's no one in the world I'd rather be with than you."

"I feel the same way, honey."

Press moved closer until their bodies touched. He kissed her cheek, her ear, her eye and then, gently, her lips. He cupped her breast in his hand, and as softly as he kissed her face, kissed her breast. He went on to her forehead, nose, shoulder and navel. While they kissed and touched and caressed, they often paused to look into each other's eyes. They had no need for words. Each knew the depth of feeling of the other, and their emotions so overwhelmed them that physical pleasure became accompaniment.

Later, she whispered into his ear, and he turned on his side and looked directly at her. "You feel it as you imagine it. It's impossible to describe—it was too wonderful."

"Can't you make a stab at it?" she prodded him.

"I don't think so."

"How about a favorite song? Which one would it be?"

"Oh, that's easy. It's 'Stay.'" He began to sing off-key: "Staaay, just a little bit longer. Please let me stay *in you*—" His rendition was truncated by a pillow.

"What's with you and the word 'stay'? Be serious for a moment."

Press grinned. "Okay, okay, I'll be serious." He thought for a few seconds. "What bobs to the top of my mind are the last words of *Turandot*: '*Gloria a te. Gloria a te.*'"

"Puccini?"

"Yes, my mother used to play the recording, and she even goaded my dad and me into seeing a Birgit Nilsson performance at the Lyric Opera. The last lines are sung by the chorus to the two lovers: '*O Sole. Vita. Eternità. Luce del mondo è amore.*' Then there's a few words I can't recall. It ends: '*Gloria a te. Gloria a te.*' Glory to you. Glory to you."

"Translate the first part."

"It's about infinite happiness—love, life, eternity. It's how I feel about us. I've never been in love before, and I've never felt anything like it before."

"I feel the same. While we were making love I saw it in your eyes." She slid under his arm, and they began to kiss and caress and whisper.

Neither grew tired in the last hours of night. At a few minutes before five, Celia got out of bed, put her hand behind the curtains, and peered out.

"Any sign of daylight?" Press inquired.

She slipped back into bed and kissed him on the forehead. "The first stirrings. If only I were Athena for a while."

"Why Athena?"

"Because she knew what to do with time. If I remember the quote, it goes like this: 'In the west the night lingered long, while in the east she reined in the dawn.'"

"Sophocles?"

"Homer."

Press laughed. "That's just great; at a time like this you bring up *Homer.*"

Celia picked up a pillow and hit him for the second time, and they laughed and rolled on the bed and covered themselves with the sheet.

13

The last eight days of OCS were devoted largely to handling the myriad details necessary for graduation and commissioning. It was a heady time. The rigidity of the past twenty-two weeks, although on the decline since week nine, now gave way to a relaxed, even giddy, atmosphere. India's senior candidates finally became not merely "short-timers"; they were, in the elaborate jargon of the military, "single-digit midgets."

Class members would buttonhole underclassmen and ask them to guess precisely how short they were. After the candidates played along, the senior would grin and crow with silly metaphors: "I'm so short I can't hoist my drawers past my ankles!"

While marching to a classroom to learn about their new pay status or how to present a calling card, the seniors would sing about the "little gold bar" which would soon adorn their shoulders or, more bawdily, about being caught in bed with the colonel's daughter and getting a "lay, ho, heave" into the Dempsey dumpster early in the morning. They sang the silly songs unabashedly, for they were on an emotional swell that few experiences could match. Even Press's spirits soared. Not only was he in love, he was sure he would never have to run until his lungs screamed, would never have to take an order from a mean-spirited sergeant or lieutenant, would never live a life so confining.

The most important event of the week for India's senior class was receiving their new duty assignments. They had completed their "dream sheets"—three top choices for posting—weeks before. Holt, still the model of detachment after all these weeks, came in one morning holding a sheaf of papers. "Gather 'round," he said. "Before I hand out your orders, I've got something interesting to tell you. According to a report I read this morning, the most dangerous jobs in Vietnam are advisors, armor crewmen, explosive ordnance demolitions, and combat engineers. Since most of you are being commissioned in the Corps of Engineers and will probably wind up in Vietnam, you should know what you may be getting into. Keep your head down when you get there." Holt's admonition collided with the doctrine of the indestructibility of youth and provoked bravado and shouts of *FEBA*.

Press, secure in his branch of service, patiently waited as Holt passed out the orders. It took several moments for each candidate to decipher the jumble of acronyms and pinpoint his next duty station. Exclamations and groans began to fill the air. Press heard Wilson shout out in agony, "This can't be right. This can't happen to me. Christ, not the asshole of the world."

"Fort Polk, huh, Rushmore?" King jibed.

"Damned hellhole," Wilson tacitly confirmed.

Press took his orders and was stunned to read that he would be commissioned an engineer. He knew immediately that he had failed to secure the top secret clearance required for intelligence, probably from taking too many courses on Marxism and the Soviet Union, perhaps exacerbated by his atheism. What mattered more, though, was where he would be going, and he searched beyond the abbreviations and acronyms for something coherent. His eyes grabbed onto two words. "Fort Dix! Fantastic!" he shouted. His assignment would be made when he reported to his new duty station. He could care less. All that mattered to him was that Fort Dix was in New Jersey—only a few hours from Celia. He phoned her that evening and told her of his good fortune. And he reminded her of the class graduation party that Saturday evening at a building just off the OCS compound.

"I wouldn't miss it for anything," she said. "Now I'll finally meet the big bad boys who have been mean to you."

"I don't mind introducing you to Holt. At least he's been professional about it. Kid Hausser is a different matter. I've got to run now, Celia. They're about to play our nighttime lullaby."

Press left the phone booth and walked toward the barracks. Still elated, he stopped to appreciate the late September moon and the quietude that pervaded the compound. Down the street a guard moved like a wraith. He thought about the months of frenetic activity that had now come to a close, and as he surveyed the shadows around him, he smiled at the serenity of the present. Then he began to laugh. Before him was the boxy silhouette of the dumpster. As taps began to sound, he walked over to it and patted one side.

He laughed again, louder this time, then turned and walked into the barracks.

The graduation party began as do all graduation parties. The India Company seniors cracked jokes, reminisced, and poked fun at one another. Those who brought wives or dates introduced them to the candidates they had not yet met and to Lieutenants Holt and Hausser and the two tac officers from the first platoon. By eight o'clock celebratory toasts were in full swing. Some candidates pledged eternal fealty to candidates they cared little for during five months of sobriety.

Wilson was telling Celia that although he and Press had had some disagreements from time to time, Press was a good guy and would do well in the Army—if he didn't cut too many corners, that is.

"You know, you haven't given a toast yet," Wilson continued to Press, his tongue a little thick. "Listen up, everybody! Patrick's got a toast."

The room fell largely silent while most waited for Press to proclaim everlasting fraternity. When he didn't say anything, a few candidates told him to get on with it.

"Actually, I didn't have a toast," Press began. "But I do now. Most of you know that a good and deserving person was recently released from the program. To the most courageous candidate of our class: To Whitworth."

Press's toast prolonged the silence and caused some head shaking and averted eyes, a few sips of already raised beverages, and a *sotto voce* comment heard by all.

"Damned fag."

Wilson retreated to less embarrassing territory while Celia asked Press who had made the remark.

"Hausser."

"Is he?"

"I doubt it very much."

"Would it make a difference to you?" Celia asked.

Press thought for a while before answering. "Why should it? I don't know what makes people queer, but I don't think they have any say in the matter. Whenever I've been approached by one, I'd tell him that I was straight, and that would be the end of it. Still, I don't think he is one."

"You knew that your toast would not be well received, didn't you?"

"Yes."

"Why did you do it, then?" Celia asked, chagrined.

"Penance, I suppose. I should have interceded with Boruff the night he let loose on Anders. Whitworth really wanted to become an officer. For me it was a strategy, and of course I'd have some control over my life—I wouldn't be the tool of a sadistic sergeant. Too bad we couldn't trade places."

"Sometimes I don't understand you, Press."

He took her hand and smiled. "That makes two of us."

Before Celia could continue the discussion, Holt approached. Relieved, Press introduced him to her.

"I'm glad to meet you," he said. "I've not always been complimentary with Patrick, but I must congratulate him on his evident good taste."

"That's very gracious of you, Lieutenant," Celia said, blushing slightly.

"Patrick has undoubtedly told you some less than flattering things about me, but I assure you that half of them are untrue and the other half blown out of proportion."

"Why, Lieutenant, *you* have come in for very few slings and arrows," she said with a crooked smile.

Holt looked toward Hausser, pursed his lips and turned to Press. "Apparently, Patrick, you feel that we made a mistake with Whitworth."

"Yes, sir, I do. Boruff lead the charge against him and prevailed. It's so ironic: One is a person of courage, and the other is a caricature of it."

"You will continue to be disappointed, Patrick. Surely you must know that the Army marches in lockstep and you in route step."

"Yes, sir, I see you found me out. Personally, I've found you to be fair and your style of leadership very effective."

"Thank you, but what exactly is my style of leadership?" Holt asked, his attention focused.

"That's like describing the color of air. Your never let us know you. You have a gift for making your point in very few words. Aside from a hint of a smile when somebody did something outlandishly stupid, you never showed any emotion. None of us could penetrate your cool exterior—you know of course your nickname among us is 'Cool Jack.' You would just stand back from all the chaos and calmly take it in. You don't know how disconcerting it is not to be able to get a handle on the person who has your fate in his hands."

Holt pursed his lips for the second time, slowly nodded his head and said, "You have the ability to become a good officer; I hope you succeed." He then faced Celia. "Candidate Patrick is very fortunate. It was nice meeting you."

Celia and Press spent the next hour and a half conversing with the other celebrants. Press was on his best behavior, subconsciously atoning for his impolitic toast. He noticed throughout the evening that all the tac officers, including Holt, were drinking heavily, almost as if a twenty-two-week burden had been lifted from them, too. At half past nine, Hausser weaved through the crowd and bumped into Celia, spilling half of his drink on her dress. He glared at her, as if she were responsible, then stumbled on.

Like most of the others, Celia and Press left the party a few minutes before its official close. They walked hand-in-hand to her car, relishing the warm evening and the warmth of being together. After twenty minutes of the standard kissing, nuzzling, and murmuring of lovers, she drove off, and he began to walk back to the barracks.

On the way he thought back over his time at OCS. He slowed his pace as a disturbing dose of reality suddenly struck him. He would now have to lead and control other people's lives. Military culture was still alien to him; after all, he preferred flowers to flags, strolls to parades, poems to weapons. He had developed no real friendships and had yet to exchange permanent addresses with anyone in his class. But was there time to develop bonds? The candidates were acquaintances with a common purpose. Do I even want to make friends? Press asked himself. Celia is enough—all I want. All I need. Need? The thought that he might need anyone displeased him.

"You lost, Patrick?" King's voice abruptly ended his self-absorption.

"Guess I was in a mental fog. Let me ask you a question, Bill. Have you got any of our classmate's home addresses?"

"Yeah, three or four. Why?"

"Just curious."

In the distance they spotted a woman handing off what looked to be an enormous pizza to an officer candidate.

"Let's wait behind the dumpster and scare the hell out of him," King suggested.

Press went along and they waited on the dark side of the dumpster until they heard the sound of scurrying footfalls.

"Evening, Candidate," King said, as he and Press stepped away from the dumpster.

"Evening, sir," the junior candidate replied, halting in mid-stride.

"What company are you from?"

"Sir, Candidate Michaels, Foxtrot Company."

"I smell the mouth watering aroma of pizza, don't you, Bill?"

"Why, yes, Press, I do. How about you, Candidate. Do you smell the tantalizing scent of pizza?"

"Sir, Candidate Michaels, yes, sir."

"We'll be graduating soon, Michaels, and we don't have an offering for the dumpster," Press began. "We were wondering if you would care to sacrifice that aromatic disc you're carrying, on behalf of the junior class, to appease the dumpster god?"

"Sir, Candidate Michaels, yes, sir. I would be glad to."

"Well, give it the old heave ho, Michaels," King ordered.

Michaels looked down at the pizza, shook his head but was stopped short of throwing it by Press's hand.

"I think the dumpster god would be satisfied with a symbolic sacrifice, don't you, Bill?"

"The dumpster god receives gifts daily, so it may be okay for Michaels here to present his gift *after* he and his classmates have made certain modifications to it."

"Sir, Candidate Michaels, *thank you*, sir."

King and Press were still laughing when they entered their barracks. After brushing his teeth, Press, wearing a T-shirt and shorts, left the lavatory but stopped near the entrance of the barracks.

"Bill," he whispered back to the lavatory, "come up here."

When King joined him Press pointed to the floor.

"Christ, that's Lieutenant Holt," King said, amazed.

Holt lay prostrate. Dribbles of vomit on the floor marked his path from the door.

"At least he managed to make most of his deposit outside," King noted. "Too bad it's not Hausser—we could piss on him."

Press, a sad expression on his face, looked down at Holt. The irony hit him full. "Cool Jack, I can't believe you lost control...of all people." And then he thought, so much for command presence.

PART TWO
14

Press sat with his feet propped on his desk, his standard issue chair resting on its rear legs. A few feet away diesel fuel dripped into a potbelly stove, the drops igniting as they struck bottom. It was warm in the small office—not an office—a shack, which served as command post for the hand grenade range at Fort Dix. Press's eyes were screwed to a page in *Catch-22*. His nose, however, picked up the aroma of freshly brewed coffee and he looked up to see Sergeant First Class Walter Trapp holding two mugs.

"Thanks, Sarge," he said, taking one.

This was their ritual. Every morning on the range Sfc. Trapp would accept a brown paper bag containing ground coffee from the senior sergeant of the company of recruits being trained that day. In the afternoon he would reciprocate by stamping the attendance cards of trainees who were on sick call or had charge of quarters' duty.

Trapp's body had become a victim of over-eating and under-exercising. He was corpulent and wizened and too fond of bourbon whisky. But he understood the Army and combat and frequently advised Press in his most avuncular manner.

Press rose and went to the window. The pine trees surrounding the range shivered in the bitter wind. "*March* is the cruelest month," he declared. "You sit through the cold and gray of winter till you can't stand it anymore. March comes along and dangles a few warm days in front of you and raises your hopes. Then the door slams shut and you're back into winter."

"Well, that sort of depends where you are, doesn't it?" said Trapp. "In my case, all my future Marches will be balmy. When I retire in November, I'm heading to Florida. My only regret is that I'll be with a bunch of goddamn civilians. Next March ought to be a lot warmer for you, too, Lieutenant."

"That's what I like about you, Sergeant Trapp, you're always bolstering my spirits. You know, we have troops in Germany and Korea and a hundred other places. It wouldn't be fair if I didn't have a chance of being sent somewhere other than Vietnam."

Trapp put his arm on Press's shoulder. "Lieutenant," he pronounced in a tone which clearly meant *son*, "there's nothin' fair in this fucking world."

Press laughed and said, "Sergeant Trapp, that's got to rank with the no free lunch adage."

He again looked out of the window and saw the trainees taking seats in the bleachers. Grabbing his jacket and helmet liner, he went out to deliver the opening presentation. He had been range officer since he arrived at Fort Dix in mid-October, after a long leave following his commissioning. For his first two weeks, he observed the instruction by the range cadre, which was straight out of the instructor's guide. The first fifty minute block was a catch-all presentation and demonstration of grenades: fragmentation, white phosphorous, thermite, and smoke. The combination of a canned speech in early morning and a still tired audience were ingredients for bleachers full of sleeping trainees.

Press had revised the presentation and began delivering it himself. When his first company of trainees had been seated, he introduced himself and the members of his staff. He then asked all those in the Regular Army to raise their hands, followed by the draftees, national guardsmen, and reservists. He jokingly told the latter two groups to take a nap, for as draft dodging, weekend warriors they would not be throwing grenades in the jungles of Vietnam. His intent was to play the different groups off one another, to create cheering sections. He poked fun at the Army, at sergeants, and at himself. He even critiqued war movies. John Wayne's grenade throwing style came in for special derision. Since he had taken over the lecture, he had spotted few nodding-off heads.

Following the oral presentation, the trainees went to the practice range, where they threw grenades with fuses but no explosives. The third and final session was the throwing of live grenades, for many trainees the most dangerous and memorable experience of basic training.

On this day the grenades arrived with an added safety device. The Army had been concerned about accidental deaths in Vietnam—infantrymen becoming entangled in the underbrush and having the pull rings of their grenades snagged in vegetation. Some of those who had seen the pin being yanked out could not jettison the grenade before it detonated.

The Army's solution was to fasten a wire clip around the neck of the grenade and the arming lever. Trainees would now have to rotate the clip before pulling the pin and throwing the grenade. Each trainee would throw two grenades.

Press climbed the ladder to the control tower, followed by Captain Petrie, CO of Bravo Company. The trainees were waiting behind a revetment, their backs to the live range. Three sergeants were stationed behind separate T-shaped concrete bays. Press broadcast the rules of procedure and safety over the loudspeaker. Soon, six trainees hurled themselves out from behind the revetment and ran across "no man's land" to the thick, three feet high concrete walls. Each of the sergeants handed a grenade to one of his two trainees, the other remaining on the opposite stem of the T.

Press controlled the order of throwing and movement on the range. The range sergeants would in turn command the trainees to: "Rotate clip...pull pin...throw grenade!" Once a grenade was airborne, four and a half seconds elapsed before the burning fuse reached the active ingredient, a high explosive called Composition B. The Comp B was encased in what resembled a shiny sheet of dimpled metal. Upon detonation the grenade disintegrated into more than 1,500 swiftly moving, white-hot fragments, unseen except for a residual puff of gray-black smoke.

During the first half-hour of the day's throwing, Press counted three dud grenades. A few minutes later, Trapp took over. While the throwing continued, Press motioned Cpt. Petrie aside.

"Something's wrong," he said. "We've never had more than one dud with any company since I've been here."

"Do you have any idea what's causing it?" Petrie asked.

"The only thing I can think of is that somehow the clip wasn't rotated on those duds."

"You're telling me that you got potentially live grenades downrange?"

"Yes, sir, that's exactly what I'm telling you. A few of us will go downrange at the end of the day and try to find them."

"I don't envy you."

"The worse thing is all the craters made by grenades detonating in the same area. See how they're all filled with water? I've been trying to get a bulldozer out here to grade the range, but the engineers won't send one out—won't send a driver, rather. Don't know whether it's too dangerous or bureaucratic inertia."

"Hell, you're an engineer," Petrie responded. "Can you drive it?"

"Well, I've never driven one, but that's probably the best way to get it done."

During the next two weeks, Press and his men found sixteen of twenty-one unexploded grenades—all but one (a true dud) with their safety clips still attached. Rainfall had been light, and the water level in the craters was receding. Meanwhile, he had talked one of the engineering NCOs into teaching him the fundamentals of driving a bulldozer. His first lesson was that you did not *drive* dozers, you *operated* them.

Press boarded the Metroliner in Trenton on the first Friday in April. He had found that taking the train to Washington, which he did almost weekly, was much more convenient than driving. Besides, unlike other single officers, who bought new, sporty cars after being commissioned, he had purchased a 1948 Dodge and saved his money for times spent with Celia.

The early evening train was packed with commuters. Press had a reserved seat but decided to go to the club car for a sandwich and a beer. He surveyed the tired faces as he walked through three passenger cars. Maybe I won't go into business, he thought. These guys slog through a day that's the same as any other day and arrive home exhausted, probably to nagging wives and children who feel put upon. As he passed one of the windows, he caught his reflection and realized that dressed in a gray herring bone tweed jacket, white shirt and black tie, he would be taken for just another commuter, and it did not sit well.

The club car was standing room only, so he made his way to the bar and bought a beer. In a sociable mood and eager for conversation, he weaved through the car until he found himself next to two young women, about his age, who were conversing with the verve of actresses.

"Do you mind if I share this table with you?" he managed to wedge in during a pause.

"Not at all," said the one on his right, giving him an appraising look. "You'll probably be bored to death, though. We're talking shop."

"You're musicians, right?"

"We're members of a string quartet based in New York."

"So you make beautiful music together," Press said, smiling.

"We do all right," said the one on his left.

"I'm Millicent," the first to speak introduced herself. She barely opened her mouth when she spoke, and her words were thrust upward, rather than outward, resulting in an irritating nasal twang, as if speaking with a head cold. "This is Kathy."

"My name's Press."

Kathy asked him what he did for a living.

Without hesitation, he said, "I'm an aid to Senator Kennedy. I'm on my way back to Washington."

Both Millicent and Kathy, who was angular and moderately attractive, seemed delighted to meet someone so close to Ted Kennedy and began to pump him for inside information on Chappaquiddick. Having been the only candidate in his OCS platoon allowed to read more than clippings, Press had devoured as much as he could of the *Washington Post* and was well-versed on the July incident. He deflected most of the questions, citing loyalty to his boss. After a creditable period of reluctance, he agreed to talk about Robert Kennedy, who had been assassinated twenty-two months earlier.

"Did you know him?" Kathy asked.

"No. I worked for Senator McCarthy during the sixty-eight primary. We all felt that Bobby Kennedy co-opted the peace movement. There was only room for one anti-war challenger without splitting the vote, and it was after Johnson withdrew—after McCarthy forced him to withdraw—that Bobby entered the race. To me he was an opportunist."

"I thought he was the most sincere man I've ever seen," Millicent protested.

Press nodded slowly in partial agreement. "He was a terribly driven man; apparently never indulged in small talk—much different from Ted, who is fairly easygoing. Bobby loved power, and he exercised it, sometimes ruthlessly, in his early years in government. He had the mind of a metropolis and the heart of a hamlet."

"Exquisite putdown, but surely you exaggerate, Millicent said.

"He changed after his brother's death. One thing that he was no doubt sincere about was his desire to improve the lives of ordinary people, especially those who just get by. He felt that one person could matter."

"Do you believe that?" Kathy asked.

"Of course—though few of them are politicians. Most are scientists, and they improve the lives of *all* people, including the rich and powerful. Look what Jonas Salk and Albert Sabin did for our generation. But they were discoverers, creators; they baked an entirely new pie. It's much harder to re-divide an existing one."

"That's human nature," said Millicent. "There are limited resources, and the pie isn't expanding fast enough."

Press nodded again, saying, "I agree, and because most people are opposed to re-directing our resources, one person stands little chance of changing the status quo."

"So politicians are useless?" asked Kathy.

"Certainly not. They pretty much reflect what consensus there is among Americans. They just don't have the impact of scientists and inventors. It's funny. You'd think that those who've contributed significantly to mankind would be universally known and admired. You'd expect people like Salk and Sabin to be heroes instead of footnotes. No. Elvis is king. Rock and movie stars and athletes are our idols, and the more outrageous they behave the stronger our attachment. I think we want to be entertained more than improved."

"In our profession we see people who want to be entertained *and* improved," Kathy interjected.

"You two must get a great amount of personal satisfaction from your work."

"Have you ever attended a string quartet performance?" Kathy asked.

"Many times."

"What's your favorite piece?" she inquired with a hint of skepticism.

"The String Quartet in B-flat by Beethoven."

"What about the Grosse Fugue?" she asked.

"It's okay."

"The fugue is so fatiguing that you're completely drained at the end," Millicent said.

"What appeals to you in the B-flat?" Kathy persisted.

"The cavatina...those gentle, subtle, pliable tones. And of course the movement preceding it—the fourth, I believe."

Kathy's angular features softened, and her wide eyes fastened on him in a new and unmistakably favorable fashion. She asked if he played an instrument, to which he answered nothing well. They discussed two more of Beethoven's works: Symphony No. 3—his favorite—and the Violin Concerto, which he said was perfect: tranquil, melodic, and optimistic.

"Optimistic?" she asked, as if she had heard him wrong.

"Yes, optimistic. It's a celebration of what the human spirit can aspire to. There's not a down note in it; you can be in a bad mood listening at the beginning, but you're serene by the end."

Kathy seemed bewildered. "This is completely inexplicable," she said. "You don't play an instrument, but you're so knowledgeable and insightful."

"I wouldn't go that far; I grew up with classical music. My mother is a member of the CSO—plays the violin, like you. She once was guest soloist playing the concerto at an Evanston Symphony concert, and she practiced in the bathroom for three straight weeks. When it didn't drive me crazy, like it did my dad, I knew I was hooked."

"Beethoven's also my favorite composer," Kathy stated. "It's a tragedy that he went deaf, although he was such a genius that it didn't seem to hinder his composition."

"An even worse tragedy was that Beethoven was never loved romantically by a woman."

"What's so terrible about that?" Millicent asked. "After all, he was a bit vulgar."

Press smiled. "Because no one could have created those sonatas without being capable of loving to the depths of his soul. I don't think that anyone who listens to the Moonlight or the Pathetique can find a more universal expression of gentle, pure, or unselfish love. What a tragedy it is for a man who could distill the essence of love in a few notes never to lie with a woman who loved him." He was looking at Kathy when he spoke, and as he finished, she was gazing at him with a fixed intensity.

Millicent laughed and said, "I think you're too much of a romantic to last in politics."

Press laughed with her, saying, "There are tougher ways to make a living than politics. Hell, I could be in the military."

"You're much too sensitive for the military," Kathy said with conviction.

He quickly changed the subject and the three talked until they reached Washington. Kathy rarely took her eyes off him and when Millicent went to the restroom before the train pulled into Union Station, she took a business card from her purse and gave it to him. "Please call me when you're in New York," she said almost breathlessly.

"Thanks, I'll look forward to my next visit there."

After getting off the Metroliner, Press said goodbye to them, and as he walked to the waiting area, reflected on the pleasant manner of passing three hours on the train. He soon spotted Celia and trotted the last few steps before embracing her and kissing her forehead, her nose and her lips. He hugged her again and kissed her ear.

Instead of a greeting she asked, "Do you know her, the tall one about twenty feet behind you?"

He swung around and saw Kathy turning away, her profile revealing a stricken expression. She retreated into the crowd, beckoning Millicent to follow. "Not really. I was talking to her and her friend on the train."

As they drove to Celia's apartment, they discussed her thesis, which examined the concentration of power by Joe Cannon, Speaker of the House of Representatives from 1903-11.

"I don't think we'll ever see a more powerful Speaker," Press remarked.

"Well, maybe not in these turbulent times, but the country will get back to an equilibrium and who knows what will happen in twenty, thirty, or fifty years."

"Politics has changed forever. People are more independent now and communications have made politicians instantly accountable. We'll never go back to the old way."

"Always so sure of yourself, aren't you," she chided. "And I thought that you'd prefer to stay away from absolutes—doors to a closed mind."

Press felt no sting from the rebuke. Instead, he seemed to delight in it. He smiled and said, "That's what I like about you, Celia. I can't get away with a damn thing."

"Tell me about the range," she said, changing the subject. "Have you crashed any bulldozers?"

"Ah, but that's the beauty of bulldozers; you're supposed to crash into things. The impromptu training's going pretty well. It's really easy to steer and change gears and all that, but it's incredibly difficult to adjust the blade in order to maintain an even grade. Sergeant Williams keeps telling me that I over-adjust all the time and that's what makes the ground look like a washboard."

"Just think, if you get good at it, you'll have a useful skill when you leave the Army."

"How right you are. I could grade roads for a living, or doze garbage at a landfill—work for the government. Maybe the war does have some redeeming qualities."

Celia parked her car in front of her apartment. As they got out, Press said, "It was kind of Lynn to leave for the weekend—I'll race you to bed."

"Okay, but if you win, don't start without me."

Their lovemaking had not become ritualized. They touched and caressed for hours, and it was as fresh and spontaneous as their first time. They finally fell asleep in each other's arms and did not wake until the next morning.

It was one of those golden April days, warm and full of the scents of spring. They drove to the Jefferson Memorial and walked among the cherry trees, now in full bloom. Press wrested a sprig from a possessive branch and placed it in her hair. "Now you'd be welcome in San Francisco. Maybe the hippies are on to something; it does give your cheeks a pinkish cast—a very kissable pinkish cast."

"Watch yourself, buster," Celia playfully replied. "I'm a proper young lady. At least in front of a thousand tourists."

They sat under a tree and talked of their first meeting almost a year earlier. "Our picnic on the Potomac reminds me of today," he said. "I didn't think I could be happier than I was on that day. I was wrong. I'm happier now."

"I fell in love with you on that day, although I'm not sure I knew it."

"You could have let on a little. You put me through the wringer getting our next date."

"You were too sure of yourself."

"I had to be. I didn't think that you'd have any interest in someone with a…a passive nature."

"That may be true, although I wasn't conscious of it."

"And now you think I'm a little too sure of myself."

She tilted her head slightly before speaking. "At times you take a position and it becomes a game to you—point-counterpoint."

He took her hand with both of his. "I admit it, but there's no game being played about us. I've been in love with you for a year." He scrunched his brow as if not sure of the length. "My God, it's been a year and yet seems no longer than a month. It's strange how we react to time. I remember wishing OCS would flash past, but it took an eternity. Now, with the months since graduation galloping by, what I would give for time to lose a step."

"It sounds like you might be enjoying the Army now that you're a grand pooh bah."

"Ha! A second lieutenant is the most reviled and ridiculed rank in the Army. I must admit, though, that it's not so bad now. The grenade range is the most interesting assignment in the training brigade."

"And undoubtedly the most dangerous," Celia added.

"There may be a connection. If we have an accident and somebody is injured, I would be relieved of command immediately. But then again I'm not a lifer, so it wouldn't matter."

"It might matter to the soldier who was injured."

"Of course, but we adhere to every safety guideline. If one of the cadre feels that a trainee is too nervous to throw or botches it on the practice range, he won't let him on the live range. I've taken many of those trainees to the demo range for a one-on-one session. One of them froze on me and dropped a live grenade. I pushed him to the ground and flipped the grenade over the concrete barrier. We tried again and he threw the grenade thirty or forty feet. He was jubilant. And without endangering others, he completed the training."

"The two of you were in danger."

"Walking across the street can be dangerous."

"Where were we before we got sidetracked?"

"How I'm enjoying the Army. I find the job interesting, the food edible, the BOQ livable, the O-club drinks reasonable, the weekends...fabulous."

"You had better say that," Celia said, tousling his hair. "Any rumors about orders?"

"The last lieutenant to get orders for overseas had a date of rank in April. If that's an indication, I won't get orders until July for a September posting."

They fell silent for a minute. Press lay on the grass and gazed at the cherry blossom canopy overhead. His mind turned to different ways of broaching the topic of marriage. He wanted to phrase it in a manner which suggested tacit acceptance. In the sales profession it is called a trial close: a car salesman trying to gauge the level of interest of a prospective buyer might ask if Celia would prefer the red car on the lot or the blue one in the showroom. While she ran a forefinger against the grain of hair on his forearm, Press rehearsed silently. How many children would you like to have? Nah. When I get out of the Army and you finish school, would you like to stay in the area or move to someplace like Atlanta or back to Seattle?

"Press, who is Kathy Petit?"

"Who?"

"Kathy Petit. Her business card was in the wastepaper basket this morning."

"Oh, *Kathy*—I didn't know her last name. She and the gal she was with are members of a string quartet, and I talked with them on the Metroliner. Remember, you pointed her out."

"What did you talk about?"

"Politics, music, that sort of thing. Why do you ask?"

"I think she was taken with you."

"Oh, com'on. How could that possibly happen in so short a time? And, incidentally, do you always snoop in your own trash cans?"

"Don't try to put the onus on me. Anyway, it was in plain view—staring up at me, actually. If there's anything I know, it's women. She saw us embracing and from her expression, she didn't like it one bit."

"Sorry. I didn't mean to call you a snoop. But you must be mistaken about her expression. We had only just met and talked for not much more than a couple of hours."

"How long did it take us to fall in love?"

"Hmmm...I still think you're mistaken."

"Did you try to charm her? That tinseled smoothness of yours can be disarming."

"Believe me, Celia. I wasn't trying to charm her." Press raised his arms in abnegation.

She tilted her head slightly and gave him an appraising look. Hesitantly, she leaned over and kissed his cheek. "Okay," she said.

15

The commander of Delta company sat in the control tower watching his men heave grenades far down the range. When Cpt. Thomas had brought his last company of recruits to the range, he had told Press that two of the reservist trainees were professional baseball players. Press had on-the-spot announced a long throw contest. Now, in the first week of May, he was once again exhorting the trainees over the public address system to throw for an air burst. This was an exceedingly difficult task because it required the grenade to remain in the air for four and a half seconds. Press would not allow trainees to "cook off" the grenades—arming a grenade and then waiting two or three seconds before throwing. He and his staff had often done it when several grenades were left over at the end of the day, but it was dangerous for trainees to attempt it.

"Great throw, Bay Two. Bay Three, you've got to throw it seventy-five yards to beat that one," Press said into the mike.

The trainee in the third bay stood and threw the grenade as if he were an outfielder going to home plate. It hit almost eighty yards down range, exploding after the first bounce.

"Outgoddamnstanding!" Cpt. Thomas gushed.

"You almost did it, Bay Three. It was a one-hopper—great throw," Press announced.

The next two grenades were also thrown long. The third landed mid-range in a crater. The water level had gone steadily down during the past few weeks, and since Press did not see it bounce or splash, he assumed it landed in the mud. Within a second of detonation, he instructed the trainees to change over. As the six trainees in the three throwing bays began to switch places with six from the safety revetment, Press noticed what appeared to be a mud ball sail toward the tower. "What the hell?" he whispered just before it detonated twenty feet in front of the Plexiglas window. The mid-air explosion sent scores of fragments into the plexiglass, disfiguring it further but causing no damage. Press looked down on the range. Four trainees and one sergeant were in casualty range. "Has anyone been injured?" he asked over the PA. The three range sergeants signaled that no one had been hit. "We're damned lucky," Press said to Thomas.

"What the hell happened?" the captain demanded.

"There's only one logical explanation. Since we've been throwing the grenades with the wire clip holding down the arming lever, we've had seven duds that are unaccounted for. I don't think they're duds. I think they're sitting in various craters—in water. The last grenade thrown landed in a crater, probably in the mud a few inches below one of those potentially live grenades. When the live one exploded, it catapulted the one above back toward the range, minus its arming lever. It must have been a pretty high trajectory, because I didn't see it until it was about twenty feet higher than the tower, and it was about four seconds from the first detonation."

"It's a miracle nobody was hurt," said Thomas.

"There's one thing for sure—it won't happen again. I'm going to ask Sergeant Trapp to take over while I arrange for a bulldozer to be brought out here this afternoon."

The dozer arrived soon after Delta Company completed training. Trapp walked up to Press as it was being off-loaded from the trailer. "You know, Lieutenant, what you're planning to do is more than a tad on the dangerous side."

Press surveyed the swath of moonscape, brutally sculptured by the daily torrent of grenades. "There's no choice, and I can minimize the risk by keeping dirt in front of the blade most of the time."

He donned a steel helmet and climbed onto the dozer. It was an old model, the blade being raised and lowered by cable rather than hydraulic cylinders. He put the transmission in gear, and the dozer, black exhaust swirling overhead, lumbered onto the range. He lowered the rusty blade into the long-beleaguered ground. The cutting edge began to shear great strips of sandy clay loam, rolling the material in front and to the sides of the machine. The prospect of a grenade detonating in front or under the 40,000 pound behemoth did not concern him. Sitting at the exposed rear of the machine, his only worry was that one would explode *after* the dozer had passed.

On succeeding passes he eased the dozer in on the sweet spot of the range and craters vanished in a roiling amalgam of dirt, water, and iron shards. His face was tense; his gaze alternated between the blade and the dozer's granular contrail. Three times he stopped to pick up unearthed grenades. After rotating the wire clips on them, he casually dropped them into remaining water-capped craters, listening for the muffled explosion as he walked back to the dozer.

Becoming complacent while finishing the central blast area, thinking more about the next weekend with Celia than the immediate task, the explosion came more as a surprise than a shock. He got up and looked over the right track and saw a small crater and mud spattered the length of the track frame. Nothing was damaged. Scratch another "dud," he said to himself and returned to the seat, suddenly surprised at how calmly he took the incident.

He completed the grading at dusk, parked the machine, and smiled wryly as Trapp approached after giving his work the once-over. "Well, Lieutenant, you ain't the smoothest damn operator, but you got balls."

Press's eyes roamed over the range for a few seconds, and he decided that it looked as though it had been scoured by a glacier. Pursing his lips in the manner of Lt. Holt, he said, "Sergeant Trapp, I appreciate the way you told me that I'm crazy."

After closing the range the next afternoon, Press drove to Basic Combat Training Headquarters. His spirits were high. He had completed a dangerous task and had not been inordinately fearful. In fact, he admitted to himself, he had rather enjoyed the experience. Two other range officers were standing near the door when he entered, exchanging stories of how close several trainees had come to cashing it in through incredibly stupid mistakes. On his way to his mail drawer, one of the officers said in a loud voice: "Looks like a pretty thick packet of papers, doesn't it, Winslow."

"Why yes, Horton, it looks like it could be orders."

"Where do you suppose Lieutenant Grenade is going?"

Press took the papers from the drawer, read the first paragraph, and said, "Italy."

"*Italy?*" Winslow repeated incredulously. "*Nobody* goes to Italy."

"See for yourself," said Press, handing a copy to Winslow.

Winslow perused the sheet. "Ha! RVN, you lying sack of shit, Patrick."

"Don't worry, Winslow, you'll get your call to arms in a month or two."

"When do you report?" asked Horton.

"I leave from McChord Air Base in Tacoma on July tenth."

"This calls for a celebration. If we leave now, we can open up the O-club," Winslow suggested.

The three range officers had been in the officers' club bar for a half-hour when Lt. Col. Hopkins, a lawyer in the Judge Advocate General Corps, entered and asked the young lieutenants if he could join them. Press had met him soon after coming to Ft. Dix, and he introduced him to the others. After forty minutes of rambling conversation, Hopkins asked the three officers if any of them had seen a woman reporter intruding on their ranges. None of them had, and Hopkins continued, "Well, this woman is from *US News*—or is it *Newsweek*—anyway, she's been trying to get permission to visit the ranges and interview trainees. The last time we denied her request, she threatened to come without permission."

"Why was she denied permission, sir?" Press asked.

"She's a troublemaker. Ever since My Lai, she's written articles attacking the Army. She's a goddamn civilian reporter who hasn't a clue about what it's like in combat."

Press briefly toyed with asking Hopkins if he was ever in combat but instead said, "Surely sir, you don't condone what Calley and his platoon did to those villagers."

"Of course not, but I understand the frustration that led to it. It's a damn dirty war with atrocities on both sides."

"There's no denying that, sir, but I think that the Army has been scraping the barrel with its inductees," said Press. "In Basic the company I was in had two guys who were incapable of coherent thought."

"Yeah, we had a couple like that, too," Horton added.

"It was a bit unsettling looking at their faces during bayonet training," Press continued. "They were like Dobermans at the ready, waiting for a sergeant's command to eviscerate the guys across from them."

"The bottom of the barrel goes for officers as well," Winslow stated. "There are more than a few like Calley in the Army."

"And you know why?" Hopkins said, becoming irritated. "It's because the educated men of your generation are copping out. They get deferments, join the country club of the guard or reserves, or run off to Canada. They eagerly take advantage of all the things our country has to offer, but they don't give a damn thing in return."

Press had a fleeting urge to admit that he would have been one of them had he acted quickly enough to avoid the draft. He decided to reason with the colonel rather than enflame him. "Wouldn't you agree that some of the draft dodgers are acting out of conscience?"

"The few that are true conscientious objectors can register that way. I'm talking about those who are afraid of getting their asses shot off in the jungles. And no wonder—every evening when you turn on the TV, there's Walter Cronkite airing some report from Safer or Bradley or Rather bringing the war right into your living room. How many recruits do you think would have signed up if in World War Two every movie theater had shown the thirty-second life span of a platoon leader on the beaches of Pacific islands. Floating corpses will make a lot of people reevaluate their patriotism."

Winslow nodded in agreement, then asked, "What do you suggest, sir, if the woman reporter pays a visit to our range?"

"Tell her she is not authorized in the training area and that she must leave immediately."

"What if she refuses; do we arrest her?"

"You don't have the authority for arrest, but you should apprehend her and call the MPs immediately." As Hopkins started expounding on the differences between arresting people and apprehending them, Press pointed to his watch, stood, and left the club.

Six days later Winslow phoned Press at his range. "Guess who's on her way over?" he said.

"Is this twenty questions?"

"Remember Hopkins?"

"Oh, Christ—the woman reporter? How do you know she's coming to my range?"

"I sent her. Told her you were a kindred spirit."

"What the hell did you tell her that for?"

"For bugging out on us last week. We had a liquid dinner with that old fart. He wouldn't let us go, and all he did was lament about the modern Army and that he wasn't going to make full bird. It took me two days to get over my hangover."

"Sorry about that. What's her name?"

"Rebecca Sperling."

"We're even," Press said and hung up.

Within minutes Press saw a feminine figure wearing an olive green base-ball cap walk purposefully up to the shack. Trapp was with the trainees on the practice range. As he opened the door for her, he decided that she was in her mid-twenties and very determined. "Good morning, Miss Sperling," he greeted her.

"It looks as though my notoriety has preceded me, Lieutenant."

He accepted her business card and replied, "Yes, you're famous and also persona non grata on this post."

"I heard that you were open-minded. All I want to do is see how you train recruits and interview some of them."

"I'd like to help you, but all the range officers have explicit orders to keep you off our ranges. By the way, how did you get on the range? I don't see your car."

"There were tire marks veering off from the entrance of your range. I followed them into the woods and parked next to an old clunker."

"Correction: vintage automobile."

"Yours, huh? Why do you park in the woods?"

"POVs—privately owned vehicles aren't allowed on the range."

"Now that we've established that you don't obey the rules, how about letting me see how you train the recruits?"

"You know, you're kind of brash for someone who should be trying to get into my good graces."

"It comes with the territory. I've got a tough job, and some men think they can push women around."

"Do I look like that type?"

"Too early to tell. Now, how about helping me out?"

"Well, look. I can't let you go out there. I would like to help you, but you're sure to get caught. We have three officers and a host of sergeants from the training company on the range today."

"What if I stay at a distance?"

"It's no good. But I may be able to help you if you tell me exactly what you need for your story. You want some coffee?"

"Thanks. I'm tracing a soldier's development—from his socioeconomic background to his training right through to his experience in Vietnam. I want to find out why some soldiers take part in atrocities. Are the origins in their training? What role do their superiors play? What—"

"Sorry to cut you off, but the S-3 is coming up the drive," Press said, gazing out the window.

"Are you in trouble?"

"You bet," he said, thinking furiously. "Maybe not." He grabbed the post phone directory, looked up a number and dialed. "Military police? This is Lieutenant Patrick on the hand grenade range. I want to report that a civilian has come on the range and refuses to leave. Right, a damn civilian. Worse than that, a magazine reporter. Right." Press put the receiver down. "Now don't get your feathers up," he said, watching the anger build in her face. "I'll get you out of this. Sit in that corner and about a minute after Major Shaw comes in, ask to go to the bathroom."

Major Shaw opened the office door and Press came to attention. "Good morning, sir."

"Morning, Lieutenant. As you were." Major Shaw's peripheral vision caught Rebecca Sperling in the corner. "What the hell is going on here, Lieutenant Patrick? What's this woman doing in your office? Is she the reporter?"

"Yes, sir. I saw her walk onto the range and ordered her to leave. She refused and I apprehended her. The MPs are on the way."

The major's stern look softened. "Good work, Patrick. Have you conversed with her on any military matters?"

"No, sir. Certainly not."

"May I go to the bathroom, or don't I have that right?" Rebecca asked, squirming in her chair.

"I will have to accompany you to the latrine. We don't have facilities for females," said Press. "Follow me."

They left the major in the office and walked toward the latrine. "You're in the wrong kind of work," Rebecca said.

"You're telling me. Look, there are two doors to the latrine. Go out the opposite one to your car. I'll meet you this evening at six at Marcello's Restaurant. It's just outside the main gate. Maybe I can give you some of the information you're looking for; I went through training with enlisted men."

"Thanks, Patrick. See you at six."

"Oh, pardon the odor in the latrine. We ran out of lime."

As Rebecca opened the door, she wrinkled her nose in almost the exact way as Celia. Press smiled, waited for three minutes, and walked back to face Major Shaw.

Press pulled into Marcello's parking lot five minutes early. Rebecca was in the waiting area. When they were seated, she asked if he had gotten into hot water.

"I told Major Shaw that you went out the other door, ran to your car parked in the woods, and sped off. I said that the MPs shouldn't have a difficult time spotting a canary yellow car. What color is your car, anyway?"

"Red."

"I thought it might be. The MPs arrived, wrote down all the information, and searched the area where you parked. They asked me if that was my car parked in the woods, and I got my hand slapped from Major Shaw. But he was more interested in seeing the grading job on the live range and the matter was dropped. Now, tell me more about your article."

Press looked at Rebecca as she expanded on her earlier explanation. Her dark hair was cut short with an inside curl at the end tucked under her cheek bones. Her eyes were set a fraction too close, but her face radiated intelligence and was fairly attractive overall. She had a large bosom for her frame, and she could not have weighed more than one hundred pounds in winter clothing.

When she finished, Press asked her if she would be doing any research in Vietnam.

"I'm trying to get permission from the magazine. The article was my idea, and it's low priority. I probably won't complete it for six months. My editor is also a little wary—he's old school, but I think I can convince him to send me."

"If you get there anytime after July tenth, look me up."

"How do you feel about going?"

"I think you've probably guessed that I'm not a lifer—a career soldier. I was drafted and given the opportunity to become an officer. I thought I could outlast the war. Nixon keeps saying that he's going to scale down the war, but instead he sends troops into Cambodia to search the Parrot's Beak for the shadowy *COSVN*. I guess they're not finding much. Hell, I'm not going to worry about it."

"These are crazy times. The slaughter at Kent State a week ago, over four hundred universities out on strike, the Weathermen and other terrorists blowing up everything in sight, the proliferation of drugs—America's going to hell in a handbasket."

"My sentiments exactly," said Press. "Tell me, how did you decide to become a reporter?"

"I've always enjoyed writing—was the editor of my high school newspaper, then majored in journalism at Tufts and worked summers at the *New York Post*. I guess I was destined to go into it. My long range goal, though, is to become a novelist."

"Hmm. So you hone your journalistic skills for years—skills that can be employed to write nonfiction—instead you turn to novels."

She reflected for a moment. "I want to use my imagination, to go beyond facts and analysis. I want to do what Hemingway told himself: 'Write one true sentence. Write the truest sentence you know.'"

126

"Hemingway's imperative no doubt inspired people to pick up the pen, but don't you think he was doing a bit of grandstanding?"

"Not in the least. He understood that writing Truth is difficult."

"Not according to Nietzsche. He relegated Truth to a 'mobile army of metaphors.'"

"Nietzsche died in a lunatic asylum."

"Touché. I surrender."

Rebecca smiled. "Speaking of mobile armies, do you know what you'll be doing when you get to Vietnam?"

"I'm in the Corps of Engineers, but I could get assigned any number of jobs."

"How about on a paper? Have you any experience in journalism?"

"I worked for the *Chicago Tribune* the summer after graduating from high school. But my responsibilities were far removed from reporting."

Rebecca leaned forward with more than passing interest and asked, "What did you do?"

"I collected past due accounts, mostly in the inner city."

"You must have some interesting stories."

"I'll tell you about one day—not that it was much different from any other. I made a collection in one of the public housing high rises in a black neighborhood. Down the hall the door to an apartment was open, and there was an overwhelmingly foul odor coming from inside. As I passed I glanced in and saw a naked toddler. She was sitting in excrement. I'll never forget the look in her eyes: no glimmer of hope and no hint of despair—if anything, indifference, the acceptance of her condition as normal.

"In late afternoon I was in a lower class ethnic Polish neighborhood. I could see four children—the oldest about seven—through the screen door. Not more than a minute or two elapsed before the parents returned, almost certainly from the tavern down the street. The father was carrying a six pack. He told me that he couldn't pay for the paper right then because he had lost at cards. The kids asked about dinner, and the mother told them they would have cereal. The oldest complained that she had promised them hamburgers. 'Shut up!' the mother ordered. 'Your dad lost the dinner money.'

"Two hours later I was at Ravinia, summer home of the Chicago Symphony. Thousands of people were sitting in the meadows on blankets or lawn chairs, eating the dinners they had brought. Many had wine, some even had candelabras and china. Can you imagine two utterly opposite worlds less than an hour apart?"

"I would say most people are oblivious to it, or don't give a damn. And I'd say you're pretty sensitive for an army officer."

Press laughed. "That's a first for me."

"I remember my dad saying he went to Ravinia when he was in Chicago on business."

"Go yourself sometime. It's sort of a spiritual place. The music captures what is possible, what is good, what is transcendent."

"You're bullshitting me."

"Would I bullshit a reporter?"

An hour later Press insisted on picking up the check. Their dinner conversation had been eclectic, roving from enlisted training and the war to the lack of self-restraint in the new culture, the recession, events in the Middle East, civil rights. He was feeling a little guilty about enjoying the company of another woman, one with whom he had much in common and was attracted to. He had promised that he would write to her from Vietnam, providing insights for her article.

"If you're in New York before you leave, I'd love to do this again," she said. "You've got my card."

"Chances are I won't make it."

"But it's so close. You don't spend your weekends *here*, do you?"

"Of course not. I go to DC."

"DC? Why would you go—you've got a girl—"

"In Arlington, actually."

"Must be serious, huh?"

"I'm going to ask her to marry me."

"Congratulations in advance, Press. Although I don't know her, I'm sure she'll accept. Don't forget to write to me when you get to Vietnam. Maybe I can get some of your observations printed."

"It was my pleasure, Rebecca. I hope I see you over there and good luck on your article."

Press was back in Washington on Friday, 15 May. Not having told Celia of his orders to Vietnam, he fidgeted during dinner with her that evening. When they arrived at his motel room, Celia sat in an armchair and gazed at him.

"What?" he asked.

"You tell me. Something's bothering you."

He strolled across the room twice, folded and unfolded his arms, pursed his lips in the manner of Lt. Holt, then said: "I've got orders. I leave for Vietnam on July tenth."

"But you said September was the earliest you would go."

"I know. The date of rank being called now is July. I'm two months early."

"How do you feel about it?"

"There's nothing I can do. I'll just go and get it over with. How do you feel?"

"There's nothing I can do about it, either. But I can't detach myself emotionally just because it's inevitable. I'll have to cope with it, that's all."

"Let's change the subject. Are we still going to your professor's house tomorrow afternoon?"

"It's a command performance for me. Spouses and friends are invited, so I thought you might want to go—relive the halcyon days before the Army."

"Is that a tear?"

"Of course it's a tear. I've lost my brother, and now you're going off to war. Why didn't I listen to myself at the start? I never should have agreed to see you. Why did I let you press me—oh, damn, now I'm making those silly puns."

"I'll make it back. Don't ever doubt that. Now, come over here…."

16

Professor Reynolds lived in a brownstone in Georgetown. Celia had been instructed to go right in and proceed to the courtyard at the rear of the house. Passing through the foyer, the energetic notes of Bach's Brandenburg Concerto No. 4 ushered them along the narrow hallway. Press poked his head into rooms along the way and stopped when they reached the library.

"Just a quick glance," he said, stepping inside. "Very impressive. Some of these volumes must have been terribly difficult to get."

He was a couple of steps behind Celia as she entered the courtyard. From the shadows of the house he saw three men engrossed in conversation. One of them, a young but distinguished looking man with dark hair and fine features, noticed her straightaway. His expression softened and his gaze lingered on her till Press emerged, when he quickly turned his head.

So that's Homer, Press thought, following Celia to another group of three people.

"Professor Reynolds, I'd like you to meet Press Patrick."

The professor, who looked to be in his early fifties, extended his hand, saying, "Welcome, Mr. Patrick. We're delighted to have you here."

"Thank you for including me, Professor Reynolds."

Celia introduced him to two of her classmates, then took him around and completed the introductions of those present. Jim Hoover was in the last group, along with Professor Smith and Dean Woolridge.

"The administration should be concerned," Woolridge stated, retrieving the conversation. "A hundred thousand demonstrators at the Ellipse last Saturday, and they weren't only students. Jim and I saw faculty members we knew from half the universities from here to Boston."

"Nixon's even got Kissinger, Colson, and others meeting with small groups of protesters," Smith said. "He's deluding himself if he thinks he can convince anybody that the Cambodian incursion is not a widening of the war."

Hoover nodded. "I think he's losing control. Last Saturday's pre-dawn appearance at the Lincoln Memorial was quixotic, to say the least. Did he actually believe he would get a friendly reception, especially after Kent State?"

The talk of the war continued for fifteen minutes, sometimes mounting in vehemence, as when Woolridge mentioned that according to the latest Gallup poll, a majority of Americans supported the war.

The question Press knew would come was finally brought by Woolridge. "You look too clean-cut to be a student, Patrick; what do you do for a living?"

"I'm an army officer, Dean."

Smith had been sipping a vodka tonic, and when he heard Press's occupation, he almost choked. Slapping a handkerchief to his mouth, he coughed twice.

Woolridge looked amused. "I would say your answer took us by surprise, although Professor Reynolds usually spices things up one way or another at his annual get-togethers."

"Like a spy in the enemy camp?" Press joked.

"Precisely," Smith retorted, recovered and unsmiling.

Celia looked uncomfortable, fearing that Press would be subjected to an afternoon of abuse. At that moment Reynolds, who was in an adjacent group, called her over.

"You're not going to tell us that you work in the Pentagon?" Woolridge asked Press, maintaining a tone of levity.

"No, I'm afraid not. I'm stationed at Fort Dix, for the moment."

"For the moment?"

"I've got orders to go to Vietnam in July."

"Well, isn't that great," Smith snorted. "Besides the tragic loss of lives, the money that would have gone for social programs is going to the war. Our taxes will be funding this career officer's adventure in Vietnam."

"Now wait a second, Alex," Hoover cautioned, "We don't know if he's a career officer, and a lot of junior officers oppose the war."

"Thank you. You're quite right; I'm not guilty on both counts," Press said.

"Nobody forced you to become an officer," Smith persisted.

"I'll let Seneca answer: 'Those who will, the fates guide; those who won't, they drag.' I'll leave it for you to guess which applies to me."

Woolridge laughed from his belly. "Score one for the Army."

Smith soon lost his appetite for skirmishing, changed the subject, and they began reviewing the sixties. Celia rejoined the group a few minutes later, while Woolridge was discoursing on the problems of accurately evaluating a period that is so close to the present.

Hoover had seemed preoccupied and said little. Now he ventured an opinion: "I think we can say it was a period of rising expectations. We thought we could do anything we set our minds to, from winning incompatible wars—the one on poverty and in Vietnam, and we won't win either—to landing men on the moon. Rising expectations also took hold in the area of rights: civil rights, Medicare, women's rights."

"Why don't you try putting your finger on the decade, Patrick," goaded Smith.

The others looked at Press while he thought. A sympathetic expression crossed Celia's face; a smirk creased Smith's. With a sang-froid kind of look, Press addressed his antagonist. "I don't think I can approach Professor Hoover's insight, but I'll try to look at it from a different angle of vision: It was a time when ideals were formed, and fought for, and killed."

"Well put," Hoover said. "You view it as the poet would."

"Thank you," Press said, impressed by his rival's generosity.

Woolridge, a somber look on his face, said, "Yes, assassinations and war have disfigured what could have been a remarkable decade. Now we're left with memories of its violent gloaming."

Celia took Press's hand and said, "Come, I promised Professor Reynolds that I would bring you back."

Reynolds had a wild mane of gray hair, which he would fling about while discussing subjects that interested him. Occasionally, he would flail his arms while making a point. Press liked him right away and enjoyed listening to the give and take between him and his students, especially with Celia, who would challenge him as often as he would her and much to his delight.

Turning to Press he said, "When Celia started her graduate work at the university, she plopped herself in a back row seat in one of my undergraduate classes. During the course of the lecture, I asked my students which is the engine of socio-political change: 'great man' intervention or process change of the dialectic. She had the temerity to rap my knuckles."

"He exaggerates. I merely pointed out—after being asked—that he set it up as an either-or question, one construct against another." This to Reynolds: "And it's great *leader*."

"She huffed and puffed that you can't look at it from a framework, that there's an interplay at work: lasting change comes from below but is hastened or slowed by a powerful leader, even shaped as his power increases. And that's the kind of discussion I was trying to generate. Here's a more recent example." Reynolds flashed a wide grin, obviously enjoying himself. "Yesterday, in fact. In the Senate Frank Church and John Cooper are proposing an amendment to the Foreign Military Sales Bill that would prohibit US military activity in Cambodia after thirty June. When I mentioned that the amendment would tie the hands of the administration, Celia jumps up and says, 'It's about time.'"

"It wasn't quite like that. I lifted my head gracefully and merely pointed out that Cambodia is a sovereign state, and that our incursion was a widening of the war."

Reynolds threw his head back. "Ah, but if we have Congress gnawing at the edges of the war, what incentive does North Vietnam have in negotiating a peaceful settlement? This could be another case of unintended consequences."

"Just as the incursion will be," Celia retorted. "The North Vietnamese took sanctuary in the border areas of Cambodia, but they have no designs on the country. Now that we've destabilized it, look out for the Khmer Rouge."

The exchange went on for a few more minutes, Reynolds waving his arms and reveling in it, Celia holding her ground.

"See what I mean about her?" Reynolds said to Press.

"All I can say is that I now subscribe to the great 'woman' theory."

Reynolds laughed gregariously, while Celia gave Press a playful push.

"I stopped by your library for a cursory look on the way out here. I hope you don't mind."

"Not in the least," Reynolds proudly answered. "What was your verdict?"

"It's very impressive, especially your volumes on political philosophy."

"You're interested in political philosophy?"

"It was my area of concentration."

"Have you come to any great conclusions? I'm always eager to hear sweeping generalizations. Debunking is a great sport of mine." Reynolds chuckled and winked at Celia.

"Okay, I'll venture one—something that's interested me for years. In fact, it has a bearing on the great leader theory. If you can debunk it, I'll be the better for it."

"Oh, good," said Reynolds gleefully, watching Celia roll her eyes.

Press pursed his lips in the manner of Lt. Holt. "Here's the question, then: What is it about human nature that largely explains the continual conflict in the world for all of recorded history? I've come up with three major reasons. The first two will seem pretty obvious. The third one I've spent some time on."

Reynolds rubbed his hands.

Press continued, "One, the need for control. Control is to humans as gravity is to nature. In its extreme—the great leader who amasses absolute power—change as we were talking about will only come from the top, none from below. Kim Il Sung in North Korea is a perfect example."

"But he can be overthrown," Celia protested. "Then change will come fast and furious."

"Not likely—look at Stalin, Mao, and the new man on the block, Castro," Reynolds said. To Press: "But go on, what's your next reason."

"We're competitive, ambitious, striving—often on the selfish side—for a better life. Freud knew what he was talking about with the id. Third—"

"Can I guess?" Reynolds interjected.

"Please."

"We're exclusive. Every tribe thought it was the chosen people. Exclusivity is everywhere: nation states, religions, country clubs."

"You've got it exactly. Two are enough for trouble. Add the third and appeal to emotions—perhaps aided by a demagogue, bad economic times, or a number of grievances, and you have anything from regional conflicts to genocide."

"I can hardly debunk what I participated in," Reynolds said. "You've made an excellent *start*."

Celia watched Press deflate. "Don't worry, Professor Reynolds does that all the time in class. He once asked us to name the most overlooked, omnipresent element in politics—a condition that has few peers. Words took wing: 'inertia, quest for power, an idea whose time has come, chance.' You know what his answer was? Ambiguity."

"Ambiguity?" Press echoed.

"Let me give you a closer look at my library, and I'll explain it to you. Mind if I borrow him for a few minutes?" Reynolds asked Celia.

Two hours later she pried Press away from the party.

"You certainly enjoyed yourself," she said, sliding in behind the steering wheel of the Beetle. "After we arrived, I thought they were going to eat you alive. By the end, even Smith came around."

"Do you know why?"

"Of course, there's not a nickel's worth of difference among all of you."

"And you're different?"

"I'm a woman."

"Thank God. Not only are you a woman, you're the most dazzling creature I've ever laid eyes on."

"That's what I mean."

"You're going to have to be more explicit."

"I'm a woman, so I'm not taken seriously. It's a sex thing. I've had to work my rear off for more than a year to get the kind of attention paid to you in an afternoon. Reynolds spent *thirty-five minutes* with you in his library."

"So that's it."

"No, that's not it. It's that it's just not fair."

"In the immortal words of Sergeant Trapp, 'Nothin's fair in this world.' Being an old salt, he used an intensifier to describe what kind of world."

"That's a perfect example. With me, a woman, you quote Sergeant Trapp. With the faculty, it's Pliny the Younger."

Press laughed. "Let's get this bug going. It's hot in here."

"See, you can't even defend your actions."

"Can we stop talking about this?"

"No."

"Before I forget, I want to tell you that I will no longer call Jim 'Homer.' He's a good guy."

"I'm glad you think so. He didn't talk much, though."

"That's because his eyes were busy, almost as if they were magnetized and you were north."

"Don't be silly."

"Cervantes has a perfect quote. You don't object to Cervantes, do you? 'The eyes, those silent tongues of love.'"

"You're too much."

"Or would you prefer Shakespeare: 'A look that is a kiss.'"

"That's nonsense."

"What do you want to bet that when I go to Vietnam, he will start an offensive? I don't blame him. After all, Sergeant Trapp's quote certainly includes love and war."

"You're exasperating, and your quotes are wearing on me. Can't you say anything original?"

They looked at each other for a moment, and he said, "Eyes so tender in love, so fierce in anger."

Her face softened. "Is that original?"

"It's from *Tosca*, but the sentiment—"

"Oh, shut up," she said, and started the car.

17

Thursday morning, 2 July broke with the all the promise of being another steamy day. Press cared less. This was his last day in charge of the grenade range. After watching several hundred thousand miniature bombs vanish in puffs of black smoke, he was ready to pass command. He would ride on his last Friday afternoon Metroliner to DC, propose to Celia on the 4th of July, and return on the 5th to begin out-processing on the 6th. He had taken accumulated leave as soon as it had become available, so on the 9th he would leave Newark airport directly for Seattle and his embarkation point. He was now reconciled to serving a year in Vietnam.

Press drove his car to the range and parked it in the woods. His replacement, 2nd Lt. Rogers, was waiting for him with Trapp in the office. "Well, Rogers, you lucked out. General Peters is coming out today," said Press.

"Who's General Peters?" Rogers asked.

"He's assistant post commander—a one star."

"Been here about three months," added Trapp.

"I'm sure he won't be here for the orientation. Since its my final performance, I thought I would do it up right," Press said.

"Well, here's your chance. Alpha Company has arrived," said Rogers.

He and Press walked out to the bleachers. After the trainees were seated, Press mounted the podium, counted four trainees with their chins already resting on their collarbones, and ordered the company to attention. "Men, for the next fifty minutes you're in jeopardy. Now I want all you draftees and enlistees on the left side of the bleachers and you reservists and national guardsmen on the right side. Move!"

Within forty seconds the trainees were separated into two groups. "Listen carefully. After about five minutes of instruction, we're going to have frequent *Jeopardy* questions—just like the game show. Each group will have a different volunteer for each question. We don't have a buzzer here, so the volunteer for all you guys going to Vietnam in about four months will shout 'On Guard' if you know the correct question. The volunteer for all of you who will be home in four months will shout 'Right Guard.'"

Press then launched into his presentation, stopping occasionally to play *Jeopardy*. The game galvanized the two groups, and they made so much noise cheering a winning question that the entire permanent party of Alpha Company drifted over to listen. This annoyed Press, as their presence caused him to cut down on his playful jabs at sergeants. When they concluded and the reservists and guards had won handily, Press told the trainees that a general would take in a portion of their training on the range. "And since you weekend warriors have won the verbal combat," he said, "I'm going to recommend to the general that *your* group go to Nam." As he stepped off the podium, the trainees stood and applauded. Should have done that before, Press thought as he waved to the trainees.

He was intercepted by the company commander as he and Rogers walked back to the office. "Lieutenant Patrick, hold up a minute. What you did out there may have gotten you some laughs, but it was unprofessional conduct. I particularly object to the way you divided my trainees against each other."

Press nodded his head slowly and pursed his lips in the manner of Lt. Holt. "Sir, how many of your trainees did you see sleeping in the bleachers?"

"That's not the point."

"Captain Burdick, that's precisely the point."

"Maybe your commanding officer will have to explain to you, Lieutenant, that this is the Army and that there are prescribed ways of doing things."

"Step into the office, sir, and Sergeant Trapp will ring him up for you."

"You're not calling my bluff," Burdick said, before turning and heading for the office.

"Good thing its your last day," Lt. Rogers said.

"Yeah, had this been earlier, they could have threatened to send me to Nam."

Rogers laughed. "Hell, I enjoyed it. Where did you get the idea of *Jeopardy*, anyhow?"

"Beats me. All I can tell you is that I used to arrange my class schedule around it in college."

General Peters arrived on the range while the trainees were throwing practice grenades at foxholes. Press and Trapp welcomed him, gave him a tour of the range, and introduced several of Alpha Company's permanent party, including Burdick. Then Press had to excuse himself to straighten out a miscount on the day's grenade shipment.

When he rejoined the group ten minutes later, General Peter's aide informed him that the general had to leave shortly for an appointment, but wanted a word with Press. As he and the general walked toward the car, Press fumed, convinced that Burdick had got to him.

"I was at a BCT graduation last week," Peters began, "and I asked a graduate what he thought of the training he received for the last eight weeks. He told me that the training was excellent, with one exception: the lieutenant on the hand grenade range did not seem to take the training, or the Army, seriously."

Press saw himself on some remote fire base in the far north of Vietnam.

"When I moved on to the next soldier, before I even asked him a question, he blurted out: 'Sir, I disagree with what was just said. The lieutenant brought life to the class. He made it the most interesting part of our training, and nobody nodded-off.'" General Peters paused and smiled. "I assume you are, well, somewhat unconventional in your methods?"

"Yes, sir, that would be a fair assessment," Press admitted with a little trepidation.

"Do you intend to make a career of the Army?"

"No, sir. I'm afraid that I'm a civilian at heart."

"The military isn't so bad, Lieutenant Patrick, although it isn't as receptive as it should be to those with unorthodox styles. It's a pity, because I think we lose creative people unnecessarily." He looked at Press for a moment and placed his hand on his shoulder. "Well, I'll be on my way. So long, Lieutenant."

"Thank you, sir," Press said, saluting.

At the end of the afternoon, Press collected his personal belongings and he and Trapp left the office. "Oh, I forgot to ask, did Captain Burdick call headquarters this morning?"

"Nah, he asked me to ring up your boss, but I told him that it wouldn't do any good."

"Well done, Sergeant Trapp. Before I leave I want to tell you that I've enjoyed working with you, and I'll miss you."

"Likewise, Lieutenant. Write us a note after you arrive and let us know what you're doing. And a little advice—Trapp's rules of survival: don't ever, under any circumstances, volunteer for nothin', stay off the beaten path, and hit the ground at the mere suggestion of incoming, like shock waves overhead, or the guy next to you farting."

"Thanks, Sarge, I'll remember that. But I read somewhere that if you hear a rocket or artillery overhead, it'll go past you."

"The one you hear will, but there may be one a second or two behind it that won't. That reminds me of one more piece of advice. Don't get close to anybody over there. I got be to be friends with another sergeant, and one day we were in the field and a mortar round came in—blew him away. Seeing a friend get it like that is not a good memory to carry."

Press nodded. "It's all going to be so new and different. Well, goodbye Sarge. Good luck in Florida."

The two shook hands and Press walked to his car, stopping at the tree line to gaze at the range one last time. It wasn't so bad, he thought. His job had been interesting, although repetitious. His weekends with Celia were tremendous. And the harassment from "by the book" superiors was minimal.

The next day the Metroliner to Washington carried as many tourists as commuters. Press was dressed in his herring bone tweed jacket, wheat jeans, and a gray tie loosely knotted around the collar of a white oxford shirt. Taking his seat, he reached into his coat pocket and retrieved a black box. He smiled as he rotated the top and gazed at a small but gleaming diamond. He failed to notice the stops in Philadelphia and Baltimore, so intent was he on rehearsing his proposal.

Press knew exactly where Celia would be waiting at Union Station. He was one of the first off the train and found her quickly. They embraced and he kissed her lips gently.

"Oh, what a sexy man you are—after six whole days no passionate kisses, just promises of things to come."

"You couldn't have put it any better, you beautiful creature. Let's go straight to the motel. After that, we can go out for pizza and indulge the other appetite."

Later in the evening Press and Celia were sitting up in bed reviewing what had taken place during the week. Celia put her head on his shoulder and said, "Lynn read an article in the paper yesterday about a returnee from Vietnam who was arrested Wednesday. Apparently, he had gone berserk in a shopping mall as he passed an arcade. A war game had made some explosions, and he went in and kicked the glass out of the game. The article mentioned that he had had some horrific experience in Vietnam."

"I wonder if he was unbalanced going in or if he was normal and the experience was too much for him? The Army's standards have been really low since the build-up. I remember a recruit named Crawford who couldn't utter three consecutive compatible words. Worse, he wouldn't bathe. A bunch of guys with bunks near his couldn't stand it anymore and gave him what we call a GI shower. They dragged him into the showers, ripped his T-shirt and skivvies off and took soap and bristle brushes to him. The message finally penetrated the gristle between his ears, and he showered every third day thereafter."

"The one in the paper had no history of mental illness."

"It's a rotten war. Some guys are going to snap, even if it's delayed reaction."

"Are you scared?"

Press sat up a little and put his arm around her. "I don't really know—I don't think I'll know until I get there. The worse thing will be our separation."

"I'm scared," she said in a tremulous voice. "I don't know how I'm going to deal with it. I'll never get over my brother's death, and I don't know how I can go back to the apartment and think of you in some jungle."

"*Jungle? Me,* in a jungle? That's preposterous! Hell, you know the ol' finagler, that part of me you don't care for. I'll be in a desk job at some big base camp encased in barbed wire."

She smiled. "Well, whatever you do, don't do anything stupid, and don't try to be a hero, okay?"

"You know me better than that."

She turned and looked at him. "Yes, I guess I shouldn't have to worry."

Press felt his face flush, but he recovered quickly and said, "Hey, let's go out for that pizza—I'm starved."

They drove to Annapolis the next morning and took lunch at a restaurant with a fine view of hundreds of small sailboats bouncing in the choppy waters of the Severn River, where it debouched into the Chesapeake. Many of the boats belonged to the Naval Academy. Unlike the square-cornered life of the quadrangle, midshipman on the Severn were sailing helter-skelter, mixing in with civilians and lacking direction and control. Occasionally a gust would peal along the wave tops and swat the sails close to horizontal. Three capsized in one burst of wind.

After walking leisurely along the narrow streets of the old town, visiting shops and reading historical markers, they found Celia's Beetle and drove back to Arlington. They had plans for an early dinner at a new restaurant in

Georgetown, followed by a drive to the spot along the Potomac shore where they had their first date. Press had purchased an expensive bottle of wine for the occasion. Under the moonlight and the stars he would ask Celia to become his wife.

The motif of the Spinning Wheel Restaurant was Early American. The dark grain woods and the spare, Shaker-like furnishings appealed to him, and he complimented Celia on her choice of eating establishments. They ate slowly, but there was little of the banter that characterized most of their meals together. She was obviously concerned about his departure the next day, and Press was nervous about proposing to her. He finally pushed back the skeletal remains of what had been a delicious roast duck.

"I'm glad we arrived early. It looks as though they've got quite a wait," he said.

"Dessert?" she asked.

"I'm fine. How about you?"

"No, thanks. The stuffed pork chop was almost too much. If you'll excuse me for a minute, I'll trundle off to the ladies' room."

Press stood as Celia rose. He watched her make her way around a few tables and then glanced at the bar. Allison Parker was staring at him and, upon his recognition of her, she flashed her eyes and fashioned a Cheshire cat gloat. He knew instantly what she was about to do and moved to intercept her, to talk her out of it. But he was too distant, and he watched her set her drink down and follow Celia into the restroom.

Two minutes later Allison left the women's room, and she looked at him and smirked. His stomach was in a whorl. The paroxysm had no equal in his accumulated years: worse than when three bullies advanced on him at age fourteen and far worse than when he totaled his dad's car at seventeen. He waited numbly for Celia to return, but minutes dragged by and still she did not appear. After what seemed to him as the better part of an hour but was in reality only ten minutes, she came out.

He stood as she approached. Her face was ashen and her words sounded like the clanging of a funeral bell: "I'll take you back to the motel."

They said nothing while they walked to the car. After shutting his door he placed his hand on top of her seat and was about to speak when she raised her hand.

"This is what she said: 'So, I see you're with Press Patrick.' Pardon me? I answered. 'Well, maybe he's not using that name. The liar told me he was an Olympic swimmer. Too bad he can't distinguish truth from fiction; he was damn good in bed, though.' I could only stammer—'You, you and Press?' 'That's right. Press and me. We did *everything*. But when I found out that he was a pathological liar, I kicked him out. Maybe you know that about him already. If you don't, I'm doing you a big favor. Don't look so down—they're a lot of better guys than him to choose from.'"

Press removed his hand from the backrest. "I'll tell you exactly what happened between us. When I first arrived at Fort Belvoir, I got an overnight pass and went to Washington. After a walking tour I came here to Georgetown—a place a few blocks away—for a beer and some dinner. I met Allison—the one in the ladies' room—and a couple of her friends. We hit it off and I wound up going back to her apartment. I was as horny as I've ever been, and it meant nothing to me—physical only. And we didn't do *everything*. Since I met you, I've been with nobody else, wanted nobody else."

"Why did you lie to her?" she asked in a barely audible voice.

He shook his head. "Well, I guess at the heart of it, opportunity conspired with weakness. She thought I was a Marine because of my short hair. She distained the military. At the time I guess I thought that she should judge me for the person I was, not the organization that I belonged to. I told her the truth the next morning."

Celia began to cry softly.

"Believe me, Celia, it meant nothing to me."

"That's what troubles me so. You have situational ethics, and they always work in your favor. You lied to that girl and tore a seam in her that's still open. There seems to be no neutral ground on how people feel about you. That girl and I are on far ends of the emotional horizon. I love you, Press, but it's a love I'm not comfortable with."

He put a hand to his brow and dragged it slowly to his chin, as if trying to wipe a stain from his face. Defeated, he asked, "I hear what you're saying; what does it mean?"

"We'll write to each other, and I'll still worry myself sick about you. Anything else—well, we'll have to sort that out when you return."

He shook his head slowly, incredulously, and said, "I can't believe this is happening. It's got to be a nightmare, and I'll wake up and it won't have happened."

They drove the rest of the way in silence. When Celia pulled into the motel parking area, Press asked if they could talk it out in his room.

"I'm sorry. I'm too wrought up about this. I won't be any better tomorrow. I think it's best if we try to work it out long-range, through letters. Please be careful over there, Press. Write to me as soon as you get settled in your new unit." She leaned over and kissed him on the cheek.

"We can't part this way. Please don't let your brother's death destroy our happiness."

"It has nothing to do with it."

"It has everything to do with it. You'll never know happiness if you're forever afraid of losing it."

"You're wrong. It's you. You live on the outskirts of morality, and that's not a place you can commute to. So please don't keep after me. I need time to think and sort it all out. Will you respect that?"

He nodded slowly and said, "I have no alternative. Take care, Celia."

He got out of the car and stood in the shadows, his outer incredulity losing ground to an inner tumult. He reached into his pocket for the box containing the engagement ring and while watching her drive off, fumbled with the lid for a second, then held the open box toward the vanishing taillights. An outstretched arm and the sigh of his gaze lingered for a moment.

'18

The following Wednesday Press was in New York City. He had completed most of the details of clearing post late Tuesday afternoon and had phoned Rebecca Sperling at work and asked her if she was available for dinner the next day. She replied that she had no plans, and insisted that he come to her apartment for a home-cooked meal. After offering to make a hotel reservation for him, she gave him her address in Manhattan and told him to arrive around six-thirty.

Press got out of his taxi a few minutes after seven. After ringing her apartment number, her voice came over the intercom. "Is that you, Press?"

"Now, is that correct radio procedure?" he responded. "A nefarious character would answer in the affirmative and could be at your door in a New York minute. After all, this is the *Naked City.*"

"Only a schmuck from the *Second City* would say that. Come on up."

He walked the three flights and met Rebecca at the landing. "Sorry I'm late. The cab driver didn't have any idea where Waverly Place was and the traffic flowed like rocks in an hour glass."

"I was beginning to think you might not show and I would have to eat this enormous dinner by myself," she said, waving her hand at various compotes and pots boiling in the kitchen.

"You didn't have to go to all this trouble, Rebecca."

"What? You're going off to war; Mars would strike me down if I didn't."

"Mars may not be on my side, but I appreciate it—the aroma's great, so tell me where to drop this bag and let me show off my KP talents by helping with dinner."

"Is that all you brought?" she inquired, looking askance at his gym bag.

Press smiled. "You didn't expect me to carry an assault rifle and jungle garb, did you?"

"No, but I carry more than that for an overnight. You'll be gone a year."

"Got all I need—my uniform, underwear, toilet kit, and, most important, a bottle of wine. I don't need a standard-issue duffel bag."

"Thanks for the wine. We'll have it with dinner. You can put your bag in the corner and then make us a drink. Surprise me."

He found a shaker and some Rose's Lime and made vodka gimlets. Twenty minutes later they sat down for dinner. Rebecca piled onto their plates generous portions of seafood fettuccine, salad, and assorted vegetables. Press opened the bottle of *St. Emilion*. "Tell me Rebecca, what's a good Jewish girl like you doing preparing a fantastic Italian dinner? You're not going through an identity crisis, are you?"

"My best friend is Italian, and I much prefer Italian over Jewish cooking—especially kosher."

They ate quietly for a minute and then she continued: "Did you have a fight?"

"No, there was no fight."

"But something, shall we say, untoward, happened?"

Press, his brow pleated, silently framed a response.

Rebecca did not wait. "You don't want to talk about it. That's okay, it's none of my business."

"No, no, that's not it. I knew when I came here that we would talk about it. It's embarrassing of course. The timing was incredible. On the same night I was going to propose, she found something out about me she didn't like."

"Does *she* have a name?"

"Celia. She said that she still cares for me, and while I believe her, our relationship may not survive for a year. She was very close to her brother, who was killed at Khe Sanh during the Tet Offensive. Now that I'm on my way to Vietnam, I think she's overcompensating for her loss. I've no idea what will happen."

Rebecca took a sip of wine. "I understand how she feels, and I think it's normal. After all, if something happens to you, she will have been devastated twice, although it's already probably too late for her. I won't blame you for not telling me, but I'm dying to know what Celia found fault with."

"Actually, it was nothing, really—just a minor human weakness. Perhaps you're right and her reaction was a defense mechanism. It turned out to be a convenient way to put off making a commitment. I'm pretty sure she knew I planned to propose that evening."

"Are you going to tell me what that minor weakness was?"

"I can see that if I don't, you'll keep asking."

"Can't help it. It's what I do for a living," she said, showing a lively smile and a twinkle in her eyes.

"What the hell. It's no big deal. Just before I met Celia, when I first arrived in Washington, I met a secretary in a bar. She thought I was a Marine because of my short hair and said she wouldn't have anything to do with me. So I told her that I was a swimmer in training. It was merely a field expedient to overcome an obstacle that had no bearing on me as a person. After that we got along and ended up at her apartment. I told her the truth in the morning, and she got mad as hell and kicked me out. Well, last Saturday night she spotted Celia and me in a restaurant, followed her into the women's room and told her about that evening, even exaggerating what we did. That's it."

"You told that girl the truth too late."

"I suppose so, but does it make that much difference?"

"Obviously it did to her. You wanted sex while she sought simpatico. She went to bed with you thinking that you were somebody you weren't. She committed to you—physically and, more importantly, emotionally. You shared the same bed but not the same dreams."

"Are you a reporter or a psychologist?" he asked, exasperated.

"Let me finish. When she found out that you had deceived her, she couldn't deal with it."

"Until I met Celia, the chase was everything. If successful, it would culminate in a night or two of passion, nothing more. I assumed girls understood that."

"They should. There is promise in passion, but no commitment."

"I'm glad you agree."

"I agree that they should, not that they do. You've never been in love before?"

"Not before Celia—infatuated a couple of times, but nothing of consequence."

"A year is a long time to wait. What if she finds someone else?"

"Of course I'll heal with time, but till then I'll have an open wound."

"I'm not saying this about you, but some guys are incapable of the kind of love that most women look for. Some men want to possess, others feel a need that a particular woman fulfills. It's a self-centered as opposed to a selfless love."

Throughout dinner, Press and Rebecca discussed the subtleties, vagaries, and the role of security in evaluating prospective mates. Although Press had often conversed on subjects of which he had no knowledge, he remained contrary to form and only occasionally offered an observation. As she poured coffee, he took the opportunity to marvel over her mastery of the topic; to which she replied: "Probably no more than most women."

"Well, I can tell you, men don't go through anything like the convoluted analysis you described. If I'm at all typical, we know who's right *a priori*. Then we take action."

"That's why there are so many bad matches. And also why women are better decision makers. I can't believe that the most important decision in a person's life would be made intuitively."

"I don't mean to say that it's sex appeal, although for some guys it probably is. Their first gaze goes to the breasts or buttocks or legs. For me, it's the eyes."

"Hmm. That's interesting. I think I see why."

"So what are you looking for in a man—in a husband? Obviously, you've given it a good bit of thought."

"I'm not actively looking. I want to pursue my career without complications for a few more years."

"When you start looking in earnest, I've got a hunch you'll ignore your dictum that security is at the heart of a woman's decision."

Rebecca shook her head. "You might be right from the financial standpoint, but what I want most of all is a secure marriage. My parents were divorced when I was ten, and it was a terrible time in my life. I refuse to have any children of mine go through what I went through."

"You certainly turned out well."

She thought for a moment. "Thanks, but you know, that's something else that might be weighing on Celia."

"How do you mean?"

"People who've suffered the most are usually the ones who understand life and respect it the most. She's suffered greatly and from what I know about you, you've sailed through life. Your blasé approach to it might be scaring her."

"You're really pumping me up as I leave for the far end of the earth."

"Sorry, but you'll be writing to her, right?" Rebecca asked rhetorically. "Time and distance might help you two to work it out."

"Maybe you're right. Anyway, enough of my problems. It's been a great dinner and you're a fabulous Italian cook. Thanks for taking the trouble."

"It's the least I could do. After all, as far as home-cooked meals go, this was your last supper."

"Yeah, and tomorrow I begin *Passover*."

She laughed. "Aren't we clever—the goy and the Jewish princess."

"Where have you made reservations for me?" Press asked.

Rebecca smiled wryly, let her gaze fall to her coffee cup and then back up to meet his eyes. "You can stay here," she said finally.

He considered her reply for a moment before saying, "In that case, let's get the dishes done."

Press lay awake at six in the morning, reflecting on their hour of lovemaking. Rebecca was the most passionate of any partner he could remember. He had been passive at first, and she had taken the lead. He had responded well, he thought, and had become drained physically. Seven hours of steady sleep had rejuvenated his body, but in spirit, he was lethargic. He thought of his love-making with Celia, of the feeling that was all-encompassing: fulfilling rather than draining, magical as well as physical. When he and Celia would separate, he would settle into a tranquility that he had never known. Now, as he lay next to Rebecca, all he felt was a nagging guilt. Ridiculous, he decided. After all, Celia had rejected him, and he was free to do as he pleased. The shrill sound of the alarm erased those thoughts. He reached over Rebecca and shut it off.

After breakfast, she elicited a promise from him to write no less than once a month describing the war and his impressions of the country. "No detail is too small," she prodded him. He picked up his gym bag and joined her at the door. They kissed as friends, and she said to him: "Who knows, maybe I'll see you over there in a few months."

PART THREE
19

As the plane took aim at the runway at Cam Ranh Bay, Press took his first glimpse of Vietnam. Several indistinct islands stood sentinel on the coast. Although they were barren and bony and no larger than the average landfill, he mused for a minute that if he had a choice to sit out his year of war on one of them, alone with only the necessities of survival, he would be tempted to do it.

His daydreaming ceased as he caught sight of the mainland, of the vast sandbar housing the American base at Cam Ranh. The pilot landed the plane as if on a carrier, exhausting the hydraulic rams and issuing a brake-squealing welcome to the passengers. Press was one of the first in line to deplane, and he was greeted by the blast of twelfth-parallel July heat. Descending the ramp, he decided that Dante's nine circles of hell had nothing on twenty steps to the Orient and on reaching the tarmac, gazed down the runway and at the makings of a mirage—an impressionist's landscape of liquid air, of asphalt, of buildings and sand, all ruffled and undulating. The welcome became ruder as he left the bus in front of the reception billet. Wind-whipped sand peened his bare arms and face, and he crouched as though making his way through enemy territory. His billet resembled a World War II tropical-style barracks, single story and screened-in along its flanks. Late that night a brief but fierce gale tore through the sprawling base. Press in a top bunk swayed with every gust, and he was swept with the spray-mist of horizontal rain. Was he embarking on an adventure or an absurdity? The uncertainty of where he would go, of what he would do, and of how he would face danger, gnawed at him. Nature's tumult, coupled with his own, playing out in a dark and alien place, left him feeling desolate. But as the slashing wind began to diminish, so too did his somber mood. He wiped the film from his face and smiled wryly, thinking this is going to be one hell of an interesting year.

The next morning, he and eight other engineer officers were trucked to the headquarters of the 90th Engineer Brigade. They spent the day in-processing and attending briefings. While walking from his billet to the brigade's small officers' club in late afternoon, he slowed and surveyed his surroundings. "Christ, what an ugly place," he said aloud, deciding that what made Cam Ranh so unappealing was its lack of color: the hues of dirty sand and weathered wood predominated, and the few trees remaining resembled warped poles with spindly leaves hiding from the sun. Only the inland hills lacked an offensive feature.

Shortly after evening mess, he was summoned to the office of the brigade commander, Col. Casten. He entered the colonel's office, saluted as if it might mean something, and stood at attention.

"Take a seat, Lieutenant."

Col. Casten's extra large fatigues fought a losing battle with his square-cornered girth. Probably one hell of a football guard in the forties, Press conjectured. His face, perspiring slightly, was on the fleshy side—or appeared that way at least, for his near total baldness presented to Press's casual eye a head full of skin. His eyes were tiny but keen and left Press with little doubt that here was a man to be reckoned with. He also had the feeling that he had seen the colonel before.

"I was reviewing your 201 file, Lieutenant, and I noticed that you had gone to the University of Chicago. My brother teaches military history there, and I wonder if you know of him."

"Of course! Professor Casten," Press responded immediately. "I took one of his courses as an undergrad. It was one of the most popular on campus. Your brother has a unique gift for combining historical insight with the funniest anecdotes I've ever heard."

"That's good of you to say. Although I've never seen him teach, he's long regaled the family with sketches of famous officers— some recent ones a bit hard-edged." Col. Casten went on to recount a few from the more distant and comfortable past. When he finished, he took up Press's 201 file once again and asked a few routine questions. His last was one Press had not expected: "What assignment do you consider yourself most suited for?"

Press answered without hesitation. "Public Information Officer, sir."

"What are your qualifications?"

"Well, sir, I wrote dozens of papers in college, contributed to the campus paper and was the command information officer in my OCS class."

Col. Casten thought for a moment. Looking directly at Press, he said: "Those qualifications are probably as solid as any found in an engineering brigade. I'll look into it, Lieutenant Patrick, but I can't promise anything. You'll be receiving your orders shortly after morning mess tomorrow."

"Thank you, sir, and good evening." Press stood and saluted. After closing the door to the Colonel's office, he tried to suppress a surge of hope. He imagined that the brigade's PIO officer spent most of his time at headquarters, venturing forth to the boonies pretty much on his own initiative. He looked around as darkness shrouded the base. This place won't be so bad, he thought—at least in the evenings.

Press finished his breakfast early the next morning and hovered near the executive officer's desk until the XO told him to wait outside. Forty-five minutes later, he felt he had waited long enough and strode briskly into the building. "Here are your orders, Lieutenant," the XO said. "Colonel Casten asked me to pass along to you that the current PIO's tour runs till October. We had to assign you elsewhere. You'll be going north to an engineer group in Phu Bai. At least you'll have a change of climate up there. Good luck, Lieutenant."

Press and four other second lieutenants boarded a C-130 cargo plane early in the afternoon. They arrived in Phu Bai in mid-afternoon and spent the evening at Group headquarters. Early the next day, he and one other second lieutenant climbed into a jeep headed for Dong Ha, a city only a few miles south of the DMZ and home to the 99th Combat Engineer Battalion. Soon they entered Hue, the ancient imperial capital that had been almost completely destroyed in the Tet offensive two and a half years earlier. Crossing over the Perfume River, they watched young Vietnamese girls dressed in white form-fitting *ao dai* walk straight-backed along the main thoroughfare. Press had never seen such slow, graceful, and aloof movement outside the stage.

"Damn good-looking female gooks, huh, sir?" the driver said to Press, who was sitting shotgun.

"*Gook* is hardly a fitting term for those girls," Press replied.

"How's that, sir?"

"Well, Specialist, to me a gook is a slimy creature who will kill you without giving it a second thought."

"Whatever you say, sir. But I'll tell you one thing, female dinks will kill you, and if they don't, they'll booby trap their babies and get you that way."

"Have you ever seen that in person?" asked Jim Weitzel, the lieutenant occupying the back seat.

"No, sir, but I heard about it enough."

They were driving past the great citadel, scene of some of the fiercest fighting during the Tet Offensive. Playing tour guide, the driver related how during Tet the American and *ARVN* (Army of the Republic of Vietnam) forces assaulted the fortress with rockets, napalm, and constant small arms fire for days before re- capturing it. Being passed down from driver to driver, Press assumed that the depiction had gathered momentum in the telling. Yet he could see that some of the walls were at least twenty feet high and almost fifteen feet thick and destruction to this once grand edifice was substantial.

They continued up the two-lane blacktop road, QL-1, Vietnam's main highway and the only north-south route that spanned the long and slender country. Running parallel to the highway was a narrow gauge train track. They passed half-size engines and railcars by the ones and twos, all motion-less and untended. So these were the threads that linked the country, Press thought. He looked overhead and added a third thread, Alternate QL-1, plied by helicopters, mostly Rangers and Huey's, the latter playing on the ear, its chords unmistakable, at once the bugle of the cavalry charge, the siren of the ambulance, the *Ride of the Valkyries*.

For a while open-air shops, huts, banana trees, and cemetery plots lined the road and people went about life in a time-worn routine. As they contin-ued north, bisecting the narrow coastal plain, rice fields sprawled luxuriantly. The view eight miles to the west revealed a land of high and harsh contours— the Annamite Mountains. Almost an equal distance to the east, past flat fields and scattered dunes, began an indefinite horizon—the South China Sea. To the north and south, not now visible to the travelers, were the settings of the struggle for hearts and minds—the towns and villages. Press fixed his gaze again at the looming hills on his left. Well, you know where you're going, he said to himself.

As if reading his thoughts, the driver said: "That's all free-fire zone—no friendly gooks in the hills. Once in a while they lob a rocket into Ben Than." Ben Than Combat Base was home for a battalion of the 101st Airmobile Division and Echo Company of the 99th Engineer Battalion. Press looked for signs of war, quizzing the driver on the likelihood of the VC planting a mine under the asphalt pavement. "It's happened before," he said. "They burrow in from the side for a few feet and string a wire to a good place of concealment. When a choice target comes along, they command detonate." He squinted at Weitzel. "I never seen it myself, but I heard they got an ammo truck—explo-sion took out the truck in front and the one behind. It's tough to dig in the hard road base, and they only have the night hours, so it's kinda rare."

Driving through the countryside chatting with Weitzel, Press kept an eye on both sides of the road. Here and there villagers labored in rice paddies, cleaning out irrigation channels. The most distinctive feature of the plain was its scent, for in the air, pervading it, was a sweetness redolent of rosemary—oven baked. It all looked so serene and for a minute, he forgot about the oppressive heat and surveyed the flat, deep green fields. He was an intruder, and a feeling of isolation swept over him. This was all happening too fast. In other wars it would take weeks on board a troop ship to journey to the battle-field, and he would know the men in his unit; some would be his friends. A few days ago, he was in the States. In a few more days he would probably be in those mountains with people he would not know. He shook the thoughts from his mind and left it to the heat alone to make him uncomfortable.

After a couple of more miles, he noticed the barbed wire periphery of a base camp up further on the left. Two plumes of black smoke drifted skyward.

"Ben Than," said the driver.

"Looks like they had a rocket attack," Press observed.

The driver spotted the smoke and turned and grinned. "Hell, Lieutenant, that ain't no rocket attack. They're just burnin' shit."

Press looked back at Weitzel. "I better keep my mouth shut for a while."

"Don't worry. I was thinking the same thing myself."

The next day the same specialist drove Press from Dong Ha to his new assign-ment at Ben Than. Press thanked him and started for the Echo Company HQ. The company area was drab to the extreme. The billets were set eighteen inches off the ground to prevent dry rot, the plywood siding painted a dispir-iting gray, and the roof capped with corrugated iron. The enormous plywood shutters were in full yawn, each propped up by a slab of two-by-six lumber. Revetments protected the exposed thirty-foot flanks from rocket shrapnel. Constructed from culvert halves and engineering stakes, the revetments were filled with red clay.

Press entered the HQ and reported to the company commander, Cpt. Marv Elkington. After a cursory welcome, Elkington told Press that he would command the third platoon. His call number was 3-1, although in most other battalions it would be 3-6 (6 the designation for commander). The company's current call sign was "Tiles."

They left his office and stood next to a wall covered with several topo-graphical maps. A hand-drawn road connected Ben Than Combat Base on the far left to Fire Support Base Ridgway on the far right. Elkington pointed to a circle on the map and began his briefing. "Echo Company's primary mission is to open a land route between Ben Than and FSB Ridgway twenty-one klicks to the west on this mountain-top. Since its construction, Ridgway has been supplied by chopper. By the beginning of October, the monsoon season will arrive and Ridgway could very well be socked-in for weeks. Two companies of the 101st Division, plus some artillery, occupy the fire base. They would be most unhappy if they ran out of food and ammo during the months of monsoon weather."

Press focused on the road as it left Ben Than. The first eight kilometers spanned the rising coastal plain, where the curves were wide on the winding road. As it entered the mountains, the curves tightened and switchbacks began to appear. The road was intersected by either dotted or solid lines less than an inch long, and each was numbered—one to forty-eight.

As if reading his thoughts, Elkington continued, "The hash marks are planned or in-progress culvert sites; the solid lines are completed culverts—forty-eight total on the road. Drainage is critical. If you've ever been in a monsoon downpour, you can't fathom what they can do to a road in a few hours' time. When it comes to road construction, Lieutenant, always keep in mind two things: drainage and compaction. If either is insufficient, the road will wash away."

"Excuse me, sir, but I think you should know that I don't know the first thing about building a road."

"Of course you don't. You're a second lieutenant. You don't know shit."

Press chuckled and asked, "How far along is the construction?"

"About fifty percent. A trace has existed for some time, but loaded dump trucks can easily travel only as far as the ford here." Elkington pointed to a stream about twelve kilometers out and a point from which the road began a steep ascent up the mountain.

"There's one more thing to keep in mind," Elkington said, returning to his theme. "As you enter the mountains, you'll be in double and triple-canopy jungle. And where there's not a canopy, it's thick vegetation, the worst I've ever been in. Never become complacent about security. You can get it from a mine, boobytrap, ambush, or mortar. There isn't very much you can do about the last two except keep your men spread out as much as possible. Oh, one other thing. There are lots of poisonous snakes. Watch where you step."

"Well, sir, I can't tell you how eager I am to start," Press said with a smile.

Elkington laughed. "I know how you feel, but I wouldn't be doing my job if I didn't tell you what you're in for. You know, Lieutenant, aside from the danger, this is one hell of a road building job. You a graduate engineer?"

"No, sir. I studied political science."

"Too bad, after your tour you'd have a hell of a plus on your résumé. Oh well, let's go over and I'll introduce you to the XO."

A first lieutenant stood as the two officers approached his desk. After Elkington introduced Mark Grieve, he volunteered him to show Press the road the next day. The executive officer then took him to the billet he would share with him and two other lieutenants. The billet was divided into four sleeping cubicles and a center section, which contained a table—home to a twelve-inch black and white television—six chairs, a large orange refrigerator, circa 1950, and a smaller table laden with liquor bottles. Playmate centerfolds blanketed the walls.

Press stepped into his cubicle, parted the mosquito netting, dropped his gym bag on the standard army issue cot, and surveyed his quarters. A couple of boards attached to a wall served as a desk. On the desk were a six-inch diameter fan, a lamp, and several magazines for an M-16 Assault Rifle. A wooden ammo box with shelves, nailed to a support, provided storage for toilet articles. A foot locker sat near the cot. Every object in the room was coated with dust. He shook his head and exhaled.

Joining Grieve in the common, he picked up a bottle of Grand Marnier and beamed with admiration. "You guys have a magnificent bar; how did you amass such a collection?"

"We all have two or three ration cards. And the stuff is dirt cheap. Three bucks for the Drambuie and Johnnie Walker Black; two-fifty for the Beefeater and Old Grand Dad."

"Looks like the OD encourages everybody to go through the war smashed."

"In one way or another. Alcohol is the drug of choice for officers and non-coms. The troops are either on heroin or a grass-beer combo—about a fifty-fifty split, I'd say. Most guys on smack also enjoy a drink or smoke, of course."

Press changed the subject. "Hope I didn't spoil your day tomorrow by your having to take me out on the road."

"Naw, Captain Elkington used to do it, but he rotates in about a month, so he might be suffering from short-timer's syndrome."

"How long you got?"

"My *DEROS* is twenty November."

"Christ, another new acronym. What does *DEROS* stand for?"

"Date eligible for return from overseas—something like that. So you're taking over the third platoon?"

"Unless the CO changes his mind. What can you tell me about it?"

"Well, it's basically a good unit, though like all the platoons, it's under-strength. And you're almost certain to have trouble with Sergeant Harlan, the platoon sergeant."

"Why's that?"

"The third platoon has been without a platoon leader for about a month, and Sergeant Harlan has been running it alone. I think he's grown fond of it. He's also been doing a good job—and he knows it."

"You mean Sergeant Harlan's not going to welcome a green second luey with open arms?" Press asked, smiling.

"Not if he stays in character. He's got fifteen, sixteen years in, and he's got his shit together."

Press started to laugh.

"If you see something funny in that, I'd sure like to know," said Grieve, looking perplexed.

"The joke's on me. I tried to stay out of Vietnam by going to OCS, but that didn't work. Then I was a whisker away from being assigned a cushy job at Cam Ranh Bay. Instead, I get sent to the far north, where I'll be building a road through mountainous jungle infested with unfriendly natives. And on top of that, I find out that I might encounter a second enemy—my own platoon sergeant."

Grieve grinned. "You seem able to handle yourself. But look on the pleasant side."

"How's that?"

"When you come in from the road every afternoon, you can drown your troubles in the finest hootch available."

Shortly past five o'clock Press heard the deep growling of diesel engines. He opened the front door, stood on the two-square-foot wooden stoop, and watched the return of the troops. Five-ton dump trucks, each carrying about eight engineers, pulled into the parking area. The troops climbed down from the truck beds before the drivers backed the behemoths into a well-dressed line. The soldiers, carrying M-16 Assault Rifles, grenades, Igloo containers, towels, and sundry field gear filed past him. One tall, muscular blond engineer, an M-60 Machine Gun resting on his shoulders, greeted Press in a Texas drawl: "Howdy, sir."

"Howdy, Specialist," Press said back. Hardly had the words left his mouth when he saw a jeep leave the road and begin weaving through the slow walking soldiers. Sitting shotgun was a sergeant first class. From his posture and imperious expression, Press knew instantly that he could be none other than Sfc. Harlan. Christ, he's propped up in his seat out-MacArthuring MacArthur, he said to himself.

Within the close of the hour, Press had meet the other platoon leaders. Al Giardi, 1st platoon, was a gregarious Virginian. After shaking hands with Press, he offered to make him a Mai Tai. Bob Coe, 2nd platoon, was reserved but pleasant. Both looked as though their skins were dyed a dirty red. They sat around the common room table and talked for fifteen minutes before pouring a second drink and leaving for the officers' showers, a forty-second walk from the back door. Grieve and Press waited until they returned, and the four lieutenants went to the mess hall for dinner.

Press turned in early and slept fitfully. His hand-me-down midget fan barely stirred the muggy air inside the mosquito net. And sleeping on a sheet of stretched canvas was not to his liking. He was still tired a half-hour after he woke up.

He went from morning chow directly to supply. Surprised that the socks were standard issue wool instead of cotton, he still asked for ten pair. He also signed for five pairs of fatigues, a pair of jungle boots, a boonie hat, and a .45 caliber sidearm. After dressing he strolled to HQ, aware that the unfaded green of his fatigues marked him as a rookie.

Grieve went to the company safe when he saw Press enter. A minute later, he handed Press a copy of the Signal Operating Instructions and told him that he could lose practically anything—his weapon, a bulldozer, anything— except the SOI. In enemy hands the NVA (North Vietnamese Army) would know all the radio frequencies and call signs of units operating north of Hue. Press stuffed it in the left breast pocket of his fatigue shirt and buttoned it.

"Oh, it looks like I won't be taking you out on the road, after all," Grieve said. "Naturally, I'm very disappointed about it."

"Naturally," Press went along.

"Captain Whitcomb radioed in a few minutes ago from QL-1. He's the CO of the 166th Light Equipment Company up at Dong Ha with Battalion. Yeah, ol' Burg Whitcomb's quite a character—senior captain in the battalion. Big sonofabitch. Anyway, he's got a platoon working on the road, and he's bringing a mint green second luey with him."

"Name's Jim Weitzel. I rode with him to Dong Ha."

"Good. When you get back this afternoon, the CO will announce that you're taking command of the third platoon, and you'll have the pleasure of meeting Sergeant Harlan."

Press decided to have a look around the company area before Burg Whitcomb arrived. Taking up about four acres on the northeast perimeter of Ben Than, it would not be a likely spot for enemy sappers to penetrate. Ribbons of concertina wire stacked high bolstered his sense of security.

He was running a thumb over the razor blade-sharp wire when he heard someone muttering a few feet behind him. Although he no longer gave any thought to the frequent interspersion of obscenities between words—syllables even—the stream of invective was so vile and persistent it demanded his full attention.

He turned and discovered the issuer of the diatribe was an engineer private, whose name tag identified him as Gonzalez. His needlepoint eyeballs and scabby, sallow, unshaven appearance led Press to conclude that the malcontent was a committed heroin user. He did not attempt to intercede, for he felt that no good would come of it. Gonzalez, finally taking notice of Press, spiced up his delivery and spat out another six or seven expletives with rhythmic propulsion, accentuating the adjectival form of the verb "fuck," usually preceded by the noun "mother." Exhausting his standard repertoire, he reloaded with descriptions of bestiality and the female anatomy, all the while exploiting each syllable, changing cadence, and misplacing modifiers.

Press listened to Gonzalez' ravings for a minute more, amazed at the difference between his experience in the stateside Army and what was taking shape during his first real day in Vietnam.

As Press returned to HQ, a jeep with the markings of the 166th was entering the company area. He saluted the captain riding shotgun. Seconds later, Captain Whitcomb stepped out of the jeep and introduced himself in a voice that mimicked the lower octave of a church organ. He was a hulk of a man, no shorter than six-foot-three, and accenting his frame was a dead, wet cheroot clamped between his teeth.

Following a half-hour meeting with the officers and First Sergeant Vernon Washington, Press climbed into the back of Whitcomb's jeep, next to Weitzel. They headed for Ridgway Road, bisecting Ben Than en route. Press admitted to himself that he may have been hasty in judging the drabness of Cam Ranh Bay. The ugliness of Ben Than was singular—red clay seemed to eclipse all else. The main base at Cam Ranh projected barely more than a two-dimensional view. Here, rises and depressions filled his eyes with a shade of red indistinguishable from dried blood. Let's see, how did Burg Whitcomb describe laterite clay? Press thought back to their meeting. Yes, *moderately granular with a hard matrix.*

As they passed the back gate, the scenery improved markedly. The low rolling hills were covered with a knee-high foliage similar to vetch. An enemy caught out here had no chance, Press surmised. It soon became evident that this was the prevailing attitude of all who worked on the road. They began to pass squads of engineers working on culvert headwalls and equipment operators grading the road with no sentries posted.

The road rose as they entered the high hills and followed a river into the interior. With the topographic change came new vegetation. Tall bushes burgeoned on the hillsides and grasses as high as eight feet covered the narrow valley they now traversed. They came upon a front-end loader and a five-ton dump truck moving on the road at idle, matching the quick step of the minesweep team in front.

"The minesweep will go only as far as the ford—less than a klick ahead," said Whitcomb. "The engineer unit on Ridgway sweeps down to the ford. When the road is open, we'll send up some dozers and graders to work mountainside jobsites."

As Press listened to Whitcomb's explanation, he looked back and saw two trucks approaching, each pulling a lowboy trailer loaded down with a bulldozer. The scale and complexity of the operation gripped him, and he silently cursed the Army for not preparing him for his new job. His only earthmoving experience was garnered through his own initiative on the grenade range.

He watched as the lead elements of the minesweep team rounded a curve. Two engineers swung their long-handled detectors back and forth in rapid fashion and in unison, like metronomes keeping one-quarter time. Impatiently, Whitcomb yanked his SOI from his left breast pocket. Flicking through some pages, his eyes settled on a frequency which he asked Weitzel to dial in for him.

He keyed the handset. "Pine Top Three-six, this is Byword Six, over."

A response came a few seconds later. "Byword Six, this Pine Top Three-six, go."

"Pine Top Three-six, what's your pos, over?"

"Byword Six, we're back at Romeo. Sweep completed three-zero mikes ago, over."

"Roger, Pine Top Three-six, that's what I want to know. Thanks much. Six, out."

He turned to the back seat. "That was Lieutenant Davidson of the 508th Engineers. He's a prick—also a Point grad—but he gets the job done. They completed their sweep. We'll continue on up the road as soon as they're finished here."

The minesweepers reached the ford and began to pack their equipment. Whitcomb asked his driver to stop the jeep next to Lt. Coe, whose platoon would be working with heavy equipment operators from the 166th on the upper reaches of the road. Infantry from Fire Base Walton, a satellite of

Ben Than, were divvied up for escort duty. Satisfied with the arrangements, Whitcomb and his student lieutenants forded the shallow stream and headed up the mountain.

They stopped at jobsite after jobsite, Whitcomb explaining why the road was cut a certain way...where box culverts were needed...how tire penetration sapped the horsepower of a vehicle. Press and Weitzel listened enthusiastically. Everything he said made sense to Press, every morsel of information usable. As they motored up the mountainside, Press noticed an abrupt change in soil conditions. The red laterite was replaced by a leached-out, sickly-looking yellowish loam. He started asking questions: "How does the loam compare to laterite after a hard rain? Does it matter if a sharp curve on a steep upgrade gets no direct sunlight?"

"Good question," Whitcomb would answer. "Loam makes a poor base and won't stand up to a monsoon. Permanent shade means the road will seldom dry out—of course there's not much sunshine anyway during the monsoon season...."

Press was also struck by the beauty of the mountain. Teak and species of meranti and seraya weaved a broken green tropical mosaic—lofty canopies conspiring to create a separate world far above the hidden floor.

The road, rough cut as it was, finally gave out. A crude trace, navigable in four-wheel-drive, spanned the last 300 meters to Ridgway. The jeep cork-screwed wildly, almost driving itself along the deep ruts. Whitcomb motioned to stop on the approach to Ridgway, a straight stretch with a sixteen degree grade. The occupants got out and inspected the area. "What do you think we're in now?" he asked.

"Pumice?" Came the incredulous reply from Weitzel.

"Right. About half this stuff is volcanic ash—fluff."

"And look at the rocks sticking out," Press added. "They're rounded, like river rocks."

"Correct. Some are over three feet in diameter—damn hard to rip out," Whitcomb said.

"Rip out?" Press quizzed.

"The dozers have either a winch or a ripper tube and shank on the back end. My boys will rip out what they can, but you will have to blast the others," Whitcomb told him.

Arriving at Ridgway a few minutes later, Press breathed the cooler air, stood a while and looked out at one of the most spectacular panoramas he had ever seen. Almost twenty miles out and 2,000 feet below, the vast cyan expanse of the South China Sea nestled against shimmering white sand dunes.

They met with the "king of the hill," Major Mack Eaglefeather, a nearly full-blooded North Cheyenne. He asked Whitcomb if one of his dozers would do a little grading on the fire base. Poor drainage had caused several of the underground bunkers to collect standing water after a heavy rain. Whitcomb declined, saying that his 34,000 pound dozers were too large for the job. Press later went into one of the water-receptive bunkers nearby. His first reaction was sympathy for the occupants, for a musty odor assaulted his sinuses. As his eyes adjusted to the darkness, he shook his head at the truly primitive living conditions: dirt, sandbags, timbers and cots filled the narrow bunker. I could have it worse, he told himself.

The engineers stopped at a jobsite on their way down the mountain. A bulldozer and a grader from the 166th were widening a switchback. Whitcomb told Weitzel to watch how the two machines worked together, while he went 200 meters up the mountain to stake the width of another switchback. "Want to hammer a couple of stakes?" he asked Press.

The two got out of the jeep at the upper switchback, and Whitcomb stood on the centerline of the road and eyeballed how far out the roadbed should extend on the outside curve. "The largest truck using the road will be a five-ton. We've got to make the road wide enough so that it can make the curve safely."

As Press hammered a stake where Whitcomb's practiced eye dictated, he asked, "Any of your men wear sandals out here, sir?"

Whitcomb strolled over and scrutinized the depressions in the soft soil at the shoulder of the road. Cigar in mouth, he said, "Looks like two of them— NVA. There's some VC along the plain but none in the mountains." He continued after only a second or two of thought: "You game for a little gambol in the jungle?"

Press peered into the thick vegetation. "In *there?*"

"We won't go far. Fifty meters max."

"Can't we radio the hill? There's got to be at least a hundred grunts up there. After all, it's their—"

"If you don't want to go, wait here with Cecil. I'll be back in a few minutes."

"What the hell," Press said. "How many guys get shot on their first day in the field, anyway?"

"You're not going to get shot, Lieutenant. On the other hand, I would keep a sharp eye out for wires. Charlie's damn good at planting boobytraps."

"After you, sir."

Whitcomb grinned and started into the jungle, a thick mass of elephant grass only for the first few steps, thinning under the canopy and offering a line of sight forty meters ahead, the floor becoming hard and covered with dead leaves, leaving no more sandal prints and no bearing for the officers. They walked slowly, looking in all directions for anything untoward, shafts of light poking here and there through the overhead cover, revealing nothing in the dim and inhospitable terrain.

Whitcomb went beyond fifty meters, but Press did not call him on it. He was also drawn on as a compelling curiosity began to displace his fear. Not that he felt no fear; he was sure his heartbeat was audible, but he was able to control it, and that, he thought, was a significant discovery. He recalled a short story that he read as a freshman in high school, "The Most Dangerous Game." He knew he was caught up in a foolish venture, for unlike the story's hero, he had a choice. He also knew that he would need all his faculties for the hunt.

They were out of earshot of the earthmoving machinery working below, and the jungle was eerily silent, a slight breeze stroking the high canopy, unheard, but given away on the floor by shifting patches of light. As they came upon a relatively flat and open area, Whitcomb slowed and then stopped. He pulled his .45 from its holster and pointed it toward the side of the mountain. Press leaned forward and saw a manmade cave with a large opening, almost fifty square feet. Whitcomb started forward again, turned to see if Press was following, saw the weapon in his hand, and whispered: "Don't shoot me in the ass."

The cave was shallow and, as they soon found, empty, barely having room for two people to sleep and shelter some gear. Whitcomb was about to put his sidearm back when they heard laughter. Although unnecessary, he put his index finger to his lips, and he and Press crept toward the sounds, watching where they placed their feet so as not to crack a twig. In the pale green filtered light they saw two NVA soldiers sitting on a log, their backs to the Americans. One was smoking; the other was putting his chopsticks on the log with one hand while reaching into his shirt pocket for a cigarette with the other.

Whitcomb whispered into Press's ear: "We'll go forward a bit and I'll yell to them. If they try to escape, shoot the one on the left. Is your safety off?" Press nodded, his composure still intact. They closed in to about twelve feet, and the encounter was stark and immediate.

"Dung Lai!" The tone and strength of Whitcomb's voice mimicked the lower notes on a church organ and even startled Press. The NVA soldiers turned simultaneously. The one on the right bolted, dashing for the cover of a large teak tree eight feet downhill. He did not make it. Whitcomb pulled the trigger as the unfortunate soldier took his second step. The soldier on the

164

left glanced at Press for an instant, caught the movement of his partner, and broke for safety in an oblique move. Press hesitated, then fired. Whitcomb fired and missed. The soldier vanished.

Whitcomb walked over to the dead soldier and rolled him over, exposing a gaping hole almost the size of a fist in his chest, where the bullet exited. After a cursory and unsuccessful search for documents, the captain turned to Press and, in a just-another-day-at-the-office manner, said, "Let's haul him back to the jeep."

Neither wanted to carry the dead soldier fireman style because of his blood-soaked uniform, so Press took him by the feet and Whitcomb by the armpits. When they reached the jeep, Whitcomb guided Press to the hood, where they set the body.

"Got any cord or rope in the jeep, Cecil?"

"A couple of feet of commo wire, sir."

"Good, use it to tie his feet to the rearview mirror."

While his driver proceeded to the front of the jeep, Whitcomb took off his belt and placed it around the soldier's neck, buckle at the throat and made it snug as a noose. He lashed the loose end around the mirror bracket on the passenger side so tightly that the dead soldier's face was firm against the windshield.

Press watched as they bound him. "As an admirer of field expedients, I'll always remember this one, but isn't it against the rules to mount a dead body like a trophy?"

"Why don't I give you custodial rights, and you can hold him in your lap?"

Press climbed into the front seat, saying, "Sir, I'm sure there's flexibility in the Uniform Code of Military Justice."

Whitcomb grinned, clamped a fresh cheroot between his teeth, settled himself behind the steering wheel, and told Cecil to hop in the back. They rode down and picked up Weitzel. As they passed back into sunlight, the brass belt buckle flashed at Press like a signal mirror and drew his gaze to the dead soldier's eyes, which were pointed at him, not with hostility, but almost as though retaining that moment of surprise. The scene was grotesque. The deep-set, startled eyes, the deformed jaw and open mouth, the buckle resembling an abbreviated bow tie—so tightly knotted that crow's feet branched over the neck—forced Press to turn his head. A minute later he reached around the windshield and closed the soldier's eyes. As they passed jobsites on their way to Ben Than, engineers scrambled for their cameras. They were too late; Whitcomb would not slow down. It was enough that they saw his trophy splayed on the hood.

The medical facility at Ben Than consisted of a building large enough for an examination table and four bunks. Seconds after Whitcomb stopped the jeep in front of the building a medic came out, looking as if he were witnessing a sacrilege.

"You, you...can't do that," he stammered, addressing Whitcomb.

"Is that the proper military greeting for an officer?" Whitcomb demanded, as he stepped out of his jeep and stood like a bison to the medic's prairie dog.

Still stunned, the medic raised a limp hand to his brow.

"For Christ's sake, Specialist, haven't you seen a dead body before? It's your goddamn *job*, isn't it?"

"Yes, sir, but—"

"Just get a body bag—he's starting to stink already." Whitcomb turned to Press and Weitzel. "It's the heat and humidity," he explained. "Can't even stand myself after a day in the field. Now, for the paperwork. One lesson both of you will learn real quick is that there's a whole lot more paper flying around here than bullets. The ratio of filed forms to dead gooks has got be to over ten thousand to one."

They arrived at the company area in mid-afternoon. After a short meeting with Elkington, Whitcomb and Weitzel left for Dong Ha. Press waited for the platoon leaders to return to the field and the daily debriefing. Sfc. Harlan would be attending for the third platoon. Press was still making notes on Whitcomb's road construction tips when they began to gather. The meeting was mostly statistical: platoon leaders reported 600 cubic yards of dirt moved and three culverts placed; the specialist responsible for communications reported two PRC-25 radios redlined. Press listened to the twenty-five minutes of reports, thinking that they were not only boring but probably exaggerations as well. Elkington then formally introduced Press to the group and announced that he would take command of the third platoon. Harlan, apprised of the appointment the previous evening, sat expressionless. As the meeting broke up, Press approached him.

"It's good to meet you, Sergeant Harlan. I've heard a lot of good things about your work."

"Welcome to Vietnam, Lieutenant Patrick. You're taking over a well tuned platoon—good boys. They know their job."

"That's what I hear. I'm looking forward to working with you and the men. I've had very little construction experience, so until I learn the ropes, I'll be depending on you quite a bit."

"That won't be any problem, sir. You'll be coordinating with the CO and the other platoon leaders. I usually lay on a hot noon meal for the boys—a good time for you to come out to the jobsites, check the progress and mix with the men."

"That's a pretty passive role you've outlined, Sergeant."

"Coordinating the work and setting priorities is important, sir."

"Well, as I said, I'll have to get up to speed, and until that's done our discussion about responsibilities is probably premature. I think it's important for us to establish a good working relationship."

"I couldn't agree more," Harlan said, showing Press a thin smile.

"Good. If you have a couple of minutes, Sergeant, I'd like to meet the squad leaders."

Back in the billet after evening mess, where the table talk centered on Whitcomb's kill, Press poured himself two fingers of scotch and chipped a piece of ice from the block in the refrigerator.

"So, how do you think you'll get along with Sergeant Harlan?" asked Coe.

"Great—for as long as I let him run the platoon. According to him, my job is behind the scenes, though he did invite me to come out with the chow truck and glad-hand the troops."

"Probably pissed at having to give up his jeep," said Grieve, laughing.

"He's a strong willed son-of-a-bitch," added Giardi.

"Did he assign a driver for you yet?" Coe asked.

"Yeah, a spec four named Snow."

"Should have guessed," Giardi said. "Snowy's the scruffiest guy in the company."

"I don't care about that," said Press. "What's his preference, smack or beer?"

Coe responded immediately. "Definitely beer. Have you seen his gut?"

"You know, you could have it pretty easy, at least until October when Harlan rotates," Giardi said.

"How's that?" Press inquired.

"Well, Harlan's got his shit together; you could let him run things while you sit back and eat bonbons."

Grieve squeezed a ribbon of cheddar cheese from a plastic tube onto a saltine. "Enough shop talk. Let's get down to important business. You play poker, Patrick?"

The remainder of the week was uneventful. Press went out on the road with the platoon but limited his role to observing and asking questions. Of those directed to Harlan, the answers carried sufficient detail, but Press sensed that they traced the edge of his patience. The three squad leaders, Art VanAcker, Bret Sondag, and Nolan Studt were buck sergeants in their early twenties. All three eagerly shared their knowledge, which in aggregate fell below that of Harlan's. One question that began taking root but Press hesitated to ask was how with the limited resources at hand could they possibly put enough stone on the road before the monsoons arrived.

The company did not work on Sunday, so Press went with Coe to the PX and bought a camera, sunglasses, a writing tablet, and two bottles of liquor. Back at the billet, he took out the tablet and wrote a letter, re-reading it before preparing the envelope.

"Dear Celia…It seems like an eon ago in another world that I last saw you, yet our parting is indelible in my mind. I can't tell you how sorry I am for what I put you though. I realize that it will take time for you to work this out, and that you may not decide in my favor, but I ask only one thing: let's not write with 'our hands against our hearts' (Shakespeare of course). For my part, you are the only woman I have ever loved—or ever expect to.

"On to lighter fare. How are things at school and work? Please keep me up-to-date on the goings-on and be sure to let me known if Scoop smiles. Also, give my greetings to Lynn and Roger.

"Not everything of late has been a travail for me. I stumbled into a great assignment here. The commanding officer of the brigade I'm in has a brother who was one of my professors at UC. He reviewed my file, called me in, and we hit it off. The Public Information Officer, a part-time assignment, is scheduled to rotate next week, and the colonel thought it would be a good fit, so I will soon be editing the copy for the engineer newspaper. He assigned me to Echo Company in the adjoining engineering battalion, where I have some executive officer responsibilities. That all means I'll remain ensconced here at the sprawling base of Cam Ranh Bay. This place is no doubt three or four times safer than the DC area, so irony of ironies, our positions are juxtaposed: I get to worry about you!

"Take care of yourself, my love, and write as soon as you can. Use the APO San Francisco address on the envelope. All mail for Vietnam goes there first. I'm thinking of you night and day."

20

As July shifted into August, Press's learning curve continued on a steep trajectory. His platoon had minesweep duty on the road, and he settled into a
routine of picking up an infantry security detail at FSB Walton shortly before
0800 and walking with the minesweep team to the ford. Sfc. Harlan would
then assign individual squads to jobsites. Press would hopscotch from site to
site in his jeep—newly stenciled *Minderbinder* on the lower windshield—Snowy
at the wheel, and measure slopes with a clinometer, note possible drainage
problems, and confer with Weitzel on cut and fill areas. He and Harlan were
cordial with each other, but Press had failed to establish the easygoing relationship he had hoped for.

On the third of August the battalion operation's officer, Major Bonds,
attended a meeting at Echo Company to review the progress on Ridgway
Road. After a late morning tour, he concluded that additional dump trucks
were needed to haul crushed stone to the stockpile located two kilometers
from Ben Than's rear gate. Returning to Dong Ha, he arranged for a platoon
of the 85th Panel Bridge Company in Phu Bai to begin hauling stone on the
16th.

Two days later, Elkington received a typhoon alert and radioed to the field
for the platoons to return to Ben Than. By mid-afternoon the engineers were
placing sandbags on the corrugated iron roofs of their billets. Many strung
wire rope over the roofs, fastening it to stakes. Echo Company's lieutenants
hosted a typhoon party for Captain Elkington and the noncommissioned officers. The center room table was covered with food sent by relatives: salami
and cheese from Grieve's mother in Wisconsin; homemade chocolate chip

cookies from Coe's wife in Oregon; a Smithfield ham from Giardi's mother, sent from Virginia.

"First Sergeant Washington," Press called from the bar. "You look like a bourbon drinker, how about a fist of Jack Daniels?"

"Good guess, sir, but not a drop over four fingers."

Press glanced at Washington, who was peeling a round of cheese as if it were a carrot. "Okay, four fingers it is, but only if you stop cutting off the green stuff. A slug of Jack Daniels will kill the bacteria." Press liked the first sergeant. Not only was he highly capable, he was fair with the men and amply endowed with a quality which Press prized: equanimity. He had an air of quiet authority, leant credence by a six-five, 280 pound frame.

"Now, you wouldn't be trying to get me both drunk *and* sick, would you, sir?"

Harlan was pouring bourbon into an aluminum beer can and listening to the banter. "What's that—the lieutenant trying to make you sick?"

"That's right," Press broke in. "I'm going to get the first sergeant as sick on food and drink as you are of answering questions."

"Impossible, sir, there aren't more than twenty bottles of booze here," Harlan jibed.

Press decided not to exchange barbs with Harlan. He made a few neutral comments and went outside to join others on top of the communications' bunker. The night air almost dripped water, and he wondered if the monsoon would come early. The only lights were those in the perimeter wire. Coe, hazily illuminated by one, practiced his latest caricature of a black power handshake. Race relations, Press knew, was second to drug use in the long list of problems facing the military in Vietnam. Although Press grew up in Chicago's mostly white enclave of Hyde Park, he felt that his lifelong association with blacks citywide gave him a realistic and sympathetic perspective on civil rights. Although discrimination was strictly forbidden in the military, racism and bigotry mirrored the civilian world. While racial tension was imperceptible in the field, where survival was the common cause, it was often palpable in base camp.

Press looked up into the night sky. He could not see the heavy, swirling clouds but felt a raindrop strike a glancing blow on his cheek. As the evening wore on, the typhoon would do the same to the coast of Vietnam.

Giardi's platoon had minesweep duty the next morning. A low-lying, gray, soupy mist cut the temperature to a comfortable level, and the standard-issue dust now took the form of tiny globules on the roadbed. Press and Snowy, riding in *Minderbinder*, were near the front of the long procession.

"You got a girl back home?" Press asked.

"I did till I got over here."

"I don't mean to pry, but how did it go south?"

Snowy shook his head. "She had no goddamn sense. A month after I unpacked, some Cornhusker tackle from the next town over knocked her up. The guy was third string, don't ya know."

"Did they get married?"

"Yeah. That's what he was angling for the whole time. He's dumb as a can of worms but smart enough to know it. He used to say, 'Da more I study, da more I get confused.' Anyway, her old man owns a hardware and feed store, so the big beef cake quit college and now he's wearing an apron, totin' sacks of feed."

"You'll find another; perhaps a better one, after you get back."

"Screw it. I've had enough of girls."

"You'll change your mind—believe me, you'll change your mind," Press said, with a wistful look.

Snowy pulled the jeep to the side of the road, next to the lead five-ton dump truck. The sun burned a hole through the haze, and Press put on his sunglasses.

"Looks like they're done with the sweep, LT."

Press got out of the jeep and walked up to Giardi, who was looking at a four-feet-deep dip in the road where a thirty-six inch culvert would be placed.

"At least we got a little running water here," said Giardi.

"Good, the mud will make it easier to excavate. What do you think, another foot before you place the culvert?"

"Yeah, that should do it," Giardi agreed, then motioned for the truck driver to pull forward and off the road. The six engineers sitting on the side boards of the bed grabbed hold as the truck began to cross over the depression. As the rear dual wheels sank into the mud, an explosion rocked the truck, launching the bed several feet in the air.

Press had taken a few steps toward the truck and was six feet away when the land mine exploded. Everything became a blur, and he felt himself being thrust backward by the blast, landing a second or two later on the soft ground a few feet from where he had been standing. Dazed, he tried to sit up. "Christ, I can't see," he said to nobody in particular. He lifted his hands to his eyes, felt his sunglasses, and removed them. His sight returned. He glanced at the glasses and saw that they were coated with mud. The entire front of his body was covered with mud. He began to run his fingers over his chest, feeling for holes. "Whew," he breathed out, finding none.

The six engineers in the truck bed had been catapulted into the air and now lay on the ground. Giardi, who had been out of the blast radii, was trying to radio the medevac unit when Press reached his jeep. Radio communication was severely limited in the river valley, and Elkington had stationed a radioman on FSB Ridgway. Press raised Spec 4 Vanterpool on his radio and asked him to radio DMZ Dust-off in Quang Tri for a medevac chopper. "Looks like we've got two down and four ambulatory," he said.

Vanterpool radioed back a few minutes later. "Be advised that a chopper is en route, but the pilot is requesting a sweep of the landing zone."

Press was surprised by the request. Ground troops walked all over the jungle without minesweeping. Being prudent was a trait he did not associate with chopper pilots. He pressed the send button on his mike: "Tiles Two-zero. This is Tiles Three-one, over."

"Three-one—Two-zero, go."

"Three-one. Tell Dust-off the sweep of the LZ is in progress. We'll pop smoke. Have him identify color, over."

A minute later the pilot radioed that he had sighted yellow smoke. Press, now in direct communication with the chopper, told the pilot it was safe to touch down at the LZ. He then hurried over to the most severely wounded engineer, one who was conscious but had limited feeling in his legs. Aware that anything more than hand-holding could aggravate the young Spec 4's injuries, he spouted some words of encouragement. A minute later two medics from the chopper politely moved him aside and began a series of questions, followed by prods and pokes on the injured engineer's limbs. After supporting his spine, they carefully placed him onboard.

Harlan approached Press shortly after the chopper lifted off with the wounded. Looking him up and down, he said, "I'd say you were damned lucky today, sir."

"I guess you're right. The blast knocked me on my ass, but I feel okay."

"The only metal in that mine was the detonator. Probably about forty pounds of black powder. If Charlie had mixed some rock with the powder, *you'd* be in that chopper now, maybe in a body bag."

"An interesting thought, Sergeant." Press wanted to tell him to wipe the grin off his face, but concluded that it would be playing Harlan's game, so he turned and walked to the ford. He took off his cartridge belt, removed his SOI and wallet, and walked into the river.

The mountain water was cool but turbid from the previous night's light rain. Press decided to rinse himself in the clear water of the tributary stream. It was only eight inches deep, so he lay down on the rocky bottom and let the fast-flowing water swish over and around him. Gazing upstream, a strange feeling engulfed him. The stream seemed to beckon, to lure him up its quicksilver pathway, along its four-foot-high banks, beside the tousled, impenetrable vegetation that closed in from both sides and nearly meshed, shutting out all but vertical light. The stream imparted mystery and danger and, inexplicably, he was attracted to it. As he picked himself up, he decided that he would walk a short distance upstream. The idea struck him after perhaps twenty steps. Here was all the rock they would need for the upper road. The haul distances were perfect—all they would need was a rock crusher. Then it came to him that it would be impossible to set up a crushing operation in an unprotected area. The NVA would destroy it in the first week. As Press retreated to the ford, he pondered ways to salvage his idea.

Two days later the minesweep team discovered another mine. This one was planted into the hard road bed and was spotted visually. One of the team members placed his detector over the disturbed clay and nodded his head upon hearing the signal. Sergeant Studt cut a block of C-4 plastic explosive in half, gouged a hole in it, and inserted a blasting cap attached to a fuse. As he lighted the fuse, another team member popped a red smoke grenade, yelling "fire in the hole" three times. Fifty seconds later, a double explosion sent a section of the road skyward, leaving a crater with a diameter of four feet. Press looked over at Harlan, who was nodding approvingly—something, Press thought, he would never get. Harlan's attitude toward him had hardened noticeably during the last week, even though the frequency of Press's questions had diminished. Burg Whitcomb had been visiting the jobsites often, and Press would invariably join him for an hour or two. Whitcomb genuinely welcomed his questions, which were becoming more challenging.

At mid-morning, while Harlan was at another jobsite, Press directed a bulldozer in an attempt to widen the road. The area contained an underground spring and as the dozer broke the hard shell of the surface, it became so thoroughly mired in mud that the tracks disappeared completely.

Whitcomb arrived as Press was literally scratching his head. "How you going to get it out?" he asked Press.

"Borrow one of your dozers and winch it out," was his answer.

Whitcomb arranged for the nearest dozer to "walk" to the jobsite, and posed another question as it arrived. "If you winch with the dozer from the road, are you going to pull the stuck one out or the one on the road *in?*"

"You're right, sir. I'll have both buried. But there's only the road—no trees or anything to dead-man your dozer to."

"Watch this, Lieutenant." Whitcomb walked over to his dozer operator and issued instructions. The operator began making a cut on the road perpendicular to the bogged-down dozer. In a few minutes he had made a nearly three-foot vertical wall in the road. He then backed the rescue dozer down the slope until it was fast against the wall. The operator then began to unreel the wire rope cable, while two engineers dragged the hook to the rear of the half-buried dozer. They wrapped the cable around a sturdy box section frame which housed a huge steel tooth. Whitcomb had explained earlier to Press that the tooth was called a ripper tube, and when lowered to the ground hydraulically, it would break hard material while the tractor moved forward.

Fastened securely, the wire rope became pry-bar-tight soon after the operator began to reel it in. "Step back," Whitcomb warned. "If that cable snaps under load, it could whipsaw and take off our heads."

Press thought that the dozer was already snug against the wall, but as the wire rope tightened, the dozer was pulled farther into the bank. The stuck dozer began to move. Black smoke puffed from the exhaust stacks as the operators opened the throttles. The noise from the engines and winch sounded straight out of the early Industrial Revolution. As the dozer slid slowly out of its burial place, the operator eased off on the winch, and the mud-covered machine began to move under its own power.

"Another lesson learned," Press said to Whitcomb. "Sorry it had to be an object lesson."

"Glad to help, Lieutenant. But I'm afraid you're on your own from now on."

"Your promotion came through?"

"Should be official today. I'm going to be Ops officer for a battalion in Qui Nhon."

Press congratulated Whitcomb, and the two officers talked for a few minutes before the new major started for his jeep. He stopped momentarily and took Press by the arm. "One more thing. You know you're going to have to lock Harlan's heels and take full command of your platoon."

"Yes, sir, I think it's time."

"Good luck, Lieutenant."

"Same to you, Major."

That evening Press opened his foot locker and retrieved Celia's letter.

"Dearest Press...I've read your letter over and over. I'm so happy that you've got a safe assignment. I think it was foolhardy for me to worry so much about you. You're very clever, and I should have known that you would charm you way into a good job.

"Everything is going well with my classes. At work, Scoop is still supporting the war, but with noticeably less enthusiasm from a year ago. No smiles yet, but he's still paternalistic with his female staffers—insisting that I be given a ride home when I worked late a couple of nights back. Lynn sends her greetings. Says to keep that handsome face out of harm's way.

"I'm still pretty mixed up in my feelings, honey. You're always in my thoughts. All I can promise is that I'll never deceive you. For good or ill, you'll know how I honestly feel. For now I can tell you that it's a struggle between my head and my heart. I liked your "our hands against our hearts" admonition, but sometimes (during the day) the sober thoughts of the mind hold sway and I have doubts about us. At night I hug my pillow and pretend it's you. Sometimes I ache for you…With love, Celia"

He put the letter down and shook his head, then went to the bar and poured himself a jigger of Old Grand Dad.

Two days after Whitcomb left, Elkington completed his tour. The day before he began his journey to the States, he sent Press to FSB Ridgway to determine the efficacy of housing a squad on the mountain-top. That would enable the engineers to begin installing culverts on the upper reaches of the road two hours earlier in the morning.

He and Snowy arrived in mid-afternoon. Snowy found a nook for the jeep, and Press started for the TOC (tactical operations center) to check in with the fire base commander. The meeting was brief. Major Eaglefeather told him there was enough room for eight or nine engineers if they split up, and then asked Press if he had brought a dozer up with him. Receiving a negative response, he dismissed him by turning away.

"Just one more question, sir. My driver and I are spending the night here, can you suggest accommodations?"

Eaglefeather wheeled around. A sergeant at the radio sniggered. "Accommodations? What does this look like to you, Lieutenant, a goddamn hotel?"

Press smiled. "Well, sir, I understand that among the fire bases in I Corps, Ridgway is four star."

Eaglefeather shook his head at Press's pun. "Bunk down with the artillery—the eight-inch battery—they've got room. Your driver can find a place with the engineers. And on your next visit, bring a goddamn bulldozer."

As Press left, a helicopter set down and two young women, clad in light blue dresses and orange hats, stepped out. He continued to the artillery battery and found a second lieutenant, who told him that they had an extra cot in the officers' bunker. Press asked him about the girls.

"Oh, some Red Cross deal," he answered. "The king of the hill put out a notice that a couple of doughnut dollies would arrive today and that everybody would shape up and dress accordingly. No showering under the fifty-five gallon drum."

"Com'on, sir, the pastry pigs might do a few tricks for us," called out a passing artilleryman.

Press laughed as he saw one of the young women pull out a deck of cards. "You can probably gauge how long you've been in-country based on how good they look to you."

"Three months ago I would have rated them a two; now, they're semi-beautiful."

"Yeah," said Press, "time does seem to soften the features and rearrange a few pounds." He suddenly imagined Celia and Rebecca standing in place of the Red Cross workers and winced. All I need is for them to run into each other sometime, he thought.

Taking his leave from the lieutenant, he walked back to the jeep and found Snowy snoozing behind the wheel. He looked around and spotted the castle insignia of the engineers nailed to a beam on a bunker only yards away. As he entered, he was reminded of the bunker he had visited on his first trip to Ridgway. The odor was offensive, a mixture of mildew and soiled socks. He made his way to a second room, an inter-sanctum so dim that it constricted his vision.

"Take a seat on the other bunk."

From a form sitting cross-legged on a cot, Press recognized the voice of Lt. Davidson. Parts of a .45 caliber pistol gradually materialized, spread in front of him on the blanket. Press had not liked him from the start, although he had only known him from the several times that his and Davidson's minesweep teams reached the ford simultaneously. Davidson had always been brusque, and the first minute of their conversation this morning would be no exception.

"Take the minesweep from here to the ford for a few weeks. We've got to build a couple of bunkers and make some gun pads," he said, while he ran a cloth coated with cosmoline oil inside the barrel of his pistol.

"You like to get right to the nub of it—no verbal foreplay before asking for a big favor," Press chided.

"Who's asking?"

"Sorry, we can't afford the time. It would negate an early start on the upper road culverts."

"We'll see what your CO has to say about it. I hear he's coming here tomorrow morning."

"This is his last day. He'll be on his way to Cam Ranh."

"His replacement will be here, along with your battalion commander."

"You running your own intelligence operation?"

"I do what's necessary to get the job done," he answered, as he began to assemble the .45. "It's what is expected of officers. By the way, how did you get your commission?"

"OCS at Belvoir."

"Five months and a gold bar," he sniffed.

"Do I detect a degree of condescension?" asked Press.

"Not if you don't think it's deserved."

"Actually, I can honestly tell you that I don't think about it at all. What I think about is getting back to the real world."

Davidson laughed sarcastically. "I thought you had a grain of intelligence. Let me educate you: the world doesn't get any more real than this. If you don't think so, why don't you take one of the paths off the road this afternoon—two, three kilometers at most. You'll find out how *real* it is. When they find your bleached bones in twenty or thirty years, they'll be real too."

"As a matter of fact, I did take a little off-road trek, and I'll have to admit your point's well taken, but it's not a normal world, and nobody in his right mind should want to be here."

"It's called duty, Patrick. You may think it sounds stupid, but if we don't stop communism now in Vietnam, it'll spread to Thailand and then to Malaysia and finally we'll be taking it on in America."

"Sorry, I don't subscribe to domino theory."

"You're no better than a goddamn politician," Davidson snapped. "Whatever is the easy way, that's the course they'll take. We can win this war if they let us." His last words were punctuated by bursts of artillery fire from a 105 mm battery just outside the bunker.

Press's peripheral vision caught movement in a corner of the bunker. Davidson raised his assembled .45 and fired. A rat, who had poked its head from an opening, had been blown back into its hole. A rivulet of blood seeping out attested to Davidson's accuracy with a weapon.

"I see you guys shoot your dinner here," Press said, as he walked out.

Late that evening, he lay on a cot in the officers' bunker belonging to the eight-inch howitzer battery. Sleep took over slowly, only to be interrupted by a body-levitating explosion. With a piercing pain in his inner ears, dust swirling in the bunker and pervading his lungs, he stumbled to the stairs and climbed to the open air.

"Sorry to wake you," the artillery lieutenant said, after seeing Press emerge.

"*Wake me?* What great deadpan. Here I am, a first-time overnight guest; you wait for me to fall fast asleep; you pull the lanyard on *Son of Egor* here"— Press pointed to the inscribed barrel of an eight-inch howitzer—"and as I come out of the ground concussed, you say: 'Oh, so *sorry to wake you.*'"

The lieutenant laughed. "It's not that bad; sleep with ear plugs and your mouth open. Once in a while one of us gets the muzzle blast. We roll over and go back to sleep."

"You guys must have cast iron ears."

"The problem is that the bunker is just in front of the barrel. We originally had one-seven-five barrels mounted, which extended past the bunker."

"What were you shooting at, anyway?" asked Press, exasperated.

"Nothing in particular."

"You mean to tell me that you lob shells out there for the hell of it?"

"It's harassing fire."

Press shook his head in wonderment. "I've got to hand it to the OD; the terrain between here and Laos has to be one of the most inhospitable areas of the country—of the world—and the Army thinks that a few rounds in the mountains will wear the enemy down?"

"I know it's stupid; you know it's stupid; but there's nothing either of us can do about it. Besides, it's nothing to lose sleep over."

Press chuckled. "Good…that's good. See you in the morning."

He had little to do the next morning except to wait for the arrival of the battalion commander and the new CO of Echo Company. Snowy was napping in the jeep. He had been "volunteered" for four hours of guard duty by Lt. Davidson's platoon sergeant. Press sat on a sand bag atop the artillery sighting bunker and looked over the curve of the earth. The morning was brilliantly clear, and the white dunes along the South China Sea sparkled. He gazed at the sea intently. Safety and sanity were somewhere beyond the horizon. What if he were given a small sailboat, provisions, and an honorable discharge; would he sail off to America? What would his chance of survival be on the open seas versus staying in Vietnam? After some minutes he decided that he would drown in the first gale. He turned his back to the sea and pulled a map from his pocket. To the southwest was Hamburger Hill in the A Shau Valley, from what he had heard and read a truly awful place to wage war; to the northwest was Khe Sanh, the scene of some of the most vicious fighting of the war. He was sitting astride two of the most feared places for combat since the *Chosin* Reservoir and Pork Chop Hill during the Korean War. He surveyed the mountainscape: peaks anchored the horizon, jutting like teeth on a ripsaw, and everywhere a deep green tangle of vegetation gripped the expanse in a stranglehold. "At least I won't have to go out there," he said out loud and felt better. Nixon was winding down the American presence, the Marines were gone from northern I Corps, and the Army now protected the populated coastal plain from a series of fire bases, such as Ridgway, strung along the eastern flank of the Annamites. It was a defensive posture designed to minimize casualties, while giving the *ARVN* time to grow strong enough to thwart the NVA.

Press repositioned himself again, and the first thing that caught his eye was a three-quarter ton truck climbing the steep approach to the fire base. It stopped near the helipad, and he watched as Davidson's engineers clambered off the sides. He suddenly sat straight as a thought struck him, then got up and started for the truck.

Davidson saw Press approaching and waited for him.

After exchanging nods, Press said, "You may feel this is none of my business, but you're taking a big gamble if you continue to haul your minesweep team back in the three-quarter ton."

"You're right, it's none of your business."

Brushing the objection aside, Press continued. "We've had to medevac six guys after one of our five-tons hit a mine. One is in a hospital in Japan and won't return. Your guys would have no chance if your three-quarter ton ran over an undetected mine."

"Thanks for your concern, Patrick. We don't have any five-ton's."

Davidson walked off, and Press waited near the helipad for Lt. Col. Fletcher to fly in with the new company commander. Fifteen minutes had elapsed when he spotted a Ranger helicopter coming in to land; seconds later, whirling blades whipped the ground into swirling clouds of dust. As the rotors stopped, the battalion commander jumped out and strode toward Press. Behind him was a captain who was wearing his boonie hat with the sides curled up, as one might who did not venture out long in the tropical sun. He was of medium height and build, and as he came closer, Press was struck by the incongruity of his face: protruding eyes, tip-tilted nose, thick lips, and a weak, irregular chin.

Press saluted the two superior officers. He had met Fletcher at Battalion headquarters in Dong Ha and was impressed by his grasp of the conditions in the field, especially on Ridgway Road. After introducing him to Cpt. Jack Durbin, Fletcher briefed the new Echo Company CO on recent operations. Their vantage point on the mountain provided an unequaled view of the road.

Fletcher waved his arm at the upper road and said, "When the monsoons come in late September, you better have two inches of gravel laid, or you may never catch up on road maintenance. It's damn difficult to work on a wet road with steep grades, for every loaded truck does almost as much damage as good. Soon you'll have the 85th Panel Bridge hauling for you, which should give you enough trucks to do the job."

Throughout the briefing, Durbin nodded at every point, but to Press his mind seemed disengaged, and he asked few questions. When Fletcher finished, Press offered his impression of the quality of gravel at the stockpile.

"Too many fines?" Fletcher repeated.

"Yes, sir. There must be two-thirds fines and one-third stone. Last week's rain washed away the fines from a section of road just above the ford, and there wasn't much stone left."

The battalion commander thought for a minute and then shook his head. "There's very little we can do about it, except for increasing the lift slightly. It's the only stone we've got. We're just going to have to make it work."

This was Press's opportunity to tell Fletcher about using river rock from the stream, but he thought better of it. To abandon the stockpile after the stone had been hauled almost twenty miles might not be acceptable at the battalion level. And if his impression of Durbin was accurate, he could be finessed.

While Fletcher used the radio in his chopper, Press told Durbin about Davidson's request and, exaggerating by half, why he turned it down.

"No way we can lose that much time," said Durbin. "I'll tell him to cram it."

When Fletcher returned, he and Durbin left to find Major Eaglefeather. Press watched them make their way to the TOC and spotted Davidson milling nearby. Okay, Snowy, he said to himself, let's get the hell out of here. As if on cue, Snowy brought the jeep down to the helipad. While they were driving past the gate, Press decided that he was no longer an interloper—on the contrary, the road was his, and neither the North Vietnamese nor higher command would determine the final look of it. He felt as Burg Whitcomb must have: confident and without fear. He had Snowy stop on some of the steeper slopes, which he marked with engineering stakes.

On the second occasion Snowy became curious. "What the hell are you up to, LT?"

"An experiment. Two of the marked-off sections are going to get a lift of stone and two with similar slopes will get a lift of river rock. We'll compare them after the next rain."

Snowy, satisfied, opened the Igloo container strapped in back, and handed Press a can of beer. He opened a Coke for himself. "I can't wait to see it," he said with a smirk.

"See what?"

"When you tell Sergeant Harlan."

"Well, let's not disappoint you. After we're finished staking, we'll go find him."

They drove to a wide area near the ford, where the company bulldozer was parked. Press hopped out of the jeep and approached Spec 4 Allen. "Is it down?" he asked, referring to the dozer.

"Hydraulic hose is leaking, sir."

"Can you run it?"

"If I don't tilt the blade. Up and down is okay."

"Good, let's take a ride."

"A *ride*, sir?"

"An engineering recon, Allen. I want to go up the stream as far as we can and occasionally push some rock up, so I can see how deep it goes."

Allen shrugged and motioned Press to climb aboard. As the earthmover entered the stream, the crystalline waters turned a dirty gray in its wake. They left the open area of the ford and entered a different world. Green on a rampage burst from both banks, so thick that, had Press reached in at arm's length, he would not have seen his hand. Advancing, the stream began to narrow and deepen, and at intervals Allen would dip the blade into the water, churning up rock and sand. Further and further they navigated upstream, a green tapestry forming overhead, thickening, and slowly shutting out sunlight, while down below water began to inch over the tops of the tracks and up to the tips of the cooling fan, causing steam to hiss out of the engine compartment and pull the engine down, down, until it cursed in a deeply guttural timbre.

"This is about as far as we can go, sir."

Press nodded, and Allen moved the transmission lever to reverse. He then lowered the blade to the maximum extent, causing the engine frame to pivot out of the water, and the fan ceased its frothy mixing. He was back-blading the stream bed, smoothing the undulations mechanically before the swift current could do it hydrologically. The engineers sweated profusely. The still, humid air, trapped under a verdant blanket, baked by the sun overhead and the engine's exhaust underneath, made them feel as though they were stirring the waters of a cauldron rather than a stream.

Press found Harlan at a culvert site near the ford. Snowy had parked the jeep close enough to overhear their conversation. Deciding on the direct approach, Press, after muted greetings, said, "I've just been upstream aways, and tomorrow I'd like to take about ten truckloads of river run from the stream and put it on the upper road."

Harlan appeared stunned.

"I gather from your expression you don't feel it's a good idea."

"If you'll pardon my asking, sir, what would you want to do a fool thing like that for?"

"You have any specific objections, Sergeant Harlan?" Press asked, taken aback by his vehemence.

"Let me name them for you. One, we've already got a stockpile of crushed stone, almost enough to cover the road. Two, river rock is smooth. There won't be any traction on slopes. Three, it's too large. Some of those rocks are as big as"—Harlan's eyes wandered over Press's head—"as a football."

Press shook off the implied gibe. "Anything else?" Harlan gave him a look which he interpreted as shit, man, I just gave you three gold-plated reasons. "Good, I've staked off two areas to dump the rock. I'll be on the upper road at 1000 hours to spot the trucks."

Press walked back from the officers' shower in late afternoon. He was wearing army-issue boxer shorts and sandals, an olive drab towel draped over his shoulders. Grieve, Coe, Giardi, and Weitzel were crowded in the center room of the billet when he entered. Freshly scrubbed and in their skivvies, they were having cocktails and appetizers before evening chow. The appetizers were usually foods with long shelf lives sent from the States by mothers and wives. Salami and cheese were daily staples. Crackers were in ample supply at the small PX in Ben Than. The young officers invariably filled up on the appetizers and took a light dinner, which with monotonous regularity consisted of dried out and tasteless roast beef—the troops swore it was water buffalo—and potatoes.

They watched the televised news on AFVN (Armed Forces Vietnam) and, sometimes, old re-runs of *Route 66* and other staples of American TV in the early sixties. Most evenings they played poker and talked. Conversations consisted in the main of their lives stateside, of wives and girlfriends—in Grieve's case, a three-month-old son he had not seen—and careers planned. No one considered making a career of the Army. Ridgway road would invariably creep into the conversation, along with problems, such as drug use, they were having in the company.

This evening, after dealing a hand of draw poker, Weitzel asked the others about Gonzalez. "Is that his daily routine—going around the company area cussing out the OD?"

"Yeah, that's pretty much SOP," Grieve answered. "I'll take three. Sometimes he comes into the office and does it there. Nobody pays any attention."

"Gimme one," said Coe. "We're trying to two-twelve him, but the paperwork is stalled somewhere."

Grieve reached to his right and grasped a machete leaning against the wall. Without leaving his chair, he raised the weapon slightly and then swiftly brought it down on a mouse. In a spontaneous move Coe turned in his chair and placed a mark next to Grieve's name on a sheet nailed to the wall.

Giardi threw his cards on the table. "Until then, Gonzalez is sort of the company mascot for the disgruntled. He's like one of our dogs, roaming the com—"

"The only one with distemper," Coe broke in, beaming with his clever word play.

"How many dogs have you got here?" Weitzel inquired.

"Three," said Grieve. "We had four until two weeks ago: Uncle Ho, Shirley, Fat Ass, and Henrietta. We think our cleaning woman coaxed Henrietta out of the base with some of Giardi's beef jerky. They went missing the same day."

Giardi picked up the story. "Yeah, that evening smoke from the vil drifted our way, carrying the aroma of barbecued dog."

Everybody except Weitzel laughed. "You guys had me believing it until that barbecue bullshit."

"Dog is a delicacy to the Vietnamese," Grieve insisted.

"If your diet was a daily dose of fish heads and rice, you'd probably take the machete to Shirley," Press said to Grieve, his eyes on the blood-stained blade.

"For as long as Mark's been in-country, he'd take something else to her first," Giardi said with a laugh.

"Why don't you extend, Mark; in six months Fat Ass might look pretty good," Coe added. "Of course, you might prefer Uncle Ho."

"First, though, make an advance on this damn pesky fly," Giardi said, waving his arm in front of his face.

Grieve, scooping up cards, growled, "*Pesky*? You're lucky you're in an engineer unit. An airborne ranger would stomp on your gonads for saying a pacifist, wimp word like that."

Giardi: "An airborne ranger wouldn't know what the word meant."

"It's not the meaning, it's the sound," Grieve countered.

"Yeah, not even your modifier 'damn' lessens your crime," Press piled on.

"Next time, say 'Smash that big fucking fly for me,'" Coe contributed.

That was how it went most evenings. It was their night life, and weekends were no exception. The gates of the base closed at sundown, and there was simply nowhere else to go. The enemy governed the night. The give and take, the talk of problems, achievements, aspirations, and shared experiences, the drinking and eating and poker playing—all those ingredients of camaraderie—were palliatives for the alternating stress and tedium of their existence.

The weather during the next three weeks produced no rain but remained humid and oppressively hot. Work on the road progressed rapidly. Lt. Hank Massie of the 85th Panel Bridge Company arrived with twelve five-ton dump trucks in mid-month and began hauling crushed stone from a barge near Hue to the stockpile on Ridgway Road. Trucks from Echo Company and the 166th Light Equipment Company were hauling the crushed stone from the stockpile to the upper road. Harlan had forgotten about Press's experiment in using river rock on the road. Press had not forgotten. He was waiting for rain, for fair weather would not determine which type of rock was more suitable for the monsoons. And he was noting the cycle times of the trucks from the stockpile to the off-load point and back again. He became certain that by loading at the ford, he could reduce the time by half.

His chance came in late August. A storm tore in from the South China Sea, and although it was brief, almost an inch of rain fell. Two days later, they began operations again on the upper road. During the late afternoon briefing at headquarters, Press presented his case.

"I'd like to propose two changes on the road," he began. "First, we stop hauling crushed stone from the stockpile and use river run from the stream near the ford."

Durbin looked around the room, searching for expressions pro and con. Harlan was looking down and shaking his head, but the others remained impassive. "Go on," he said.

"Most of you know that we put down a lift of river run on two steep sections of the road several weeks ago. When I inspected them after the rain, there was no erosion. And when we hauled stone today, there was very little rutting of the roadbed. That's not the case on similar slopes covered by crushed stone. There's a good bit of erosion and loss of stone, and most severe of all, deep rutting by the twelve—it was twelve trucks today, wasn't it, Al?"

"Right, we started with thirteen, but one was redlined early on," Giardi confirmed.

"Anyway, the road's torn up where there's stone or just dirt and in pretty good shape where there's river run. Al, Bob, and Jim can verify that."

Durbin saw the nods of agreement from the other platoon leaders. "This might not go down well at Battalion."

"Why does anybody at Battalion have to know?" asked Press, rhetorically. "In our sitrep we'll say rock instead of stone. Nobody's going to pick that out."

"What if Major Bonds comes down?" Durbin asked.

Press thought for a second. "How does that old saw go? Oh, yeah: 'I'd rather ask for forgiveness than for permission.'"

Amid silence, Durbin indecisively tapped a pencil on his notebook.

"Come on, sir. You don't have a choice," Grieve almost barked. "If Press is right, and it sure as hell looks like he is, you can either take the credit for getting those convoys up to Ridgway in the monsoons or take the blame when they get stuck halfway up the mountain. You don't think Charlie won't have a field day with a bogged-down convoy?"

"All right, already," Durbin said, irritated. "Just keep it among ourselves for a while."

"Thank you," Press said. "There's one more thing. We've got a helluva job to do in less than a month of good weather. There's no way we can cover all of the upper road with enough rock in that time. I think we should do a visual minesweep every day the road is dry and hard. I don't think there's any way the NVA can dig a hole, place a mine and cover it so that it's not noticeable."

Harlan almost leapt from his chair.

"That's taking a pretty big risk," Coe stated. "I agree with you about visual detection, but if they get one by us—even if we don't take casualties—there would probably be a court martial."

The words "court martial" and the lack of support for Press's proposal induced Durbin to speak firmly: "No goddamn way, Patrick."

Grieve caught up with Press after the meeting broke. "Durbin's a real study, isn't he?"

"Yeah," Press agreed. "What Churchill once said about an opponent certainly applies to him: 'He prefers the discomfort of a fence to the horrors of a decision.'"

"That's true, except for minor decisions; he's always making those. Did you notice Rinaldo in the head shack this afternoon?"

"Yes. I wondered what he was doing behind a desk."

"Because Durbin moved him to headquarters—intends to reform him, get him to swear off drugs."

"I guess as long as Durbin doesn't interfere with what we're doing on the road, he can drive First Sergeant Washington crazy with his incremental interference."

"For what it's worth, Washington told me at the door that you're the kind of officer he'd like to serve with."

"That's good of him. He's probably alone, though."

"Don't worry about Harlan. He's fighting a losing battle. Just as long as you don't screw up—"

"You mean like conducting a visual sweep?" Press asked, as they entered the billet.

"Name your poison," said Coe, who was at the bar.

"Johnnie Walker Black," Press answered.

"I'll have some of that yellow stuff, even though it looks like they get it out of the pisser," said Grieve.

"Galiano it is."

"I've noticed something odd since I've been here," Press started in. "You'd think the jungle would be a giant aviary, but there just aren't that many birds out there."

"I heard they sprayed the area with Agent Orange a couple of years back," Coe said.

Grieve shook his head. "It's a defoliant, and if they sprayed it, it was ineffective, except for some of the trees at the top of the canopy."

"Maybe the snakes are keeping the population down," Giardi offered. "The fuckers are everywhere."

Massie was sitting at the table savoring his drink. "You know, I've just made my own astute observation. None of us smoke."

"You can't get anything past these panel bridge guys, can you?" Giardi marveled.

"Well, you know, you just don't find a group of five guys and none of them smokes—not in this man's army," Massie protested.

"Smells like piss too," said Grieve, his nose in the lidless beer can containing the Galiano.

"Let's drink to our non-smoking health," Press proposed.

Giardi laughed. "It's a good thing we drink, or this place would drive us to smoke."

"Worse yet, we don't even have sex, unless you count the steam 'n' cream at Phu Bai one Sunday afternoon a month," Grieve lamented.

"You can't count a hand job as sex," declared Coe. "Although the plump gal with the big tits has a great stroke. Last time down there I came twice."

His words were capped off by an explosion in the adjacent compound of one of the periodic nuisance rockets fired by the NVA from the western hills.

"That must be mess call," Massie joked. "Who wants to take the first cold shower?"

Following the minesweep the next morning, Press sent a bulldozer and a front-end loader a hundred meters upstream of the ford to begin stockpiling rock. He put a second dozer to work cutting an access road parallel to the stream so that the trucks could travel by road to the stockpile, where they would be loaded, and return to the ford via the narrow stream bed. After two hours of work on the service road, Allen, the dozer operator, complained to Press that he encountered a type of clay—clay rock, rather—that was so hard he would have to rip it. This piqued Press's interest, and he watched the ripping operation with mounting enthusiasm. The loose clay compacted so tightly after a few passes with the dozer that running water from a spring did not turn the surface into mud.

"Fantastic!" Press shouted, his exclamation lost in the din of iron scraping against rock, hot gases surging past ports, and fan blades cleaving air. He had not related to Durbin at yesterday's meeting that the trucks often lost traction on the slopes covered with river rock. Harlan already knew this and would no doubt inform the CO. If Press could mix some of the clay with the rock, it might stabilize the rock and provide needed traction.

And it did. When the access road was cut and the stockpiles shaped, Press began routing the trucks up the road and back down the stream, half of them filled with hard clay, half with river rock. The fully loaded trucks would puff and cough as they climbed Ridgway Road in first gear. For several weeks of constant hauling, the hill dwellers of FSB Ridgway would look out at the South China Sea through a diaphanous haze, what had once been the yellow loam of their mountain.

Word soon reached Battalion what Echo Company was doing. Major Bonds phoned Durbin one morning and told him to be at the ford at 1100 hours. Durbin arrived a little early in order to get a look at the operation.

Sgt. VanAcker sidled up to Press. "Sir, what the hell is *he* doing out here?"

"Well, Sarge, I think he got an invitation from the major. I hope he can answer Bonds' questions."

As the major's jeep came into view, Durbin approached Press and told him to stay at his side. Seconds after Bonds hopped out of his jeep, the two junior officers saluted.

"Lieutenant Patrick, why don't you brief Major Bonds on the experimental operation here."

Press launched into a detailed explanation of the advantages of using the combination of clay and river rock, both in road improvement and daily production. Bonds listened with arms folded over his chest.

When Press was finished, he said, "So, Lieutenant, what do you intend to do with all that crushed stone back there?"

"Salute it every morning as I drive past, sir," Press responded reflexively.

Durbin turned scarlet and emitted a nervous chuckle. "Lieutenant Patrick has a civilian sense of humor, sir. Of course we're going to use the crushed stone. Like I said before, this is just experimental."

"Let's take a ride up the road, gentlemen," said the major.

Forty-five minutes later they returned to the ford and the two junior officers got out.

"What's the lesson learned here, Lieutenant?"

Press looked at the major and thought for a second. "Field expedients move mountains, sir."

Bonds smiled. "It's this: never go past a stockpile of crushed stone without saluting."

After the major had driven off, Press said to Durbin, "You want to celebrate by going for a swim?"

"Are you kidding, the river's muddy as hell."

"I'm talking about the stream."

"The *stream*? You must be crazy, it's not six inches deep."

"It'll be as high as its banks in a few minutes. I promised the boys a swim after lunch, and it's time."

Press and Durbin walked up the stream for a hundred meters, and Press signaled to the dozer operators, who were relaxing near their machines. Within minutes the two dozers had pushed up six feet of rock. Spec 4 Ken Powers then maneuvered his front-end loader onto the sandy stream bed, which appeared naked without water. Four engineers climbed into the bucket, and Powers began moving the machine up the pile of rock while pulling back on the lever controlling lift. The bucket moved slowly upward. Soon, it was above the water, which was already four feet deep behind the dam. The engineers dove into the water, and Powers returned to get more swimmers.

"Hey, sir! Com'on in the water, it feels great," Allen yelled to Durbin.

"It ought to feel great, it must be ninety-five in here," Press added.

Within five minutes the water, now almost six feet high, began seeping through the gravel, and the swimmers climbed onto the cleared bank. Still standing below the damn, Press half-turned, warning, "It's going to break."

It went with a suddenness that shocked him. Water gushed toward the two officers. Press began his sprint downstream, but Durbin hesitated and was caught at the knees and thrown on his backside. He scudded along the bottom, striking an occasional rock, wincing and flailing his arms and legs in the air. He got to his feet after a ride of sixty feet and rubbed his buttocks. Press, convulsed with laughter and tears in his eyes, looked away. He felt certain that Durbin would never set foot on the road again.

21

On a Sunday afternoon in mid-September, Press started a letter to Rebecca.

"Greetings from a land where reality overshadows appearance, where substance surpasses style (good thing you don't read with your lips). I know it's been a while since my first letter, which admittedly wasn't much of a letter as far as commentary on the war goes. I'm still pretty green, although my fatigues are beginning to fade a bit. I better explain that. Anyone parading around in new duds, even if he is a short-timer, is automatically suspect. I must add, though, that a short-timer would rarely discard his boonie hat: the true badge of a veteran. It could be in tatters but that would only increase its value to the wearer. It says to all who glimpse it: 'I've got my shit together.'

"I'm still a second luey, and no matter what the condition of my apparel, I can't be trusted. When you're green everybody seems to let you know that you haven't paid your dues. That sentiment goes triple for lifers, especially sergeants with 15 or 20 years in. I've got two squad leaders—buck sergeants—who went to NCO school (much like the school I went to become an officer), and they take flak about it continually. Everybody calls them 'shake 'n' bakes,' but my two are smart and good guys. The only person I have trouble with is my platoon sergeant. He left today to go on R&R, thank God.

"I still wear my .45 pistol. Remember my first letter about the NVA soldier I came face-to-face with and didn't have the guts or hatred to aim at him. Well, it turns out that he stood a better chance had I tried to kill him rather than shooting willy nilly.

"I made this discovery the other day when Snowy and I parked a mile from the closest jobsite while I gulped down a beer (3.2 beer and it tastes terrible, but it's better than soft drinks). Anyway, I engaged in a little target practice—an empty can at ten feet, then eight, then six. I got it with my third shot at four feet.

"I should discard the damn thing, but by now it's grafted to my hip. Anyway, I need it for paymaster duty. I have to go up to Dong Ha and get about $10,000 in MPC (military payment certificates). If I'm robbed, I'm still responsible for the money.

"OK, the real reason I carry the thing is that it looks good on me. I'm playing war. How many kids would love the chance to wrap a cartridge belt (with a holstered .45) around their waists every morning, throw an M-79 grenade launcher (a snout-nosed weapon that lobs grenades or fires shot) into the back seat of a jeep, and then drive off to war. That's the problem with us males, the kid is always scratching at the surface. I wonder how many draft dodgers will regret later on not having the experience? Probably more than we think. Even though this is a stupid, accessory war and I hate it, I'm being tested like I never would be in civilian life. I don't know if I'll be stretched to the limit, but the rack in war is standard equipment.

"A footnote to the war, but one you might be interested in, is that every report—like body counts—seems to get inflated. We make daily situation reports (sitreps), and if we moved as much material as we say we do, there would be one less mountain in Vietnam. A more personal observation: I use a lot fewer abstract nouns and intransitive verbs than I did during college days (how far off they seem now!). And all my direct objects seem to get loaded, dozed, or graded. There's nothing passive in this place.

"The country is fertile ground for all varieties of field expedients. Major: I'm betting that smooth rock will work better than crushed stone on the road. Minor: We don't have a corkscrew, so when I buy wine, other than Mateus with its Champagne cork, I have to resort to two wood screws and a pliers as a substitute.

"Remember the comment in my letter about the drug problem over here? Two nights ago, one of our malcontents, a fellow named Gonzalez, overdosed on pure heroin. A medic took him to the med shack, where he received treatment. Two hours later, while the medic on duty was apparently napping, Gonzalez woke up and walked out—in the wrong direction. He woke the guards when he began caterwauling in the wire coils of the perimeter fence, and they mistook him for an enemy sapper and shot him. Gonzalez died an hour later. No one mourned him, and there wasn't even a memorial service. He was one of those lost souls who existed only on the Day Report. All he did was walk around mouthing obscenities—the worst imaginable—waiting for his two-twelve, his 'walking' papers. No one stopped him, or remonstrated with him. As Giardi remarked, 'Gonzalez could have been one of the company dogs.'"

Press wrote for a few more minutes, then picked up a book and went out to sit under his banana tree. It was still living a week after he had Powers dig it up in the jungle with the front-end loader and transplant it outside his billet.

The week of Harlan's rest and recuperation in Hong Kong was one of the most productive on the road. Press had broken up the work assignments into smaller teams, eliminating some of the stand-around time associated with squad strength. Major Bonds arranged for a platoon of the 831st Land Clearing Company from Phu Bai to remove vegetation near the river rock work site in the stream. The platoon and its special application bulldozers would arrive the following Tuesday.

On Saturday Press's platoon found three containers of unusable ammunition that had been dumped near the road. They were a mile out from the back gate, and VanAcker unpacked a block of C-4 plastic explosive while some others stacked the ammo in a depression.

"Get out a red smoke grenade," he told one of the men. After a brief search, the engineer reported that none had been brought out.

"What should we do now, sir?" VanAcker asked Press.

Press thought for a minute. "Blow it. Throw some white smoke out."

"But, sir, white smoke marks where you want to spot artillery or gunship rounds."

"True, but we'd have to call a fire mission or request a gunship first."

"Why not use some other color?"

"Let me ask you this, Sarge. If we lit a fuse with a thirty second burn time, what could possibly enter the blast zone without us stopping it?"

VanAcker did not hesitate: "Could only be a chopper."

"Right," Press confirmed. "Now, say you were piloting a chopper and you saw white smoke; would you fly over it?"

"Hell, no."

"Neither would I. Short-fuse it and pop white smoke."

"Yes, sir."

The real detonation occurred on Tuesday, when Harlan returned from R&R. Stopping Press outside the headquarters' building, he drew himself to full height, rocking slightly on the balls of his feet. He was two inches shorter than his superior officer but stoutly built, and he was livid.

"You're wrecking the platoon," he blurted out, his chest intruding on Press's comfort zone.

"How so?"

"By splitting the squads. You took men out of the squads and made assignments where there was no NCO supervision. What if they had come under fire. In case you don't know it, there's a goddamn war going on out there."

"I've got a pretty firm grasp of the obvious. The reason for making smaller work teams is legitimate. We were like a government road crew back home. How often have you driven by a crew filling potholes—two guys wielding shovels and three standing around? As to security, the two work teams without an NCO were on the coastal plain, which is safer than any large city in America."

"Another goddamn thing. You could have got them killed with that stupid goddamn stunt you pulled with the white smoke. You're lucky they didn't open up on you from Walton."

"You must think that I'm the dumbest second lieutenant you ever met."

"By far."

"You know, Sergeant Harlan, you're being insubordinate as hell. I could bring court martial charges against you."

"I don't give a damn what you do, Lieutenant."

"Tell me, Sergeant, when's your *DEROS*?"

"In six weeks."

Press pursed his lips in the manner of Lt. Holt. "I suggest you find something to occupy your time till then. You'll not take one step out on the road." The exchange of glares between the two seemed interminable but lasted only twelve seconds, when Harlan shook his head and turned.

On the way to his billet he turned back briefly and snarled: "This will not stand."

It was cocktail hour when the door to the lieutenants' hootch opened and Press squinted to make out the silhouette standing against the back light.

"Don't tell me you've gone anti-social, as well as the deviant you've always been," said the voice from the shadow.

"Bill King!" Press exclaimed. "And I never gave you my address after OCS."

"Too bad. I'd have turned down this TDY assignment."

"Welcome to the pleasure dome of Kublai Khan," Press said, shaking hands with King. "So you've got the land clearing platoon."

"Greased and ready to fell trees at a single swipe."

Press introduced him to Giardi, Grieve, Coe, and Weitzel, who were sitting around the table.

"How long have you been in-country?" Weitzel asked.

"Seven weeks."

"How are Anne and Ginny?" Press inquired.

"Great. They're back in Cleveland for the duration."

Grieve rubbed his hands, saying, "Now we've got enough for split-the-pot games. You play poker?"

"My CO at Fort Lewis made it T,O and E, so I had to contribute weekly," said King, referring to the Table of Organization and Equipment organic to military units.

"Only a hustler would say that," Giardi posited.

Within minutes King was a welcomed member of the club, joining in the ritual banter: Grieve was answering Coe's question on how he had met his wife. "No, it was my junior year," he corrected himself. "I had a top-floor apartment with a view of one end of the roof of the Pi Phi house two blocks away. One afternoon in April, I noticed two of the gals sunbathing topless— at least two were in my line of sight, so I pulled out the old telescope—my roommate's of course, a professional snarker—and waited for them to switch sides and lie on their backs. I had to wait almost a half-hour for the first to turn over, but when she did, it was an eye-pop. I even took a second to glance at her face, so I would recognize her with her clothes on."

"What about the other one?" King asked.

"It was about ten minutes later when she rolled over. Her tits were pretty good, but she had a couple of strands of hair—about two inches long—at the outer edge of her areola. It was a real turn-off." He shook his head in self-commiseration.

A hurt look surfaced on Coe's face. "My wife has hair there. I don't see what's—"

"Geez, these cookies taste like shit. We ought to take them back to the PX," Giardi said, spitting into a tissue.

Weitzel: "That'd be tough to do. My mother sent them."

Giardi grimaced. "Sorry, I really didn't mean it; I was just trying to change the subject."

Press poured himself a large scotch. "You hear my conversation with Harlan?" he asked Giardi.

"Yeah. It was incredible."

"I wonder who's making the bigger drink? Hell, he's probably chugging the bottle."

"How come you let him get away with it?"

"Hmm, I don't know. For me, the Army's an interlude. For him, it's his life. And that's the part I don't understand. He's got the ability and time left to be a first sergeant. He knows I'm going to write his efficiency report in two weeks, and yet he attacks me. It just doesn't make sense. I'm convinced it wasn't the white smoke or the work parties—"

"You were taking over," Giardi stated matter-of-factly.

"That's what I think it was. He was no longer in control, but with only six weeks left why would he risk his future?"

"Who knows? But I still think you should have locked his heels," Giardi insisted, stabbing a hunk of Vienna sausage with the fork tool of his Swiss Army knife. "I'll give you another couple of months...you'll change."

"Yes, you could become like Captain Morrison," Coe added, holding an issue of *The Stars and Stripes*. "Listen to this—it's his address at his former high school during last June's commencement: 'Nine years ago, as a graduating student, I had the honor of addressing the graduates and their families from this podium in this hall. Nine years ago President Kennedy said the following in his Inaugural Address: "Let every nation know, whether it wishes us well or ill, that we shall pay any price, bear any burden, meet any hardship, support any friend, oppose any foe to assure the survival and the success of liberty."

"'In 1961, few people ever heard of Vietnam. In 1970, it's all we seem to hear about. In the early years of the war, Americans supported our efforts to assist a people in their struggle for liberty. We took a stand against oppression and the spread of communism in Southeast Asia. Now, many Americans have either turned against the war or have grown tired of it. I'm not here to try to reconcile differing opinions. We all must decide for ourselves.

"'In a few weeks, I'll be returning to Vietnam for a second tour. People ask me why I'm doing it. I answer that our cause is righteous and our commitment still valid. I answer that it is dishonorable to cut and run when conditions become difficult. I answer that when a person—or a nation—sacrifices honor—'"

"Stop before we start humming the national anthem," Giardi blurted out, holding up his hand. "Don't tell me—he's stationed in Ben Than—"

"No, he's permanent party in Arlington, Virginia."

"He's at the *Pentagon*?"

"The *cemetery*," Coe said, putting down the paper. "He was killed three weeks into his second tour."

After initial silence, Press leaned back in his chair and said reflectively, "He died for honor, but I wonder if it wasn't also a wasted, stupid death. Can it be both?"

"I can't help comparing Morrison to Calley—two officers about as different as you can get," King offered. "Always seems like the good guy gets it."

"It's easy to condemn Calley," Grieve jumped in, "but I think you have to experience something to appreciate it."

"Nonsense," Press replied. "Calley didn't just cross the line, he leaped over it. I'm ashamed to be anyway connected with him."

"Oh? How many of your men have been killed?" Grieve shot back.

"So that gives him the okay to execute children and old people? You didn't see the newspapers during the height of the publicity. The welcome back was a little different from prior wars; some were even called 'baby killers.'"

From Weitzel: "The worst one I heard was that some gal asked an amputee where he lost his arm. 'In Vietnam,' he says. 'Serves you right,' she tells him."

"And I thought clearing jungle was fun," King said with a laugh. "Is this a nightly occurrence for you guys, or do you set aside time for a little rumination?"

"That means *thinking*, Mark," Press quipped.

"I don't need a wimp who can't discipline his platoon sergeant tell me what it means."

King brought the conversation back to the article. "Morrison conceded that we all have to decide for ourselves what is right. It reminds me of what I saw on the way home on leave from Fort Lewis, after I got my orders for Nam. Anne, Ginny, and I were driving through Canada. We must have passed twenty Volkswagen vans carrying hippies across the prairie. I don't know if the males were evading the draft, but they didn't seem to have a care in the world. Here they were in a communal lovefest, and there I was about to leave my wife and daughter for a year. And I kept thinking...*what if they're right?*"

"It's something they'll have to answer for themselves—in about twenty years," Coe said with finality. "It's time to dress for dinner. Who wants to trudge to the showers first?"

22

The first hard monsoon rain descended on them as they were preparing to go to the field one morning in the third week of September. For the first hour it was like any other rain—enough to keep the engineers in their billets, but not to take much notice of. Gradually, the intensity increased. Reaching torrential downpour status by ten o'clock, it forced Press, who was on his bunk reading, to put his book down and listen to the pounding from above. The sound was not that of a short-lived, wind-whipped cloudburst, but a steady, vertical emptying of the heavens, and it was unnerving. The corrugated metal roof seemed to sag from the volume of water, and the tresses underneath creaked and groaned as if in pain. When the sun later climbed to the top of the sky, the rain so bent, broke, or absorbed its light that on land, midday was as dim as dusk.

Nature's fulmination went on for three more hours, relenting only intermittently. When Press looked out at three o'clock, water had advanced to within yards of the billet. The coastal plain east of Route QL-1 was inundated. But the remainder of the day would not be idleness indoors, as Press found out when Durbin entered the billet. He told Press that he had received an urgent call for help from a Military Assistance Command - Vietnam compound in a village south of Ben Than. A convoy of Army trucks traveling north along QL-1 had been caught in the flooding. The road in some areas was covered by three feet of water.

Press had VanAcker's squad gather emergency supplies and load them quickly on a five-ton truck. They started off and turned south on QL-1, and the road soon disappeared from view, and all ahead was submerged in an inland sea. They plowed through water until the driver could no longer see the centerline stripe, and Press dispatched two engineers to walk out front and guide the truck. They tethered themselves to the five-ton with ropes to avoid being swept away. After a half-hour of slow progress, they came upon an exposed stretch of pavement. Press counted seven bodies lined up on the shoulder, as if in formation. A medic was busy putting them into body bags.

He shouted to Press: "The convoy's just ahead. There may be some survivors. We don't have a head count, but we figure five or six are still missing. We need a ground search."

"You got it," Press responded, and the driver gunned the throttle. Medevac choppers circled above, their crews searching for swimming or floating GIs. As the five-ton entered the water once again, the convoy of perhaps thirty trucks, mostly flat-bed ammo trucks or deuce-and-a-half, were clearly visible in waist-high water. The scene was surreal, like a modern sculpture on a grand scale, the trucks appearing to be implanted in a giant mirror. As they drove closer, however, the surface was anything but placid. The current, contained near the main frames, formed rapidly moving eddies along the front and rear bumpers. An ammo truck lay on its side off the road. Only a fragment of its rear frame jutted out of the water. Press told the driver to stop, and he got out of the cab and climbed into the bed.

"Should we search it, sir?" VanAcker asked.

"Yeah, we need to check the cabs of all submerged trucks."

"Why do you think the convoy tried to drive out of it?"

"Who knows? Maybe they thought they could make it to Ben Than, or maybe the water was rising rapidly and they thought they would surely drown if they stayed."

VanAcker looked west. "Christ, it's charging out of the mountains, and there's nothing to stop it."

Press followed his gaze and although the mist cut off the mountains at the waist, he imagined the gathering flood: rain lashing the eastern slopes and spilling down the jungle floor, first in harmless rills, then in fractious rivulets, etching and sloshing and then overwhelming stream beds and, finally, sending whole trees skidding into the river. Press had seen the river many times but did not recognize it as he put binoculars to his eyes. The watercourse had grown a hundred fold in volume and tenfold in width.

He then looked east. Barely visible in the gray backdrop was a thin line of dunes, undoubtedly porous but with sufficient bulk to slow the rush to the sea. This was his first exposure to a panorama of destruction—of the stark reality of nature's duality. A moment later, he shrugged and turned to speak to one of the engineer outriggers. "Skrine, you got enough rope to get to the cab?"

"Thirty feet at least, sir."

"That's plenty. Can you swim?"

"I was raised on the Mississippi."

"Good, dive down to the cab and see if there's anyone in there."

Skrine nodded and waded to the shoulder of the road. "Here goes," he said as he reached the fore slope of the ditch and disappeared. Twenty seconds later his head bobbed out of the water. "There's a bro down there," he shouted to the occupants of the five-ton. "Throw me another rope."

Skrine went down again with the rope in an attempt to tie it around the chest of the drowned GI. After resurfacing he dove again and yanked twice on the rope. As several engineers slowly brought in the slack, Skrine guided the corpse out of the cab. One of the chopper crews spotted the activity and redirected the craft to a hovering position above the truck. An engineer passed the rope to a crewman, and the chopper began to ascend. The limp body rose from the water and twirled several times—first one way and then the other. The crew delivered the dangling corpse to the waiting medic on the road.

On their way back to drop off the rope, one of the crewmen motioned frantically to the engineers. Press looked around and saw the floating log. "Tucker!" he yelled.

Tucker, the pathfinder on the right front of the truck, looked to where Press was pointing just as a two-foot-diameter hardwood struck him. The force of the impact pushed him back. Instinctively, he draped his arms over the log and was carried by it toward a two-and-a-half-ton truck. As he hit the chassis, air from his lungs hissed out of his mouth, and he gasped for breath. Skrine acted quickly, swimming toward the near end of the log. Using leverage from the truck, he pushed the log sideways and made his way along the flank of the truck to where Tucker was pinned. He slid the log past its fulcrum at the bumper with one arm while holding the still breathless engineer with the other. The current took the log toward the sea.

After two engineers hauled Tucker onto the truck bed, Press apologized to him for all eyes being fastened on the chopper. He turned to Skrine. "Great reaction. Good thing no grunts saw you playing point; they'd be asking for your transfer."

"Wasn't nothin', sir. Give me water every time over jungle."

"If you're feeling up to it, we still have quite a few trucks to search," VanAcker said.

"I'm your man," Skrine shouted with exuberance.

The squad found two more drowning victims before the convoy gave out. Searching for a place to turn the truck around, they continued south until they reached a built-up section of the road—the approach to a timber trestle bridge. Press got out of the truck and walked onto the span. A dragline, parked near the center of the bridge, plucked logs and whole trees from upriver, where almost one hundred meters of debris had piled up against the trestles, swung the load over the deck, and dropped it downstream. He approached an intelligence officer, who was watching the bridge-saving operation intently.

"Hell of a log jam," the officer commented. "One of the old men in the vil says that this was the worst flood he can remember. Gauged it at almost a meter of rain."

"Before today, I would never have imagined something like this."

"Yeah, this stretch of road has not been kind to the people. Bernard Fall wrote about the area in his book, *Street Without Joy.*"

"He was killed not too long ago, wasn't he?" Press asked.

"That's right. Land mine got 'em...seems like there's an awful lot of ways to die in this place."

The next day Press and Snowy drove out on Ridgway Road. There had been no minesweep, so to avoid land mines, Snowy kept the wheels on the crown and the shoulder of the road. When they approached the ford, Press shook his head in disbelief.

"This is incredible," he said. "How fast do you think it's going?"

"Don't know, but I wish I could get *Minderbinder* to move like that," Snowy responded, patting the steering wheel.

The stream had been transformed into a torrent, seventy feet wide and nine feet over its banks. Its surface was littered with jungle vegetation, including entire trees. Press took his binoculars and scanned the visible areas of the upper road.

"Jesus," he whispered.

"What you gaping at, LT?" Snowy asked, slumped in his seat and tearing open a candy bar wrapper.

"It's gone—a whole section of road's gone—sluiced down the mountain. Here, look up there at that yellow loam. It's all over the place."

Snowy took the glasses but set them on the passenger's seat. He took a bite of his candy bar, and his expression registered complete indifference. "I can see it from here. It looks like the mountain puked."

"Do you know what the implication—"

"If you don't mind me saying, you're getting a tad too close to this god-damn road."

Press canted his head slightly and laughed. "That's a first—me being accused of taking something too seriously."

Snowy stroked his three-day growth and pursed his lips, imitating the way Press imitated Holt. "I can prove it," he said.

"Fire when ready, Gridley."

"Huh?"

"Go ahead, prove it."

"Okay, we're sitting out here, just the two of us, no security, and it's not even a work day. The little people who left those sandal prints in the mud"—he pointed to the shoulder of the road—"could be back any minute. If they are, our asses are grasped. Probably watching us right now. On the way back in, we could run over a mine. What I'm saying is that in the next couple of minutes we could get killed because of your love affair with this fucking road."

"How come you didn't tell me how you felt before we came out here?"

Snowy hunched his shoulders. "Guess I'm a dumb shit."

"Guess I am, too. You want a beer?"

Snowy nodded, went to the rear of the jeep, and retrieved two cans of beer from the container. On the drive back to Ben Than, Press sought to be honest with himself. Could his singularity of purpose be linked with devotion to duty, the underpinning of the military credo? Could any of it be ascribed to selflessness? Not letting down the platoon? The company? No, he told himself. Then, after a minute's reflection he mumbled: "Challenge."

"What'd you say?"

"I was thinking out loud. When people are confronted with difficult challenges, they respond with greater determination than they would if the challenge was either insignificant or insurmountable. There's a famous history professor in Britain who makes a living writing about challenge and response. The simple fact is that getting the road in shape is a challenge for me."

"Looks like I got an even bigger challenge: keepin' you alive and *Minderbinder* running—not necessarily in that order," Snowy said, grinning.

The next week brought little rain, and the engineers were able to repair much of the damage to the road. Sections with a surface layer of river rock had fared well. Several sections with crushed stone only had either washed out or suffered erosion. Toward the end of the week the battalion reported an increase of enemy activity in the area. Giardi suggested that as soon as the minesweep squad entered the hilly area, it conduct a recon by fire. The request went up the chain of command and was granted.

Press armed himself extravagantly with several hand grenades fastened to his cartridge belt, the ever-present .45 snug against his hip, and his chest festooned with two crisscrossing belts of grenades for his M-79 Grenade Launcher.

"Well, look at this," Giardi said to Coe upon seeing Press leave the billet. "All he lacks is a sombrero."

"Hey, what do you expect—I've a million years of hunting-gathering in my genes," Press responded. "Besides, today's the day to make Vietnam safe for democracy."

"Ah, he's going to celebrate making first lieutenant," Coe said, noticing the black bar insignia on Press's lapels.

"Damn straight, I worked hard for the automatic promotion. You guys can't kick me around anymore—I've been officially de-greened."

"Wait up, I'll take the sweep with you," Giardi said. "A little frustration-aggression on the flora and fauna can't hurt."

When Press, Giardi, and the minesweep squad entered the hills an hour later, they opened fire. Being under no fiduciary obligation to conserve ammunition, the engineers and their infantry security detail fired their weapons promiscuously. They raked the hillside on their left with a relentless barrage. The passage from the firecrackers of early youth to live ammunition was palpable: they fired from the shoulder and the hip, they sprayed and shot singly, they wise-cracked and they whooped. The tall blond Texan signed his name on the hillside with his blunderbuss, an M-60 Machine Gun. No one, after the first minute, believed that the NVA would be waiting in ambush, yet each engineer marched up the road with his trigger finger fully employed. It was a great frolic.

A LOCH helicopter soon joined them. The diminutive machine flitted around the hills ahead of them like a hummingbird. The pilot would take the craft within feet of dense vegetation. As the greenery flounced in the wash, the observer would peer into potential hiding places. Maneuverable as the LOCH was, an uncovered enemy would almost always have the first shot and could swat it out of the air at point blank range. Press had for some time felt that courage under fire had a tenuous correlation with character and perhaps less with judgment. But observing the LOCH crews, whatever their ethics and acumen, he marveled at their unblinking bravery.

Davidson was waiting at the ford when the Echo Company minesweepers arrived. "Jesus Christ, this isn't Saipan," he said to Press, exasperated with Echo's profligacy.

"Relax, Davidson, the boys are just having some fun. That's probably against your religion, but—"

"Stuff it, Patrick. Did you get approval for recon by fire?"

"Of course. I'm surprised you didn't request it. Your men—"

Press was interrupted for a second time. The explosion occurred more than one hundred meters in their rear. Both men flinched but each sensed that the explosion was not incoming and remained standing. A five-ton truck had crossed the last unfinished culvert site on the lower road, and like the previous mining, its rear duals had sunk into a muddy depression, detonating a buried sack of black powder. The two officers ran to the truck, stenciled "Humpin' To Please." No one had been riding in the bed, and there were no injuries.

"Damn. Now we've got one less truck for a few days," Press said. Replacement of equipment declared a combat loss was much faster than equipment destroyed through negligence or accident, but Press did not want to wait for even a few days. Mostly out of exasperation—partly to bait Davidson—he said, "There must be a way to make peace with these guys."

"Have you gone mad?"

"Gone mad? Has Kissinger gone mad? He's trying it, why can't I?"

"You don't have the authority. Your job is to do what you're told." Davidson continued his lecture for the better part of a minute, when Press walked off.

Within a half-hour the truck loading operation commenced. Spec 4 Powers operated the control levers of his front-end loader with great skill, shuttle shifting the machine in the stream, first to fill the bucket with rock, then to reverse direction while raising and tilting back the bucket, next to approach the truck and roll the bucket forward, finally to pause momentarily while the wet rock spilled noisily into the truck bed. He made it look smooth and effortless.

Press sat on the bank and watched the equipment work. It reminded him of the construction activity he had seen as a boy on Eden's Expressway north of Chicago. His most ardent career goal in the early 1950s was to drive one of the monstrous earthmovers, hauling great gobs of dirt at break-neck speed. He now realized that he was running a bona fide construction job, albeit much smaller than the building of an expressway. From here he traveled to the upper reaches of the road, where the trucks dumped the rock. A bulldozer and a one of Weitzel's road graders spread it evenly over the dirt surface.

As he returned to the ford, a feeling of satisfaction came over him, and he thought of Major Dedson's prescient comments at Fort Leonard Wood.

Watching truckloads of rock leaving the stream, he was proud of his ingenuity and determination— especially his determination. While he had not handled Harlan well, he had not backed off early on when faced with Harlan's derision. His musings continued until Powers shut down his front-end loader and pointed to a tiny stream of water flowing out of a hole in the bucket. The suspension of noise from the machine must have roused Snowy from his dozing, as his head involuntarily jerked away from its nesting place in his jowls. After a couple of sidelong glances, he heaved himself off the seat and ambled over to join Press and Powers at the bucket.

"It can't be more than five or six millimeters in diameter," Press observed.

"I can tell you one thing, sir," said Powers firmly. "It wasn't there until a minute ago."

"What's going on, LT?" Snowy interjected.

"We're trying to solve the riddle of the mysterious hole in the bucket," Press said.

"Maybe Charlie is having a little fun," Snowy surmised.

Powers glanced up at the hills and said, "With all this noise around, they could be taking pot shots at us and we wouldn't even know."

"Until they hit one of us," Press said flatly.

Snowy rubbed the stubble on his cheeks. "Not a damn thing we can do about it, don't ya know."

"I don't think it's for amusement," Press said. "This is the first time that we've had a recon by fire. They could have easily killed one of us, so maybe it's a warning not to do it again."

Powers nodded in agreement. "That's the way I see it, sir. We're not a direct threat to them, at least not till this morning."

The three fell silent for a moment, then Press spoke. "What kind of hootch you think they like?"

Powers gave Press a quizzical look. "What you got in mind, sir?"

"*Sake*," Snowy volunteered.

"That's the Japanese," Press corrected him. "Tell you what. Drive on back to Ben Than, go into my hootch and bring back a fresh bottle of Johnnie Walker Black—no, make it Red Label. The color's appropriate and they won't know the difference in taste."

Press was talking to VanAcker, when Snowy returned forty-five minutes later. "...and don't tell Sergeant Harlan about this. Battalion will be on my ass before dawn. As a matter of fact, we better wait until we pack it in this afternoon and get our security on a five-ton. There's a raft of grunt lifers at Walton who would not take kindly to a little civility shown the enemy."

"You got that right, sir. If you would permit me, I'd like to do the honors."

Later in the afternoon, after dispatching the security detail, VanAcker walked to the center of the road only yards from the ford and fired a shot in the air. He then thrust the bottle of scotch overhead, gripped in his right arm. He rotated slowly, coming full circle, and deposited the bottle on the road. Stepping back, he climbed into the rear of Press's jeep a second before Snowy gunned the engine. The road again belonged to the NVA. The next morning the minesweep squad found a piece of paper skewered by a twig planted in the road. On it was written one word: "*Merci.*"

The tacit agreement of a separate peace was too juicy not to spread ripple-effect up the battalion food chain. Harlan, who had been reassigned and remained in base camp, expedited its delivery to Dong Ha. He had only two weeks until *DEROS*, and word got back to Press that he had spent a day at Battalion making the rounds.

Three days after the event, Fletcher rang Durbin on the land line and asked if there was any merit to the rumors circulating Battalion regarding Press's behavior. Durbin replied that he had begun a full investigation and would report his findings early next morning. Fletcher told him to have Press at Battalion no later than 1100 hours *this* morning.

As ready as he was reluctant, as confident as he was diffident, as steady on the outside as he was shaky in the inside, Press knocked twice on the door frame. Beckoned, he saluted crisply as he came to a halt two yards in front of the battalion commander's desk. Putting him at ease, Fletcher recounted the story being bantered around battalion headquarters and asked Press to confirm, correct, or deny the rumor.

"The physical facts are true as you related them, sir. It's the motivation that's wrong."

"Explain, Lieutenant."

"Well, sir, I had two concerns. First, we lost a five-ton truck to an NVA mine that morning. That cut down on our productivity by fifteen percent. Knowing how critical it is to have the road open for re-supplying Ridgway, I tried to think of some way to postpone any further hostile acts. Moreover, sir, and maybe it's my parsimonious nature, but I feel responsible for the equipment in my care, and I know how expensive a five-ton is. Well, I thought that if we were able to trade a two-fifty bottle of scotch for a future 25,000 dollar five-ton, it would be a pretty good deal.

"Second, and more important, I figured that if we could find a method of intelligence that would indicate when they were in the area, we'd be extra careful, especially around likely ambush sites. An occasional bottle sitting on the road would be like having a salt lick in the field."

He looked straight into Fletcher's ever-widening eyes during his presentation. Just as Press felt the sockets could no longer support his elastic gaze, his eyes narrowed. Now, with Press finished, his eyebrows began to bunch, and Press could read his thoughts without him having to utter a word. Fletcher parted his lips, then compressed them. Moments later he began to speak in a restrained manner.

"Lieutenant Patrick, never in my nineteen years in the military have I heard such obvious and blatant, self-serving crap. Your tongue was side-slipping all over your mouth and for a second, I thought you might choke on it."

"Sir, I must respectfully inform you that your interpretation can only be conjecture. The only person that I related my concerns to about this matter was my driver. In fact, on the drive up here we were discussing the chain of events and my motivation, and we are in agreement that it happened just as I explained it. He's outside in the jeep, sir, if you would like to verify it with him."

"I have no doubt, Patrick, that his story will be in lock-step with yours. You have used up all your credits, Lieutenant. If it weren't for the fact that you've taken the initiative and made good progress on the road, I'd strap an Article Fifteen on you this minute. Let this be a warning that if you pull one more smart-ass trick; if you screw up one more time—if it's only half a screw-up— I'm going to throw the book at you. Your oily tongue won't get you out of it. Do you understand?"

"Yes, sir." Press saluted smartly and quickly left the building.

Snowy started the engine after Press told him they were going back to Ben Than. "Shiiit, you mean I shaved for nothin'?"

The monsoons of October were sporadic and never reached the heavens-emptying production of the September deluge. Harlan had packed his duffel bag in mid-month and left Echo Company unceremoniously. In the evening of the day he departed, Press began writing to Celia.

"Received a letter from you today—the one dated Oct. 9—and wasted no time in taking it back to my office, plopping my feet on the desk, and reading what's new on the home front.

"I was not shocked by your decision to date on occasion. It would be unfair of me to expect that you wouldn't. Although I'm not going to argue with your promise not to let your relationship with Jim go beyond the friendship stage, I don't want you to feel that you have to keep it on my account. I trust your instincts and judgment, and I know that whatever happens, it won't be by accident.

"On to other things. The sergeant I've worked most closely with since arriving here returned to the States today. He made memorable my few field trips to gather information for the articles appearing in the *Castle Courier*. Not only did he show me the ropes, he made me realize that each day has its own temperament. To most soldiers here, the days exhaust themselves and drift interminably from one to the next. It's called base camp boredom. But if you attend to the day, you see how different each is: the local fisherman hauling in the catch during my morning run, the sight and smell of the sea as it breaks against the sand, the bustle in the harbor when the supply ships dock, the fulsome grins of soldiers boarding a plane back to the States, the well crafted story of the courage and competence of an engineer platoon in the field, the taste of a fresh blue crab at evening mess, the infrequent USO show delighting the troops—this compared to villagers in mud up to their knees tending rice paddies on the western fringe of the base, desultory work parties waiting for the ships to dock, the assailing whiff of night soil and buffalo dung carried on a land breeze, a sparse article requiring bulk, a salty, dried-out hunk of roast beef for dinner, a shoot-'em-up film shown in the open air theater. All of this can happen on successive days.

"So, farewell to the sergeant who made my days more interesting and individual. As to your request for a copy of the newspaper, I'm enclosing the last issue. You won't see my name mentioned, as my job entails selecting and editing stories and sending them on to Engineer Command Vietnam in Long Binh."

It was late and he wrote for several minutes more, then prepared to turn in, wondering the whole time how close imagination could capture reality.

As Press stepped out on the road the next morning, he felt no tension for the first time since his arrival in Vietnam. His mood was buoyant, and he joked with VanAcker during the minesweep. "You know, Sarge, you swing that thing almost like it was an appendage of yours."

VanAcker lifted the four-foot-long pole of the mine detector, gave it the once-over in mock examination and retorted, "LT, I *don't have* an appendage this short." A few minutes later he told Press to look back at Snowy driving the jeep. "I swear he's snoozing," he observed.

"He's been on these sweeps so many times he probably thinks he can leave it in idle and Minderbinder will steer itself," Press laughed. "Guess we ought to wake him before he gets to the next curve."

"That's what I like about you, sir. You're always thinking about the welfare of the men."

As the minesweepers neared the ford, Press radioed Davidson and learned that he was more that a kilometer away. Press wanted to send the trucks up the mountain as soon as they could be loaded, so he decided that the minesweep team would continue until it met Davidson's.

The walk uphill went slowly, and the men had gone only 300 meters before their counterparts strode into view. Press and Davidson were civil when the two teams stopped on a level portion of the road. Press watched as the 101st Engineers loaded their equipment in the three-quarter ton truck. Walking back to his jeep and with Snowy in earshot, he shook his head and said, "I've got a feeling that something bad's going to happen to that Tinker Toy truck."

"Maybe Davidson has a bad feeling about Minderbinder," Snowy retorted.

"Davidson doesn't have feelings. In any event, the NVA would rather take eight casualties than two."

"You may be right, but tell me what kind of mine they're gonna plant in the road that can tell the difference between a three-quarter ton and a jeep."

Press did not have time to answer. The blast occurred on the periphery of his vision, and as he turned he saw the three-quarter ton flip over end. A spray of AK-47 fire then ripped into the side of the truck. At the same instant, the Echo engineers dove for the ditch on the defilade side of the road. The dull rapping of AK-47 fire ceased abruptly, before the engineers could return fire.

Fear grazed his bowels, as Press crawled back to the jeep. He radioed to Ridgway and requested the dispatch of Medevac choppers. He then changed to the Medevac frequency and heard Davidson speaking directly to the dispatcher. Press dropped the handset and ran to the truck.

He was shaken by the scene. The mine had detonated under the right rear axle, and the wheel nearest the explosion had been blown off. It was obvious that when the truck rotated over end, the canvas covering trapped most of the men inside. The engineers sitting near the rear of the truck had been thrown clear, for three of them were lying on the gravel among many of the sand bags which had previously lined the bed. Davidson and another engineer—the driver, Press assumed—must have bailed out of the cab, for they were unhurt and were checking on the engineers trapped under the bed of the three-quarter ton.

Two medevac choppers arrived within five minutes. The medevac crews took over the rescue, as those remaining under the truck suffered from both bullet wounds and horrible orthopedic injuries: limbs askew and many broken bones.

Press watched the choppers lift off six minutes after they landed. He felt as though a lick of flame bounded through his insides, and he flushed with shame at the thought of his stunt with the bottle of scotch may well have influenced the NVA's choice of targets. That he had warned Davidson against using the three-quarter ton mattered little. Those mangled young men may well be whole if he had not tried to outsmart the Army and had just done his duty.

Nearby, Davidson was speaking rapidly into the handset of his radio. As soon as he finished, Press approached, shaking his head. "They're gone, Davidson—at least a klick away by now. Gunships won't help."

"You don't know what you're talking about. The bastards are still here— watching us, and I'm going to roast their ass." He dropped his handset and waved Press off.

The sky was overcast and ugly, mirroring Press's mood. He looked at the wet, pliant surface of the road, whose base had to be well compacted and therefore difficult to burrow into from the shoulder. Yet, he suspected that the mine had been command detonated; if not, it probably would have exploded when the truck first traversed the road on the way down, empty. But how? After rummaging around on the shoulder of the road, he uncovered a wire leading to elephant grass. He scratched his head in amazement that the NVA could cut, plant, and suture a road without leaving a scar.

He looked up to see two Cobra gunships breaking through the clouds. Davidson was in direct contact with the two-man crews and directed their fire. Rockets cleaved the air and pitched into the jungle. Skeins of black smoke and noise from the detonations eased the pain in Davidson's expression, but to an objective eye the jungle lay undisturbed. After the choppers flew off, Press walked over to Davidson and told him he would have a dozer come up and drag the truck to the ford, where they could load it onto a lowboy trailer.

Press sat alone at the table late that evening. He poured himself another generous dose of Drambuie and took up his pen. "Dear Rebecca," he started. "Thanks for your 10 Oct. letter. Sounds like the real world is working quite well without several hundred thousand expatriate GIs although according to your clipping, Nixon is planning on withdrawing 40,000 of us by Christmas. He talks a great game on Vietnamization, but he must certainly know the fate of the country when all of us leave.

"I envy your hike in the Adirondacks. Ah, to stroll in the red and yellow sequined hills (as opposed to perpetual green), carefree and whimsical (as opposed to edgy and suspicious). I remember well how those simple pleasures were so easily taken for granted.

"Actually, things have been going so well here that I'm considering extending my tour. Why, just today, I can probably take credit for killing or maiming five or six soldiers. As luck would have it, they were our own. It began when I paid tribute to the NVA." Press went on to explain the train of events that culminated in the morning's mining incident.

"Although I've been in my hootch for five hours now, my mind resides twelve kilometers away, over green hills, and over a heap of self-scorn—well justified, as you now know—the end play of a smart-ass game. I think that in war hubris is a leading cause of casualties.

"Sorry about the self-pity. It was welling up inside and none of the wine bottles here have a stopper stout enough to suppress it. I can't unload on Celia or my parents, but being a journalist I know you'll read the account with a dispassionate eye.

"On your continuing interest about the war, I have an observation to make. One of the reasons we're not winning is that we're all too often shooting, bombing, strafing, etc. where the enemy isn't. So far in the war, our side has dropped more bombs than we had in all of World War II. If you get over here, you'll see what I mean. It's like what Davidson did this morning out of sheer frustration.

"On a personal level I'm now fully habituated to living a life of inconvenience. I was going to say primitive, but the men living in the mountains west of here are the ones leading primitive lives. Inconvenience is the daily cold shower, foul smelling latrines, cramped quarters. Minor irritants.

"I must stop. My hand's frozen."

Press signed the letter. He would mail it in the morning.

Major Bonds had left for the States the week before and his replacement, Major Shannon, scheduled a visit and briefing with Echo Company on a Saturday morning in November. After a long, hard rain on Friday night, Durbin canceled all work scheduled for the road.

When Shannon arrived at 0900, Durbin greeted him and introduced the officers and senior NCOs. Following the obligatory briefing inside, he and the new S-3 left for a tour of the jobsites in Ben Than.

Press was leaving the mess hall early in the afternoon, when the two officers returned.

"Lieutenant Patrick," Durbin called out, his jeep still rolling to a stop. "Major Shannon would like to see how work is progressing on the road. Why don't you round up Snowy and take him out after we grab some chow."

The universal joint on *Minderbinder* would on occasion disintegrate, so Press suggested that they take two jeeps. Within the hour he and Shannon stood on a badly eroded section of road not far from FSB Walton.

"What do you suppose caused this much of the road to wash out so quickly?" Shannon asked.

"For one thing, sir, we can't get the tolerance between the culvert pipe and the headwall close enough, so when the runoff builds up—fifty acre feet of water sometimes—it's going to start eroding behind the headwall, even if the laterite is well compacted. It's a matter of almost constant maintenance during the monsoons."

By the time the party reached the ford, Press was convinced that Shannon knew the answers to most of the questions he was asking. The major impressed him as being highly professional, with none of the overbearing demeanor he had seen in a few of the middle grade officers.

"Running the trucks in the stream doesn't affect their braking ability on the road?"

"No, sir, it doesn't seem to, possibly because they're going uphill and are spread far apart, so there's no need to stop until the brake pads dry out."

Shannon, who was tall with a medium build and intelligent eyes, gazed around the site, taking in the scope of the operation. Drawing a knife, he chipped at the surface of the access road, then remarked, "This material sets up like concrete; have you considered using it to backfill head walls?"

"Yes, sir, but I decided that the upper road took priority and—" Press did not get a chance to finish. An explosion rent the air and, almost simultaneously, the officers hit the ground. The shell had detonated forty meters from where they stood talking, and an equal distance from where the two drivers were seated in their jeeps.

After a few moments without a second incoming round, Press and Shannon ran to the jeeps. The drivers needed no orders, reversing their vehicles the instant the officers were aboard. They backed the vehicles ninety meters to Ridgway Road, where Snowy, whose full attention was now focused on the task, pulled abreast of the major's jeep.

"That's quite a welcome somebody arranged," Shannon quipped.

"It's a first—lucky we didn't have the troops out here," said Press.

"Do you know where it came from?"

"It had to be a 105 round from Ridgway. If you don't mind, sir, I'd like to investigate this while memories are fresh."

"Not at all, Lieutenant. We can't have our own artillery shelling engineer work sites. Let me know what you find."

Press uncovered little. The 105 battery commander at Ridgway radioed that he received a *courtesy* clearance from FSB Walton to fire on a set of coordinates matching that location. Officers at Walton acknowledged issuing the clearance, but the source of the order and the reason for targeting a friendly jobsite—one for which they provided security—could not be distilled from the self-serving doublespeak he encountered in their TOC. What he found most disturbing was their casual disinterest, and he wondered if they had been living underground too long.

That evening, most Echo Company members were watching a movie, *Midnight Cowboy*, which Press had seen with Celia. The film had been pummeled by repeated showings and after the eighth break, Press vacated his place at the picnic table and strolled toward the headquarters staff's billet. Passing a hootch belonging to the first platoon, he was engulfed by the pungent aroma of incense, universally used to disguise the sweeter odor of marijuana. He entered the next billet and looked into several cubicles for the company clerk, who had recently finished reading a book Press wanted to borrow. As he approached the center cubicle on the right, he stopped abruptly and scowled. Stacy Rinaldo may well have felt the heat from Press's gaze, for he glanced up and while saying "Evening, sir," quickly opened his foot locker and threw the syringe he was holding inside. Three young soldiers from the 101st Division stood awkwardly in the cubicle, sleeves rolled up and arms at the ready. One of them, seemingly straight off the farm with a face as wide as a plow and eyes full of surprise, slowly moved a shovel-like hand to his sleeve. He watched as Press approached the entryway, blocking egress.

"Open your foot locker and stand away," Press ordered Rinaldo.

Rinaldo complied to the first order but instead up standing clear, he scooped up several vials and charged directly at Press. He was short and stocky and his shoulder struck Press's sternum with enough force to knock him aside. He rushed to the exit, where Press caught him from behind, but before he was dragged back he threw the capsules as far as his tethered arms would allow. The capsules came to rest on some sand bags twelve feet away.

VanAcker was rounding the far side of the billet as they struggled, and he hastened over to assist his platoon leader.

"Let's get him into his cubicle," Press said between breaths. "I caught him as he was about to shoot up some of our green-twig neighbors. I expect we'll find them gone."

Gone they were. Press left Rinaldo sitting on his bed and VanAcker sitting on Rinaldo's foot locker, which they had moved to the entrance. When Press found the CO, Durbin expressed shock that Rinaldo could be involved in drug dealing.

"I'm afraid it's conclusive," Press told him.

"Well, what do you think we ought to do about it?" asked Durbin naively.

"We should call CID."

The captain squirmed a little, but he had no choice. Half an hour later, Warrant Officer Borders of the Criminal Investigation Division arrived. He collected the evidence, including additional vials in Rinaldo's foot locker, and took statements. It was an evening without shadows as midnight approached and Borders closed his notebook and climbed into his jeep.

"This is about as open and shut as I've seen it," he remarked to Durbin and Press. "We'll have the lab results back from Japan in two or three weeks."

The two officers stood in the darkness and watched the jeep's shifting cone of light illuminate a line of dump trucks, perfectly dressed, beds tilted skyward in silent salute to the passing warrant officer. Just as they turned to go back to their billets, an explosion ripped into the night. Press knew immediately the identity of the weapon used—a one-grenade salute of good riddance. He and Durbin ran to the sound. As they turned a corner, they saw Borders standing next to his jeep, stabbing the dark with the beam of his flashlight.

"The bastard," he exclaimed. "Almost got me." His lone light was joined by several, then a score. They poked into the darkness while shouts from their holders filled the heavy air.

"Looks like it detonated in that depression," Press observed, his eyes following an arc of light.

"You'd better go," Grieve said to Borders. "We'll never find out who threw the grenade."

"Roger that," Borders agreed.

Grieve turned to Press and put his hand on his shoulder. "You know what this means, don't you?"

"Of course. I could get the same treatment."

"Be careful."

"Right."

A few minutes later, the company area was again silent and cloaked in blackness.

A week after the incident, Grieve returned to the States, Giardi became XO, and Durbin made Press project officer with responsibility for all of Ridgway Road. Coe would be going home in late December, leaving Press first in line for the desk job in January, Giardi's *DEROS* month. His tour, then, would have a fair balance of almost seven months in the field and five interminable months of monotony—*safe* monotony, in the office.

"Two days till Thanksgiving," Press said to Snowy in an offhand manner, as the jeep idled along the last kilometer of the morning minesweep.

"Yeah, a day off and a decent dinner," Snowy responded.

"Don't tell me that you've lost your appetite for water buffalo?"

"Five days a week of that dried-out shit is too much."

"Breakfast is what eats me—no pun intended—with bacon on the grease and soggy toast."

Army cuisine in general, and cooks in particular, came in for a few more minutes of lambasting, until Snowy pulled off the road at the ford. The routine was time worn by now—truck drivers and the operator of the front-end loader took their equipment up the access road for clay and river rock; half a squad of infantry secured the work area, while the other half remained aboard a five-ton to accompany the engineers to a jobsite on the upper road. Coe joined Press at the ford.

"You expecting any visitors?" Coe asked.

Press turned and noticed Lt. Davidson walking towards them. "I'd rather see Colonel Fletcher. Wonder what he wants?"

Davidson dispensed with the formalities. "I need your security."

Press was incredulous. He shook his head as if to shake off the words. "So do I," he said, finally.

"Look, Patrick, I'm not going to stand here and argue with you. I've got a job to do and no security. I need yours. After all, they're part of my battalion."

Press, still afflicted with guilt over the Johnnie Walker fiasco, tempered his antipathy toward Davidson and sought to reason with him. "If I give the security detail to you, I'd have to pack up and go back." He motioned with his arm at the elephant grass fronting the work site. "Certainly you'll agree that with the noise of the machinery, my men would have no chance, even against a sniper."

Davidson glanced down at the M-16 cradled in his right arm. Raising his head, a look of desperation formed in the recesses of his eyes. "What's your date of rank?" he asked in a flat voice.

"September—you're not going to pull rank on me, are you?"

"June. I out-rank you, and I'm ordering you to turn over the security."

Press, not having looked deep enough into his eyes, said, "Date-of-rank might be worth a dry fart at the Academy, but it doesn't cut it out here."

Davidson took a few seconds to make up his mind, and then thrust his M-16 into Press's abdomen. "Turn over your security," he ordered.

"Remove your weapon from my gut," Press said in a determined tone.

"Listen to me, Davidson," said Coe. "What you're doing is a court martial offense. Surely you're not going to shoot another American over a security detail?"

"Are you going to turn them over?" Davidson asked in a demanding tone.

"No, now remove that goddamn thing from my stomach."

Davidson considered his next move, then let the rifle swing toward the ground. He walked off without another word.

Press and Coe looked at each other for a second. "My, my, he certainly has a combustible temperament," Press said.

"Crazy bastard," Coe remarked. "You going to press charges?"

"I should, but I won't. He's had a tough time of it, and the worst of it may be my fault."

23

Press heard about the convoy by accident, while buying sundries at the PX. Two lieutenants in the 101st Division were discussing the stand-down of troops on FSB Ridgway and when one remarked that replacements would be brought up in a convoy of more than twenty-five trucks, Press entered the conversation. He learned that the convoy would leave Ben Than on the day after next, 8 December.

The day was like all others of late: a stew of clouds and fog hung above a ceiling of 200 feet. Press had arranged for two bulldozers to accompany the convoy, and he and Snowy drove to FSB Walton to pick up their security detail. Inside the tactical operations center he cleared his request with a company commander. He turned to go and came face to face with a lieutenant colonel who was, to the eye, the archetypal officer. His name tag identified him as Griswold and with the first movement his stiff neck and the promontory that was his jaw, Press knew he would be in for the second dressing down of his non-training military career.

"Where in the hell do you think you are?" was the first rhetorical salvo. "And you're supposed to be an officer—brace when I talk to you. Take that flimsy goddamn headgear off that stub sticking out of your fatigues." Press removed his boonie hat. "Nobody—I say again—nobody comes on my fire base without wearing a goddamn steel pot. A battalion of body bags, stuffed with idiots who didn't wear combat gear, has already been shipped home in this war. And I'll tell you this: no engineer lieutenant is going to take any of my combat infantrymen from this fire base without setting an example." Griswold snorted away for another half minute before he turned and climbed the stairs to the exit.

"Is he always like this?" Press asked a staff captain, whose face showed sympathy.

"No, it's just that he's been under a lot of pressure recently."

As Press climbed the steps, he again heard Griswold's blistering invective. His last words were to the effect that Snowy was undoubtedly of porcine ancestry and a disgrace to the uniform. Press waited for a few moments of silence, then walked out of the TOC smiling. "I see you met Colonel Griswold."

"Yeah, he tried to talk me into re-upping."

It was almost eleven o'clock when the lead jeep of the convoy stopped just short of the ford. Press had briefed the three-man security detail, telling them to stay at the rear of the convoy, that they would be needed to escort the dozers back down the road after the convoy reached FSB Ridgway. He then strode over to the jeep and exchanged salutes with a Major Reading.

"Morning, sir. I'm Lieutenant Patrick of the 99th Engineers and project officer for Ridgway Road. I've brought a couple of dozers along to assist your convoy."

"That's very good of you, Lieutenant. Do you expect any problems?"

"Well, with this many trucks, the tail end of the convoy may have some trouble reaching the fire base. The road is still pretty wet from the intermittent rain and no sun in the past few weeks. I expect the first fifteen or so trucks will make some pretty deep ruts, especially on the long slope just below Ridgway."

"I see. We'll appreciate any help you can give us," Reading said with sincerity.

Press looked down the line of mostly 2.5 ton trucks, each loaded with grunts or supplies. "The convoy won't make it past the first klick, sir, unless the drivers let half the air out of their tires—the rear duals, anyway."

"Half?"

"It'll double the coefficient of traction with more tire on the ground."

The major shrugged. "I'll see to it."

Twenty minutes later, the convoy, a bulldozer in the lead, began crossing the ford. A LOCH bounded haphazardly below the low-lying fog and cloud, poking close to swishing vegetation. Press had changed the frequency on his radio and was following the traffic of the convoy commanders. He asked Snowy to pull off at a location which afforded a view of ten or more trucks negotiating a steep and winding slope. The engines seemed to gasp for air, as diesels do under heavy load, and the noises they made, besides rendering the radio useless, competed with their smoke-signaling black exhaust to alert any enemy within mortar range.

This is it, Press said inwardly, the culmination of months of work. All they need to do is knock out one or two of the lead trucks. The rest will be a shooting gallery, but of course they would have to know beforehand—Christ, what if the road gives way, a side-hill cut collapses, a couple of trucks roll down to the first teak trees. We'd never get the convoy to Ridgway before nightfall. Why didn't they start at first light? He leaned over and shouted into Snowy's ear: "Piece of cake."

It was stop and start for the first hour, as Press brought the dozers in for minor straightening and towing, but as the convoy inched further into the mist, the wet air began to hug the tires, making them slick and less tractive. As the center of the convoy reached a strip of road that had been covered only by stone, deep ruts appeared, and Press called in the following dozer to scrape off eighteen inches of mud.

"LT, you got your proof now," Snowy said, chuckling. "Rock is better than stone."

"Go tell that to the captain over there, the one with his eyes alternating between me and his watch."

"He's looking up toward Ridgway now. Too bad he can't see shit."

In mid-afternoon Press and Snowy watched as one side of a truck slipped into the ditch which separated the road from an almost vertical wall of earth more than ten feet high. The side of the truck scraped the sodden loam, and a cubic yard of it fell into the truck and just behind it. The troops sitting on the right side were covered in the tawny muck. Standing, they attempted to wipe the mud from their bodies; they succeeded in smearing it, and only the outlines of their helmets and the orbits of their eyes were recognizable. After a half-minute of continuous laughter, Press radioed for the lead dozer. Putting the handset on his lap, he uttered, "Who said war is hell?"

Another hour was eaten away by minor holdups. The lead trucks arrived at the long, final grade as the first shadings of twilight, though difficult to discern, began to encroach on the convoy. Press was thankful that all the twisting and maneuvering was near an end, but he feared what might happen on the steep, straight last leg. The stretch was so unstable that its substructure could be turned into mush by a few stubborn wheels. The first trucks had no problems, but each drive wheel tore away a rock or two, and the cumulative effect after little more than half of the convoy had passed was to expose the volcanic ash underneath. Moreover, the gooey remains of the surface were beginning to permeate into the ash. Press stopped the convoy and signaled Allen on the lead dozer to travel to the top of the grade and take a deep cut off the road on his return. He also radioed for the tailing dozer to be brought up.

Minutes later, he motioned to the truck drivers to continue their ascent. The fifth in line bogged down, followed by the sixth. Press signaled the second dozer operator to give them a push. Darkness was closing in, and the remainder of the convoy could not be pushed up in ones or twos; the likelihood of having an accident on the narrow road after dark was too great. He briefly considered that the Army could hold him financially responsible for his next decision. Shrugging it off, he briefed his dozer operators and then went from truck to truck, the remaining twelve. In quick order the trucks closed in on one another, bumper to bumper, and the soldiers sitting shotgun got out and chained them together. Allen hooked on to the first truck in line; the operator in the rear dozer nestled his blade against the bumper of the last truck. Press raised his arm, kept it high for a second, and then brought it down sharply. Exhaust shot through the stacks as fourteen engines roared. The daisy-chained line began to move. There was none of the swaying or swerving that a single truck would undergo. Whenever a driver would ease off a bit on the throttle, one glance at Press's twirling arm prompted him to flatten the pedal. The final furlong was fantastically noisy, the scream and roar of engines and exhaust intermingling with the crunching and scraping of steel, the trucks now pushing or being dragged, depending on the gripping or spinning of wheels, flying mud signaling progress, a pass in review so utterly opposite of a parade. While still twirling his arm almost from inertia now, Press looked at the passing faces of sergeants, privates, specialists, lieutenants, and captains: all were passive and expressionless.

Then they were gone, lost in the fog but safely beyond the gate, and an eerie silence settled over the mountain. He stood on the road, feeling an elation which was altogether different from anything he had experienced before. This sublime moment was heightened by his surroundings, for the mountain seemed to be dissolving in the fading light and silken mist. He had overcome so many obstacles: a job for which he had been unprepared, the traditional way of doing things, the monsoons. It was as clear as an epiphany that he had succeeded in the most consequential undertaking of his life. His thoughts turned to Major Dedson. The crack from a 105 on Ridgway carried as if someone had pulled the lanyard only yards away, and it brought him out of his euphoria.

Snowy, his rain slicker glistening, was slouched in his seat, smoking. "Looks like we should of brought our toothbrushes, don't ya know, unless you figure on making a break for it," he said, as Press walked to the jeep.

"You think I'm crazy? I already told the operators to spend the night. Let's go down and pick up our security and get our carcasses back up to Ridgway."

Snowy drove the short distance to where they had told the security detail to wait. After looking around for a few minutes, he asked Press if the trio might have started walking back to Walton.

"I wouldn't think so; it's too far to walk and dangerous as hell, but who knows—they didn't walk up to Ridgway. I guess we could ride down another hundred meters or so. You want a beer?"

Snowy had all he could handle trying to avoid high-centering the jeep shuffling between ruts, so Press held both cans of beer while scanning the sides of the road. They were half way to the ford when he said, "We'll never make it back up to Ridgway. I'll radio Walton." He nestled one of the beers between his knees and checked his SOI. "Sonnet Five, Sonnet Five, this is Maple Three-one, over."

"Maple Three-one, this is Sonnet Five, over."

"Sonnet Five, this is Maple Three-one. We're the pioneers who escorted your folks up to Romeo. Three members of a security detail from Whisky were with us, but we can't locate them on Romeo Road, over."

"Maple Three-one, this is Sonnet Five. You can't find them because they were deserted and picked up by an ambush team. I'm going to jump in your shit, mister. I say again: I'm going to jump in your shit. Do you copy, over?"

"Sonnet Five, this is Maple Three-one. It was a little garbled, but it sounded like you just called yourself a shithead—self-deprecating wit, no doubt. Anyway, I'll come to your pos tomorrow and accept your thanks for saving your collective asses on Romeo Road today. This is Three-one—out." Press, fuming, threw the handset into the back seat.

Snowy retrieved his beer. "You want me to gun it when we get to the ford?"

"Yeah, if anybody guns it, let it be us."

As the jeep sped along the lower road, the radio crackled and a voice blared desperately: "Contact! Contact!" The sound of small arms fire accented his next words, the coordinates of his position, which Press figured was on the mountainside.

Snowy glanced at Press. "If those boys from Walton are there and any of 'em get killed, you know you're dead, right?"

"Yeah, let's see...what would be a fitting punishment? Of course! They could send me to Vietnam, give me a field job in a free-fire zone, somewhere really nasty, like mountainous jungle. What a punishment that would be."

PART FOUR
24

"Happy New Year!" Press wrote to Rebecca on 4 January. "My best to you for 1971. I hope your holiday season was as joyous as mine. I've always wanted to go south, someplace warm, for Christmas. You mentioned in your last letter that you had been invited to the Guy Lombardo dinner dance on New Year's Eve. I trust the *Royal Canadians* were up to snuff. A little staid for your tastes, perhaps, but your new boyfriend sounds as though he's the serious type. Not bad R—a copyright lawyer, handsome (but your tastes are in doubt), from a wealthy family, and Jewish to boot. Sounds like he's a real mensch.

"You may have danced to Guy Lombardo, but I laughed with Bob Hope. His Christmas show was in Phu Bai. My biggest laugh stemmed not from Uncle Bob, but from what I heard from an infantry officer I know from Ben Than. Here's what happened a week or so before the show: Snowy and I drive out to a fire base to pick up some grunts for security. As I go into the main bunker, the commanding officer becomes enraged with me for not wearing a helmet on his chunk of real estate. This guy's appearance is the sum of all clichés on military bearing—square jawed, ramrod straight, etc. He flays me on the spot, then walks out and berates Snowy. Meanwhile, a captain tells me that the CO is under great stress. When I emerge from the bunker a minute later, Snowy's usual lethargic demeanor seems intact, but I can tell he's seething inside by the way his whiskers are standing at attention.

"Anyway, who do you think I see sitting by himself in the last row at the Christmas show? None other than our preternatural professional soldier: Mr. Army Universe. At intermission, I point him out to the fellow I mentioned above and he says, 'What, you don't know?' I assure him that indeed I don't know. So he continues: 'The reason he jumped all over you is that he was about to be relieved from command—he was caught in the sack with a Spec 4.'

"Caught in the sack with a Spec 4! I couldn't stop laughing. I'm going to have to overhaul my thinking about queers. I would have bet my $760 monthly stipend on him being straight—and a hefty side bet on being a despoiler of fair maidens.

"December was a busy month. Snowy and I and a couple of dozer operators helped a convoy from the 101st make it up to Ridgway. One of their desk jockey staff captains blamed me for abandoning three of their grunts on the mountain as darkness was closing in. They were picked up by an ambush team and promptly ran into a few NVA. Lots of lead flew but no fatigues were penetrated. The captain backed off the next day. There were still fireworks of a sort, though. Snowy and I were leading the convoy down the road late the next morning, when an explosion a few yards away almost shook us out of the jeep. Snowy slammed on the brakes and we bailed out. It turned out to be a lone gunman letting loose with a rocket propelled grenade. The RPG hit a teak tree, which suffered grievously. Lesson learned: never travel with grunts, or any hunters, for that matter. The NVA are professionals, and they would prefer to expend precious ammo on the Americans that are out to kill them. What concerns me is that we're an easy target, always available.

"Now, for the important stuff. Echo Company moved up to Dong Ha two days ago. I'm writing from new digs, although appearances remain the same. Scuttlebutt has it that the reason for the move is because a major operation is imminent. Lending credence to the rumor is that enough culvert sections to build a road from here to Laos were dumped in the company area yesterday. If you're going to get to Vietnam, you better start working on it—and head north to this area.

"I'm about to celebrate my six month anniversary in this fine country. The musical chairs rotation is in full swing. Coe left just before Christmas, replaced by Brad Benischek. Giardi leaves for home in two weeks, and I'm in line to be the next XO. It may be a boring job, but it's a safe boring job.

"If you make it out here R, I know a great Vietnamese restaurant—okay, food stand—in Quang Tri, only eight miles south of here. Till then—yours ever, Press."

Dong Ha was slightly uglier than Ben Than, and on the whole, depressing. Its single virtue was a strategic location, embracing QL-1 on one flank and QL-9 on another. During the waning days of January, the rear of Echo Company's area was filled with thirty-six inch diameter culverts strapped together in neat packages of three. Skeletons of the M4T6 Bridge lay in line next to bundles of bridge decking near the airfield at Quang Tri. Although speculation about the coming mission was running rampant, not a word was whispered, apart from rumor. The troops were on edge anticipating action, preferring in a way the finality of hell to the wait in purgatory.

Press missed Giardi, who had left for home in mid-month. As usual, the evening prior to his departure saw numerous shouts of "Fire mission!" as champagne bottle corks flew amid toasts and promises of fealty forever. Two new platoon leaders had reported for duty in January, Lieutenants Lee Darnell and Jason Scogland. The morning Giardi left, Press presented himself at headquarters to assume the executive officer's position. Benischek was in Durbin's office, and they had both averted their eyes when he entered. Apologetically, Durbin explained that although Press had more time in-country, Benischek, having gone to ROTC, had an earlier date of rank and thus would become XO. Press did not protest. One lesson he had learned well in the Army—and reinforced by Celia—was never to get carried away by expectations.

Press was back in Durbin's office late in the month, on the penultimate day of the CO's tour, after his request for a six month extension had been turned down. Press asked him for the cause of delay in Rinaldo's court martial.

"It doesn't matter," he stated matter of factly. "He's going home—a medical discharge. Hepatitis. He'll be gone in two or three days."

Press sought to control his anger. "You sat on it," he said finally. "Bill King was right. He told us that when you two served together in the same battalion at Fort Lewis, the word was that you could get into your fatigues without breaking starch."

"Now hold on. You can't talk like that to me."

"I can't? You want me to take this up with the colonel and tell him how I risked my life trying to prevent three eighteen-year-olds from becoming heroin addicts? And that you, or the Army, or both, screwed up? You know how I feel about the OD. How goddamn ironic is it that I've become a sterner disciplinarian."

"Wait a second. Calm down," Durbin said, his eyes moving jerkily. "Rinaldo fucked up and he's gonna pay for it, but whatever kind of guy he is, he's not the kind who's gonna frag somebody. And about his court martial— I'm not sitting on it. You know that this is a goddamn paper war. His court martial is competing with a hundred thousand other pieces of paper."

Press looked closely at Durbin, searching his face, which revealed nothing behind his darting eyes. "It's no use," he said after a few moments. "Good luck as a goddamn civilian."

The new company commander, Ron Padgett, took over on 28 January. He had spent nearly a year in-country, knew that a major operation was imminent, and extended his tour for six months in order to participate in the mission. That evening Major Shannon called a meeting at company headquarters. Captain Padgett brought the officers to attention, as the battalion operations officer entered the building.

"As you were. Bring your chairs close to the table, and we'll get started," Shannon began. "I know that everyone in I Corps is speculating that a major operation is imminent. And it is." The S-3 waited until the five officers of Echo Company were perched on their chairs with heads thrust forward before continuing. "We're going to reopen QL-9 to Khe Sanh, the old Marine combat base deserted in sixty-eight. I can't tell you any more about the operation, except to say that it's major and surprise is crucial. As the junior officers digested his opening statement, he passed out topographic maps and aerial reconnaissance photos. "The mission commences at midnight on Thirty January. At 0300 tomorrow, D minus one, the battalion will leave Dong Ha for Vandegrift Combat Base, here, just south of the Rockpile"—he pointed to an obscure location on the map, the site of an abandoned Marine base—"and a couple of miles south of where the paved road ends. Once you arrive at Vandegrift, you will be engaged in upgrading the road and the base itself." Shannon spent some minutes going over the orders for D-1 and D-day. Echo would lead on D-day. The 3rd platoon would be the spearhead, minesweeping the old French-built road, now completely overgrown. Lt. King's platoon from the 831st Land Clearing Company would follow, removing vegetation and making bypasses around downed bridges, while elements of mechanized infantry would comprise the bulk of the combat force. The bridge and culvert sites were numbered on the map and assigned contiguously to each of Echo's platoons. At first light helicopters would ferry the bridging equipment and culverts to the appropriate sites, where they would be assembled. The objective for D-Day was the opening of the road ten kilometers.

"Have we got a magnifying glass?" Press inquired during a pause. "The road is a little hard to make out."

"It's covered with elephant grass—doesn't show up well in the aerial photos," conceded Shannon. "You may stray off it from time to time, but with hills on your right and the Quang Tri River on your left, you won't stray far."

"What about illumination?" Benischek asked.

"None. It's too dangerous."

Shannon delved into detail for another fifteen minutes and wound up the meeting with a disquieting assessment: "It is very much in the interest of the NVA to interdict as early and as often as they can. That's why secrecy is vital—why we're starting off at midnight. If the mission has been compromised, it could be very rough going the day after tomorrow."

At 0300 on 29 January, the rolling stock of Echo Company clogged the dirt road leading to QL-9. Press and Snowy sat in their jeep, waiting for the signal to move out. The convoy passing in their front clamored for attention—moving parts roaring and squealing, depending on the source of emission. "You'd think the mech boys would grease the tracks," Press said after a passing armored personnel carrier clawed its way, rather than rolled, along the road.

Snowy took a deep draw on his cigarette and agreed, saying, "Sounds like a damn cat fight. Charlie can probably hear it on the DMZ."

"The engines are okay, but those damn tracks are worse than a hundred flutes in high register."

Snowy snorted, not at all enchanted with Press's analogy.

"You know, I think I've discovered a phenomenon not recognized in natural law," Press said, waving away a ribbon of smoke. "No matter where they're situated in relation to each other, smoke always drifts from the smok*er* to the smok*ee*. Should be a corollary to the laws of thermodynamics."

Snowy grinned, pulled hard on his cigarette, and coaxed four nearly perfect smoke rings from his mouth. "Hope you don't mind me saying this, Boss, but you got more bullshit than a herd of water buffalo."

Padgett stepped out of his jeep at the head of the line. "Listen up," he shouted. "Our turn's coming in a couple of minutes. Go ahead and crank your engines." He then said a few words to his driver, who strolled to the gate. After tugging on a chain, he returned to the jeep. Padgett shook his head and looked to the rear.

"Looks like the need to know didn't extend far enough down," Press said. "Go on down and ask Sergeant VanAker to send someone up with a bolt cutter and cut the lock."

Echo was only three minutes late leaving and easily caught the slow moving convoy. They traveled west along the paved section of QL-9, stopping frequently. At dawn villagers began to line the road. Years of war had worn them down, and it was reflected in their faces: blunt, inert, saggy-eyed. This was the neighborhood of Cam Lo and Con Thien, a battleground during the five years that the Marines had operated here. Press felt like an intruder. Their dwellings were tiny and depressing for an egalitarian eye, being constructed of bamboo and straw or concrete and corrugated iron and furnished with scavenged materials: sheets of plastic, strips of aluminum, scraps of plywood.

All the inhabitants ever wanted was to be left alone. The words *Saigon* or *Hanoi* meant little to them. It's all about control, Press reminded himself. Someone always knows what's better for you and will coerce you or kill you if you resist. These people don't even resist and still they get killed. All they want to do is raise kids and grow rice.

He tried to shake his thoughts as they cleared the gauntlet of grim faces, but only two kilometers past Cam Lo he surveyed a set of new faces. They were Montagnards—mountain people—and they were standing near the turnoff leading to Camp Carroll, an outpost on the fringe of civilization. The Montagnards were a strange and primitive-looking people, never assimilated by the Vietnamese. It was a chilly morning and Press was wearing a field jacket. They wore very little, which amazed him. Most were even shorter and thinner than the Vietnamese and almost devoid of body fat. Many were smoking foul-smelling cigarettes, and Press wondered whether it was the cigarettes or the chewing of betel nut that discolored their teeth.

The convoy traveled another twelve kilometers before the road began to swing south. A granite monolith came into view and seized Press's eyes. "Spectacular," he murmured.

"What? You mean that hunk of rock up ahead?" Snowy responded.

"That hunk of rock is an almost perfectly symmetrical outcropping about 600 feet high, probably formed by differential erosion, garnished with tropical flora and stained with the blood of not an inconsiderable number of US Marines—it's the Rockpile."

"You think you're so damn smart. How do you know it's symmetrical; you ain't never been to the other side," Snowy retorted, flashing a victory grin.

"Here, eyeball this circle," Press said, handing Snowy a topographical map.

"Huh, well, maybe you'll get by."

"It's a damn shame they had to fight in such a beautiful place. I know a guy who crawled around those clefts and crannies...he hates the place." Press kept looking back at the Rockpile as they continued driving south.

They were being funneled into a narrow valley, ideal for ambush. The heightened tension could be seen beyond the lined and wary faces of those in the convoy: grunts pointing .50 caliber machine guns at the hillsides, silence replacing sporadic conversation. They all knew that the operation was aimed at striking deep into NVA territory, at their supply line, and they knew that the NVA would strike back. But where would it be? At this juncture in the war, no one underestimated the cunning or the combat qualities of the North

Vietnamese. With several divisions waiting or en route, it was obvious that hard fighting was in the offing.

The convoy reached Vandegrift—a wide, flat, former stream bed covered sparingly with stunted vegetation—in mid-morning. The engineers spent the day upgrading approaches and in site preparation. After evening chow, the members of Press's platoon checked out the minesweep equipment and prepared for their midnight march. Padgett convened a meeting with the officers and went over D-day objectives for the final time. As it broke, he told them that they might like to write a letter home and then get a couple of hours of sleep.

"You know, I didn't bargain for this," Scogland said to the other platoon leaders as they entered their tent. "You'd think that as green as I am, there'd be some time for OJT."

"You're an interchangeable part," Darnell reminded him.

"Do you think the CO knows more than he's letting on—you know, telling us to write home?" asked Scogland.

"Nah, it's just not an everyday deal going through jungle that you can't see on a road that's not there, not to mention doing it making the loudest possible noise," Press piped in. "You'd have to say that Padgett was just being prudent."

"Aren't you scared?" Scogland asked Press. "After all, your platoon is the trail blazer."

"Look at it this way: how many guys get to lead one of the largest operations of the war. I'm honored to serve my coun—"

"Don't expect to get a straight answer from Press," Darnell broke in. "He's as nervous as any of us. Now, what do you say we get to our letter writing and catch a couple of Zs."

None of the platoon leaders was able to sleep, and at 2300 they left their tent and began to form their platoons in the marshaling area. Two minesweepers took point; Press, King, and VanAker stood behind them, followed by two of King's 34,000 pound bulldozers equipped with special land-clearing blades; then came a Sheridan tank, a mortar APC, another bulldozer and a long line of tracked combat and engineering vehicles. Interspersed among the gray iron were hundreds of mechanized infantrymen and engineers.

The battalion chaplain, Captain Hayes, moved through the assemblage, talking quietly with the engineers. Press picked up a few words, and he turned to King and said, "So, looks like we'll have an incantation—I mean a prayer."

"God is going to get you for that," King whispered back.

Hayes was upon them in a moment. "I just want to wish you fellows good luck," he said with sincerity. "May God be with you."

At midnight the entire lead element—engineers and the mechanized task force—moved out. For the first two minutes they walked on a trampled roadway and strode across a recently laid bridge span. They halted there while some snafu was worked out. Then they stepped out as if into a hole—a forbiddingly dark hole—and were swallowed by the jungle. The two minesweepers were inching forward tentatively, jabbing at the vegetation with their detectors, unable to execute the rhythmic swing so natural to them.

The going was extraordinarily slow. With ambient light squeezed from the sky, they had no reference points. A cold mist was seeping into the river valley and, given their position on the 17th parallel, the coming chill would soon disabuse the soldiers of there being an absolute association between the words *warm* and *tropics*.

Press had tied a handkerchief over the working end of his flash light and fixed it to his cartridge belt at the small of his back, so that the dozer operator would keep his direction and distance. He was certain that those in the very tip of the spearhead felt an especially acute responsibility for succeeding in this first crucial stage of the operation. He leaned toward King and shouted, "*Heart of Darkness* is my favorite short story—I never thought I'd be living it."

"Yeah, the river is somewhere to our left, maybe we ought to be taking it," King replied.

Press laughed. "If we only had—Christ! What's that?"

"I got 'em," VanAker yelled, gripping the collar of one of the minesweepers, whose left foot was poised over an abyss.

"It's an abutment," King said. "One of the downed bridges."

As VanAker pulled the minesweeper to safety, Press took out his map and King illuminated it. "We're not making enough progress. At this rate we won't make four klicks by dawn," said Press.

"We're going as fast as we can, unless we use lights," King replied.

"That's right. That's what we have to do."

"We've got orders. We'll have to radio higher to get permission."

"We've got orders not to break radio silence. And if we do they might say *no*."

"Let's ask the mech CO," King suggested.

Captain Packard stood between the Sheridan tank and the APC talking with his first sergeant. Press and King approached and explained the predicament. Without hesitation Packard replied: "I'm with you; hell, let's turn 'em on."

Within a minute the work lights of the dozer illuminated an area extending twenty yards to the front. The operator then turned his machine to the right and plunged into heavy overgrowth. The blade swept aside everything in its path, and soon the dozer crossed a dry gully skirting the bridge abutments. Once again on the trace the column picked up speed, but the minesweepers still could not maneuver in the high grass and, after another short conference, the detectors were thrown into the rear of the APC. A tank slipped a track and was moved off the road.

While clearing the road, the column made steady progress. Yet when it encountered the steep, soft banks of an intermittent stream—usually one with no flowing water but whose bottom was laden with stinking and sucking black muck—the bypass operation could easily consume a half-hour. Time was the crucial element, assuming that first-day operations would be unopposed, and cutting bypasses around bridge abutments was the key variable.

Press was losing track of time as he walked behind the dozer. His surroundings were seducing him, and every nerve and every sense became tuned to this surreal and forbidding land. He was a wayfarer in a wilderness of forms and shadows. A stand of bamboo at road's edge—caught in the suffused light thrown by head lamps into the mist—leaned toward him as if at parade rest: leafy, emerald staves, sentries of the jungle. And he watched in awe the scissoring of the great grasses as the dozer's blade skinned the ground—stalks flickering in front of him, like a newsreel at the end of its length. He felt profoundly, flamboyantly alive.

When the gray-misted dawn finally arrived, the intensity of their time on the road and the mounting hours with no sleep caused the marchers to move along with wear-worn steps. The outline of two hillocks on the far side of the river began to take shape. Press fumbled with his map in an attempt to align the crests in the hazy distance to the contoured topographic lines at hand.

The radio operator scurried up to Press and told him that the battalion commander wanted to know their position. Fletcher had rotated in December, and Lt. Col. Stewart Cunningham had taken command. Press took the handset and depressed the sender key. "This is Acorn Three-one, over."

"Acorn Three-one, this is Trumpet Six. What's your pos? Over."

"This is Three-one. As far as I can tell, we're about eight klicks from start, over."

"This is Trumpet Six. Well done. As soon as the fog lifts we'll be airborne and will have a look. Six out."

Press was doubtful that they had made eight kilometers, but the only other landforms that approximated the height and spacing were only four kilometers from start, and he was certain that despite the many bypasses and delays, they had walked more than four kilometers.

Within a half-hour the visibility was sufficient for low-flying choppers, and Press heard the familiar whipping of air above. Within seconds he was again on the radio with Cunningham. "Roger, I copy, only four klicks from start...Roger, I know that's not very far, but the going has been pretty tough... Roger, we should be able to make much better time in the daylight...Roger, out."

And progress they made. The lead dozer often ran in third gear while on the road, and the troops behind had to step up the pace proportionately, increasing their exhaustion. Soon the sky began to fill with what would become an armada of choppers carrying the materials of war on an aerial highway over the river and on to the Khe Sanh plateau. There were howitzers, bridge bundles, conexes, culvert sections, ammunition crates, small dozers, rations, and bundled tents dangling from slings five or ten degrees behind plumb. Back on the road where they had trod hours ago, the marchers now saw plumes of yellow and purple smoke from canister grenades mix with the dust kicked up by chopper blades swirling high over the river. The ground troops gazed skyward, took in the enormous sweep of the mission, and felt rejuvenated.

In late morning Press had his map out and realized that they had crossed into his area of operations two bridge sites back. "I must have been sleepwalking," he said to King, explaining his error.

"You going to send a squad back?" King asked.

Press was about to answer when his RTO approached. "Don't tell me, it's Trumpet Six."

"He wants a sitrep, sir."

"Trumpet Six, this is Acorn Three-one. We're about one klick into my AO and getting positioned to receive bird droppings, over."

"This is Trumpet Six. Real fine, Three-one. Your first loads will soon be lifting off, over."

"Roger, Trumpet Six. Would you send my jeep along as soon as conditions permit? Over." After a six second pause: "Did you copy my last? Over."

"Do you picture him shaking his head, half in disbelief, half in disgust?" King needled Press.

"We'll send your jeep out with the other vehicles. Till then stay on your feet, over."

"Roger, Trumpet Six. Just wanted some mobility when the shit hits the fan—all those bridges and culverts coming my way, over." When they signed off, he turned to King. "We'll leave the first two sites for last; it doesn't say anywhere that they've got to be dropped in order."

"Obviously, pissing off Cunningham doesn't bother you."

"Why should it? I'm already anchorman on the org chart."

The next two bridge sites were only a short walk ahead, and Press had work teams waiting at each when the chopper pilots radioed that they were over the river. Within seconds green and then yellow smoke rose from the road and the choppers swept in to deliver H-frames and decking. The next three craft carried culverts, and the engineers had them set down in stream beds where they would not have to be manhandled.

During the next two hours, Press kept one eye on the sky and one on the road, looking for Snowy. Two of the last three bridges would have to be placed four kilometers back, and everyone now was thoroughly exhausted. "We're running out of time; those choppers will be lifting off any moment," Press remarked to VanAker, as they watched a dozer spill dirt over two culverts.

"I believe help is on the way, sir. There's an antenna driving along the road, and I'd bet good money there's a jeep under it."

Press squinted hard in the direction VanAker was pointing and picked out the moving antenna just before Snowy rounded a curve and emerged from the elephant grass. "Great, grab two of your men and jump in the back." He then turned and greeted Snowy. "You the first one out of the box?"

"Yep. The colonel told the CO that you were screwing things up out here, so they sent me out to save your ass."

"If I weren't so goddamn tired, I'd take umbrage at that."

"There you go again, talkin' big. Umbrage...hmmm—"

"Turn the jeep around, Snowy," Press cut him off. "We've got to move."

He was on the radio within two minutes of Snowy's arrival, a chopper pilot asking, "...are you making smoke? Over."

"This is Three-one—negative. We haven't quite reached the pos, over."

"This is Buffalo Eight. Is that you in the jeep with the drunk driver? Over."

"That's most affirm—wait one...the driver says to tell you that he's taking umbrage at your remark, over."

"Say again, Three-one—he's taking what?"

"Umbrage, Buffalo Eight. He's taking *umbrage*, over."

"I'm impressed Three-one; must have a college boy at the wheel, huh? Over."

"Buffalo Eight, we're pulling up to the pos and will pop smoke over the abutment. Please identify, over."

A few seconds later: "I see a *bilious* yellow, over."

"Com'on in Buffalo Eight. This is Three-one, out."

VanAker and his two men were not out of the jeep three seconds before Snowy floored the throttle and raced around the bypass to the next bridge site. The timing was perfect. But, unlike the Chinooks of earlier deliveries, a CH-54 Sky Crane, which resembled a giant dragon fly, descended. Press jumped from the jeep and ran almost blindly through the whipped air to the bridge frame, stepping on a beam as the assembly was lowered onto the abutments. He could only open his eyes fractionally, for he was caught in a stinging, cyclonic swirl of dust and pebbles. He groped for the sling and then the shackle and fumbled with the retaining pin. It seemed to take forever, but he finally released the Sky Crane from its cargo and stood head bowed, listening to the mounting pitch of the engine and the blades furiously clawing the air. He picked up his hat on the way back to the jeep and sank into his seat, grimy and spent.

The platoon worked the remainder of the afternoon accepting bridges and culverts—assembling the bridges and covering the culverts with two or three feet of dirt. When the final bridge frame was on its way, Press had no one at the site. He tried to think, and rubbed his forehead and hollowed-out eyes to encourage the process, but fatigue was his sole sensation. He had it dropped where he and some others stood.

All D-Day assignments were completed at dusk. As if by prior arrangement, the disparate units of the operation gathered on a hillside, scattered in groups of two or three, and broke out C-rations. In their now-sedentary state, the cold was becoming increasingly uncomfortable. Packard, King, and Press discussed security arrangements while they ate. Each knew that everyone was exhausted beyond measure and that assigning guard duty would be futile. Still, Packard left to deploy his men shortly after finishing his meal. Press and King talked for a few minutes, mostly about what they would be doing this evening were they home, but soon their words became thick and slow, and in silent submission, they reclined on the cold hard ground. Even though Press was wearing a rain slicker over his field jacket, he felt the chill penetrate. None of the discomforts, however, could match his need for sleep, and within seconds, he drifted into oblivion.

Dawn came early to their defilade position on the northwest slope of a hill fringing the Quang Tri River. Press opened an eye and gazed through the filtered light. The eye was uncomprehending at first, for his dreams had been thousands of miles away and in a far more agreeable setting. Gradually, he focused on King, who was spooning out ham and eggs substitute from a tin of

C-rations about three meters away. "Bill, you got any C-4 to heat instant coffee?" he asked in a pleading tone.

"No time. I could sure go for a nice warm fire, but we're going to have to get our asses in gear if we're going to open the road by noon."

"You're speaking with the exuberance and can do attitude of a lifer."

"Ha! How about you with Ridgway Road. I ought to write to Celia and tell her she had stiff competition for a while."

"She thinks I'm living the easy life in Cam Ranh."

"Is she joining you on R and R?"

"Hope so. How did Anne and Ginny like Hawaii?"

"They loved it. We went to a secluded resort—the Hanalei Plantation—on the island of Kauai. Fantastic place. Go there, if you can talk Celia into going. You'll thank me."

After writing down the information in a notebook, Press said, "Well, I guess we ought to get back to business."

"Today's objective is a good bit easier than yesterday's—open three klicks of road down to a switchback, where we meet up with the engineers airlifted to Khe Sanh yesterday."

"From a distance standpoint yes, but look out there." Press drew King's attention to where the road made a ninety-degree turn south. The spreading dawn and thinning mist unveiled a string of interlocking hills, several with seventy or eighty degree slopes which dropped headlong into the river; and somewhere, serrated in the wild overgrowth clutching their flanks, was the remnant of a road. The river below was shallow and wide, with clear water rushing down the channel, scouring the limestone bed, and both men were taken by the winking and glimmering of its continuous cataracts.

After a half-hour of refueling and greasing the dozers and front-end loaders, the engineers went to work on the road. Press was busy installing culverts when a Huey approached and landed close by. A lieutenant colonel motioned for Press to climb aboard and, once airborne, told him that there was no bridge assembled at the switchback ahead. Within seconds they flew into a deep canyon, where a narrow and fast flowing stream—a tributary of the Quang Tri River—held sway. QL-9 was carved into the sides of the canyon, and Press could see the skeletons of two prior bridges—one probably built by the French—sprawled across the stream bed underwater. This was the most critical and difficult location on the road to defend. The NVA could lob mortars onto the switchback from anywhere on high ground.

"I understand that the switchback is supposed to get an AVLB," Press finally told the colonel. An Armored Vehicle Launch Bridge, carried by a tank-like vehicle, could be hydraulically unfolded and laid out sixty feet in only minutes. It was one of the more innovative post-World War II engineering creations.

"*Where* is it?" the colonel asked, harshly.

"Beats me, sir."

"Lieutenant, a good many vehicles waiting at Vandegrift will be crossing over the switchback later today, so we're gonna need a bridge soon."

"Well, sir, an M4T6 should work until the AVLB arrives. We could have the frame airlifted in place and install the decking and be open for traffic by noon."

"That's what I like to hear, Lieutenant. Get to it."

The bridge was assembled and usable by 1140, and the road was open as far as Khe Sanh. Still, there was no letup in work. Fatigue again wore the men down, and Press rested them often. During one break, he went into the jungle to urinate and caught sight of a natural cistern, resembling a wall-mounted, cathedral-size tub of holy water, sequestered on a hillside and fed by a spring from the rocks above. He stripped off his cloths, took a bar of soap he had been carrying for the occasion, and climbed to the landform. Inhaling sharply as he sat in the very cold seven or eight gallons of water, he cursed the war several times and then splashed and lathered. Two minutes later, famished, he donned his street sweepings masquerading as fatigues.

"Snowy," he hailed from a distance. "I've got the appetite of a stevedore. We got any more chocolate or pound cake?"

"Jesus, LT, you went through a dozen boxes of C-rats picking out that stuff; why not eat one of the six cans of spaghetti, the four of ham and eggs, or the two of beef we got in the back seat?" Snowy pealed open his field jacket and patted his portly mid-section. "What you need is some bulk—a few rolls of reserve to get you by."

Press, whose face now showed fatigue, ignored him and rummaged through the C-ration cartons, finding pound cake. He fished a P-38 out of his shirt pocket and began to open the tin. Having roughly the length and width of a long postage stamp, only thicker, the P-38 was the most prolifically used tool in the field, equally good for stripping commo wire, as a screw driver, or a can opener. Press opened the lid and stuffed a chunk of pound cake into his mouth. He was burning calories rapidly warding off the cold and eating continually to maintain his energy.

That evening, instead of bedding down for an uninterrupted night of sleep, the platoon was twice called out to make emergency road repairs. Press had noticed that the few vehicles making the run to Khe Sanh were doing so without lights, and he would explain to each unit commander he saw that this stretch of the road was far too treacherous to drive without headlights. Orders, they countered. This proved disastrous the next two evenings when convoys of more than a hundred trucks each made their way along the serpentine route near the switchback. The radio in Press's jeep would crackle and fizz, and a voice would shout out for help. Most of the calls originated from an area where the road was carved into a limestone cliff, no more than ten feet wide. Whenever a front-left wheel veered off-line more than two feet, the truck—it was usually a deuce-and-a-half—plunged off the road, rolled over two or three times and came to rest on the river bank forty feet below, killing or seriously injuring the driver and the soldier sitting shotgun.

It was early on in the mission when Press's platoon went into the salvage business. During the morning of D+2 VanAker reported that a jeep belonging to a captain in the Military Police had been abandoned on the road. Press, perhaps influenced by the movie *M*A*S*H* he had seen at Fort Dix, inspected the jeep and told him to have it pushed into the jungle, where they could later stencil-in new numbers. The captain returned a few hours later to recover his jeep, but everyone he approached shrugged his shoulders and feigned ignorance. The next serendipitous find was an A-frame shed fitted onto a trailer. It was loaded with boxes of C-rations, but Press saw a potential use for it as a future sleeping compartment. An unwelcome and frequent find was a pallet or two of artillery rounds, mostly 175 millimeter, which had slid off a flat bed truck while it took one of the curves near the switchback.

Apart from the MP captain's jeep, the discards of war wound up inside the company's night defensive perimeter. Other than the base at Khe Sanh, it was the most protected outpost between Vandegrift and the Laotian border. With dozers clearing and stacking vegetation into high dense windrows, engineers strung six coils of concertina barbed wire around the inner perimeter. The weakest area was a portion of the north flank which fronted a stream with almost vertical banks. The eastern edge of the NDP hugged the road, now almost in continual use. The dust kicked up by traffic was a constant irritant to the engineers of Echo Company.

Padgett told Press in the morning of D+3 that his platoon would have to guard two bridge crossings for the next two nights. Press informed the squad leaders at noon chow and divided the unit into two teams. He would stay with the team responsible for the strategic bridge at the switchback, while VanAker and the other half of the platoon would guard a bridge closer to the NDP.

Press was cleaning his mess kit in a stream when Spec 5 Schade approached, wearing a nervous but determined expression. Clearing his throat, he said, "Sir, I have twelve days and a wake-up left in-country, and I don't think I should be pulling duty to guard a bridge."

Press thought for a moment before he spoke. "I know you're a short-timer, Schade, and if you had a week to go, I'd let you sit it out, but I can't do it at twelve days."

Schade inhaled sharply. "I'm not going to guard that bridge. If Charlie hit us, we'd get slaughtered."

"Look, I know it's dangerous and none of us would volunteer for the duty, but we simply have no choice. You've got an outstanding record; certainly you don't want to risk a court martial and possibly the stockade, or at the very least a dishonorable discharge."

"I'm prepared to risk it," Schade countered. "At least I'll still be alive."

"Let me ask you this: is it just the switchback bridge you're refusing to guard?"

"Both, sir."

"You're an E-five, Schade, and what, twenty-one or twenty-two?"

"Twenty-two."

"Have you thought about the long-term ramifications of taking this step?"

"I'm prepared to take a court martial, if that's what you mean."

"That's not what I mean. This reaction of yours is typical of short-timers—you've almost got it made and there's a fear in you that in the last few days in the field something will happen. In all the time I've known you, you never blinked an eye at danger—not till this moment. If you give in now, it will begin to wear at you—maybe not right away but soon, like some chronic, insidious disease. You may never be rid of it. It's the way you are, Schade. Your conscience isn't strong enough to lug around the doubt, regret...shame. I'm asking you—for your sake—not to do it."

"Sorry, sir, I've made my decision."

Press, with half-shuttered eyelids and an expression of disgust forming on his face, took almost half a minute to make his decision. "Okay, then. I want you on the first truck back to Dong Ha. You'll stay in base camp till you leave for Cam Ranh."

"Yes, sir. Thank you for understanding."

"You misinterpret, Shade. I've just sentenced you."

That evening, Press spread his guard team along the south bank of the stream. A few boulders provided some cover, but the narrow river valley was exposed on all angles. He reasoned that if the NVA attacked with mortars, it would be from a defilade position high on the north slope. Calling in artillery would be useless. Although he registered their position with the artillery unit responsible for the lower road, he set the jeep radio to the Medevac frequency.

Blackout restrictions for the evening convoys had been lifted the day before, and now, as a convoy passed through in the thickening darkness, it was no longer a skulking low crawl to Khe Sanh but a twinkling, confident procession. A minute after the taillights of the last truck disappeared around the south hill, an uneasy silence returned, and Press propped himself against a boulder, feeling on his face the first moist beads of a mist creeping up the valley floor.

As he sat there, he tried to reconcile the two conflicting emotions vying for supremacy: apprehension and boredom. How was it possible to feel both? Sitting in the darkness without talking or reading or listening to the radio made time pass slowly. Knowing that there was a possibility of combat in the hours ahead only made the passage less palatable. He escaped for a while in thoughts of Celia, but soon the specter of Schade's fear began to weigh on him, and he sensed the NVA closing in from above. As the stream gurgled close to his ear, he realized that a handful of engineers stood no chance against veteran attackers—they would descend like wraiths, shadowy figures firing AK-47s and hurling satchel charges, seconds later vanishing into the night, leaving behind the broken bodies of amateurs.

At two past midnight small arms fire erupted out of the north. The sounds, grave and frightening, lasted less than a minute. Then a plaintive voice on the radio called for a medevac chopper. A voice at the other end responded that a DMZ Dustoff would be en route in seconds. Press pushed a ball-point pen from its slot in a fatigue pocket and wrote the coordinates as they were given and repeated: 4045 and 9132. Placing a rule on his map, he turned on his flashlight, plotted the coordinates, and quickly called out to his team leaders to wake anyone who was sleeping and keep a keen watch on the hill to the north. The fire fight had taken place 200 meters from the top of the hill facing them.

Press shook his head in wonderment as he listened to the distant sound of chopper blades. What kind of crew would take the terrible risk of flying blind to what would almost certainly be an inaccessible location? The radio traffic picked up, and he learned that the wounded was a member of a long range patrol. The chopper was quite close now, probably over the river, and the pilot radioed that the visibility was too poor for a rescue attempt. They would have to turn back. The LRP leader realized the folly of an attempted air-land rescue and thanked the crew for its efforts. The two unhurt soldiers would try to carry the wounded member to the road, where he could be evacuated by an APC. The engineers could provide no help; the north slope of the hill was too steep to negotiate in the dark.

The rest of the night passed quietly, and, at first light, Press woke from a hard, four-hour sleep. He reached into the stream with his mess cup and filled it with clear water. He then sliced a block of C-4 plastic explosive into several bite-size chunks, lighted one in the recess of piled stones, and rested the mess cup on the makeshift supports. Similar fires flared up among the boulders. The C-4 burned quickly and white-hot, and Press fed the fire until the water boiled. If instant coffee can ever qualify as an elixir, it does on a chilly morning when sleep fades grudgingly. Press, Snowy, and Retherford, a newly arrived squad leader, stood around the jeep eating C-ration scrambled eggs and savoring their brew, which warmed the body and soothed the spirit.

"One of the things I would like to do before the convoys run all day is to widen the road here—make it easier to turn onto the bridge," Press said, initiating a discussion of business.

"We'll have to get more explosives," Retherford stated.

"Not if we use a few of the one-seven-five rounds scattered about. Three or four of them should fit into that cavity," said Press, pointing to a gap in a rock wall facing the bridge approach.

"Geez, I want to be a mile away when that blows, don't ya know," Snowy said.

Early that afternoon, with the platoon formed back into squads, VanAker salvaged a crate of 175 mm shells and hauled it to the switchback. Several engineers dragged four of the rounds to the rock face and placed them in the crevice. They unscrewed the nose cones, removed the fuses, stuffed the cavities with C-4, and connected the four rounds with detonation cord, an explosive almost identical in appearance to a plastic clothesline. Other engineers had strung electrical wire for more than a hundred meters. Still others stopped traffic. While a lone engineer taped a blasting cap to the det cord and ran back to the group, Snowy set off a red smoke grenade. VanAker connected the wires at the far end of the length to the blasting machine and attached the handle. An engineer in the rear shouted "fire in the hole" three times, and VanAker asked Press if he would like to do the honor.

"No, go ahead."

"Okay, let's have a blast." As Snowy shook his head, VanAker gave the handle a quarter turn twist and almost simultaneously the rock face lifted upward and outward, followed by the swirling black residue of Composition B and the gray dust of ages. Almost a half minute later, long after the roar of the explosion, smaller pieces of rock were still falling not far from where the engineers were standing.

"Jesus Christ, I'll bet that carried to Khe Sanh," someone shouted.

As the engineers were cleaning up with a front-end loader, Padgett appeared, nodding his head at the widened approach.

Press saluted and said, "Didn't see you arrive. Is third squad still down by the NDP?"

"Just left them. They're winching out a deuce-and-a-half that went off the road night before last. Tell me, what's going on with Schade."

"I sent him back to Dong Ha yesterday. He refused guard duty last night, because he's going home in eleven days."

"He refused a direct order?"

"It was direct enough. How did you find out about it?"

"Got a message about a half-hour ago that he wants to come back. A few months at LBJ ought to straighten him out," Padgett reasoned, referring to Long Binh Jail.

"I'd prefer not to press charges. Schade's no coward—or if he is, he's a highly inconsistent one. This is the first time he's flinched from any nasty duty. I think he felt he was owed a break by being short. When I told him that twelve days was not short enough, he became obstinate. With a little time to reflect, to fully understand that he let his buddies down at a dangerous moment, he'll sentence himself—for a long time."

"That's all very nice psychoanalysis, but the Army is run by regulation. It's our duty—"

"Forgive me for interrupting, sir, but that's bullshit. Regulations are enforced so unevenly that it's making a mockery out of military justice. I caught a pusher in the act—to me a more reprehensible crime than Schade's—and the Army sent him home because of self-inflicted hepatitis. Where's the justice in that?"

"Cool down, Lieutenant. I'm not going to overturn your decision. What happened to you would not have been tolerated under my command." He grimaced and shook his head. "Discipline has gone to hell in this war. But you're wrong about Schade's offense; deserting your unit at a time of danger is among the worse. He should face court martial."

"He'll face worse punishment, and practically speaking had we been overrun, Schade's presence would have only meant one more dead body. You know what the NVA are like in a night attack."

The captain did not respond, except to say, "Carry on," as he climbed into his jeep.

Shortly after Padgett left, Press and Snowy set off to visit the third squad. Stopping at a proposed culvert site, Press surveyed the embankment and wrote a few lines in his notebook.

"Don't look now, but I think somebody's watching us from across the river," Snowy said, trying to sound matter-of-fact.

Press looked up quickly, reached into the back of the jeep, and seized an M-79 Grenade Launcher. He fixed his eye on a tree limb that flexed for no apparent cause, while stuffing a round into the wide mouth of the barrel. "No friendlies on that side of the river," he said as he closed the breech and aimed at the limb 110 meters away. He pulled the trigger and watched as the round sailed across the water and disappeared into the tousled vegetation. The explosion was muffled, but black smoke rose in sieve-like threads.

"You need to correct your windage," Snowy joked. "You were three meters to the—Christ, what's that?"

A look of self-revulsion gripped Press's face, as he watched a red shanked douc langur drop from the tree and land on the limestone at river's edge. The monkey seemed disoriented, but after a few moments, was able to sit up and look at where his right arm had been. Instinctively, he placed his left hand over the shoulder in a futile attempt to staunch the flow of blood. He looked strangely human with longish white hair bristling from his cheeks in the style of an 1830's politician. A dark mat of hair covered the top of his head to within an inch of his eyes, which were wide and uncomprehending. Slowly, he reclined on the river bank as the loss of blood depleted his strength.

Press threw the weapon into the back seat. "So, it's come to this...."

In the waning light of the day, Press sat on the sand bags covering his culvert domicile and opened a tablet. He had decided to invite Celia to Hawaii over Easter, to the resort recommended by King tucked away somewhere on the lightly populated island of Kauai.

He started his letter with the standard palaver about base camp boredom and then inquired about her job and Lynn and Roger. He paused for a minute and then began his third paragraph. "I'm more than half way through my tour—a seasoned pro by any account here—and it's time I made arrangements for R&R. My choices are: Hong Kong, Bangkok, Sydney and Hawaii. As much as I would like to visit the first three cities, there's nothing in the world I would rather do than meet you in Honolulu in early April. I'm told that there's a resort on an enchanted corner of the island of Kauai that juts out into the sea and has a distant but dazzling view of Lumahai Beach (many of the scenes of

South Pacific were filmed there, including Mitzi Gaynor singing 'I'm Going To Wash That Man Right Out Of My Hair'). You can do likewise by declining my invitation, but if the struggle between your heart and your head is at all close, I'm asking that you give your heart sway. I'll send you a money order to cover the cost of the airline tickets."

After several interruptions and a trip to the slit trench, with darkness skewing his script, he closed the letter with a modified line from Herbert Trench: "'By starlight and by candlelight and dreamlight, you come to me.'" He then crawled under his culvert halves and into an all-consuming sleep.

The days on the lower road drifted into each other, each very much the same as the day before and memorable by only one or two events. During the early hours of D+7, two soldiers on guard duty, alone in an armored personnel carrier filled with mortars and situated ninety meters from Echo Company's NDP, seriously wounded themselves when they blew up the APC in what they hoped would be taken as an enemy rocket propelled grenade attack. Press was sleeping the sleep of the outdoorsman, on an air mattress in the hole covered by culvert halves. The explosions of the mortars cooking off did not shake him from his slumber.

Two days later a stalled *ARVN* deuce-and-a-half threatened chaos. It occurred on the most confined area of the road, just short of the switchback. After a thirty minute wait, an MP rushed up to Press and asked for help, citing the scheduled departure of a US convoy from the opposite direction in an hour. Looking the situation over, Press said to VanAker, "Are you thinking what I'm thinking?" VanAker grinned, and he continued, "Tell Allen to push the truck into the river."

At first, the Vietnamese soldiers in the truck refused to vacate. But as Allen positioned the bulldozer blade against the left front bumper and gradually pivoted the truck, metal screeching against metal, the occupants scampered off. He then repositioned for a broadside and pushed the truck into the stream.

The convoy began to roll on, and when the last truck took the turn at the switchback, a jeep carrying an MP lieutenant pulled up at the bridge. "You Lieutenant Patrick?" he shouted.

Press thought he was going to be questioned about the stolen MP jeep. "Afraid so."

"Got a message for you."

Press walked over to the jeep and took a scrap of paper from him. He bit down on a chunk of chocolate and read the note. It was the fifth request he had received from Schade to return to the unit. He wondered for a second how many messages went undelivered, then crumpled the paper and threw in into the stream.

25

On the twelfth Echo Company received orders to decamp and move to Khe Sanh. Press had often wondered what lay beyond the ribbon of road and river that he knew so intimately. Now, as he and Snowy ascended the high hill on the south side of the switchback, he began to marvel at the difference. Where the lower road was often sunken and confining, dark and mist-shrouded, the uplands basked under a vast and brilliant sky. They rode along a narrow corridor lined with giant tropical trees and more haphazardly, countless rubber tress. Press remarked to Snowy that this must have been the Michelin plantation rumored to be in the area. The view was spectacular. At one point the corridor was so narrow that he could see each flank plunge almost perpendicularly hundreds of feet and then rise gradually. In the distance, mountains pushed against the horizon. Khe Sanh was to the northwest, taking up the better part of an elongated plateau and offering from this vantage point no hint of its history nor foretoken of its future. It merely resembled a great flat heap which eclipsed the valleys and was in turn dwarfed by the mountains.

After a few more minutes of driving, the road spilled onto the plateau. The sparkling beauty glimpsed from a kilometer or two back and a hundred meters down belonged only to the fringes of the eye; immediately to the front was a disfigured and denuded plain. The road was covered with a good three inches of laterite dust as fine as chalk powder, and it rose like a rusty red curtain with every passing vehicle. Press and Snowy were coated with it when they motored into the area Echo would be occupying on the southern perimeter.

Press surveyed their immediate surroundings and then gazed into the distance. "Did you ever think, Snowy, that everything we touch here turns ugly?

Look at what nature's done with a hundred square miles all-around and compare it to all the bases we've known and the square mile we're standing on."

"Don't mean nothin'. Only thing that counts is gettin' closer to *DEROS*."

"You've got the heart of the poet, Snowy," Press chucked, as he unhitched his "house" trailer. He then set up his cot and air mattress inside and arranged his books, candles, and radio. Having so few possessions was to his liking. He knew full well that he would begin accumulating them soon after leaving the country—a car straight-off, then stereo and sports equipment. But even then he would probably equate mobility and freedom of action with owning only what could be stowed in two suitcases. He was tucking a blanket under the air mattress when Snowy reached through the small opening and handed him a letter from Rebecca. It was short and businesslike. Her editor was sending her to Vietnam for a story on the enlisted soldier's perspective of the war. She would be arriving in Da Nang on 14 March and would fly to Quang Tri the next day. Would he be able to meet her in Quang Tri, and could she travel with him to Khe Sanh?

He smiled and placed the letter in *The Arms of Grupp*, then climbed out of the shelter and walked the short distance to the headquarters of the 87th, the 99th's sister battalion. The S-3 was to turn over to him an assignment which had originally been the 87th's, but had not yet been started.

Major Fox greeted him warmly and asked him to sit. He then began a detailed explanation of the assignment. Distilled to its essentials, Press was informed that helicopter parking space was at a premium—they were now crowding the airstrip—and a 100,000 square meter helipad was to be constructed on the south end of the base. There were a few "impediments" to the construction: an old Marine minefield for which no map could be found; a few hundred meters of perimeter wire to be cleared, much of it booby-trapped by the Marine defenders in 1968; and scores of dud mortar and artillery rounds scattered about. Press's platoon would have two weeks to clear and level the site and apply a coating of oil to minimize blowing dust.

The platoon arrived at its new work site early the next morning and assembled on the road fronting the minefield. Press addressed the engineers with a stern warning: "The S-3 of the 87th says that there's some stuff in here that'll make holes in your fatigues—grenades strung in the wire, which we have to clear by hand, and all kinds of dud rounds in the grass. So be very careful where you step. If you walk into a tripwire, run about ten steps and hit the ground. You'll have four-and-a-half seconds in the event it was a boobytrapped grenade. If it's a claymore, it doesn't matter what you do. You new guys—stay behind somebody who's been here a while, but don't bunch up. If something's going to happen, we don't want multiple casualties. And don't think for even a second of going anywhere near the dozer. It could easily arm a grenade by crushing the lever.

"Now about the minefield—I'll order up some Bangalore torpedoes. With the priority of the operation, they'll probably arrive before I get off the radio. On second thought—they'll probably fall off the truck down by our old NDP. Anyway, until they arrive we'll stay away from it. Any questions?"

"We're out of electric blasting caps," VanAker said.

"Thanks, Sarge. We'll order some. Until we get 'em, we'll short-fuse. Let's get the detectors out now and sweep behind the minefield."

The engineers embarked on their task with some trepidation, clearing the field cautiously. The grass was dead scraggly stubble, not much more than waist high and spaced several inches apart, so the laterite clay, and anything lying on it, could be seen fairly well. The men found tens of dud rounds and anti-personnel mines with Chinese and Russian markings and stockpiled them in a hole at the northeast corner of the field. Whenever a detector picked up a metal object below the surface, the engineer tore off a small piece of C-4 and detonated it in-place. Jerome Allen on the dozer cleared the dead vegetation from areas already swept. In mid-afternoon of the third day, he lowered the dozer blade a few inches into the ground to smooth out a rise. Press was watching the operation and the obviously-tired operator, when he saw a cloud of smoke rush out horizontally from the blade and then rise, wispy-white into the clean air. The roar of the explosion followed immediately and Allen, without a change of expression, stopped his blading work, stepped out of the operator's compartment and walked casually along the right hand track to the front of the machine. He leaned forward and peered at the slightly twisted front edge of the blade, nodded his head, and returned to resume operation.

Press was relieved that no one was standing nearby. Many fatalities of the war occurred in incidences similar to this. He went on to think of the difference in the reactions of higher command between someone getting killed here or in the States. Here, there would be a cursory report and expressions of regret and *c'est la guerre* all around. In the States, there would be safety people sniffing about, reports ad nauseam and, in many cases, the officer in charge being relieved of command.

On the following morning the platoon began to take out the minefield, using Bangalore torpedoes. The front section of the torpedo had a nose cone, which made it easier to push the three-inch diameter tube along the ground. Additional sections were added to the cylindrical bombs until they spanned the minefield. Press then went through the chain of command and obtained permission to detonate the explosives. Forty-five minutes later, he received the all-clear from the air traffic controller. While red smoke drifted overhead and shouts of "fire in the hole" echoed in the air, one of the new platoon members, Aaron Garrison, a freckled-face lad from Texas, was given the honor of turning the handle on the blasting machine.

"You eighteen yet, Garrison?" Press asked.

"Almost, sir."

"You sure you want me to turn this over to a minor, LT?" VanAker joked.

"Have you read the appropriate field manual on how to operate the blasting machine?" Press quizzed Garrison.

"Can't quite recall if I have, sir."

"In that case we'll give you a little OJT. Take the machine with one hand and grip the handle with the other." After Garrison took the machine from VanAker, Press continued. "Listen carefully, now. This is a one count movement. When I say "turn," rotate the handle in a clockwise manner; you got that?"

"Yes, sir."

"Ready...Turn!"

Nothing happened. "Okay, Garrison, try again, but remember to turn it *clockwise*."

Two hundred meters away, coal black smoke from the exploding Composition B flared upward, followed immediately by billowing gray dust. The engineers heard two distinct detonations: the mines went up in a secondary explosion, almost a tenth of a second after the Bangalore torpedoes. The mixture of powder and dust raced upward, resembling a vast, vertical cumulus cloud, and smelling of incinerated earth.

Garrison's jaw dropped at the spectacle. "Gee, I never seen nothin' like that before." After a few more seconds of gaping at the sight, he turned to Press and said, "Sorry about the first time, sir. I remember now that we're still north of the equator."

Following a decent interval, Press strode over to Sgt. Retherford, Garrison's squad leader. "Sarge," he began in little more than a whisper, "take Garrison under your wing and make him a supernumerary on dangerous details for a while."

Something had caught Retherford's eye, and he said with urgency, "Move gradually to your right. A Bamboo Viper is within striking distance of your left leg."

Press did as Retherford suggested and looked down to see an emerald green snake, no more than two feet long, with an out-sized viper head and golden, cat-like eyes. "Thanks, Sarge. You don't live two minutes after a bite from one of those."

"My pleasure, sir." With that, the sergeant took two steps forward and smashed the snake's head with his rifle butt.

Just as it happened on the lower road, the days began to blend together with a routine of sorts. Hot food was served regularly. The weather was warming and becoming clear, morning mists giving way to brilliant skies. The dust, however, was ubiquitous and made driving on the clogged perimeter roads misery. It irritated and reddened the eyes and nestled into pores. And everyone was certain he had inhaled enough dust for a lifetime.

The evenings were much better for Press than those spent at the NDP or guarding a bridge. When he was not playing poker in the command tent, he was in his trailer-house reading by the light of three candles. He received two English speaking stations on his portable radio: Armed Forces Vietnam (AFVN) and the North Vietnamese propaganda station featuring Hanoi Hannah—a throwback to Tokyo Rose—who, between pop recordings, would attempt to stir racial discord and wear on the morale of enlisted soldiers.

On each evening spent in the candlelit enclosure, shadows playing along the walls, apparitions to an inattentive eye, the AFVN theme would come on the air, an eerily haunting emotive strain that invariably prompted Press to lower his book and think of Celia and of the great distance between them. Not only was she on the opposite side of the world, but she was attached to him in the most tenuous way, by emotion. He worried that her rational side would take hold and she would cast him off before they would see each other. Apart from writing there was little he could do.

During one of those somber moments on a pleasant February evening, he opened the letter from Celia he had saved from earlier in the day. It almost certainly contained her response to his invitation to join him on R&R. As he unfolded it, he realized that the dread of a refusal was more pronounced than any fear induced by the enemy. He glanced nervously at the plywood walls, where the candle flames danced grotesquely. He turned from the silhouettes to the letter.

Dearest Press,

The deepest part of winter is behind us here, and soon we'll be seeing the first stirrings of spring. The weather where you are and farther north must be very different. I don't normally watch the war news on TV, but I did see one report showing the troops near the Laotian border dressed in heavy jackets, while those somewhere down by you were wearing T-shirts. I much prefer the change of seasons to distinguishing months by the calendar, as you wrote you do at Cam Ranh.

I've always known that you would have R&R sometime during your tour, but I've only thought about it in the abstract until your last letter arrived. For several days now I've thought of little else. I'm fully recovered from the grand funk that woman put me in, although it's taken some time. And I no longer blame you. I had no justification for feeling betrayed by an act that occurred before we met each other, and of course I knew that you were not "inexperienced." Lynn says that I should not hesitate in accepting your invitation. She also admits being prejudiced in your favor.

You know that I've been dating on occasion. What you do not know is that you seem to be right there with us, not obtrusive or hovering—you're in that creaky chair in your office, rocking away while you edit. I guess that's how I think of you over there. Anyway, I owe it to both of us to see if what we had still exists, and I will be happy to join you on R&R. Besides, a girl would have to be crazy to turn down a free trip to Hawaii.

Press put his head back and breathed a prolonged sigh. He quickly read the last page of the letter, then retrieved the information he needed to make the necessary reservations in Hawaii.

The helipad was cleared and graded by the end of February, not a day too soon according to the operation commanders, who were stacking choppers along the flanks of the airfield. Before Press turned it over, he sought permission to detonate in-place the motley collection of land mines, artillery and mortar shells now piled in a pit on the edge of the helipad. In a departure from the norm, clearance was granted almost as soon as requested and Press radioed the air traffic controller to coordinate the timing. He put his handset away and told Snowy to drive to the far side of the helipad. He then turned to VanAker. "We've got clearance, Sarge; you got the shape charge ready?"

"Yes, sir, but we're again out of electric blasting caps."

"Then we'll have to short-fuse it." There was no need to specify the length of fuse needed, both men having used explosives almost daily.

VanAker cut six inches of fuse, enough for about thirty seconds of burn time. He inserted one end into a blasting cap and placed it in the receptacle on the shape charge.

Press set off a smoke canister while VanAker lit the fuse, and both watched it burn for a few seconds before dashing through the curling red smoke to a concrete pipe twenty-five meters away. Twenty seconds passed...thirty.

"It should have blown by now," Press remarked, looking at his watch.

"That's what I hate about fuses," VanAker stated.

Press waved to Snowy to bring up the jeep and said, "Let's wait five, and I'll radio air traffic control." A few minutes later, Press replaced the handset for the second time, and he and VanAker walked toward the pit. When they were twenty feet away, he told VanAker to stay while he checked out the fuse. Although he was certain that either the fuse or the cap was faulty and the charge would not detonate in his face, his heart punched the walls of his chest as he neared the atomization zone. "This is stupid, creeping like this," he blurted out.

"What's that, LT?" VanAker asked.

"Just talking to myself," Press said, as he reached for the fuse. Pulling on it gently he noticed the unburned stub. "Okay," he yelled out, "let's try it again."

VanAker repeated the procedure, this time cutting the fuse an inch shorter. They both watched it burn for a couple of seconds before dashing back to the pipe. Red smoke and shouts of "fire in the hole" again filled the air as they took their position in the pipe. As they squated, their eyes were drawn to the sky, prompted by the unmistakable stabbing sound of rotors.

"Jesus Christ, he's coming in right over the hole," VanAker exclaimed.

Press was already waving frantically from a foot outside of the pipe, but the pilot seemed to be focusing on a landing spot near the end of the airstrip. The Huey was approximately one hundred feet above ground when the pilot noticed the swirling crimson smoke. He passed top dead center as the shape charge detonated and a blast wave swept upward, propelling the red smoke before it and engulfing the chopper, shaking it violently. Press was transfixed by the spectacle, and he had not taken cover. Seconds later, shrapnel began falling from the sky, and he quickly jumped into the pipe.

"Unbelievable!" VanAker shouted, watching from the other end. "He made it—he's gonna land."

Snowy drove the jeep up as Press stepped out of the pipe. "You almost knocked him out of the sky, don't ya know." He picked up the sender and handed it to Press. "Here, the air boss wants to talk to you."

Press grabbed the handset. "This is Acorn Three-one, over."

"Acorn Three-one, this is Neptune Four. The Huey that just flew over was not monitoring the proper—wait one, over."

"Roger, Neptune Four." Press released the send button. "Damn close, wasn't it. That would probably have been a first in the annals of combat engineering."

"He's got to have some holes in that bird," VanAker added.

A minute later, Neptune Four returned. "That was the Huey pilot; be advised that he's a little hot and after he checks his bird for holes, he'll be on his way to see you, over."

"This is Three-one; we're always ready for a courtesy call, but we're a formal bunch—can't receive him without a calling card, over."

"This is Neptune Four. I believe it's strapped to his side. Good Luck. Neptune Four, out."

The Huey pilot stamped across the wasteland with his head straight and his features fierce. He was not a big man, but his flexed walrus mustache was good for an extra ten pounds. He was fifteen paces away when he opened up at the group of engineers standing around Press's jeep. "You shitheads damn near shot me down."

"You were supposed to see red while you were in the air, not on the ground," Press retorted.

"I don't know what bullshit you're trying to pull, Lieutenant, but I can tell you one damn thing—I've got two months left in my second tour and this was the closest I've come to buying the farm—and from my own goddamn side!" Perhaps partly from anger and partly from the burden of his mustache, the pilot's upper lip quivered when he talked, and the engineers strained to decipher his words, lip reading being out of the question.

"Now Bartlett," Press read his name from his flight suit, "don't tell me you've served two tours without reading *Catch-22?* Christ, man, you're lucky to be alive."

"What the hell you talking about?" Bartlett snapped.

"Anyone who's read *Catch-22* would know that not only is the enemy trying to kill you, '*your own side is trying to get you killed.*' This lesson may save you in your last two months."

Bartlett's mustache twitched. "You're totally fucked up, Lieutenant, and your battalion commander is going to hear about it."

"Bartlett, *Bartlett*," Press rolled out in his most patronizing manner to the warrant officer. "Don't you know what you're going to be doing till your *DEROS?* You're going to be flying between here and the Ho Chi Minh Trail, ferrying *ARVN* troops in the advanced stage of the big collapse. You might get it from any side: the NVA, your own, or the *ARVN*."

"That's it, Lieutenant, your ass is grasped. I'm making a full report on you."

"Be sure to give higher my compliments. And Bartlett, stiff upper lip—it's going to get hot up there."

Bartlett did not report the incident, and ten days later Press's platoon was sent half way to the Laotian border with orders to build a helicopter landing zone.

26

Press woke automatically at six o'clock. He washed and shaved, put on a clean pair of fatigues and socks (he had stopped wearing drawers early in his tour, as they chaffed and were slow to dry after wading in streams), laced up his jungle boots, and went out for morning chow. The coffee was bitter, which was standard fare, but he had grown used to it. The bacon was sopped in grease as usual and the scrambled eggs watery, but hot.

He put his mess kit on the draft frame of the potable water trailer and looked out. The day was docile, the warm air stirring subtly, and all that surrounded the plateau—arching hills and slump-shouldered mountains—stood benignly, showing no trace of a contrarian past. While he ate, he wondered what the North Vietnamese were having for breakfast. It couldn't be much, he reasoned, a few ounces of rice and perhaps some dried vegetables. How could they possibly hold their own against an army that could feed its soldiers hot meals so far from base camp? But they had done it for years now, and they would continue to suffer privations and even the terror of saturation bombing until the *Americans* had had enough. Nixon's Vietnamization policy was on schedule, and this operation was the test case for the *ARVN*'s ability to confront the NVA.

Snowy made his way over to Press and sat down heavily. "Mornin' Boss. Nice day, huh?" Press's canteen cup was high over his mouth, and he nodded as he gulped his coffee. "So we're still going to Quang Tri to pick up your correspondent friend?"

"Right after we get things running at the LZ. The CO told me that higher wants it completed *ASAP.*"

Snowy nodded. "You want me to stay at Dong Ha on the way back, you know, rest up for the big departure?"

Press gulped another mouthful of coffee and said, "Damn, I forgot you were getting so short. How many days, now?"

"Five."

"*Five?*"

"Five and a wake-up."

"Well, I guess it's best that you...that you sit it out at base camp," Press stammered. "Maybe get prepared for civilian life, buy a 'House and Home' or some magazine and get reacquainted with a flush toilet or some other modern convenience."

"They don't sell those kind of magazines. 'Playboy' might have a toilet—you know, some chick lounging in the tub next to the toilet."

"Yeah, well, why don't you pack and we'll get on the road."

"Pack? You sound like I got something to take back. There's only one essential possession in life—geez, I'm even starting to talk like you—a toothbrush." With that he twirled his toilet kit.

"Okay, let's get on the road, then."

"I can stay a couple of more days if you want. Escort you and the magazine gal around."

Press thought for a moment as they stood up. "Better not. If you stayed, I'd be responsible for you."

"Seems to me that it's been that way since you got here, don't ya know."

"True, but there's a big difference. If you'd been blown away yesterday, I'd certainly feel sad. But if it were to happen tomorrow, I'd feel sad *and* guilty."

"I'll just stay at Dong Ha, then, and you won't hear me askin' to come back like Schade," Snowy said, grinning.

"His last note was the day before he left for Cam Ranh. I think it'll be some time before he forgives himself."

They drove to their work site, an LZ bordering QL-9, near Lang Vei, a former Special Forces outpost which had been overrun by an NVA battalion in 1967. Bill King's platoon had nearly completed clearing the trees and overgrowth. Press's platoon had been grading the LZ, and much of it was already in use.

The two platoon leaders greeted each other and discussed their objectives for the day. Press then asked if King knew the reason why the operation commanders were insisting that they complete the LZ by the next day.

King thought for a moment and said, "Some of the pilots who came in late yesterday afternoon told me that the *ARVN* are getting it even worse than last week. The NVA has tanks and apparently they're damn hard to target from the air."

"Sounds like it might get busy here in the next couple of weeks. We'll have an oil truck tomorrow, so we'll give it a good coating of peneprime. But on to important matters. How's the pig roast going?" One of King's men shot a boar while clearing a patch of jungle and several of the engineers who had taken R&R in Hawaii were cooking it luau-style.

"Not bad. It sat out a few hours while they got the rocks super hot, but steam is coming out of the ground, and the aroma is starting to whet our appetites."

"You going to share it with the arty boys?"

King laughed. His platoon was bivouacked with a 175mm howitzer battery. "They can have any leftovers. We'd be more generous if they didn't keep us up at night blasting away in Laos. Hope they're taking out more NVA than *ARVN*."

Press and Snowy arrived at the Quang Tri airport just before noon. Rebecca was standing in the main building, a depressingly shabby waiting room filled with heavy dark wooden benches and a musty odor. She was wearing fatigues and, except for a lack of insignia, would easily be mistaken for an army nurse. She saw Press stroll into the room and walked quickly to him, greeting him with a hug and a kiss on his cheek.

"It's so good to see you, Press," she said warmly.

"You look great, Rebecca, and fresh, although you must be exhausted from the journey. How long have you been waiting?"

"Less than an hour, and I'm not tired. I've had two whole days in Da Nang and plenty of rest between visits to the Press Center. I'm ready to see the war."

"Well, I'd like you to meet one fellow who won't be showing—"

"You've got to be Snowy," Rebecca cut in. "I'm very glad to meet you. I've heard a lot about you."

"This is Rebecca Sperling," Press said.

"The pleasure's all mine," said Snowy with a sideways glance at Press. "But what's this the lieutenant's been telling you?"

"It's all good. He always writes how lucky he is to have you."

Snowy beamed and said to Press. "You know, LT, I wouldn't mind staying an extra day, just so you don't have to drive yourself."

Press thought for a moment and said, "We came through the war this far together. I guess one more day won't hurt."

"This is your duffel bag, Miss Sperling? I'll take it to the jeep." Snowy grabbed the bag by the strap and hoisted it to his shoulder. "Mighty heavy for such a small"—glancing at her fatigue shirt— "er, short person."

"You don't know how women travel," she laughed. "I consider it traveling light."

"The only western females Snowy has seen in a year are a few USO entertainers and a couple of Red Cross pastry—doughnut dollies," said Press. "Looks like the boys in Da Nang equipped you pretty well."

"They were all very professional, although they tried to dissuade me from coming up here unescorted."

"Doesn't look like you had any problems with connections."

"Not at all. Quite a few supply planes were headed here. I even had a choice."

"Let's go join Snowy and get on our way. I know a place where we can grab a quick lunch."

The place was a drab mess hall in Dong Ha. The food was heavy and bland, except for the fried potatoes, which left an oily aftertaste. But the conversation was good. Rebecca filled Press in on the details of her life of late, most notably that she now had two men interested in her. Her magazine had finally printed the article she wrote on the Army's practice of filling its ranks with mostly lower class and lower-middle class inductees, and it had been well received. The government, she had argued, carried out the policy with the complicity of the upper middle class. Both preferred to continually lower standards rather than curtail student deferments or call reserve units to active duty.

"I remember one of the passages in the draft you sent—the one where you drew an analogy between the Roman Army and ours," Press said, waving a fly away from his face. "The decay of the Roman Army and then of the Empire began when the Army started filling its ranks from young men in the provinces—surrogate soldiers."

"You don't agree?"

"Well, my contention is that when this war finally ends, the Army's going to do something about standards and drugs and discipline. It can't let what's happening become permanent."

"What about the proposals floating around for an all-volunteer army? If that happens, the present state of the enlisted ranks may become institutionalized," she reasoned.

Snowy stood and rolled his eyes. "I'll let you two argue this out alone. I'm going out to the jeep and have a smoke."

"We're right behind you," Press said, rising.

They walked out of the mess hall as more than a few eyes followed Rebecca.

"Most of those guys haven't seen a female round eye for a while," Snowy explained, settling himself behind the wheel.

"So I better get used to it, right?"

"A size larger fatigue shirt wouldn't hurt," Press offered.

She ignored him and turned to Snowy. "I meant to ask you when we left Quang Tri why you've got sand bags in the jeep?"

Snowy peered at the single layer of sandbags resting on the floor boards. A triumphant grin spread over his face. "Psy-cho-log-i-cal," he replied, as if prolonging the pronunciation deepened its meaning.

Rebecca arched her eyebrows.

"He's just showing a little ankle," Press quipped from the back seat.

They drove west along QL-9, turning off at Camp Carroll to give Rebecca a tour of the Montagnard village. "They're so different," she exclaimed. "They look like some primitive tribe in the rain forest."

Press thought for a moment. "I don't believe they've ever intermingled with the Vietnamese, at least not wholesale. They were brought down here from the high hills, from where we're going. It's like two different worlds, down here and up there. You may think what you saw on the way is subsistence farming, but the coastal plain is the rice bowl. In the hills and mountains it's damn tough to scratch out a living, so the Montagnards have traditionally been left alone and isolated."

"I've heard they're pretty tough, better fighters than the South Vietnamese."

"Think of it this way. The South Vietnamese Army is a jelly donut, the Montagnards a toasted English muffin, and the North Vietnamese a frozen bagel. There's that much difference in the hardness scale. Between the North and the South, it's difficult to imagine how one people can be so different."

"What he means to say," Snowy interpreted, "is that the NVA is kicking butt."

Rebecca laughed. "You're like my editor—wring out the excess words and get to the point."

Snowy swung the jeep around and drove back to QL-9. Press pointed out the Rockpile and recounted the misery of the Marines who were so often given the task of rooting out the NVA from its inner reaches. "In most wars," he added, "you take a place once, maybe twice. In this war it's a moveable farce of taking and retaking."

They came upon a column of trucks stopped on the road about a mile south of the Rockpile. Many of the drivers were standing on the shoulder staring at a billowing stream of black smoke several hundred meters ahead. Press left the jeep and talked briefly with a sergeant. "A tanker truck was hit by a mortar about twenty minutes ago," he explained, when he returned. "Six rounds were lobbed in; they got lucky with one."

"Anybody killed?" asked Rebecca.

"The driver and shotgun got out all right. Fortunately, the truck was carrying diesel fuel. Had it been JP-4 or gasoline, it probably would have blown at once."

"I assume we're in disputed territory—I mean the whole country is disputed, but the area we're in now is more so?" Rebecca asked.

Press nodded. "I think since the Tet offensive the NVA and Viet Cong have pretty much conceded the coastal plain, where the bulk of the people live. The VC is a skeleton of its former self, so all the action is with the NVA. And really all they have to do is wait till we leave."

"So you believe that the real reason for the operation is to see if the *ARVN* can take the fight to the NVA?"

"Exactly, but with our air support, it's not an even match."

"That's not what they told us at the Press Center."

"You probably got the standard stuff about destroying supplies on the Ho Chi Minh Trail to thwart an NVA offensive this year."

Rebecca changed the subject. "How long do you expect we'll be here?"

"Another half-hour or so. They'll get a bulldozer or tank retriever or something from Vandegrift and push it off the road," Press responded.

"Well, I'll just soak up the sun then; it's so nice and warm. March in New York is dreary beyond measure—all concrete and cloudy."

It was over an hour before they skirted Vandegrift and began driving along the river valley. The sun was low in the sky, perched now just above the hills, and they passed through the thickening shadows of bamboo and elephant grass. It reminded Press of the midnight mission to open the road, now seemingly so long ago. His thoughts were summoned to the present when the left front tire hit a hole and Snowy hit the steering wheel with his palm and issued a curt "goddamn."

"What was that?" Rebecca asked, inquisitive rather than alarmed.

"Oh, just the sound of a U-joint destructing," Snowy answered. He brought the jeep to a halt, got out and retrieved a couple of wrenches from the tool box, then slid under the chassis.

"Happens about once a month," Press said casually. "We'll be on our way in a couple of minutes—in front wheel drive."

"Looks like *Minderbinder* has been through a couple of wars," Rebecca remarked.

"You're probably right. We've got a newer jeep in reserve at Khe Sanh, but Snowy has an affinity for the old Ford."

"Ford? I thought *jeep* was a trade name."

"Officially, there's some long military name describing a general purpose utility vehicle and its weight, but everybody calls it a *jeep*, no matter who makes it. Remember the old movie reels of World War Two—those humpback Chevy or Ford staff cars with two small rear windows? They looked like they had the outer shell of an insect. And then a jeep would go by—basically the same jeep that we spend hours in every day: driving, radioing, writing sitreps, drinking beer in. We could have inherited *Minderbinder* from soldiers in the Philippines, France or, more fittingly, Italy. The thing is timeless."

Rebecca laughed. "You're as fond of it as Snowy. When you start looking at it longingly, I'll know you've been here too long."

"You know, it does have nice lines and I haven't looked at anyone longingly since July—"

"Shh," Rebecca whispered. "Snowy will hear you."

Press was having fun, and he had no intention of stopping. "Of course now that I can eyeball both, *Minderbinder* doesn't stack up—forgive the pun—'to a girlish, womanly, female, feminine dame'"—the lyrics sung off-tune.

"Don't try to *South Pacific* me; I'm not a naive nurse."

Snowy pulled his head out from under the jeep. "So, does that mean you two won't be making beautiful music together?"

"I suppose you heard the whole exchange?" she sniffed.

"As the LT would say, *Minderbinder* has the acoustics of an opera hall." Snowy picked himself up, dusted-off his fatigues, and resumed his place behind the wheel.

They were nearing their old night defensive perimeter as twilight embraced the valley. From their vantage point, they could see a column of dust queuing up at the edge of the river about a half mile ahead of them.

"Truck convoy," Press said matter-of-factly. "We probably ought to spend the night at our old night defensive perimeter. A troop from the fifth mech has it now; from the way we strung wire all over, it's safer than driving to Khe Sanh in the dark."

"If I weren't along, would you be stopping?" Rebecca inquired.

"Not if I were alone. But with you here and Snowy extending for a day, I'm not taking any chances."

Press went to the CP after Snowy pulled into the familiar perimeter. He returned a few minutes later and told Snowy that one of their former shelters—Press's—was available. Then he asked Rebecca if she had ever slept in a hole in the ground. She had not. "Well," he said, "it's covered by culvert halves and sand bags and not too bad with an air mattress. Snowy and I will be on either side. If there's anything you need from your duffel bag, better get it out now. You won't be able to even light a match, and it's going to be very dark tonight if we get ground fog. Oh, one other thing—when nature calls, there's the slit trench; just wait till it's dark enough."

"Too bad I can't go like the Vietnamese woman I saw out in the field, standing with one pajama leg rolled all the way up."

"I know. I was amazed at the first time I saw a mamasan pee—a stream as straight as a man's and parallel to the leg."

While Snowy rounded up some chow, Press gave Rebecca a tour of the NDP. "Is that a tank or an artillery piece—the one with the long snout?" she asked of the first track vehicle in view.

"It's a tank, of sorts—a light tank, called a Sheridan. It's really paper mache disguised as armor," Press said, pointing to the turret. "It's fast, but speed in the jungle is not exactly an asset." Changing the subject, he said, "You can see the men taking up positions on the berm just inside the wire. They'll rotate guard duty with the guy next to them."

"I can't imagine anybody crawling through all that wire," Rebecca said, impressed by the stacks of concertina.

"If the guards stay awake, sappers will never get through."

They sat down near the CP and ate their meals. Snowy gobbled his and went off. Press and Rebecca watched the last trucks of the convoy wend their way past the NDP. "This is so different from the last time we spent the night together," she said. "It seems like both yesterday and some distant yesteryear."

"For me, New York is in another world, and everything prior to Vietnam is another time."

"There's no *yesterday* in your memory?"

"Of course there is. I think of it more than I should; you shared a difficult moment with me and helped me face a dismal prospect."

"And now you're helping me get a perspective on the war that would have been impossible otherwise," she said appreciatively.

"One thing's for certain: you can't get a view like this in New York...or anywhere."

The road had been eclipsed by a rolling stream of dust parallel to the river, its billowy fringe iridescent in the last glimmer of light over the rapids.

Press and Rebecca sat motionless, enlivened, transfixed, as they watched the two utterly incompatible forms of dust and water silently and harmoniously flowing away in the dusk.

They turned in early in the evening, as fog began to creep up the narrow river basin. The last sound Press heard before drifting off was the snoring of the off-duty guards. He was in deep slumber when the explosion shook the NDP. Had it not been so near, he might have shaken it off. Instead, Press reached for his .45 and rolled onto his stomach. Several flares were fired simultaneously, and their brilliant flames illuminated the deepest shadows in the darkest time of night. With his right eye open, he glanced at the perimeter and glimpsed two figures in the blinding light, one of whom was throwing something into Snowy's former shelter. It was all so fast: shouting to Rebecca to stay down, the satchel charge exploding, and the sapper racing back to the wire. In seconds the explosions and small arms fire ceased, replaced by shouts, curses, and a few screams. Press went over to the shelter, then called for a medic. A few minutes later he returned to Snowy and Rebecca and related the GI's condition. "The blast severed his leg. He's in shock, but the medic says he will live."

"How did they get in?" Rebecca asked, "It looked impregnable."

"They cut the wire next to the stream. The guards must have been asleep," he reasoned.

Snowy cleared his throat and said, "I'll tell ya, Boss, that's one doozy of a send-off, don't ya know. When we get to Khe Sanh, I'll be getting on the first truck out."

They rose at first light and surveyed the damage. A rocket propelled grenade round had hit a Sheridan tank, scarifying the soldier inside. One of the tankers remarked that the medics had to pick body parts stuck to the inner walls. There were only two casualties, and the tankers were now going about business as usual.

As they got into the jeep, Rebecca shook her head and the expression on her face was of incredulity. "How can they be so blasé about it? He was killed so horribly," she protested.

"It's probably protection against fear. Because there are no front lines here, everybody in the field is constantly at risk—from an ambush, a sniper, an RPG, a land mine, boobytrap, mortar, rocket, artillery. You can be a victim of any of those at any time. The point is"—Press paused for effect—"fear is ever-present, like some insidious disease, and either you manage it or it will manage you."

"So tell me, are you like that? Blasé, I mean."

"I think for almost everybody who has been out here for a while it's an acquired taste. How about you, Snowy?"

"I don't know about that taste BS, but the LT is right, except for a lot of guys when they become short-timers. Look what happened to Schade. Christ, he was so short, his ba—his chin was dragging on the ground." Snowy went on to tell Rebecca of Schade giving in to fear.

"Why didn't you let him back, even for a day?" Rebecca asked Press.

"Well, that's just like a woman."

"What's like a woman?"

"The way you're chiding me for being too hardnose. If I screwed up, it was in his favor. What he did probably would have gotten him shot in other wars, or in prison."

"Will the real Press Patrick please stand up? What happened to the nonchalant, the—"

"You know, you've got a lot of chutzpah," Press cut her off. "I do have a serious side, even though there's little reason for it."

Rebecca laughed. "Chutzpah, huh? I know you've got a serious side; in fact, I think you cut a wider swath with it than you'd agree with."

Snowy turned to Press, stroked his three-day growth and said, "Hey, Boss. I don't know what language you two are going at it in, but I'll bet a ten spot she's gettin' the best of it."

Press leaned forward. "Now look at what you've encouraged. He's got his eyes off the road and one hand on the wheel in a place where ten or twelve trucks have landed in the dying cockroach position not so long ago."

Rebecca peered almost straight down at the river bank forty feet below and, noticing their proximity to disaster, sucked in her breath.

"I've been on this stretch so many times, I can drive it with my eyes closed, don't ya know," Snowy joked.

"When we get to the Khe Sanh turn-off, he might as well drive with his eyes closed," Press added. "You know when you go into a room that hasn't been cleaned for a while, and the afternoon sun plays on dust floating in the air? Well, last week Snowy and I watched a convoy go by, kicking up a billion sun-flecked particles, and each passing truck damn near dissolved in the dingy light."

"He's trying to make it easy for me to leave," said Snowy, looking at Rebecca.

It would not be easy. Shortly after arriving at Khe Sanh, they washed and ate breakfast. Snowy then ambled to the jeep, retrieved his toilet kit, and joined Press near his trailer. He pursed his lips imitating Press imitating Holt.

With mounting emotion, he said, "Good luck, LT...Good luck, Press. It's been a helluva partnership."

Press placed his left hand on Snowy's elbow. With equal emotion, he responded, "I can't believe you're actually leaving. This damn war won't be the same without you."

"Don't worry, you're all broken in now and don't need nobody."

Press laughed and put his arm around Snowy's shoulder. "Well, I'm sure as hell going to miss you, don't ya know."

"Ditto." Snowy reached in his breast pocket and handed Press a piece of paper. "How 'bout dropping me a line, just to let me know you got out of here in one piece."

"Will do. Take care, Snowy. Oh, when you get to Cam Ranh, you might want to shave; just so they'll let you leave country."

"Naw, I'll get a profile." He extended his hand a last time and said with feeling, "Goodbye, Press." He turned and waved to Rebecca, who was standing a few yards away. She returned his wave and blew him a kiss.

Press took Rebecca to the press tent at the western sector of the combat base. After checking in and dropping her duffel bag, they toured the airfield and visited the broken remains of a C-130 cargo plane.

"How did it happen?" she asked.

"A rocket got it as it was taking off in sixty-eight. See the exposed rock on that mountain? It's called rocket ridge. The NVA doesn't use it anymore, but they still fire on the airstrip once or twice a day from somewhere up there."

"You mean they could fire right now, while we're standing here?"

"We're almost on our way. Ready to see a live work site?" She nodded, and he began to pull out, but stopped before reaching the road.

"Changing your mind?"

He pointed east. There, not one hundred feet above and close to them, was a heavy dark cloud dragging a wet tail across the plateau.

"By all means, let's wait for our friend to pass."

The drops made popping sounds as they plopped into the hot, dust-glazed ground. The cloud passed over inconsequentially, and they set off for the LZ work site with a contrail of dust. Arriving in early afternoon, he explained the type of work his platoon was engaged in on the site. Rebecca then interviewed several of the engineers, who were glad for the novelty and the work break. An hour later they walked to the far end of the LZ, where the land clearing operation was continuing. King greeted them and offered each a can of soda from a large igloo container.

"You got a couple of dozers down, Bill?" Press asked.

"Five of my guys were medevaced early this morning—stomach poisoning. Apparently, the boar wasn't cooked long enough or hot enough in a couple of places." He went on to relate for Rebecca's benefit how the wild pig became yesterday's evening meal.

She asked him about his men, his opinion of the war, his life in the states. Revealed in their discussion was a joint acquaintance—a close friend of hers from college had been a classmate of his in high school. After the exchange of a few anecdotes, he fished for his wallet and showed her several pictures of his wife and daughter.

"How you must miss them," Rebecca said, after admiring the photos. "When do you *DEROS*?"

"I see Press has educated you in military jargon. I've got six months, three days and a wake-up," he said with a smile and the exactitude common to almost everyone serving in Vietnam.

"Somehow I knew there'd be a *wake-up* in your answer." She turned to Press. "How far from here is the Laotian border?"

"About nine kilometers, wouldn't you say, Bill."

"Yeah, nine or ten."

"Can we drive there?"

Press thought for a moment. "I guess it's all right, as long as we get back to Khe Sanh before nightfall."

"There was an ambush on the road two days ago," King cautioned.

"You still want to go?" Press asked her.

"Sure," she said without hesitation.

"We'll catch you tomorrow, Bill," he said, and he and Rebecca started for the jeep.

"Can I have a word with you before you go?" King asked Press.

"Sure." And then to Rebecca, "I'll be back in a minute."

When they were out of earshot, King gave Press a quizzical look. "What the hell's going on here?"

Press explained quickly how he met Rebecca and why he was escorting her during the operation.

"You mean to tell me you haven't been screwing her? Does Celia know about her?"

"No, I'm not screwing her and no, Celia knows nothing about her. Besides, Celia's dating someone else. She found out that I had a one-night-stand before we met, which confirmed her doubts about me."

"I can't believe she's going with another guy."

"She says it's platonic…is that possible?"

"No, and that's why I believe there's something going on between you and Rebecca."

"Believe me, Bill, this is purely professional. I'll see you tomorrow, okay?"

"Yeah, but be careful out by the border. The NVA is getting bolder."

Press walked back and started the jeep. They bounced over the rough terrain for a minute and then turned west on the road. The scenery near the Laotian border was different from the area of Khe Sanh. The red clay was no longer ever-present, sharing the landscape with a drab tawny loam. The countryside flattened as the road poured out of rolling hills and into a river valley. Almost as a counterbalance to the horizontal scrubland, there appeared a vast limestone escarpment a mere two kilometers distant on their left flank.

"Oh, it's stunning," Rebecca gasped. "Stop for a second, for a quick picture, will you?"

Press stopped in the middle of the road and gazed into the tree-line on both sides. "It's called *Co Roc*, inside Laos. We'll run parallel to it for a few klicks. Anybody who still believes the earth is 6,000 years old only has to look at that—600 feet of limestone cut away by a second rate river."

Rebecca took several shots of *Co Roc*, and they resumed their drive to the border. A sign from Press's battalion welcomed travelers to Laos; another warned US military personnel not to cross into Laos. Ahead a little was a small stone pyramid—the official border marker—placed by the French long ago.

"This is it?" Rebecca asked, obviously expecting more.

"It is rather nondescript," Press agreed. "But it's the demarcation line, at least for ground troops between Dewey Canyon Two and Lam Son 719."

"They told us in the Da Nang briefing that Lam Son was the name for the *ARVN* incursion, but we were never told what it stood for."

"It was the village birthplace of a famous Vietnamese who defeated a Chinese Army back in the 1400s."

"You'd think they'd get tired of calling every operation Lam Son something."

"Well, when the North wins, every future battle will become a sequence of wherever Uncle Ho was born."

"So they're fighting it out down that road?" Rebecca asked.

"About fifteen klicks in. Do you hear the artillery fire? It's faint, but if you listen carefully, you can hear the queen of battle at work."

"Queen of battle?"

"That's what Stalin called it, probably because it causes the most casualties in war."

"You're full of historical tidbits. Maybe the Army should keep you on."

Press was about to respond when he saw a three-quarter ton truck coming toward them from the Vietnam side. It stopped at the border, and a tall man with a narrow face and a sallow complexion, perhaps in his late twenties, hopped out. He thanked the driver and watched as the truck turned around. "So this is where you're hiding," he said to Rebecca.

"Press Patrick, meet Sid Miller from UPI," was her curt introduction. "Sid and I were at the Press Center together in Da Nang."

The two shook hands and Press offered the correspondent a ride back to Khe Sanh after he had had his fill of the border.

"Thanks, but I'm not going back."

Rebecca looked down the deserted road and with a pained expression asked, "You're going into Laos?"

"Of course, that's where the action is," Miller stated matter-of-factly.

Press stood in the center of the road, his hands on his hips, and looked down at his feet, shaking his head. He understood immediately how Miller's stroll toward the Ho Chi Minh Trail would kindle Rebecca's competitive instincts. With a grave expression he gazed directly into Miller's eyes and said, "The NVA has already killed four journalists so far in the operation. If you walk down that road, you may be presenting them number five as a gift."

"I appreciate your concern, and I'm aware that there's an element of risk involved."

"You were probably told that the *ARVN* is holding its own. It's not. There's nothing but chaos on the Trail; shells are flying everywhere, and there's no protected or safe real estate—hell, you're not even carrying a damn canteen."

"Just the same, I'll take my chances." If Miller's equable manner cloaked an inner uneasiness, Press saw no hint of it.

Rebecca then tried to talk him out of going, but he put her off in the same polite but firm way he did with Press. They watched him walk into Laos with an indifferent, loping gait.

"I realize that you can't take me, but maybe if I got a ride with the next Vietnamese truck—"

"Don't even think about it, Rebecca. You're not here on that assignment, and with your looks and appeal, the *ARVN* would gang rape you no more than a mile in."

She stood watching, lips compressed, as Miller disappeared around a bend in the road. "He sure has pluck," she finally said.

"*Pluck*? Come on, Rebecca. Pluck doesn't get you killed. The guy's deluding himself. A reporter looking for a scoop couldn't do any better than talking to chopper pilots at an LZ or two—they're way stations of information."

Her face brightened. "I know it's not my assignment, but I wouldn't mind contributing. Lieutenant, lead the way."

Later in the afternoon, at the nearly completed LZ, Press sent his engineers back to Khe Sanh. Bill King returned with his men to the NDP they shared with an artillery battery. Press and Rebecca sat in his jeep talking, as they waited for a helicopter to land. They did not wait long. At a few minutes before five o'clock, they heard the distinctive sound of a Huey.

"Jackpot!" Press shouted, as the chopper came into view.

"Oh, my God!" Rebecca exclaimed. "They're hanging all over."

The Huey cleared the trees with almost a score of *ARVN* soldiers stuffed in the crew compartment and hanging from and standing on both skids. One of the soldiers fell as the chopper hovered twelve feet above ground. He scrambled out of the wash as the Huey landed. Press and Rebecca made their way to the craft once the blades stopped, and the pilot told them that he had radioed Khe Sanh and a truck was on the way for the *ARVN*. "Lost two or three on the way," he said, with no apparent regret. "It's pretty hot right now—lot's of shit being thrown." Rebecca was writing rapidly and when the pilot was finished, she went from crew member to crew member slaking her omnivorous appetite for detail.

Press sat in his jeep, his feet propped on the flattened windshield, drinking a beer. It was a sparkling afternoon, the sky scrubbed clean of clouds and warm, slanting sunbeams filtering through the stirring leaves of perimeter trees. He finished his beer and was about to nod-off, when he heard a muffled explosion, perhaps a kilometer to the west. Within a minute a scream leapt out of his radio. "Help! Help!" it pleaded. "They're dead, oh my God, they're dead." Rebecca heard the cry and came running. Press gunned the engine the second she was seated, and they bounced violently over the undulating LZ. They continued to listen to the anguished voice as they raced toward the scene of the tragedy.

Press saw the engineer, a dozer operator, gripping the handset, now calling for a medevac. He braked immediately, jumped from the jeep and ran to him. "Where?" he shouted. The engineer pointed to an area behind the parked bulldozers. Press dashed to the rear of the closest dozer and quickly looked away, the color draining from his face. His stomach began to feel as though it was being threshed. Rebecca came up, saw his look of infinite desolation, paid no heed to his warning to keep back, and almost stumbled on a leg severed near the hip. She began retching violently, vomit spewing over the ground. Press took one more look, making sure that all were dead, including Bill King. He lead Rebecca back to the jeep, then walked to the adjacent artillery unit, where the reaction bordered on indifference. It was too bad, but they *were* dead, weren't they? A medevac was on its way with body bags—they were out. No, they didn't hear the incoming, must have been in an acoustic shadow, whatever that meant.

After the medevac left with the bodies, Press and Rebecca drove back to Khe Sanh in silence.

"Why don't I come by in a couple of days," he suggested. "You can talk to the troops here and get all you need for your story."

"Yes, I guess that would be best." In a barely audible and tremulous voice she went on, "Oh, Press, it's so terrible."

He took her in his arms and they stood for a minute, before he said, "My last words to him were trivial...sorry, that's a selfish sentiment." He let his arms fall, took several steps toward the jeep and turned her way for a moment. "We'll probably never know, but I hope that it was theirs, not ours."

27

The next morning, Padgett informed Press that a sergeant first class would be reporting to the company, and he intended to assign him to Press's platoon. He was still digesting the news as Sfc. Terry Banks strode into the HQ tent, dropped his gear on the ground and, in a voice that drowned out the whine of the generator outside, reported for duty.

Banks was short, not over five-seven, just a sliver on the beefy side, but with a quick eye and an affable manner. Press liked him immediately. Banks explained that he had come over on a chopper from Quang Tri and was ready to go to the field straight-off. On the way to the LZ jobsite, Press learned that Banks had been born and raised in Texas, was married, had no children, and that this was his second tour in Vietnam. By the end of the day he became convinced that the young E-7—he would be thirty in three days—would some day be a command sergeant major.

Early the following morning, Press, accompanied by Allen, the dozer operator, parked his jeep near the press tent and waved to Rebecca, who was chatting with two other journalists.

"Good morning," he said, as she excused herself and walked to the jeep. "How was your day, yesterday?"

"True to form. We heard how the *ARVN* were interdicting the Trail successfully, although the fighting was fierce. A half a dozen of us went to Lang Vei, where an APC and a helicopter were hit in an ambush on Route Nine near Lao Bao. When an armored cavalry unit at Lang Vei was ordered to retrieve them, fifty-three soldiers refused. Apparently, they used pretty strong language with their officers."

Press introduced Allen to Rebecca and said, "I don't think you ought to go on the road anymore. The NVA are obviously getting bolder. Our first platoon was working out past Lang Vei and lost a dozer to a land mine. Padgett wants me to see if I can wangle a replacement from headquarters."

"Anyone injured?" she asked.

"No, but it destroyed one of the tracks. You care to come along and scope the place out?"

"Wouldn't miss it for the world: Press Patrick insinuates himself into the good graces of the major domos."

Headquarters was in a house, one of the few structures to survive years of war. They walked into a large central room, and Press talked to several of the enlisted staff about acquiring the dozer parked out back. While Rebecca surveyed the room, he approached a captain, who listened to his request for a few seconds and then cut him short: "Lieutenant, you can't just walk in here and requisition a bulldozer like you do toilet paper. It doesn't work that way."

"What way does it work?" Press asked, noting that the captain was wearing unfaded fatigues, and wondered if this was his first tour.

"Fill out the combat loss report and apply for a replacement. This is our only bulldozer, and we may need it for an emergency. Maybe we can get you one from Quang Tri in a week or two."

"Captain, you don't have anybody capable of operating a dozer; in an emergency, you'll be calling on us."

"Sorry, that's the best I can do."

"Do you mind if I go over your head, to a major or maybe a colonel?" Press asked, exasperated.

"Look, goddamn it, Lieutenant, yes, I mind. You can't have that dozer, and that's final."

A brigadier general had walked out of an office while the staff captain was upbraiding Press and, after pausing a few moments, approached them and asked what the dispute was about. Press spoke while the captain's first word was still in his mouth and explained why Echo Company needed the dozer parked outside.

"Take it," the general said.

Press thanked him and strode to where Allen was waiting. Grasping him by the arm, he said, "Jerry, get on that dozer just as fast as you can and walk it to back to the company area." When he and Rebecca were in the jeep, he said, "I believe I may have underestimated the Army—some officers, like General Sweeney back there, probably do rise to the top on merit."

"You certainly know how to make friends and influence people," she said.

"I'm still stunned. I can no longer believe what Catherine the Great said about generals: 'They deal with paper. We deal with human skin.' You know, we may finally be out of reach of official stenographers, praise singers, and paperweight bearers."

"Is there no other road to use?" she changed the subject. "The dust is suffocating, and it's so terribly difficult to get clean around here."

"I've got a remedy for that. There's a magical place down by the end of the runway. Remember those Tarzan movies with the waterfall where Tarzan and Jane would frolic? Well, we have our own waterfall, and you get to play Jane. I'll take you there at dusk for a shower, when there won't be anyone around."

They drove to the new helipad, where Press detailed the impediments his platoon faced during construction. Only twelve choppers were there now, but more than one hundred would park there overnight, he told her. The rockets and ammunition were stored in a depression on the northwest side. He became voluble during the tour, and Rebecca soon asked him if he rather liked it here. "No, no," he exclaimed. But after a moment's reflection, he tempered his protestation. "Let me put it this way. One, the work is challenging—not boring, like base camp would be. Two, we don't have any drug problems. Three, the lower road was constricting and the weather foul, so it seemed sometimes like we were working in a tunnel. Up here it's wide open with the horizon bulging at its seams. And it's often bright and warm with sunsets of cinnabar."

"You sound like a travel agent promoting a vacation spot."

Almost as a punctuation to her sentence, rockets began to slam into the airstrip. "No need to duck," Press advised. "The runway's just getting its daily dose. Rockets aren't very accurate, but they generally stay within a hundred meters or so of the strip. They haven't hit anything of note since we re-opened the place."

"You may be use to it, but they're a little too close for my comfort zone. How about showing me something on the periphery?"

They got into the jeep and drove to the *MASH* unit located on the western edge of the base. No one challenged their entry into the vast olive drab tent, and they stood in a corner watching the surgeons preparing the wounded for airlift to the medical station at Quang Tri. The four patients being treated were helicopter crew members. The one closest to them had been hit by a large caliber round, which had traveled along the length of his inside upper arm, between the elbow and the shoulder. His hand was tethered to a stand, and his arm hung limply. A surgeon stanched the bleeding and wrapped the entire limb in clear cellophane. The patient's eyes, dulled by morphine, were fixed on his devastated arm. Minutes later, he was whisked to a chopper for the next stage of treatment, then perhaps to the hospital ship *USS Sanctuary*.

As promised, Press took Rebecca to the waterfall at dusk, stopping briefly at the company area for soap and towels. The stream that fed the waterfall was only eighteen inches wide. They stepped over it, and he led her down a pathway through a stand of bamboo and short, spiny-leafed trees clumped together, exiting beyond a dense damp canopy at the base of the falls. "Don't stand in the middle of the stream while you shower," he cautioned. "It may only be a ten foot drop, but the water will hammer your head and shoulders... and your, well, you know."

"Oh, I know—you stand guard and keep anybody from glimpsing the *you knows*."

"Yes, ma'am. I'll be waiting at the top." Press retraced his steps and stood vigil. He did not expect to encounter anyone, as most troops would be at evening mess.

He looked at his watch several times while waiting and after about ten minutes shouted, "You okay down there?" He heard no response over the steady sound of falling water. Shadows, thrown haphazardly across the ground, darkened perceptively. He let two more minutes pass, then repeated his call. Hearing nothing, he walked halfway to the falls, keeping his eyes to the ground. "Rebecca!" he shouted again. He took a few more steps, glanced down the path and, although his view of the falls were obstructed, caught sight of her fatigues draped over a rock. The next moment she stepped into view, her arms arched about her head, wrapping the army issue towel around her hair. She looked up at him before he had a chance to turn away. He merely shrugged his shoulders and climbed back up the path.

"I never figured you for a voyeur," Rebecca said, joining him at the jeep.

"I'm really sorry, but nobody spends fifteen minutes under that cold water, and I called to you several times. We *are* outside the wire, you know."

Rebecca looked at him askance for a moment and said, "It's noisy down there, and of course I had to wash my hair. Oh, well, it's not like this is the first time you've seen me in the buff."

"I can assure you it did me no good; it took all of the self- control I had to look away. I've never needed a cold shower like I do now, so wait here at the jeep and I'll be back in a few minutes."

When he returned in eight minutes, she grinned playfully. "Tell me, what's red and white and wet all over?"

"Red and white?" he began.

Rebecca laughed. "You under the waterfall. Your face and forearms are red, the rest of you is milky white."

"So, you got even."

"Oh, I just wanted to test myself."

"Did you pass?"

"Not even an up-tick in the pulse rate."

Press had intended for Rebecca to join Echo Company for evening chow, but the hot meal had been consumed and pots and pans were being scrubbed in the field kitchen.

"LT, we got some water buffalo leftover, if you and the lady are hungry," one of the cooks called out as twilight drew the day down.

"No thanks, Reggie. I've got some edibles in the trailer." Turning to Rebecca he said, "If you take Scotch without ice, I've got Johnnie Walker Black or, if you prefer, red wine."

"Wine is fine."

"Wine it is," Press said as he opened the door and climbed into his trailer. He came out with Vienna sausages, cheese and crackers, a bottle of claret and the last two pieces of a cake his mother had sent. He lifted ammo boxes for a table and chairs into the bed of a five-ton dump truck, spread a towel over a box and then helped her up.

"I've got to hand it to you, Press. Who would ever think of dining alfresco in a dump truck?"

"It's closer to the stars. Wait till it gets a little darker; you'll be able to touch them from here."

Pastels ran their palette on the horizon, and it remained warm in the unfolding evening as they ate and drank leisurely and talked animatedly. Later, they angled their "chairs" against the truck sides, leaned back and gazed upward. The air was dry and clear and the stars incandescent; even the dwarfs appeared emboldened, basking in the blaze of giants.

"I've never seen so many stars before," Rebecca said with emotion.

"Hell, you've got to get out of New York once in a while."

"Oh, I get out often enough—not like you though, getting to spend a whole year rusticating in the wilds."

"I know, some people have all the luck."

"I read somewhere that on a normal cloudless night you can see a thousand stars, but up here you can watch a thousand square pinwheel across the sky."

Their eyes lingered on the heavens for a time, and then Press broke the silence. "Why don't you stay here tonight. It's a little late to travel back to your quarters and my trailer's probably more comfortable."

"Are you propositioning me?" she asked, smiling.

"I'm sorely tempted, but no. I'll sleep in the command tent."

"When was the last time for you?"

"With you, in July."

"You haven't been with a Vietnamese girl?" she asked, incredulously.

"No. The closest I've come was a hand job at a steam 'n' cream in Hue."

"I'll ignore the pun...you must be horny as hell."

He smiled sheepishly, then shrugged.

She thought for a moment. "If you change your mind, I suppose it's all right—just for this one night."

Starlight defined her face, and he suppressed an impulse to kiss it. Battle lines formed: gratify the immediate desire or the lasting one, enliven the moment or exercise restraint, embrace the code of conduct of the war zone or the code of conduct of the conscience? He said, finally, "I don't know what's going to happen—whether I'll survive my tour, what my relationship with Celia will be—and I'm trying to prove a point."

"When do you see her?"

"Ten days."

"Well, if she rejects you, she'll be the loser."

"Thanks for the sentiment, but there'd be no winners."

While Rebecca went to Hue for two days, Press stayed with the platoon, which was engaged in several small jobs along Route 9. Each time he drove past the site where King and his men were killed, he felt a profound sadness. He considered writing to his widow, but what could he possibly say to diminish her grief: "Bill never knew what hit him?...he exemplified the finest in military tradition?" This is where religion salved the mortal wound with the promise of salvation, of everlasting happiness; for believers there could be no greater comfort. He hoped Anne was a believer.

His sadness was partially displaced, however, by two circumstances. The immediate one was the capability and leadership displayed by Terry Banks, which rendered his frequent absences during the past few days inconsequential. And his imminent trip to Hawaii and five days with Celia buoyed his spirits. His thoughts of her, however, were crimped by her lingering uncertainty of him.

Rebecca returned to Khe Sanh on the 23rd. She would be leaving the next day and wanted to run through the notes of her article with him. They had evening mess at Echo Company and afterward sat and talked next to a Coleman lantern in the headquarters' tent. Press asked her how she gauged the mood of Americans toward the war.

"It looks now as if a majority is against it—fifty-one percent in a poll this month. I don't think it matters much, though; Nixon will fight a skillful rear action and the boys won't be home by Christmas."

"I will, at least. I suppose I ought to be happy about it—I'm sure I will when the time comes—but this damn thing is total immersion—"

"What's that?" Rebecca broke in.

"Small arms fire. Either the troops are trigger happy, or we're being attacked."

Padgett rose from the poker table fifteen feet behind them, glanced at a machine in the communication's set-up and calmly announced, "Red alert. Let's get to our positions."

"Wait here," Press told Rebecca. "I've got to go to the perimeter." Dashing out of the tent with his M-16 before she could utter a word, he began to run the short distance to his platoon's sector. His eyes had not yet adjusted to the darkness and the berm beneath his feet disappeared unexpectedly. He hit hard on the ground, his lungs deflating with an agonizing hiss. Press lay there fighting for his breath. He finally gulped enough air for him to feel the pain in the knuckles of his right hand, which had struck the ground with the stock of his rifle in his grasp. When he rolled onto his back, Banks was standing over him.

"Sorry, sir," he said while extending Press a hand. "I modified the berm this afternoon to improve our field of fire. You okay?"

Press nodded, then said, "Just a face wound. If you don't tell anybody, I sure as hell won't." A few of the engineers who were already in position on the berm chuckled.

Banks helped Press to his feet and observed, "Looks like we've got sappers on the airstrip perimeter." The firing of small arms was concentrated along the flank of the runway, and a profusion of orange-red tracers from the rifles of the defenders ripped into hill beyond the wire. Artillery-fired flares illuminated the night sky, appearing for a while to be suspended hundreds of feet overhead, before slowly floating earthward.

Press told Banks that he was going to get a better view of the action and climbed onto the bed of a nearby dump truck. No more than a minute had passed when he heard, "How about a hand over here?"

"Rebecca? Christ, you can't come waltzing out in the middle of a fire fight—go back to the tent."

"No way. I saw you up there drinking it all in. I'm the reporter, remember, now help me or be responsible for a broken bone or two." Press reluctantly pulled her up on the bed and they watched as the firing trailed off.

"Do you think they got in?" she asked.

"I've no idea. It takes incredible finesse and patience to get through all that wire. If they got caught in the first line of wire, the answer's no. But Charlie is as good at infiltrating as we are bulling our way in. To paraphrase Balzac, we 'go in like a cannonball, they go under like a plague.' You've got to admire the bastards. If I had to do it, the sound of my heart beating would alert the guards."

"I think they've stopped."

"Look above the helipad," he said, pointing.

"At the flare?"

"That's not just another flare. It was fired on a flat trajectory, and it's not going to linger and burn out in the air."

"You think it might land on a helicopter?"

"Let's watch and see." They waited for almost a minute before Press shook his head and whispered, "Oh, shit."

"The re-arm pad?"

"Dead center. 2,000 degrees Fahrenheit. There's going to be hell to pay in a minute or two." His prediction was accurate, the burning flare igniting boxes containing rockets, the ensuing blaze setting off a pyrotechnic extravaganza.

"This is better than the Fourth of July," Rebecca said. "And it's all so random, you never know what direction the rockets will go."

"Well, if one comes our way, we'll have about two seconds to duck."

But none came their way. Most rockets made high stately bell curves, although an occasional one would corkscrew wildly, much to Rebecca's delight. Many of the projectiles landed on the helipad. So brilliant was the white-hot nucleus of the conflagration that its light reflected off the windshields of scores of choppers, which were lined-up in parade ground fashion facing the spectacle. Smoke rose profusely, so thick that rockets cooking off from the far end of the re-arm pad could not be seen until they emerged from the sides of the distended pale gray plume.

As they watched in fascination, he turned to her and said, "I recall a line in Faust that's fitting: 'It's like a living ember gleaming...And flashing, through the darkness streaming.'"

"I've heard it all—first Balzac, now Geothe while all hell's breaking loose."

"Geothe, at least, was damn prolific when it came to hell."

"There's probably a lot of scribbling going on near the press tent."

"What do you want to bet that they say Charlie did this?" He teased her.

"You don't think my esteemed colleagues saw the same thing we did?"

"They're not nearly as close."

"I'll make an announcement at breakfast. I'll even put it in my article, but that probably won't be for two weeks."

"The fire will burn for hours—you want a snack?"

"I'm starved. What have you got?"

"My mother sent me a cake—tastes like she doused it with double rations of grog. It'll probably knock you on your tush."

The red alert ended shortly after they climbed down from the truck, and they went to the tent to eat. Padgett uncorked a bottle of Drambuie and poured generous amounts into empty beer cans for Rebecca and Press and the returning card players. As he handed one to Press he said, "This is for medicinal purposes, for the walking wounded." While the others laughed, Press explained to Rebecca how he took a fall.

She watched him munch on a piece of cake and follow it up with a sip of liqueur, his feet propped on a cot. "War is hell," she said.

"I'll drink to that."

The next morning Rebecca arrived at the company area just as the engineers were finishing morning mess. She thanked the jeep driver and walked to a newly assembled culvert, where Press was sitting drinking coffee.

"Morning," he greeted her, rising. "Have you had breakfast?"

"Just finished."

"How about coffee, then? It's not good, but it's hot."

"Love some, thanks." He got her coffee, and they sat down on the culvert. "Last night was quite entertaining. You guys really know how to put on a production."

"Yeah, it's a specialty of the Army—better than a USO show. Who says friendly fire can't be fun?"

Rebecca ignored his remark. "I'll never forget it—my whole time here. It's so awful, yet there's another dimension, something I don't want to admit to, but I think it's in every journalist."

"Soldiers too. It's job related. Of course, no one forces you to become a journalist."

"You may be a reluctant soldier, but you still feel it."

"That's because of the high stakes. If you screw up in most regular jobs or are unlucky, you get fired. If you lose a game, you shrug your shoulders, maybe feel bad, or settle the wager. If you screw up or are unlucky out here, you're likely to wind up in a body bag. There's a disturbing fascination with the prospect."

"I think that the fascination is normal."

"So do I. That's why I said *disturbing.*"

"You mean that people will cause death and destruction because it fascinates them?"

"I guess what I mean is that after the last couple of thousand years of recorded human experience, there's still a hell of a lot of us who *enjoy* it. Some of the greatest minds—Plato, Rousseau, Jefferson—believed education would civilize mankind. It hasn't. We're no better now at the core than we were at the beginning."

"That's a very dark outlook."

"You've already seen a very dark example."

She scrunched her brow and said, "Bill's death affected me deeply. I didn't know him as well as you, but I liked him immediately. I plan to phone his wife when I get back, for what good that will do. The point of what I was saying, though, is that this is where the action is, and it's very different from anything I've experienced before. You can't control your reaction to it. I'm trying to be honest about my feelings, that's all."

"And I'm not?"

"That's hard to say, because you seem to operate on two levels. There's the philosophical plane, the sweeping generalizations and hand wringing about the greater good of man, and there's the nitty gritty you. I suspect your feelings aren't deeply rooted. I don't know if you have the capacity for great emotion. Your skepticism, and it may be a defense, gets in the way."

He studied her for a moment. "The next time I lose a bulldozer, Rebecca, I'll ask for you."

"Hah! You could get run over by one and you wouldn't feel it. It's just that I don't think anyone knows who you are. Not even you. I certainly don't."

"It's simple. I'm the sum of my past and the vision of my future."

Rebecca sighed and said, "Okay, let's change the subject. You were right about the press pinning the cause of the explosion on the NVA. No one saw the flare, and they didn't take my word for it. A *Life* photographer has a time exposure that makes it look like Armageddon."

"Did you learn how many were killed?"

"Three GIs and fourteen NVA."

Rebecca no sooner finished the sentence than Banks called to Press. "Sir, you gotta see this," he yelled from the road.

He and Rebecca joined Banks at a three-quarter ton truck and looked into the rear compartment. She gasped but did not turn away. The bodies of the fourteen North Vietnamese sappers, limbs akimbo, eyes and mouths open, presented a grotesque sight. "They were just thrown in," she said.

"Probably by the buddies of the GI's killed. They wouldn't be in any mood to stack 'em," Banks said.

"Poor dumb bastards. They had to know that their chances of survival weren't much better than a kamikaze pilot's, yet they went in," Press said. "That's what happens to true believers—no doubt convinced that when the North takes over, life will be better."

"Starting to smell a bit gamy," Banks commented. "The burial detail is probably here for a machine. What do you think we ought to send, the loader or the dozer?"

Press pondered for a few seconds, pursing his lips. "Guess it depends on how far away they're going to bury 'em. If it's more than a klick, I'd send a loader."

Banks answered "Roger that" and started off for the three-man crew, who were drinking coffee and chewing on greasy bacon.

With a twist to her mouth, Rebecca asked, "Is there an SOP for grave digging, or is there some field expedient at work in your decision?"

"You can retract your talons. I recommend only what to lend the burial party, if that's what they are and what they're here for, and it's based strictly on marginal utility. A dozer will dig a fourteen-man slot trench a lot faster, but it travels a good bit slower than a wheel loader. I figured that a klick would be the break-even point."

"Utility? How can you be so callous? Maybe James Jones was right. 'War doesn't turn a boy into a man; it turns a man into an animal.'"

Press pursed his lips. "Jones does a great injustice to animals."

"I can see it's time to leave—your attitude is starting to work on me."

"I plea guilty only to rational observation."

"They're coming back," Rebecca said, looking at the burial detail. "My camera's packed; will you take a picture of the truck before it leaves?"

"You mean of the human debris. Sorry, that's a court martial offense."

"Oh, I see how it goes—selective allegiance to the paper war."

They walked away from the truck and sat back down on the culvert. "What day are you leaving for R and R?" she asked.

"I'm not sure. I have to hitch a plane ride to Saigon, which could take a couple of days. I'm scheduled to arrive in Honolulu on April first."

"Let me know what happens."

"What happens?"

Rebecca peered down at her feet briefly, then said, "You know, between you and Celia."

Her studied her for a moment. "What if we found it's not going to work?"

Rebecca blushed. "You never know. You may get a craving for home-cooked Italian food."

Press smiled and changed the subject. They talked for several more minutes before he took her back to the press tent, where they saw Sid Miller hunched over a typewriter.

"He only made it as far as some landing zone about half way in," said Rebecca. "Had a lot of competition getting a spot on a Khe Sanh-bound chopper."

"Pretty soon you'll be on one bound for Quang Tri. You've seen a lot in a short time, Rebecca. I hope you'll remember some and forget some."

"I'll remember it all for the rest of my life, just like the guys who've fought here."

"The remainder of my tour won't be the same without you. Have a safe trip to New York and take care of yourself...send me your articles."

"*Mazel tov.*"

Press kissed her lightly on her lips, got into his jeep, and drove off.

28

As the plane began its approach to the Honolulu airport, Press glanced around at the faces of the servicemen nearby—faces checkered with excitement, anticipation, nervousness. One of those surveyed, Spec 4 Holloway, with a neck more or less hinged to his shoulders, bore a likeness to Ichibod Crane. His eyes seemed the size of half dollars, and he blinked with the steadiness of a metronome, appearing as if he could not come to grips with his impending reunion. Press wondered what kind of girl he would be meeting.

He had been fortunate with the course of his trip thus far. Three days previously he had stepped into the waiting room at the Quang Tri airfield, and was there only an hour and a half before climbing aboard a twenty-seat Air America prop plane. The flight arrived early that evening at Ton Sun Nhut Airbase, now one of the busiest airports in the world, just north of Saigon. He had quickly hitched a ride to the Officers' Club on the sprawling base. Becoming reacquainted with indoor plumbing in the men's room, he spent a few minutes laughing at stall-door graffiti, especially two with an historical flavor:

To do is to be   Plato, circa 400 BC
To be is to do   Aristotle, circa 350 BC
Do be do be do   Sinatra, circa 1965 AD

I came
I saw
I ran
    Julius ARVN

The dinner special was steak and lobster, and he was tempted to order twice. Throughout the meal, he deflected looks of disapproval made by several senior officers at his boots, which had not been polished since January. Leaving the club he walked on sidewalks along paved streets past two movie theaters on his way to a bus stop. "Unbelievable," he said out loud.

The next day, he phoned a boyhood friend, a captain in the Air Force, who showed him around Saigon. Against regulations his friend shared an apartment with his girlfriend in a residential area of the city, and Press stayed in his billet on base until he caught his flight to Honolulu.

When the plane landed, the servicemen were bused to Fort Derussy. From his window seat, Press could see the wives and sweethearts standing on the grass adjacent to the parking lot. His eyes swept the crowd several times, failing with each pass to find Celia. He felt a sinking sensation, and he raised himself slightly off the seat and searched in earnest. She was there, in the rear, half-hidden behind a tree, talking to another woman. He settled back in his seat as the bus stopped, waiting for Holloway to take a place in line. Getting off just ahead of the tall, young serviceman in wrinkled civilian clothes, Press occasionally glanced at him, amused by the quickening wiper motion of his eyelids.

Holloway stopped thirty feet from the bus. His eyelids slammed against the stops of his brow and the blinking ceased. As he swallowed, his Adam's apple rose to greet his chin. Press grinned and followed his gaze to a tall, thin, redheaded girl. She, too, had large eyes, frozen open. She looked as nervous as he, but the sight of him apparently galvanized her and she rushed to him and hugged him with long arms.

As couples embraced around him, Press strode up to Celia, smothered her with his eyes, and kissed her softly on her lips. "I didn't think it was possible for you to be more beautiful than the way I saw you every day and every night, but you are," he said. "You look magnificent."

"You haven't forgotten how to sweep a girl off her feet" —seeing a wince cross his face she continued, "How can you look in my eyes and so misread my intention?"

"Sorry, I guess it's the memory of our last time together."

"It was a compliment. Anyway, you look great, all tanned and everything."

"Thank you." Press was uncharacteristically nervous, and he could see that she was too, although perhaps less so. They talked inconsequentially for a few minutes, then he suggested that they start for the airport. It was not until they were on an Aloha Airlines turboprop en route to Kauai that they settled into comfortable conversation. Celia was now helping to draft some of

Senator Jackson's speeches, which she enjoyed much more than answering mail. She and Professor Reynolds had settled on the subject of her thesis: FDR and the Supreme Court, 1933-42.

Press swallowed a glib remark about the spellbinding nature of the subject and asked, "Will you have the time to do all the research and writing and still work for Scoop?"

"I'll reduce my hours a little, but not so much that I'll have to ask my parents for more money."

"If it's ever a question of money, just let me know."

"You know I couldn't accept a loan or gift of money from you, Press."

"I knew you'd say that, but there'd certainly be no strings to it."

Celia gave Press a cautious smile and said, "Before I forget, one of the women in the office has a son in Vietnam. He was transferred from Chu Lai to Khe Sanh in that Laos invasion. She's worried, especially after seeing the ammo dump explosion in the paper, and she asked me to ask you if you knew what's going on up there."

"I understand that it's winding down. The *ARVN* are bugging out and will no doubt declare victory. Tell her he'll be fine."

"You sound so sure."

"I was talking to a couple of guys on the plane. They just came from Khe Sanh and told me that everyone will be out of there in a week or so."

Celia broached a new subject, and when they landed at Lihue, Press rented a car. The views were resplendent on the drive to the remote north coast. The ocean on their right stretched endlessly east to the horizon, while on their left a mountain loomed, immediate and irregular. Rain clouds—the only clouds in the sky—swirled around the summit. Press pulled the 1968 model Toyota off the road at a scenic lookout. They left the car and marveled at the vista, smiling broadly and taking deep breaths, as if intoxicated with their surroundings.

"I don't think I've ever seen you so...so—"

"Ebullient," he finished.

"Yes, ebullient. A penny..."

"Oh, a penny is it?" he laughed. "Any twelve-year-old would know."

Celia blushed. "Men."

"What a view," he exclaimed, changing the subject. "Tell me what you see." He spread his arms and turned full circle.

"Is this going to be another word game?"

"Not this time. Let's go for description; maybe a story."

She was silent for a long time. "Well, I see nature at its most creative: a sea as blue as can be and gentle, reassuring, timeless; and a mountain that provides a counterpoise, dark and earthy and brooding." She pointed to the cloud-cupped summit to make her point. "But the mountain serves to connect the sea and the sky, so that nature links everything and nothing stands alone. Your turn."

"That was wonderful. I also see a serene sea, and a pliant one, for it yielded, or rather was pushed aside by the upstart mountain. As the mountain grew it thumped its chest, proclaiming superiority over the ocean. But then its lifeline moved away, and its growth was arrested. Now the mountain is trying to find sustenance from above. What it doesn't know is that the water belongs to the sea, and the sea, in its infinite patience, is wearing it down—not only from the head but also from the waist."

"That's a sad way of seeing it, not at all a reason for ebullience."

"True," he admitted. "But it's only yin and yang—the cycles of nature. And right now, nothing is so natural as us being together." He kissed her forehead and added, "I'm definitely back to being ebullient."

Press walked out of the Hanalei Plantation office and returned to the car. "We're down toward the end," he said. "Remember my letter mentioning *South Pacific*? This is where they filmed the patio scenes."

"I can see why. This *is* paradise. Separate cottages and lots of flowers—"

"And a tremendous view."

Press parked the car next to their cottage, which was surrounded by a profusion of color: bougainvillea, hibiscus, jacaranda, anthurium, and frangipani—all posturing for advantage, like eager beauty contestants. "How do you find it?" he asked, after carrying in the luggage.

"It's so friendly and bright and airy. You've chosen well."

"You know, we could be standing on the very spot where the French planter sang 'Some Enchanted Evening.' I think he had something there with the lyrics, 'Once you have found her, never let her go.'"

"You do, do you?"

"Oh, I most certainly do," he reaffirmed and took both of her hands in his. "Whenever a soldier leaves for R and R or the States, among his parting words are: 'The second thing I'm gonna do is put the bags down.'"

She stepped back a little and said, "Could we wait till this evening, Press? It's still a little sudden for me."

"Of course we can wait, but Celia, it's not like this is our first time."

"I know. I know. But after not seeing you for so long, I guess I'm a little, well, shy."

Press nodded his head and released her hands, then after a few moments of hesitation said, "There's probably not a good time to discuss this, but I have to know. Do you, ah"—he glanced away momentarily, reddening—"do you feel any differently about me regarding, you know, regarding my character?"

Celia took his hand and they sat on the bed. "I've only had one truly awful time in my life—when my brother was killed. When you left for Vietnam, I was in turmoil...not only worrying about you but devastated by the episode in the restaurant with your one-night-stand. Till that moment, I had been at the center, or very close to it, of those things important to me—family, school, friends—and I was sure that I held that place with you. All of a sudden, it was like I was in a centrifuge, circling and unable to concentrate on anything. Coupled with that was your leaving. I was terribly afraid for your safety for weeks and weeks, even after I received those first letters assuring me that I need not worry. You seemed to bask in your good fortune, and I suspected you were saying you were somewhere that you weren't."

"You were right to think that. If I hadn't been fortunate in my assignment, I would have made up one."

"Did you?"

Press chuckled. "Of course not. Wives, mothers, and sweethearts all seem to think that their loved one is in constant danger over there. But most are support troops in well-secured base camps, so the odds of being sent to the boonies aren't that great."

"That may be, but every time you turn on the TV news or pick up a newspaper, you see jungles and napalm."

"That's because boredom has no appeal. But I interrupted. You were saying?"

Celia mustered her thoughts and continued. "In mid-September I started talking to Lynn about it. Basically, she took your side, saying I had no right to expect some pure, fairy tale romance, someone appearing magically with no past—that no one loves a perfect person. If you had cheated on me while we were going together, that would have been different."

"Lynn is wise beyond her years."

"But you deserve a full answer to your question. I...There's still that part of you that I'm unsure of—the part that has to do with being grounded, committed, serious. Your contempt for religion bothers me."

He waited a minute before speaking. "Thank you for being direct. I'll work on moderating my view of organized religion. As to becoming more serious, I believe Joseph Campbell is right and 'life is the act of becoming.' I'm not the same person I was last year. This I also know: You've brought happiness to me in a thousand forms, from catching your smile across the chapel courtyard to our most intimate moments. If I weren't so selfish that would probably be enough."

Press walked to the door, opened it, and broke off a stem of hibiscus, placed it her hair and kissed her forehead. She smiled, and they began to converse about more mundane subjects until dark, when each showered and dressed for dinner, which they took at the resort.

After a stroll near the water, they returned to their cottage feeling much less tense, partly from the Mai Tai's at dinner and partly from the zephyr sweeping the bay. They kissed slowly and temperately. No signal or words passed between them to begin undressing, which they began to do simultaneously. They followed their established pattern of lovemaking, but by degrees more searching and less consuming. It was past two o'clock when they gave in to sleep.

After breakfast that morning they started off for Waimea Canyon and drove past pineapple and sugar cane plantations. The Toyota strained on the steep grades, slowing to ten miles per hour. Press predicted that Japanese-made cars had a dim future in the US. They hiked along one of the trails high on the rim of the expansive canyon, which fell a half mile almost straight down. Time and the path of the Waimea River had formed the lava slopes in horizontal rings, and it would have been easy to mistake it for the stratification of sedimentary rock except for the uniform reddish-brown color. Splotches of green clung to the slopes. Press was so taken with the reliefs that he blurted out, "Makes the mountains of Vietnam look gentle."

Celia, who was walking in front, turned and gave him a puzzled look. Recovering, he went on. "I get to see the whole country from my desk. You wouldn't believe the number of pictures and aerial photos that get routed through the office."

From Waimea Canyon they went to Kalalau Lookout for the spectacular view of the serrated Na Pali coast. They marveled at a high sloping ridge, smothered with vegetation, linking the mountain and the sea. It appeared to Press that the ridge was wafer-thin and would totter without being buttressed by tens of volcanic rock spines, resembling roots of the pandanus tree, which rose up several hundred feet from the valley below.

Taking Celia's hand, he inhaled deeply at the stunning expanse before him and the state of euphoria within him. He wanted to tell her of the contrast between the past months and the present and spout insipid platitudes, such as how he would never again take things for granted, that love and beauty and tolerance are the anecdotes for war.

She searched his face and said, "So, where are you now?"

"Oh, just thinking. This is the perfect present, and I don't want it to end."

"It's beautiful here, and so tranquil. Whoever recommended Kauai, give him my thanks."

Press's involuntary flinch was slight, but visible enough to cause a bewildered expression on Celia's face. She chose not to remark on it and said instead, "I'm looking forward to dinner tonight at the Coco Palms; after that snack we had for lunch and our long hike—I'm famished."

"I guess we should be leaving soon. We've got to drive about 300 degrees around the island to our hotel, then double back for dinner."

"Thank God it's downhill."

They arrived at their cottage at dusk. Press turned the shower on and stepped out of his clothes. "We don't have much time, so if you want to join me, you'll get a free back scrub."

"Okay, but don't start anything or we'll miss the show."

Celia undressed, wrapped a towel around her hair and joined Press. "My God, you're bleeding," she cried.

"That's not blood," said Press, laughing.

She looked closely at the reddish residue swirling at the drain. "If that's not blood, it's the stuff they use in movies to imitate it."

"It's clay—red clay, and it clings to your body like plastic wrap."

"There was never any mention of it in your letters. All you wrote about was the blowing sand."

"Well, of course, but it's not *pure* sand. About ten percent of it is laterite clay, and that's the stuff that sticks," he said, hoping that he sounded convincing.

Celia shrugged, slid past Press and said, "I'm going to stay upstream."

They left for the Coco Palms as darkness descended. Visibility was slightly impaired from the rising vapor on the highway, but the headlights illuminated small oblong shapes, slightly darker than the bleached asphalt. As the tires ran over the shapes, they heard squishing sounds. Celia leaned forward and squinted. "*What* are we running over?" she asked.

"Mr. Toad." Press answered.

"They're all over the road, hundreds of them."

"They like the warm pavement, and there are so many of them because snakes are not indigenous to Hawaii."

"This is awful; I don't think I'll be able to eat," she said, revolted.

"The stupid things just sit—sit there and get pounded."

When they arrived at the resort, Press and Celia strolled around the torch-lit palm grove until it was time for dinner seating. They talked continuously—neither brought up the subject of toads—until dinner was served. Celia regained her appetite, and they ate heartily and drank Mai Tai's and after dinner watched native Hawaiian dancers perform in the grove.

"It's amazing how they twirl and throw those torches around without getting burned," she observed.

"I've only had one eye on them; the other won't leave you. Have I told you how captivating you are, how alluring, ravishing even, in your Hawaiian garb?"

"No, you haven't. But you're rapidly making up for it."

"I'll tell you more when I return—the men's room's calling." Press slipped out of the booth and walked only a few yards when the loud, familiar crack of a detonation reached his ears. In the first snip of a second he started for the floor; in the next instant he recovered, realizing it was part of the act, and resumed his normal gait. Wondering if Celia had seen his involuntary start, he casually glanced back while turning a corner. She had a ferine cast to her eyes, tracking him but otherwise expressionless. "Damn," he whispered.

She said nothing when he returned, and he resisted saying okay, we get a rocket in about once a month, or, you know, we simulate attacks on Cam Ranh all the time. The show ended a few minutes later, and they drove back to their cottage, squashing few toads on the cooling pavement.

Late next morning—their final day in Kauai—they picked up a box lunch and drove the short distance to Lumahai Beach. "It doesn't look to be a public beach," Celia observed, seeing no parking spaces.

"When's that stopped us? Let's park on the shoulder and try to find a place to walk down." The side-hill highway wound thirty feet above the beach, and the vegetation between the two reminded Press of Vietnam. They found a path through ironwood trees and made their way to a spot just beyond the lapping line of surf, where they spread their towels and deposited the lunch boxes. Although the water offered no shock, it was invigorating, and they swam for a half-hour before eating lunch.

"I'm going to look for shells," she said, after replacing the plastic plates and utensils.

"The pickings look a little slim but go ahead; the sun's been working on me and I'm going to submit to it." He watched her go and thought about their remaining day and a wake-up. Scooping a handful of sand, he picked out a few of the black granules and gazed at their source, a volcanic rock outcropping just off-shore. Time, he thought. So much of it for you, so little of it for us. He then lay back on the blanket and in two minutes began to doze.

He was awakened by cold water splashing on his chest. Celia stood over him, giggling. "Come on, sleepy head, let's beach-comb." He got to his feet and they started off toward the Na Pali coast.

When they returned an hour later, Press said, "Stop here. This could be the very spot where Emil professed his love for Nellie."

"Emil and Nellie?"

"*South Pacific.*"

"I should have known."

"You remember the story, don't you? They are wildly in love and he proposes to her but, because of something in his past, she rejects him. He then goes off to war. She, realizing that he's a pretty good guy, decides upon his return to marry him." Celia bit her lower lip gently while looking at him intently. He took both of her hands in his and continued. "If a blotch in my past hadn't surfaced on a certain evening last June, I was going to ask you to marry me. I suppose you already knew that?"

"Yes, I was pretty sure, but when you started putting your hand in your coat pocket every five minutes, I was certain."

He smiled. "I was so sure of myself...it's ironic. I've never believed in absolutes, and so few things in life are sure things, but after meeting you and getting to know you, I was absolutely convinced that we were right for each other. Here we are now at such a very propitious place, but Emil wasn't successful until he finished his war, and I'm not finished with mine. Of course with my job, you know that my coming back is almost a certainty."

She kissed him softly on the lips and said, "Honey, I don't know that at all. What I know is that you have a reflexive motion when a fire cracker explodes; I know that my brother wrote me from Khe Sanh and complained that the red clay packed his pores and wouldn't wash out and his letters had red fingerprint smudges just like your last letters; I know that you grind your teeth in your sleep, something I've never heard you do before. I could go on."

Press blanched and tried to think of a rebuttal, but Celia preempted him. "And I know how difficult it must be not to share the pain and frustration of your experience over there. I could see it in your eyes several times. You wanted to tell me things but swallowed the words. Nothing you can say in that facile way of yours will change the fact that you're going back to a dangerous place. I will have to deal with it. I will deal with it. All I ask is that you don't take any chances—don't do anything stupid."

"You're looking at the most careful soldier who ever put on the uniform."

"Good. Now, do you think we would desecrate the scene of your favorite movie if we spread our towels under the banyan trees and made love?"

"Not at all. The spirit of the film was make love, not war."

29

The pilot set the chopper down on the huge helipad at Khe Sanh. As the rotors slowed to a halt, the occupants saw a puff of black smoke over the airstrip. "Charlie's been pounding the place pretty good the last few days," the crew chief shouted to Press. "Don't know why, there's hardly anybody left. It'll be all his in a day or two."

Press thanked the crew and stepped out onto the almost deserted helipad. He walked to the company area, where the engineers were loading several five-ton dump trucks. The headquarters' tent was down, but he found Padgett directing the loading of the generator set.

"Welcome back, you're just in time to pick up all those bridges your platoon put down; we're bugging out."

"So I see. Any disasters occur while I was gone?"

"Same old. How was R and R?"

"About as good as life can get. It's almost unimaginable that within twenty-four hours you can be in two utterly different worlds."

"Especially in one if you're shacking up every four hours," Padgett joked.

Press ignored the remark. "Celia knows I'm not in Cam Ranh; I didn't tell her about Khe Sanh. Her brother was killed here in sixty-eight."

"Looks like if you get it, it won't be here. Down the road is a different matter. The First of the Fifth reported two ambushes yesterday, both near bridges."

"It feels so good to be back."

Padgett thought for a moment. "Once we return to Dong Ha, there's nothing but maintenance activities scheduled. You might sit out your tour in base camp."

"Sounds all right to me. So what's on the docket for today?"

The officers got out their maps, and Padgett showed Press the location of the night defensive perimeter the company would be setting up in late afternoon. During the next two days, the engineers would disassemble all the bridges between Khe Sanh and Vandegrift, taking the furthest out and working east. Although they would have security up and down the road, the battalion commander issued strict orders for all personnel to wear flak jackets and steel pots.

Press left after the briefing to find Banks. At the moment he found him, a rocket slammed into a deserted bunker not far away, detonating inside. "Welcome back, sir," said Banks. "They're using delay action fuses now. Really messes up the inside."

"Good to see you, Sarge. The CO tells me you did a great job while I was away—said I could have been gone another week."

"Appreciate that. Too bad he didn't tell you that before you left."

"Looks like we get to spend a few days on the lower road. At least it will be warm this time. I know a good place to swim in the Quang Tri River. You've got to go down a long way before hitting bottom."

"Doesn't look like there will be time for that, sir."

Press shook his head. "Suppose not. Why don't you bring me up-to-date on the platoon, then we'll get on the move."

Two hours later, they were leaving Khe Sanh. Press looked back from the abandoned rubber plantation and found himself reflecting on the operation. He would have assorted memories; some, he decided, would provide proud, perhaps rarefied moments, whenever a prompting word or image would send them gliding into his conscious mind: the midnight opening of the road and taking out the minefield and booby-trapped wire without casualties among the most welcome. Much further down memory lane lay one so dark that he feared it would breach his sleeping mind. And of course his waking hours would always be open to hearing the word *king*, or any of a hundred lesser associations, invariably precipitating a journey to that dreaded spot along QL-9. He was still gazing at the receding plateau when the jeep began its deep descent to the lower road.

It was four o'clock when they reached the NDP, situated between QL-9 and the Quang Tri River, a kilometer south of Vandegrift. "Looks like this is home for a few days, Malone," Press said to his new driver.

"Looks like a gravel pit," Malone observed.

"Best the Army can do on short notice. When you were a boy, maybe four or five years ago, didn't you want to camp on a river bank, rise at the crack of dawn, and throw out a line for trout?"

"Yes, sir, I did want to do that. Only I didn't want to get my nuts shot off in mid-cast."

"Ah, you're not a true fisherman then, Malone."

An advance party had already thrown a curtain of wire along the perimeter, so the arriving engineers busied themselves with setting up camp, cramming down evening chow, and sending out security in the descending dusk.

The next morning, they retraced their route and began to disassemble the bridges for which established bypasses existed. AVLB tractors were driven out to retrieve the bridges they had put down early in the operation. To Press, it seemed as though the road was being reeled in. Soon it would be swallowed by the jungle.

The air barely stirred, and the stagnant mid-afternoon heat collected in the valley, causing discomfort among the engineers. Press and Banks arrived at the bridge being taken in by the second squad. Davis, the new front-end loader operator, was sitting in the seat smoking a cigarette, waiting for the squad members to finish stacking the decking on the bucket. Banks caught his attention and motioned for him to put on his flak jacket, which was draped on the back of his seat. Davis gesticulated, as if to say, "Com'on Sarge, it's hot sitting on this machine." Banks shook his head, and Davis shrugged his shoulders and complied.

A few minutes later, Malone was repositioning the jeep to drive Banks and Press to another bridge site, when an explosion rocked the area. The occupants of the jeep threw themselves out simultaneously, while others hit the ground in what resembled precision drill. Davis jumped off the loader on the protected side of the machine. Press watched as he fingered the collar of his flak jacket and removed a sharp metal fragment which had penetrated the outer lining. The hole in the collar was aligned with Davis' carotid artery. Press yelled out to determine if any squad members had been hit. All responded in the negative.

"You saved his life, Terry," Press said, getting up. "RPG, most likely—a tweak, at least for now."

"Let's hustle a little and get the job done before they get through in numbers," Banks suggested.

"Let's hope the grunts up there earn their combat pay," said Press, pointing at the hill rising above the road.

Later in the afternoon, on yet another site, Padgett drove in from the west, and the dust kicked up by his jeep rolled unabated in the still air toward them. Rays from the sun, beginning its retreat behind the massive bulkhead of Hill 242, filtered through the dust and broke on the press of spring grasses and new bamboo flanking the road. Padgett walked up briskly and took Press by the elbow. "Think you can retire Bridge Six before dark?" he asked.

"Without breaking into a sweat."

"Good, a platoon of the 166th was ambushed forty-five minutes ago. It was a real quick hit and only one casualty. Weitzel took an AK forty-seven round in the foot."

"Much bone damage?"

"Yeah, it looked like it, but there was no way of telling whether he would lose it or not. One thing's for sure, he won't be back."

"He and I came in together—drove up on a jeep from Phu Bai. Glad I didn't know then one of us would be carried out."

"That may be a little premature...you still have three months."

PART FIVE
30

Press dated his letter to Rebecca May 20, 1971 and scribbled a greeting. "Thanks for your packet," he continued. "And thanks for sending your articles—very interesting and compelling reading. Especially enjoyed how you interweaved first hand experience. I was surprised, though, that not once did you use "hubris" or "zeitgeist"—not even a "gestalt"—in your articles. Oversights like that can cost you your press card—at the very least cafeteria privileges. After six or seven weeks of base camp boredom, my platoon arrived this morning at the target range for NVA gunners, a.k.a. Bravo One, a fire base in the rolling scrub about 15 kilometers south of the DMZ. I had thought that Dong Ha could never be surpassed in sheer, stark ugliness, but this place wears a hideous red scowl and is little more than a huddle of bunkers hunched in fear. It's a legacy of the 'McNamara Line'—remember the string of fire bases McNamara proposed to construct from the South China Sea to some point in Laos in order to cut NVA infiltration and supply lines? The top brass ridiculed the idea—especially the Marines (they hate a static defense)—and only a handful were constructed between the mountains and the sea just south of the DMZ. (From here we can see the last one built—FSB Fuller—in the high hills to the southwest.) By the ferocity with which the NVA fought to keep open the Ho Chi Minh Trail in Laos while you were here, it would seem McNamara's plan had some merit.

"There's one facet of our current mission that does appeal to me: it's only for a few days. We're repairing gun pads for a 175 mm howitzer battery, and we're commuting from Dong Ha. The arty boys are keeping the guns pretty busy although, I'm afraid, they're making more noise than damage. The good news is that the NVA isn't doing much better. They've got a stockpile of 122 mm rockets in the hills about ten or twelve klicks west of the fire base, and every so often send some our way. If you're looking west, you can see the tiny silver flash from the ridge—visible for only an instant. Radar picks up the missile and a siren alerts the troops. You have about ten seconds to take cover, though there's probably nowhere to hide. They flung their last of the day at us about eleven this morning, the siren blared and we ducked inside nearby bunkers. The thing sailed over the east fence and detonated out-of-bounds.

"Remember the generally fine weather we had while you were here? Well, the sun's now at its zenith—immense and close and in such a rage that the surface temperature on the barrels of the big guns varies little before and after firing. Next month it will bound off the Tropic of Cancer and land in our laps once again. In a former life I recall fondly something called air conditioning.

"Received a letter from Celia yesterday. She's doing fine—busy as hell with school and work. Told her I was settled in for the duration of my tour in base camp. At the time I thought I would be. Still, the war is winding down for me (only 70 days and a wake-up), and it's winding down for the US. All that's left is an epitaph."

Press wrote several more paragraphs, then signed and folded the letter and stuffed it into an envelope.

He awoke the next morning, leaving his fan on to stir the heavy stagnant air inside his cubicle, pulled on his fatigue pants, socks and boots, and took his towel and ditty bag to the shower shed. As he entered, he noticed a Vietnamese woman leaving one of the hootches which housed his platoon. She was ugly, bone-thin, and looked severely worn. He shook his head in disgust and when it came time to wash his face, he scrubbed vigorously.

During formation after morning mess, he scrutinized the twenty-six engineers standing at parade rest. VanAker had gone in April; in fact, all the squad leaders of the Ridgway days were gone. Nixon's Vietnamization of the war had taken hold, and there were many fewer Americans in Vietnam now than there were when he had arrived.

After Padgett dismissed the company, Press kept his men in place. "I'm not going to subject you to a sermon," he began, "but from the conduct of some of you in the last twelve hours, you need one. The whore many of you passed around until dawn this morning probably has six or seven varieties of VD. Some of the strains going around are damn hard to knock out. If you have to have a whore—by the way, I'm not giving my approval—use a rubber. That old gal you had last night looked like she had sperm up to her eyeballs. I suggest that all of you who went skinny dipping stop at the med shack right after formation. Captain Horner and his assistant will be expecting you.

"That's enough about the whore. We've got two more days at Bravo One. If we take more in-coming, don't get complacent; jump inside a bunker. At least you'll have cover from shrapnel. Questions?" He paused for a few seconds, then to Banks: "Take over, Sergeant."

Bravo One was little more than one square kilometer in size. Living was exclusively underground in forty-eight bunkers. Five bunkers, located on the southeast periphery, had been vacant since the Marines moved out in 1970. Centered on the southern end, between the self-propelled howitzer battery and the vacant bunkers, was a battery of 155 mm howitzers. Two companies of mechanized infantry occupied the north end. No one at the fire base expected a ground assault. The North Vietnamese would almost certainly not risk being caught in the stubble of vegetation covering the undulating terrain, where they would be decimated by fire from artillery and helicopter gunships. They would have to settle for the harassing fire of rockets, rather than the headline grabbing assault and overrun. This no doubt suited their strategists, patience being a virtue long prized and practiced. Having waited years for the Americans to leave, they now watched them depart wholesale. The NVA soldiers in the hills to the west would endeavor to give the Yanks a memorable send-off.

It was late in on a rainy day and the platoon, except for Press and Banks, had already left for Dong Ha. Press and Lt. Galecki of the 175 mm battery were standing on a gun pad talking about the intricacies of siting the big guns. "But every time you fire, the gun moves; what do you do—"

The wail of the siren cut into Press's question, and he instinctively started for the nearest bunker. "This way," Galecki stopped him and began trotting toward the tower.

"Isn't this a little exposed?" Press asked, half way up.

"Other than the TOC, it's the safest place."

They reached the top and heard a faint swish high above, then an explosion off to the east, outside the wire. Galecki continued talking, paying no attention at all to the explosion. "The rockets all have delay action fuses, so even if the tower took a direct hit right here—" he pointed to a spot on the fifty square-foot deck— "it would travel right through and detonate near the ground. And if you're standing in the middle of the deck, you're pretty well protected from the shrapnel of a rocket hitting anywhere in the area."

As they talked, Press and Galecki watched small groups of soldiers leave their bunkers and walk toward the mess hall. "Do you think the NVA can see where their rockets detonate?" Press asked.

"They'd have to have a spotter damn close by, living in a spider hole...I don't think so, because even then you can't direct them like you can artillery. Rockets are good for large area targets, but that's about—"

"There goes another," Press interrupted.

The siren sounded and they watched the troops return to the bunkers they had just vacated. This time the swoosh was louder and closer, but there was no following explosion.

"Oh, God!" Galecki exclaimed. "Look!"

Press had been looking eastward for the impact area; what he saw was a bunker waver for a few seconds, then collapse into itself. He stared in disbelief, saying "No, it can't be, it can't be. That's the one they all went into."

Both officers raced down the steps and toward the bunker located 150 yards away, calling for help as they ran. Tens of rescuers swarmed into the depression and began digging through three feet of overburden, removing sandbags, posts, and broken lumber, groping for bodies. In a much shorter time than it seemed, they pulled the first dead soldier from the floor of the bunker. The sun had disappeared under the horizon, and lights from parked vehicles illuminated the scene. Every so often, they would pull another body until, hours later, twenty-nine soldiers lay dead, some killed by shrapnel, some crushed to death, the majority buried alive.

The rescuers rotated, and Press sat down on the ground, filthy and weary, physically drained from the consuming effort. He heard someone crying and turned to see a Spec 4 slumped on the ground with his hands over his face. The young soldier must have sensed someone standing nearby, for he raised his head and opened his eyes.

"He was my best friend," he said, without looking at Press. "We started together...thirty-one days, that's all we had left, thirty-one goddamn days. This fucking war—I hate this fucking war." He wiped his tears with his sleeve and continued. "I went to get us a couple of Cokes. Phil said he would go, it was his turn, but I had to piss, so I said 'no, I'll go.' The siren went off on my way back, and I jumped into a bunker.

"We promised that if one of us got it, we would visit the folks of the other. What do I tell them—that I lived and their son died because I had to take a *piss*? Oh, God, why did he have to die?"

Press wanted to console the grief-stricken soldier, but he could not find the words. Instead, he sat down next to him and put his arm over his shoulders. They sat together until Banks came up from the hole, drenched in sweat and exhausted.

"I hate that smell," he said, referring to the pungent odor of cordite.

Press struggled to get to his feet. "Let's get washed and fed, then find a place to stay with the one-seven-five battery." He put his hand on the shoulder of the disconsolate soldier for a few moments, before starting for the latrine in a slow, uncertain step.

The sun had lost its infernal intensity by the time Press arrived in the company area late the following afternoon. Walking to the officers' hootch, he gazed at the western sky, where reclining rays of light ruddied distant mountains and tinged the wispy oblong cirrus clouds that in Press's imagination were a thousand bloody boot prints marching off the horizon. He sighed and entered the billet. Darnell was at the table cleaning his M-16, a weapon notorious for jamming when dirty. "If you haven't seen the sunset, throw your head out the door."

Darnell glanced up and said, "Saw it when I came in a few minutes ago. There must be a helluva lot of dust over the mountains—B-52 strike probably."

"At least that would finish the day with some symmetry—blood in the hills, blood in the mountains, blood in the sky," Press rasped.

"That must have been tough at Bravo One."

"Twenty-nine families are going to go through hell in a day or two."

"I still can't believe that so many were in one bunker," Darnell said, shaking his head. "They must have gone in on a conga line. No survivors?"

"Only those taking cover in the entrances. The twelve-by-twelve support in the center had been taken out months ago so they could watch films, and the bunker caved in. Who knows whether the missing post would have saved it. I saw it collapse; it was like one of those underground nuclear explosions in miniature: the top of the bunker wavered for a few seconds, then imploded. Most of the guys were either crushed or died from asphyxiation...there was collateral damage."

"Bravo One should have been one of the first fire bases handed over to the *ARVN* under Vietnamization."

"Ah, yes: *Vietnamization.* Doesn't sound like it ought to be a word, does it? You know what it really means? Definition one: Nixon's surreptitious ceding of the South to the North under the guise of peace with honor. Definition two: the granting of victory to the North under the installment plan."

"You need a drink," Darnell said.

Press went into his cubicle and in a few minutes came out wearing shorts and sandals with a towel draped around his neck, carrying a bar of soap and a bottle of shampoo. He had a perplexed look on his face as he walked.

"If something's not where it should be, but you can't put your finger on it, look at the table again," Darnell advised.

"The TV's gone," Press said, after glancing at the table.

"Stolen. That's a pretty brazen act, going into the officers' hootch and walking off with the TV."

"Stupid, too, with only one station to watch and meager fare at that. Too bad he didn't steal Padgett's tape deck, or at least the Janis Joplin tape. I'd rather listen to gravel scraping against the bed of a five-ton than 'Oh, Lord, won't you buy me a Mercedes Benz. My friends all drive Porches, I must make amends.'"

"He wasn't so stupid in the way he pulled it off. He went through three or four hootches in the company area and nobody questioned him. Know why?"

"No, why?"

"He was carrying a goddamn clipboard...What's so funny? Com'on, what's so goddamn funny?"

The water was tepid in the shower, which in May was not nearly as uncomfortable as in January. Press stepped out of the shower after five minutes and felt better, as if some of the horror of the day before had been washed away with the grime.

That evening, Padgett, Benischek, Darnell, Banks, Scogland's new platoon sergeant, Williams, and Press played poker. Scogland, who had contributed without stint for three months, kibitzed. Banks wore an eye shade, but the accessory failed to induce his strongest opponent to drop in three attempts at bluffing, and an hour into the game, he was down twenty-five dollars.

"Low spade in the hole," Padgett announced and began to shuffle the cards. It was his favorite game. Each player was dealt seven cards, three of them down: in the hole. Whoever revealed the lowest spade in his down cards at the end of the betting split the pot with the best poker hand. Split-the-pot games spurred betting and, with pot limit, often spawned big winners and losers.

Padgett and Williams bet on the first two opportunities, each player having four cards. Banks had the three of spades showing. Scogland circling.

"Jason, grab that bottle of Drambuie behind you, will you?" Press asked Scogland.

"Throw me a can of beer while you're back there," Padgett said.

"By the way, you got guard duty tomorrow night," Benischek told Darnell.

"Christ, I just had it last month."

"It was two months ago."

"Great. Nothing's more fun than walking the wire waking the zonked or the zoned."

"I had the duty a few weeks ago," Press said, "and only found three asleep—one lost in the ether, but he must have shot himself up before he got in the hole; no needles or vials around."

"Could be a lot worse," Padgett pronounced. "We could actually be somewhere where there's a remote chance of attack. Most of the VC have been killed off, and the regulars aren't coming out of the mountains."

Darnell shook his head. "Don't forget about the ammo dump at Quang Tri; the blast woke us all up, and we're fifteen klicks away."

"I'm not saying that there's not a sapper or two out there. There aren't enough to overrun us, like they did at Mary Ann," Padgett explained.

"The army's a lot different than it was during my first tour in sixty-six," said Banks. "We had discipline and hardly any drug use. It's so fucked up now that I'm thinking about becoming a goddamn civilian."

"That surprises me, Sarge," Press said. "You're the most upbeat person I know in the OD, a shoe-in for sergeant major, and you're thinking of chucking it?"

"I'm questioning whether it's worth it. Forty to forty-five percent of the troops in-country are dopeheads. There may be a few lost souls among 'em, but the bulk are, are—"

"No damn good," Press finished.

"Exactly," Banks agreed.

There was a murmur of accord and Padgett began to throw out more cards. "Queen for you," he said to Benischek. Turning a card for Williams: "Nothing going there, Sarge,"—to Press— "Seven, possible flush...Pair of tens—looking good, Lee...Sarge, a jack, no help. Damn!" he exclaimed, dealing himself the deuce of spades.

"That makes the four good," Scogland said, needlessly.

"You ought to sit in, Jason," Darnell said.

"I've got to save my money. I'm going for my MBA when I get out."

"It's the passing moment that's important, and you're missing it," Press said.

"That's easy for you to say—a guy who's keeping only a hundred a month. What are you doing with the rest of it?"

"I see you're not going to be goaded into playing," Press replied.

"Ten's bet," said Padgett.

"Dollar," Darnell said.

"I'm in," Banks said.

"Your dollar and one more," Padgett upped the bet.

"Your dollar and your dollar, and I'll bump it two more," Benischek blurted.

"Christ, Brad, you might as well have the four of spades shellacked to your face," Press said.

"I'm out," Williams said.

Press threw in his hand, while the others saw the raise. The betting continued. Throughout Benischek leaned back in his chair in an aura of complacent neutrality. Darnell pursed his lips, though not in the manner of Lt. Holt. Banks repeatedly peeked at his down cards, as if double-checking a straight or flush. Padgett remained expressionless, but his eyes were at work, poking and prying at cards and faces.

After the final bet, Banks laid out a small straight, beating out Darnell's three tens and Padgett's two pair. Benischek took half the pot with the four of spades.

Padgett re-stacked several piles of poker chips in front of him and suggested that they turn on the cassette player.

"Yeah, how about Janis Joplin," Press offered.

"You hate Janis Joplin," said a suspicious Padgett .

"I'm in a good mood. Tomorrow is our last day at the wasteland."

"Is it her voice or is it personal with you?" Scogland inquired.

Press considered for a moment. "Her voice grates on my ear, but that's not it. With fame and financial security, she had neutralized any outside control of herself, at least any *unreasonable* outside control."

"How do you define unreasonable?" Padgett asked.

"Let's say her record company wanted her to record a sappy song that didn't fit her style. That would be unreasonable and she wouldn't have to do it. If we were ordered to do an engineering recon in the hills near Fuller, it would be unreasonable but we'd still have to go. Of course the military is all about control, so that might not be a good example. Here's a better one: An employee plans a big dinner for his wife on their wedding anniversary, but his boss insists that he work overtime. The guy is screwed—can't even control his dinner. All Joplin had to do was exert a little control over herself; instead she relinquished it, and it killed her."

"Self-control aside, aren't you really talking about power—who's got more power?" Darnell asked.

Press squinted in thought, then said, "Power is nothing without control, except maybe a runaway train. Control is the exercise of power. It's like gravity; you don't often realize it, but it's always acting on you. While I have no desire to control anybody else, the most important thing to me is having as much control over myself as possible, and maybe it's a dark corner in my character, but I've no respect for anybody who casually discards it."

"Okay, give me the discards; I control the deal," Benischek said with a laugh. "Seven—Twenty-Seven."

Scogland pressed a button on the cassette player and Janis Joplin's voice leapt out of the machine:

Unchain my heart
Oh, let me go
Unchain my heart
'Cause you don't love me no more....

31

Press and Galecki sat in the underground mess hall at Bravo One eating the noon meal. Press was soaking a piece of bread in the grease his meat loaf was floating in—not to consume, but to sponge away as much of the liquid as possible. He was listening to Galecki predict the likelihood of an artillery duel with the NVA.

"With our static defense, it's going to get even worse. Unless we have grunts out there in those hills, Charlie might bring up some arty." Galecki pressed the tip of his forefinger on the table to underscore his point: "And then we'll almost certainly have a duel."

"What do you call what's happening now? They fire off rockets and you respond with artillery."

"Well, for one thing, the rocket launchers are so mobile that you can't get any kind of sustained fire on them. Our guns hit them where they *were*. And, of course, their rockets are so inaccurate that it's almost the same outcome for them. In an artillery duel both sides have the range, and they slug it out, like two fighters in the last minute of the final round."

"Sounds like the ultimate contact sport."

"If it happens, and I don't think it has very often in the war, we'll be ready for it. We're switching to eight-inch barrels. With a good observer we can drop the third round into their baggy shorts."

"Sorry we won't be around to see it," Press said with a smile.

"That's right, you guys are pulling out this afternoon. Thanks for your work on the pads."

"See the captain who just walked in?"

Galecki nodded. "What's he doing here?"

"He's our CO and he's no doubt looking for me." Press waved to Padgett, who walked over to the two officers. After introducing him to Galecki, he and Padgett sat down at another table.

"So, what brings you up here?" Press asked.

"Thought I better do this in person. Major Shannon called me in this morning and told me that Group headquarters received an order to reinforce the bunkers at Bravo One."

Press closed his eyes and stemmed an urge to lose his temper. "So we stay," he said.

"Afraid so. Apparently, Abrams is mad as hell about the twenty-nine KIA here. Word's out that any commander who permits bunching up or any slack behavior and takes casualties will get relieved. AFVN is saying that there's great political pressure on the military to minimize casualties during the troop withdrawal. Group's sending a couple of staff officers to inspect each bunker and determine what's needed in the way of knee braces or additional support to bring them up to spec."

"*Knee braces*? They can't be serious," said Press, astounded. "Beefing up the interior may or may not prevent a collapse, but that's not the point. How would you like to be in a bunker when a rocket detonates at your feet? Would you rejoice that it didn't collapse?"

"I know what you're saying; I was thinking the same thing on the way up. We'll need to pour a concrete cap on the bunkers."

"Yes, sir. That's the only way to stop a rocket."

"I think I can get a half-dozen cement mixers from Battalion. We'll have to see about the cement."

"We can pull water and gravel from the Cam Lo River."

"Right. Bring your platoon on in and we'll get everything organized. You can move into the old Marine bunkers along the southeast perimeter."

Press nodded and they stood. "You know, deep down inside I knew I wouldn't see the end of this cesspool until *DEROS*."

"You don't have to tell me what it's like; I was here from October to January."

"I can see why you extended your tour; it would have been too large a leap to be here one week and home the next."

Padgett bunched his brow for a few moments before speaking. "I don't know what to tell you, Press. You're too experienced for platitudes and a pat on the back but, who knows, maybe you'll save some lives."

"Good try. I just hope I don't *lose* any."

At mid-morning three days later, Press's platoon drove north along the dusty road the Marines had built in the mid-sixties and passed through the gates of Bravo One. They stopped in front of the vacant bunkers and off-loaded their gear. Banks quickly assigned each squad to a bunker. He and Press took one in the center. Minutes later the engineers walked individually to the self-propelled howitzer battery, which now carried eight-inch guns.

A lowbed trailer stacked with bags of cement on pallets was parked near three operational cement mixers. Although covered by plastic, months of storage in the unsparing humidity of the coastal lowlands had turned most of the cement block-hard. While Press talked on the radio, Banks, undeterred by the poor state of the cement, organized the men into work groups. Two of the groups began to salvage the usable cement, while three groups went to work scraping the insides of the mixers. He sent Powers, the front-end loader operator, to a stockpile of clay and told him to take what he needed and construct a ramp near the mixers for the water trailer. With the trailer above the mixers, they only had to attach a hose to feed the mixers by gravity flow.

The work was completed by mid-afternoon, and the platoon left for the Cam Lo River, only a few kilometers south of Bravo One. It was wide and shallow with a firm bottom of sand and stone, which they loaded into the five-ton dump truck for use in the mixers. The river was also the fill point for the water trailer. Press watched the engineers work and remembered OCS, where the wet bulb temperature had occasionally saved the candidates from debilitating boonie runs. There was no wet bulb in Vietnam, only common sense and frequent breaks. Working in the cauldron of the Cam Lo, the engineers found respite every few minutes by flopping down in the foot-deep water. Rising, they again felt the full brunt of the sun, which not only poured on them from above but bathed them from below with reflected rays.

After they had loaded the truck and cleaned their pioneer tools in the river, they took a break under a shade tree. Almost before he sat down, Press was approached by a Vietnamese boy carrying pineapples.

"GI, you want to buy pineapple?"

"How much do you want?"

"Piaster or MPC?"

"MPC."

"Four dollar."

"Four dollars? That's too much. I'll give you one dollar."

The boy looked shocked. "No way, GI. Three dollar—best deal."

"I'll tell you what; I'll take all three for six dollars. You will be a big hero in the vil for your sales skills."

"You got a deal, Lieutenant."

Press took the pineapples from the boy and tossed two of them to platoon members. He paid the boy and asked him to sit down. "How old are you?" he asked.

"Twelve."

"How did you learn to speak English?"

"We have English in school. But mostly I learned from Marines. Marines number one. I was gofer—boots, errand, you name it."

"I'll bet you were good."

"Fuckin' eh."

Press laughed and cut a piece of pineapple, which he handed to the boy.

"You no dummy, either," said the boy before gulping the piece down.

"Well, you never know," Press reasoned. "Tell me your name and tell me about your family."

The boy talked enthusiastically. His name was Trinh, and he was the youngest of four children. His father had been deputy district chief in Cam Lo before he was killed by the Viet Cong in 1968. The VC were mostly gone now, and life was quiet in the village where the family moved a year after his father's death. They lived in a one-room, concrete block structure. Press had seen countless similar hovels, mostly furnished with the discards of the American military: plastic sheets covering the open front in winter, ammo boxes providing seating and storage, shell casings used as containers. His mother worked in the rice paddies with the extended family. While Trinh was not in school, he peddled the produce his uncle grew on a small plot.

When he finished, Press and Banks looked at each other, both obviously impressed. Press told him to come by every day at four-thirty, and he would buy pineapples. The boy agreed happily, and the platoon began the short return to Bravo One.

Unlike most of the bunkers at Bravo One, the four that housed Press's platoon were built on the upper edge of a swale. Laterite clay excavated for the foundation was used as cover material for both the top and the exposed side of each bunker. Press did not get a good look at his bunker that morning, when he and Banks had stowed their cots and footlockers. Now, after evening chow, he inspected it closely. The bunker was illuminated by two candles burning on his footlocker and by the flashlight which he used to inspect critical structural members. He could only cast a beam projecting a few inches, for the dark creosoted timbers seemed to absorb light. "It would take a hell of a blast to knock out these twelve by twelve posts and caps," he observed.

"I'd just as soon not put it to the test," Banks joked.

Press doused the beam and sat on his cot. "What's your pleasure, Sarge, vodka and orange soda or Drambuie? Too bad we don't have ice."

"I'm very disappointed in you, sir. Only two choices? At Khe Sanh your bar was well stocked. Ice, though, is probably even beyond your means."

"I'll bet you there's ice at the TOC," Press said, pouring vodka into an empty beer can.

"That's right, the king of the hill probably has ice."

"Did you see him this morning, standing in front of the TOC being interviewed by CBS?"

"Must have missed it. Do you know what he said?"

"I was too far away, but I'm sure it was about the casualties last week. He looked like a recruiting poster—shoulders squared at gut-sucking attention, steel pot clamped at right elbow arms...his head sixty percent jaw, the rest of it shaved clean."

"You really don't like this fellow, do you?"

"Not if appearance is more than skin deep. I could be wrong, maybe he's a good guy. Anyway, here's a screwdriver," Press said, walking over to Banks' cot in the southwest corner of the bunker.

They talked for a while longer, then Press picked up his paperback, *Les Miserables*, and read for forty-five minutes in the candlelight. Banks was snoring rhythmically when he blew out the candles. The bunker was plunged into darkness, and he could see nothing, not even his hand two inches from his face.

Press lay on his cot insensate. The first stirrings were subliminal, the second soft rustling, the third came in waves, subaquatic to start, then rolling into the brackish backwater of semi-consciousness, and finally breaking against an eyelid. He opened it and saw nothing. Moments later he identified the noise as chirping, and it was becoming louder and louder, accompanied by the sound of tiny feet scampering somewhere on the stringer above—multiplying feet—going in one direction and then reversing course, then a misstep, and something falling on his stomach, squealing and scampering off his cot, landing on the bunker floor, where it squealed again. Press was now fully awake and alert. He swore savagely and groped for the matches somewhere on his footlocker. "Sarge, wake up!" he shouted twice while striking a match. An anemic flame appeared at the tip and although it barely cut into the darkness, the rats took notice and vanished into hidden recesses.

Over his swearing Press heard a sleepy voice from the far corner of the bunker: "What's going on—we getting hit?"

Both candles were now burning, faintly illuminating the interior. "Christ, Sarge, you didn't hear the rats playing rugby on the stringers? There were enough of them to form a league—back and forth, back and forth, and then one of the little rodent bastards fell on me."

"Never heard 'em. But you ought to be grateful; it could of been that Goliath we saw foraging by the gate this morning. Nothing like an American-fed Vietnamese rat," Banks quipped with equal measures of jest and awe.

Press poured himself a generous dose of vodka. "Good thing these candles will last the night," he said and gulped down half of the spirits. "Promise me this, Sarge," he continued. "Don't let it out that I'm using a night light."

"Wouldn't dream of it, sir," Banks said with a chuckle, then rolled over in his cot and quickly went to sleep. He began to snore softly as Press simmered silently.

Several days of only sporadic interruption ensued, and the platoon settled into a work routine. The engineers would begin at first light with a benign, nearly horizontal sun. Three teams would stoke the mixers and fill the bucket of the front-end loader, whose operator would deliver the heaving cargo to a fourth team waiting at the target bunker. This team would spread the concrete in a three inch layer over the entire bunker. No one knew precisely what thickness of concrete was necessary to prevent a rocket from penetrating the hard shell, so whenever the engineers came upon a discarded tank or APC tread—many littered Bravo One—they would drag it to a bunker for use as reinforcement.

The work was exhausting, and the pace slowed as the liquid sun inched ever higher. They broke for chow at mid-day, when the sun cast no shadow, taking a half-hour to eat and relax in the relative cool of the bunker. The mixers ran steadily from one to almost four o'clock. They flushed and scraped the mixers, then drove to the river, where they cleaned out the loader bucket, filled the trailer with water and the five-ton with sand and gravel. They finished their workday by washing themselves in the shallow water.

Trinh, pineapples in hand, would wait for the platoon at the river, and Press was always pleased to see him. At their second meeting, Trinh had asked Press to help him to improve his English, which he began to do for twenty minutes each day.

The platoon would arrive back at Bravo One in time for evening chow. When the sun reached its evening repose, Banks would dispatch three engineers for guard duty. The others would drink beer and play cards or go off and smoke a joint or two of marijuana. Press knew of no one using heroin, even though there were even fewer diversions here than in base camp. Perhaps it was the grinding work in somnolent heat; all were so exhausted that by eight o'clock, most were fast asleep.

The weather changed on the third day of June. As Press and Banks emerged from the mess bunker under lightening but sulking skies—misty sheets of low gray clouds with no promise of rain—Banks remarked favorably on the turn of weather. Press listened but seemed unconvinced. "Well, you may not buy into it, but I'll take a warm, overcast day over the damn sweltering heat every time," Banks finished.

"It's not the temperature I'm concerned about," Press responded. "Look over there," he continued, pointing to the west. "Tell me what you see."

"Clouds. Lots of 'em."

"What don't you see?"

"The hills."

"Right. We've been only taking four or five hits a day for the past week. I've got a strange feeling about today."

"Well, even if we can't see the launch, radar should still pick them up," Banks reasoned.

"I don't know. They'll still have the advantage."

They walked to the cement mixers, where other platoon members were gathering. For security purposes no formations were held. Communication was informal, and most announcements or directives were generally passed to squad leaders and from them to their men. Both Banks and Press were always accessible and rarely taken by surprise, despite the increasing rotation of engineers.

It was not yet nine o'clock, and Press was sitting on top of a bunker writing a letter to the US Immigration and Naturalization Service. From his perch he could survey the work in progress. For areas in which the front-end loader could not maneuver, the engineers used a wheel barrow to haul the concrete. It was exhausting work, especially when negotiating a rise. Press put his letter down when he saw Garrison take the handles of the wheel barrow and place it under the shoot of the mixer. The last time Garrison had hauled concrete, he lost control and turned over the wheel barrow half way to the target bunker, eliciting a round of hoots, guffaws, and snickers from the onlookers. Now, he lifted the handles and steered the load along the beaten path, picking up speed on a down slope. He passed midpoint and shoved the wheel barrow along a moderate incline. Engineers at the mixer and those waiting on a bunker grinned and nodded to each other approvingly. A glimmer of self-satisfaction appeared on his face as he negotiated a seventy-degree turn and shouldered the wheel barrow close to the bunker. His foot slipped on a patch of wet concrete as he was making a final turn, but he recovered and set the wheel barrow down in front of the team waiting with shovels. The engineers smiled and several at the bunker patted him on the back. As Garrison beamed, Press and Banks exchanged thumbs up.

Press went back to his writing and carefully constructed three sentences before pausing. The explosion sounded like the crack of lightning splitting a tree. The rocket had struck the ground near an eight-inch howitzer at the edge of the jobsite. While the engineers scattered to various bunkers, Press ran to the artillery tower. Galecki was already on deck, gazing west into the clouds with a detached, clinical look on his face and a sprig of beef jerky clamped between his teeth. "What kept you?" he asked rhetorically.

"I had to fold a letter and put it in my pocket."

Galecki flexed his mouth in what Press construed to be a grin. "Interesting," the artillery officer muttered, without looking away.

"I know what you mean: Nothing changes so much as a cloud."

Galecki ignored the remark. "They're so low—almost kissing the ground. The Montagnard call it *crachin*: a soupy blend of cloud and fog. This is not going to be a good day."

"Well, Tom, I hope you don't calibrate danger as well as you do howitzers," Press said as he put his hand on Galecki's shoulder.

They talked for a few more minutes, Press watching the jobsite and waving several of his men who had ventured out of the bunkers back inside. Two more rockets exploded nearby.

"Why don't they ever target the north side of the fire base?" Press said in irritation.

"Because this is where the guns are."

"I should have taken my mother's advice. She always told me that I'd get into trouble associating with the wrong crowd."

Press took another look at the glowering sky and left the tower. He found Banks waiting in the entryway of one of the bunkers and told him that the platoon would stand down for the day. Banks then organized a detail to wash out the mixers and equipment and directed the rest to go back to the platoon's bunkers singly.

Shortly after nine o'clock, the sporadic shelling turned into a fusillade. Press and Banks made the rounds of the bunkers, visiting each squad in turn.

While they were with the second squad, several rockets burst in the swale between the engineers and the 155 mm battery. Two more gutted the flat ground a few feet beyond the bunker, then one to the left and two to the right in quick succession. They were bracketed. Sgt. Johnson, a normally easygoing squad leader, began to shake uncontrollably.

"Easy, Sarge," Press said. "They won't get us."

"Sorry, sir, I can't help it. I'm scared to death."

"We all are; you're just the first to admit it," Press reassured him as he surveyed the faces of the squad members. Several had turned ashen, others wore grim expressions. Everyone was standing, and no one joked or spoke above a murmur, perhaps in the illogical fear that it would give their position away. Johnson still trembled, and he began to pray in a half-tone.

The explosions were deafening, and as soon as the shock waves from one would dissipate, another would detonate, often only feet away from the bunker. Press knew that the rocket tubes could not be better placed for the destruction of the platoon's bunkers and the chances were fair that he and many of his men would die at any moment. He thought about the conversation he had had with Rev. Browne and realized the time had come to test the adage about there being no atheists in foxholes. He felt only fear. He knew that if he was wrong, he could very well be on his way to hell in the next minute. But the acceptance of God would have to be sincere and unconditional. He could not do it.

The rocket attack subsided half an hour after it had started in earnest, and Press stepped out of the bunker and looked around. One of the powder storage bunkers of the 155 mm battery was burning furiously. The fire could not reach the ammo bunker, but if it were put out soon, some of the powder would be saved.

"The engineers to the rescue," Banks said from behind.

Press turned and saw Spec 4 Powers leave the third squad bunker and climb the steps of his front-end loader. "Looks like Powers is seizing the initiative," he observed.

"Yes, sir. Finest tradition of the Army."

"I guess you never can tell, you know...how Johnson reacted."

"It got pretty bad there for a while—worst than I've ever seen it."

Press nodded. "Now we've got a hint of what some of those guys went through in World War Two with the rolling artillery bombardments. It all boils down to this, Terry. We're underpaid."

They both laughed and continued to watch Powers fill the bucket with dirt and dump it on the blazing bunker. Occasionally, the fire would reach a new powder bag, sending a lick of flame skyward. It was no match, however, for the suffocating load of nearly two cubic yards of dirt every forty-five seconds. Soon, the fire was extinguished, and Powers parked his loader and strolled nonchalantly back to his bunker.

Press and Banks were counting the dwarf craters surrounding the platoon's bunkers. "It's a damn miracle none of 'em were hit; maybe we should cover ours next," Banks said with a hint of sincerity.

"If we stay in range, we probably should, but it would hardly be in the finest tradition of the Army."

"My own words used against me."

"Com'on Sarge, let's see how the third squad is getting along."

The rocket attack continued intermittently, and the occupants of Bravo One, being unable either to gauge its reappearance or prevent it, remained holed up. They ventured out only to dash to the mess hall for the noon meal or to relieve themselves. Press and Banks had rotated among the men until three o'clock, when they returned to their bunker.

Banks began to pace the floor while Press took up a book. "I'd go crazy here if I didn't have anything to read," Press said. Hearing no response, he lifted an eyelid. "Something on your mind, Sarge?"

"Sort of. It's my wife, actually."

Press sat up on his cot and asked with concern, "Is she okay?"

"Oh, it's nothing like that. We've only been married for a few months—rushed it a little on account of my orders for Nam. Anyway, I got a letter from one of my brothers the other day. Well, the gist of it is that she might of committed bigamy. I knew she was married before, but my brother believes that her divorce hasn't been finalized. You know anything about these matters?"

Press wiped a hand over his forehead and cheek. "Hell, I can't even *get* married, so I'm probably the last one to ask. I don't know—I suppose it's a matter of doing nothing—letting the divorce come through while you're still here and as long as nobody outside the family knows. Does her ex-hus—er—does husband number one know you and she are married?"

"Don't think so. But there's another problem: she's seeing somebody else. I guess I should of waited till I got to know her better before...." Banks reproached himself in a voice that trailed off.

"I'm sorry to hear that, Terry. You don't need to be worrying about things like that while you're over here getting pounded by rockets."

"Thanks, but it doesn't bother me as much as I thought it would. At least it won't cost me much to get out of."

"You're a better man than I. If I knew Celia was sleeping with somebody else, I'd be seething. I don't mean that in the machismo sense—you know, she's *my* woman and all that. It wouldn't be so bad if it were just for physical pleasure. But she wouldn't do it for pleasure—her heart would have to be in it. That's what would be so awful. Tell me, did you mean it when you said it doesn't bother you?"

"No, I guess I don't. I still love her. I hope my brother is wrong about her shacking up. I hope there's still a chance for us."

"One of the most frustrating things about being here is that we're powerless to do anything at home. Hope is all we have."

Banks paced the floor for a minute then sat down on his cot and opened his footlocker. "You play cribbage? I've got a board here and a deck of cards—"

"It's been years—I played in grade school."

"Want to have a go, two out of three?"

"Why not," Press said, and he got up and took a seat on the far side of Banks' footlocker, leaving the side near the cot as a playing surface. Banks reviewed the rules of the game, set the pegs at the head of first street, and dealt the cards. Press took the lead from the start. As he advanced onto second street, he had a double run, counting "Fifteen-two, fifteen-four, fifteen-six, fifteen-eight and sixteen for twenty-four."

"My God," Banks cried, "You're killing me."

Press widened his lead going down fourth street and was home with Banks having only a single peg in the first hole on third street. "Almost a double skunk," he said gleefully. "We should have been playing for money."

"You want to play another—dime a point?"

Press considered playing one more game, but slowly shook his head. "I don't think so...a skunk is two out of three. I believe I'll get something to eat at the mess hall."

"Hell, it's only four o'clock, the mess hall won't be open."

"Maybe I'll get lucky. I'll be back in a bit, Sarge."

Banks stretched out on his cot, his pillow partially propped against the bunker wall. "Think I'll take a little nap," he said.

Press climbed the double row of steps out of the bunker. Sergeant Retherford was standing next to the jeep reviewing the guard duty roster for the evening. "You been out here long, Sarge?" Press asked.

"Only a few minutes," sir.

"It's not the safest place to be."

"Sir, there is no *safe* place."

"You're right. See you later; I'll going to the mess hall."

"I don't think it'll be open, sir."

Press shrugged his shoulders and turned to walk down the path into the hollow beyond his bunker. He was only about forty feet past the bunker when he heard the whoosh of a rocket over his left shoulder. The sound was swallowed up by the dirt in front of his bunker. "Whew, a dud," he said, after hearing no explosion. He turned and walked upslope toward the bunker where a cursory look at the point of entry showed an eight-inch diameter hole in the dirt leading directly to where they were playing cards. The rocket was no doubt buried somewhere in the eleven feet of clay protecting the bunker. He decided to tell Banks how lucky he was.

He continued up the slope and reached the steps. Before he took his first step down, the unmistakable odor of cordite invaded his nostrils and filled him with dread. He raced down the steps and stopped short. Where Banks' cot had been was now occupied by three feet of clay from the partially collapsed roof. About six feet of the bunker wall had been blown out. Press shouted twice for Retherford, then swooped down on the pile of dirt and began scraping it away with his hands.

"He's over here, Lieutenant," Retherford said a few seconds later.

Press turned to his left and saw Banks sprawled ten feet away, his legs spread-eagle, flung apart by sudden acceleration. His head was swelling rapidly, and his partial of four upper front teeth was protruding from his mouth. He struggled to breathe.

"I don't want him to die down here; let's carry him up," said Press in a voice overcome with sadness.

They put Banks on the ground near the jeep, and then Press radioed for the medics, who ran the 200 meters from their station. When they arrived, they crouched over him but soon stood up. The senior of the two shook his head and said, "There's nothing we can do for him."

Banks' head continued to swell, and he made several almost indistinct sucking sounds.

The junior medic unrolled a body bag, but quickly put it away after a withering glance from Press, who was feeling as helpless as he ever had in his life.

Press watched as Banks took his final, labored breath, still finding it difficult to comprehend the passage from a person to a cadaver.

The senior medic checked his wristwatch and removed one of Banks' dog tags. Dictating to his subordinate, he said, "SFC Terry Banks died at sixteen-twelve—what the hell is today's date?"

"The third."

He began again: "SFC Terry Banks died at sixteen-twelve on the third of June of wounds suffered in enemy action."

As Press watched the medics put his platoon sergeant into a body bag, he was thinking that they were playing cribbage together only fifteen minutes earlier. Then a second thought shook him to his depths. What if he hadn't beaten Banks badly in cribbage? He hadn't played the game in years—what luck! Was it luck? If they had played two out of three, would he have been killed too?

Press did not want to go back into the bunker, but he found himself on the steps and once again inhaling the stench of death. Down in the bunker he searched for the footlocker. How could something so large...don't look for large, he chided himself. It was there, scattered over the floor, the smallest fragments match stick size. Had he played on, they would have needed two body bags. He left the bunker and inspected the path of entry of the rocket. Goddamn Marines, he said to himself—how could you build a bunker and not compact the cover material? Had the Marine engineers compacted the outer few of the twelve feet of laterite clay protecting the exposed side of the bunker, the rocket blast would not have penetrated the bunker wall.

Retherford met Press at the jeep after Press had radioed the news to Battalion and reported Banks' death personally to Lt. Col. Forbes, the fire base commander. He listened sympathetically while Press railed against Forbes for his brusque and indifferent manner.

Retherford obviously had something on his mind, and when Press let go of Forbes, he said: "Sir, I know your eating habits pretty well, and I've never seen you go for chow at 1600."

"I guess it was out of the ordinary, but this is no ordinary day."

"Do you mind me asking a question?"

"Go ahead, Sarge."

"Were you hungry?"

Press thought for a few moments, then slowly shook his head. "No, I wasn't hungry."

"I can't help but feel you weren't alone this afternoon, if you get my drift, LT."

"I get your drift, Sarge. All I know is that I'll never be able to explain it."

Retherford left a few minutes later, and Press sat in his jeep reflecting on how the turn of a few cards and an inexplicable departure almost certainly saved his life. He looked skyward, where children were taught heaven was, and just as he began to speculate on the metaphysical implications, a rocket slammed into level ground sixty meters away. A clod of dirt hit the white star on the jeep's hood dead center and rolled off onto the ground. Press made a *hmmph* sound, and although the inside of a bunker was the last place he wanted to take refuge, or to see ever again, he decided he would be safer joining one of the squads.

Darkness did not settle on the fire base in the usual stages, dusk being day long, and Press was surprised to find that he needed a flashlight so soon after returning from evening mess. He went from bunker to bunker, talking to the engineers and giving falsely-felt assurance on the prospects for the next day. He completed his round and started for his jeep, when Retherford approached. "Sir, Garrison hasn't shone for guard duty," he reported.

"Come to think of it, I didn't see him in any of the bunkers."

"I double-checked. He's not here and he's not at guard duty."

Press swore silently, knowing that there were no distractions, nowhere to go, on Bravo One. "Let's break out the flashlights and search the area. Be sure your people don't bunch up; this hasn't exactly been our day."

In very short order, no more than four or five minutes, a voice shot out in the darkness, "Over here! Over here!" The shout came from below Press's old bunker. By the time he reached the same path he had taken on his aborted trip to the mess hall, four engineers were standing in a semi-circle with their lights pointed outward.

"Don't look, Lieutenant. It's terrible, a direct hit," said Retherford, his voice full of emotion.

Press of course did look and what he saw in one pass of the beam through the haze repulsed him. "He had a birthday coming up; did he ever make it to eighteen?"

"I believe he did, sir," said a voice in the darkness.

"I'll go to the TOC and report it and have the medics come over. Meanwhile, fan out and search for body parts and his dog tags; we can't establish that it's Garrison—not to Graves Registration's satisfaction, anyway," said Press.

"Roger," Retherford said.

When Forbes saw Press enter the TOC, he grimaced and said, "Don't tell me you lost another, Lieutenant."

"Yes, sir. Private Garrison. He left his bunker sometime after evening mess, probably going to guard duty, and took a direct hit by a one-twenty-two."

Forbes shook his head severely and said, "We don't need any more god-damn preventable KIA's on this fire base."

Press was stunned by his reaction. "You make it sound like it was his fault for getting killed."

"Watch how you talk to me, Lieutenant."

Press flung a cold look at Forbes who, with eyes as hard as marbles and a scant fringe of hair on his lower head, epitomized all he had come to detest in the Army. The fire base commander was now being evaluated by his superiors chiefly on his record of casualty prevention, and every death chipped away at his chance for promotion. For whatever reason, Forbes could not extend himself and express an insincere compassion. Press, managing to keep his tongue tethered, turned slowly, offensively, and walked out.

On the walk back he watched the tight cylinders of light sweep the ground, and it reminded him of a scavenger hunt at the summer camp he attended in Wisconsin when he was twelve, a stark contrast to this night: sober shouts to raucous revelry, picking up body parts to pulling clues out of dark places.

As the medics arrived, the searchers congregated around the blackened trunk of Pvt. Garrison. No identification nor anything of substance had been found. Touching the torso as little as possible, they eased it into a body bag and with the help of two engineers, hauled it away.

At first light the next morning, Press and the squad leaders, each carrying a shovel and a box which until recently contained C-ration cartons, searched a broad area near their bunkers. It was on the fringes of their search that Press found a forearm and hand, a liver, and a piece of skull, which at first he mistook for a coconut shell—pure white on the inside, the outside covered with tufts of hair. He knew it would be a long time, if ever, before he would eat coconut. Johnson retrieved a boot with a foot inside, and Retherford came up with Garrison's wallet, which, despite cuts, was whole.

Press opened the wallet and looked at the identification card. "He did make it to eighteen," he said. "Old enough to go to war."

After a few seconds of silence, Retherford peered inside the container. "Goddamn rats," he said.

Press put his shovel in the ground saying, "Let's bury it right here."

In early afternoon of the next day, the platoon returned to Dong Ha for a memorial service. Without having the briefest acquaintance with either of the deceased, Chaplain Hayes assured the assemblage that the souls of the two fine soldiers were in a state of holy grace. Press, gripped by an unrelenting lassitude, divorced himself from the service. He thought of the journey Banks and Garrison were making together—how embarrassed Banks would be by the company he was keeping. A wave of shame overcame him, and he felt himself turning scarlet. His thoughts then drifted to his own mortality. The next thing he knew, he was standing alone near the two empty helmets. He felt a hand on his shoulder.

"Come sit down a moment," the chaplain said. "You're not a religious person, are you? I've never seen you at a Sunday service."

"No, I'm not religious."

"I could see you were suffering; lost within yourself…I just want to know if there's anything I can do?"

Press was silent for a moment. "I should have died with Terry Banks. By some incredible luck in a card game, followed by inexplicable behavior on my part, I survived."

"Believe me, you're not the first to experience something like that. Have you ever considered that God may have a purpose for you?"

"For what? I've been against Him. And why me? I'm insignificant. Why would God pick me when He has refused to intercede in billions of acts of egregious barbarity throughout history?"

"I can't answer that, but those who have died that way may have a special place near Him. Maybe the transient hell they went through on Earth is being made up for by an eternity in heaven."

Press lowered his head, as if in contemplation. "There was this young soldier on Bravo One. His friend was killed and he blamed himself for living. One thing I'm certain of—I'll not be imprisoned for the theft of time, for stealing a future. I'll earn a pardon." He got up slowly, looked at the chaplain and smiled. "Ah, that's too serious. So, for the present, I'm going back to the hootch and find a special place near Johnnie Walker—Johnnie Walker *Black*." Several seconds later: "That was uncalled for. I'm sorry."

Hayes smiled. "That's okay, black humor doesn't offend me."

"You're all right, Reverend. Stop by some evening. We've got a few lost souls who are down on their luck. You play poker?"

32

Press was sitting in his jeep at seven-thirty the following morning, and his thoughts were mundane: where was Sfc. Gutierrez, his newly appointed platoon sergeant from Charlie Company? Press had convinced the chain of command that the flight path of the NVA rockets endangered the lives of his men beyond an acceptable risk and had received permission for the platoon to move back to Dong Ha and commute to Bravo One. He glanced at his watch and noted that the rest of the platoon had been gone for ten minutes. Pfc. Jasper, his new driver, sat behind the wheel, absorbed in a sex magazine.

As he was about to step out and search for Gutierrez, he felt the jeep sway and caught sight of his platoon sergeant taking a seat in the rear. "Okay, Jasper, let's get on the road," he ordered.

The cooling effect of the artificial breeze and the lack of dust made the drive west along QL-9 pleasant. But as they made a right turn onto the dirt road near Cam Lo and slowed down, Press began to hear mumbling from the back seat which he could not decipher but caused him to feel uneasy. He canted his head backward to catch an intelligible word and found himself listening to a tongue scuffing against a mouth. He did not look back, but strained to pick out fragments of the slurred monologue. He concluded most of it was profanity with an occasional reference to officers and the Army.

Press closed his eyes and while continuing to listen to Gutierrez' drunken diatribe, attempted to quell the emotions swirling inside: disgust, helplessness, shock at the realization that Banks had been succeeded by his reciprocal. Jasper glanced nervously at Press several times during the remainder of the drive to Bravo One, but gained nothing from it. Press had made a decision and kept silent and expressionless until they entered the fire base.

"Pull up in front of that bunker," Press ordered, pointing to one of the artillery bunkers that had been covered with concrete. "Come with me, Sergeant," he said, looking at Gutierrez for the first time since formation. After the sergeant climbed out of the jeep, Press told Jasper to join the platoon. He waited till Jasper drove off and then turned to Gutierrez, fixing him with a fierce gaze. "Go into this bunker and sleep it off, Sergeant. Do not leave it except for mess until I come for you at 1700. I expressly order you not to have any contact with the men; you are no longer a member of this platoon. Do you understand what you are to do, Sergeant Gutierrez?"

Gutierrez looked defiant, but he would not challenge Press. He nodded and disappeared into the darkness of the bunker. Press walked a hundred meters to the jeep and called Padgett on the radio. After explaining what had transpired, he told the CO bluntly that he would not keep Gutierrez. Padgett replied that he would go to Battalion and see what he could do. They signed off.

Press knew well the recycling expedient employed by the Army. Problem NCOs were passed around to various companies in the battalion, either with the dim and self-deluding hope of eventual rehabilitation or by the desire to postpone the daunting procedure of involuntary separation under section two-twelve of the Uniform Code of Military Justice. Perhaps both. Whether Gutierrez' morning embalming was brought about by his sudden and humiliating transfer from Charlie Company or prompted by the prospect of a journey to perhaps the most dangerous American-occupied parcel of land in-country, Press would never know. By sunset Gutierrez would be someone else's problem.

Few rockets would strike the fire base during the next ten days, and progress covering the bunkers was rapid. The engineers refined techniques and improved coordination to the point that the project flowed as smoothly as the concrete. Press was not only pleased with the platoon's effort, but also with the attitude and behavior of the men. The morale of troops country-wide was degenerating. Fewer than 200,000 remained, and for most of those it was a garrison war. Base camp boredom was a contagion with heroin use endemic. Press also felt fortunate with the lack of racial tensions in the platoon. Two of the seven black soldiers under his command were squad leaders, and neither showed any favoritism nor were treated with a lack of respect by other engineers.

The hour each day spent at the Cam Lo River was especially agreeable for Press. He was slowly converting Trinh's "Marine" English to a less spicy variety and was delighted by his appetite for new words. None of his inquiries regarding Trinh's immigration had yet been answered, but he was undeterred, writing to both his senators and congressman in Washington DC. To ensure that he was pursuing a goal which Trinh also shared, he had obliquely questioned him on the subject: "You have studied many countries in school. If you had a choice, what country would you most like to live in?" Trinh's immediate response was that he wanted to go to America, make money, and drive a GTO.

One afternoon in mid-June, while they were sitting under a shade tree snacking on pineapple, their attention was drawn to the hills in the west. Fire Base Fuller, now manned by *ARVN* forces, was being pounded. They were accustomed to seeing only the initial flashes of launched rockets; now, with the glint from the sun and their transverse direction, they streaked through the sky like spears of lightning.

"Looks like the NVA might try to take Fuller," Press speculated.

"Good, the more they fire at Fuller, the fewer they'll fire at us," Retherford reasoned. "Dink against dink—that's how it oughta be."

Trinh gave him a disagreeable look, and Press shook his head in silent reprimand.

"Sorry," the sergeant said. "Dink against *ARVN*."

"Does your family have a plan to leave this area when the NVA cross the DMZ next year or the year after?" Press asked Trinh.

"You think they will come?"

"Yes, after the Americans leave, they will attack. And they will win."

Trinh thought for a while. Finally, he said, "Fuck that."

Press laughed. "I see we still have work to do on your grammar."

The next day at Bravo One, Press and Galecki sat in the artillery officers' bunker taking a break from the insistent, suffocating heat and listened to the opening of Beethoven's *Eroica* Symphony. "I'll have one more of those rum cookies, if you don't mind," said Press.

"Help yourself."

Press reached into a large cardboard box containing an assortment of cookies and picked out the largest of the rum cookies. "Eat enough of these, and you'd get stoned."

"My wife says she used a whole fifth of rum in the recipe."

Press pointed to one of the flaps on the box on which the words *I'M HORNY* were written with a marker in four-inch strokes. "What does that do for your morale?" he joked.

"Drives me crazy."

"When's your *DEROS*?"

"Not till November, but if the rumor's true, I'm looking at August."

"What rumor?"

"There'll be a big pull-down in August and Bravo One will be history."

Press whistled and reached over to shut off the tape player. "That was the first movement. It broke the rules of classical music at the time and really pissed off the purists. Couldn't you feel its power and exuberance? It's like a giant wave rolling toward the beach—slightly menacing, irresistible, unstoppable."

Galecki crossed his eyes and said, "Think I'll have another cookie." They both laughed and stood up to leave. "Some *ARVN* unit will take our place," Galecki continued with the subject that interested him.

"I've got to find a way to get Trinh to the States this year. There's no way the *ARVN* will hold."

"Did you watch the change of command ceremony at Fuller yesterday?"

"Yeah, the NVA pulverized it."

"And we pulverized it for four hours last night. The *ARVN* are going to retake it, but there won't be anything left. Just think what will happen when the NVA flings a couple of divisions across the DMZ."

They stepped out into vertical sunlight and winced, despite wearing sunglasses. A slight breeze warded off some of the debilitating effects of the heat, but, nonetheless, their emergence into the hottest part of the day caused Press to remark that with another degree or two, the air would scorch their lungs.

The heat promised not to be the fiercest enemy of the day. Within minutes of resuming work, the siren blared and rockets soon dropped from the sky. The artillery responded, both the 155 mm and the eight-inch track howitzers. Press took in the tumult from the siting tower: the peeling roar of the big guns and black blurs of torn air, then wheezing sounds as the heavy invisible shells hurtled toward distant hills, soon lost to the ear with no hope for the eye of any finality. Occasionally, a synchronous blast from an incoming rocket and outgoing artillery would shake the tower with an ecumenical explosion.

It was not an artillery duel in the pure definition, but in the practical sense it was every bit a duel and they crossed swords for the better part of an hour, before gradually subsiding. After five minutes of nervous quiet, Press made his way down the steps, meeting Galecki at the base of the tower. Galecki spoke, but Press did not hear. "Say again?" he asked.

The artillery lieutenant laughed and said in a loud voice, "You need ear plugs for times like this. Incredible, wasn't it?"

"I should probably feel honored. I'm sure not too many people have been caught in an artillery duel and watched in relative safety. I kept expecting your eight-inchers to take a deep breath after exhaling those 200 pound shells."

"Maybe if they did, we wouldn't have to replace the barrels so often."

"Any casualties?"

"None in our area."

"It's a damn miracle. I counted six craters just around the tower. One hit about two feet to the left of your bunker, but the soil obviously wasn't compacted and it must have burrowed pretty far before it detonated—might have done some damage inside."

"Let's have a look," Galecki said with concern, and they walked to the bunker, entering from the right side. The interior was in shambles. The blast had been funneled down the length of the narrow bunker, leaving the internal buttresses intact, but damaging or destroying all else in its path. Dirt and debris covered upturned cots and floor boards. A phonograph which had been on a table near the blast point lay demolished against the right wall. Galecki's tape player was scattered in small pieces at their feet.

"Sorry about your tape," Galecki said.

"Don't worry—you can't kill Beethoven. I don't suppose the OD will reimburse you for the loss of personal items."

"You suppose right," Galecki said, peeling a cookie off of one of the supports. "I didn't have much; too bad, though, we didn't get further into the cookies."

Press had never seen a B-52 Bomber run before the last days of June. His chance came during the late morning of the twenty-fifth. The NVA had fired more than 150 rockets at Bravo One the previous day, and the report had been passed quickly to higher commands. Galecki had spotted the planes and alerted Press. The bombers were flying at a great altitude—much too high to be heard. From the ground they looked like sewing needles flashing through the air for a minute before becoming lost to the eye. The gray bombs did not reflect sunlight and fell unseen. Minutes after the B-52s turned west, back to Thailand, the bombs began to strike, but unlike the pandemonium of the artillery duel, only muffled sounds resembling distant thunder reverberated off the western hills, shock waves too distant to feel, but with dust rising in great sheets, very much like a rain shower in the distance, only from the ground up. Artillerymen and engineers in the area were on their knees, smiling and bowing with arms extended to the west.

"Too bad we don't have the ingredients for a toast—it's definitely time for a bottoms-up," Press said with a grin.

Galecki's jaw slackened with awe as he viewed the columns of dust. "Damn, it's like a giant curtain closing off the horizon. You know, this may cool the earth a degree or two," he said, laughing at his hyperbole. "I'll bet Charlie took some lumps today. B-52's are their worst nightmare of course. They absolutely shit in their pants when the bombs drop. I remember reading that a captured NVA said that a near miss was enough to collapse their tunnels."

The B-52 attack had a devastating effect on the NVA. They were able only to respond with desultory fire in the weeks ahead. The curtain that Galecki saw on the 25th of June closed the war for Press. In early July he returned to Dong Ha for his final week in-country. Several days before departing for Cam Ranh Bay, he began a letter to Celia.

"Love and war—the two most emotional experiences a person can have. I happen to be in both, but let me tell you, my love, that by the time you read this I'll have given up one—forever. And I'm going to remain in the other—forever.

"In three or four days, I'm leaving for Cam Ranh Bay, and will probably arrive three days after that at Ft. Lewis, Wash. It should take less than two days to muster out, then it's on to DC and you. I still can't believe that I'm going home. My two years, eight months, and seventeen days posing as a soldier will seem like one long floating moment. No they won't. It didn't occur to me until I wrote those words that I am a soldier—a flawed one no doubt—and will in many ways always be one. And the memories of this place will always be distinct and fresh.

"Now, Celia, to where I've been. I spent my first seven months building a road in the mountains; the next two, at Khe Sanh. I especially did not want you to know that I was there. I know that you suspected by R&R that I was not where I said I was, but I just could not put that additional burden on you by telling you what kind of work I really did. In one of my recent letters, I explained that I was sitting out the war in base camp. That didn't last long. For most of the last two months I was on a tiny fire base a few miles south of the DMZ. That place will always be a source of sadness for me."

He wrote a few paragraphs describing how he met and formed a friendship with Trinh. Continuing, he wrote, "I have written to the INS and other agencies about getting him a student visa, so he can live in the US. I've not received any replies. He now lives dead center in the invasion route the North is sure to take after our forces pull out. His father was a government official murdered by the VC, and if Trinh survives the invasion, his future looks bleak. The mobility of civilian life will enable me to do much more for him than I've been able to accomplish sequestered in the military. It may sound crazy to you, but I plan to return to Vietnam as soon as I can obtain some official backing for Trinh. At the very least I'll get his family to Saigon and take him back with me. Then I'll find a job in the DC area, where I'll be close to you and will be able to work on sponsoring the immigration of the remaining family. While I don't have a lot of money, I've saved almost all of my overseas pay. As you know, my needs are not great. I could live very frugally and, with an occasional glimpse of you—it would be enough to draw the same air—very happily.

"I realize that I've never lacked for confidence, probably without having earned the right, but I leave here convinced that I've accomplished much—and it's just the beginning.

"It's time to fold this up and get it on its way, my love. I'll phone you when I arrive in Tacoma. Thoughts of you are as food is to life...or a smile on your gentle lips."

He signed the letter. Sealing it, he felt he was doing the same on a life forever removed.

33

The cheering erupted spontaneously the moment the aircraft wheels touched the runway at McChord Air Base. As the plane taxied, Press was mulling over the quote attributed to Winston Churchill: "There's nothing so exhilarating as being shot at and missed." Yes, there is, he said to himself. Coming home after a war is much more exhilarating.

Twelve of his OCS classmates were on the airplane, including Wilson, Ortiz, and Petras. Most had gone to Vietnam in October 1970 and qualified for an early out based on date of commission. While they were returning home up to three months prior to their original *DEROS*, the wind-down of the war curtailed Press's tour by one day.

They were all in a euphoric, jaunty mood as they left the plane late on a Thursday evening and boarded the bus that would take them to the barracks-style bachelor officers' quarters. After drawing bedding supplies, the former classmates made arrangements to meet at the officers' club the next day for dinner. With any luck they would complete most of their mustering-out activities on Friday.

Press could have slept longer, but got out of bed at six o'clock, eager to attack the day. After morning mess, he grabbed his personnel file and began going from building to building and line to line. At mid-afternoon he was just completing his medical check-up, when he saw a notice about the post blood drive. He had time, so he walked to the appropriate section of the building and after a few minutes, was on the table. The nurse who had prepared him woke him fifteen minutes later.

"Must have dozed off," he said. "Sleep comes with the closing of my eyes."

"Just return from Nam?" she asked.

"How did you guess?"

"When I cleaned your arm with alcohol, a layer of red dirt came off."

"Sorry, I showered this morning, but I suppose it'll take weeks to get out."

"It's very thoughtful of you to donate blood—just back from Vietnam."

"That's why I'm doing it. I could have donated once or twice over there, but I passed up the opportunity."

The nurse laughed. "One thing before you leave. You told the clerk that your blood type is B positive."

He reached for his wallet and pulled out a dog tag. "See for yourself."

"It's wrong. We checked it twice while you were napping. You're O negative. Good thing you didn't need an emergency transfusion." She glanced at the dog tag once again and continued, "And with no religion, you wouldn't have had a prayer."

Press laughed heartily. "That's very good, and so quick." There was a time when he would have added, "And so pretty." But he did not.

The nurse smiled, saying, "Well, you know your blood type now, and I don't imagine you'll be needing your dog tags. Stop by the refreshment table and have a cookie and some juice."

Press thanked her and picked up some refreshments to take to the pay phone, where he dialed Celia's phone number. After ten rings, he replaced the receiver. Walking back to the BOQ, he wondered where she was at seven on a Friday evening.

One of the permanent party officers had told Wilson late in the afternoon that the officers' annex would have a live band playing that evening, so at six o'clock, the classmates climbed into three taxis and drove several miles to the shore of Puget Sound. The two-story annex, a plain but sturdy building, was popular with junior officers. A fair number of people were already present.

After finding a table large enough to accommodate their party, ordering beer, and drinking the first toast, Press made his way to the entrance and a pay phone. A few seconds after dialing he heard a female voice. "Celia, is that you?"

"Press?"

"Lynn? Yes, it's Press—I'm back in the States."

"Welcome home. Are you local?"

"No. I'm at Fort Lewis, Washington."

"Celia's not here right now, Press."

"Hmmm...out with Jim, I suppose?"

"Is there a number she can call when she returns?"

He gave her the number and said, "It's a pay phone. Please tell her she doesn't have to call tonight; this place is going to get a little noisy—a lot noisy. I'll phone again in the morning."

"She'll be so relieved and happy you're back. It will be great seeing you again, Press."

He rung off and returned to the table. After pursing his lips in the manner of Lt. Holt and pulling on a can of beer, he considered Celia's date with Jim. He had no claim on her. Still...

He did not dwell on the matter and was soon drawn in by the camaraderie of the group and the catching-up of recent histories. At eight o'clock and many toasts later the band assembled.

"Listen up," Petras shouted. "Anybody hear the scuttlebutt on what happened to Hausser?" After no one spoke, he continued. "Wait till you hear this. After we graduated, he became a senior tac officer and one day ordered some unfortunate retread into the dumpster while the rest of the platoon goes to the boonies. About two hours later, the regimental commander is giving a tour of the OCS compound to some brass from the Pentagon, explaining how they've cut down on hazing and are concentrating more on skills development. When they round a corner, the retread sticks his head out of the dumpster, looking for his returning platoon, which he hears in the distance. He turns his head only to face the assorted brass. The regimental commander, somewhat taken aback, asks him what he's doing in the dumpster. The retread, trying to protect Hausser, tells him that he's looking for something he had accidentally thrown out."

Petras was forced to interrupt his account of the demise of Lt. Hausser until the uproarious laughter around the table subsided. "So the regimental commander asks the retread for his name and unit and tells him to return to his barracks. As the brass continue on their way, the platoon double-times past like conquering heroes. Meanwhile, Hausser veers over to the dumpster and yells, as if somebody's inside, all under the gaze of the commandant."

Tears were now streaming down the faces of most of the classmates. Petras stood up and shimmied around the table. "Next day, the very next day! Hausser is told that he's a goddamn civilian."

It started with Ortiz to the tune of Waltzing Matilda. Soon, they all were singing the same refrain: "Goddamn civilian, goddamn civilian, you come a waltzing civilian with me. Goddamn civilian, goddamn civilian, what kind of wretch do you take me to be?" They began to add stanzas, and soon the band provided accompaniment. With that the returnees scoured the annex for dancing partners, some appropriating the dates of fellow officers. No one protested; on the contrary, they joined in the celebration and began to clap and sing. Press approached the nurse who had taken his blood in the afternoon and asked her out to the dance floor. They introduced each other on the way. What they and the others did for the next half-hour skirted the rough edges of "dancing." The club seemed to gyrate with jubilation while the band played along with the newcomers' bawdy tunes.

Just before taking a break, the band played a ballad popular from World War II, "I'll Be Seeing You." Many of those at the table sang while the young officers home from Vietnam danced. Press held his partner at an appropriate distance at the start. But from the beer and the moment and the fragrance of the very same perfume Celia wore and with his eyes closed, his perspective wavered and he drew her close. When the dance ended he complained of the smoke and asked her to walk with him outside.

"So, what do you plan to do after leaving the Army?" she asked, as they left the club and began a stroll to the water's edge.

"Ah, Carol, you know how to hit a guy with a tough question. All I can say is that my future is far from settled. What about you? Will you stay in the Army after your three years are up."

"I've been thinking of going back to Chicago, but unlike you, I've got another year to sort it out. Who knows, I may see you there—on State Street or the Magnificent Mile."

"Or in a small cafe."

"At a wishing well."

Their banter went on for another twenty minutes. Press was feeling the intoxicating blend of beer, stress relief, freedom, and the promise of a future. He was enjoying his conversation with Carol and was at his most charming.

"...so it was like viewing everything from a fun house mirror. Then a terribly attractive nurse woke me and I realized where I was."

"Now that you're back in the real world, you're going to have to be careful on moonlit summer evenings."

"How's that?"

"Well, here you are, all tanned and with those blue eyes and white teeth and a nice smile; you just might sweep some unsuspecting girl off her feet."

Press turned and looked out over the water. "I'd very much like to try tonight," he said, after a long silence. "But I'd be a scoundrel to you and to the girl who's waiting for me—I hope she's waiting."

"And on top of that, an honest man. Most guys returning from the war would try to take advantage in florescent light and lose all inhibitions in moonlight."

"I guess I finally decided that when I'm old and sitting comfortably in a rocking chair—looking out at a lake—and memories crowd upon me, I don't want to be ashamed of them."

An awkward silence ensued, and she said finally, "I guess we better be getting back."

Wilson intercepted them as they approached the club. "Patrick," he yelled. "You were paged a couple of minutes ago, and I took your call. It was Celia. She's waiting for you to phone."

"Thanks, Jim."

"Don't mention it, Press."

Press turned to Carol. "Thanks for sharing some time with me. Maybe we'll run into each other in Chicago."

"Good luck to you. I hope everything turns out well."

Press changed some bills at the bar and dialed Celia's number on the pay phone. She picked up the receiver almost immediately and said, "Press?"

"Celia—yes, it's me."

"Oh, Press. I can't believe you're actually back."

"I've got to pinch myself occasionally to remind me it's true."

"When do I get to see you?"

"I'll wind-up my out-processing late tomorrow morning. There's a military flight leaving McChord tomorrow evening, arriving at Andrews at dawn on Sunday. It'll take fifteen higher ranking officers to bump me off the flight, so there should be no problem."

"Call me as soon as you arrive, and I'll come get you."

"No, no. I'll wangle a ride into town and take a taxi. If you put the coffee on at seven, it'll still be perking when I arrive. I'll call if I'm going to be any later than seven-thirty."

"I'm sorry I wasn't here when you called earlier. I went to dinner with Jim."

"That's okay, Celia. I know I've got competition."

"With all the background noise, it sounds like I might, too."

He explained how so many of his OCS classmates happened to be mustering out at the same time. "Anyway," he continued, "I've had my fill of drinking and celebrating, and it isn't really necessary. I don't think I could ever describe the feeling of euphoria. I think perhaps that when I see you, the combination will be too much for an ordinary mortal."

"Oh, Press, I still can't believe you're back. I was so worried—"

"Please deposit two dollars for three more minutes," interrupted the brittle voice of the operator.

"I'll sign off now, Celia. See you in little more than a day."

"Coffee will be on the table—and breakfast."

They rang off and Press walked back to the table, where his classmates were standing on their chairs singing boisterously and out of tune. He good-naturedly joined in, but he was right: no amount of celebration could heighten his elation. During a moment of acuity and introspection, he thought of Major Dedson. Should he thank him or curse him? Or both?

"Sir, it's time to wake up; we're landing at Andrews in a couple of minutes."

"Thanks, Sergeant," said Press, rubbing his eyes. "What time is it?"

"Oh five-forty, sir. You've had a long sleep."

Press looked around the terminal after landing, but no vehicles were going into town. Luckily, one of the air force officers was going off duty at six o'clock and offered to take him to Alexandria. After being let off at a gas station, he phoned for a taxi and at six-fifty was standing outside of Celia's apartment building. He set down his duffel bag, breathed in the warm damp air, and lolled for a minute on the tree-lined street. His thoughts went back twenty-six months, when he came here for the first time. He recalled the shuttered light of the setting sun and the way the trees elbowed each other in the gusty breeze. The leaves were fuller now, and a deeper green, and silent in the still air.

"Getting cold feet?"

He heard Celia's voice from her front window and looked up and waved. "I was trying to steady them. I'm on my way up." He threw the strap to the duffel bag around his shoulder, entered the building and bounded up the three flights of steps. She was waiting at the door. They looked at each other for a moment and embraced, then stood there for minutes holding each other, as if unable to comprehend that they were together. When they finally released, they talked volubly—Celia asking questions about his return trip, Press catching up on her activities in prior weeks. After twenty minutes, Celia asked him if he would like to go to Ft. Belvoir for Rev. Browne's nine o'clock service.

"That's a very good suggestion. I'd like to see Reverend Browne—promised him even that we'd be back to see him. And the old ladies. It'll be nice to see them too. Why don't I slip into the shower—"

"And I'll make breakfast. Bacon and eggs sound good?"

"Fantastic," he said, following her into her bedroom. "Mind if I empty my duffel bag out on your bed? I've got a change of uniform—which reminds me; this afternoon we go shopping for civvies."

She laid out a towel and washcloth for him, as he sorted his belongings on the bed. "I'll iron this for you while you're in the shower," she said, taking his folded uniform out of the room.

"Somehow, the mess hall could never capture this aroma," he said when he joined her later in the dining area.

"I know the competition's tough, but here it is, your first civilian meal since Hawaii."

They ate quickly, then drove to Ft. Belvoir, arriving a half-hour before the service. Celia parked her Volkswagen near the chapel, and they walked, hand-in-hand, to the courtyard.

He looked around, smiled and said, "I've often thought about the times we spent here. It was a sanctuary, so far removed psychologically from OCS and, like now, so peaceful and pleasant."

"I've been back here while you were away," Celia said, turning to face him. "Four times. Nobody was here and I went into the chapel—it's not kept locked—and prayed for you. I couldn't help it; I knew you were in danger, and I had these terrible forebodings, especially the last time. It was the same feeling I had before my brother was killed."

"When was your last visit?"

"It was early June, around the fifth—wait, I can tell you exactly. I remember mailing the power bill that day from here." She reached into her purse for her check book and leafed through it. "No, not the fifth, it was the second."

Press looked stunned.

"What's wrong?"

"The third in Vietnam is the second here."

"When you wrote about a place that was a source of sadness to you, did something happen there on the third?"

"Then you got my letter—why didn't you say?"

She wrinkled her nose a little and said, "Oh, I've got my reasons."

"What do you think of my plan to bring Trinh here; and eventually his family?"

"I think it's wonderful."

"You do?"

"Yes, but I think you'll need help."

"What kind of help?"

"Well, to start with, it would be helpful if you were married."

Press was stunned for the second time in less than a minute. Recovering, he reached for Celia and kissed her.

"Well, aren't you going to propose or something?" she said, after they pulled apart.

He grimaced and said, "I've been carrying an engagement ring around for over a year and now, when I need it, it's on your bed."

"No, it isn't. It's in my purse." She reached into her purse and withdrew a ring box.

He removed the ring, saying, "Marry me, Celia. Marry me."

"Oh, yes, my love, I will."

"I can't believe it; we're actually engaged. I'm dying to know: is it because I'm safely home?"

"Not at all. It's what you wrote in your last letter. After I received it Friday, I told Jim that I was going to marry you if you asked me."

"What I wrote in my—?" A look of comprehension swept over his face.

They were on time for the service. Rev. Browne smiled and nodded to them from the pulpit. The widows Whiting and Raymond beamed in delight and whispered back and forth. When the mass concluded, Press and Celia returned to the courtyard and greeted Rev. Browne and the ladies. Having seen the ring, they congratulated the couple on their engagement and asked Press when had he returned.

"Early this morning," he said.

Mrs. Raymond looked over his uniform. "I know the Army gives you ribbons for being in Vietnam."

"I saw four or five stuffed in his duffel bag—one with a star," Celia said.

"How much longer will you be on active duty?" Rev. Browne asked Press.

"Officially, three more days, then I'll be in the Reserves for a while, but for all practical purposes, I'm a—a civilian."

The widows engaged Celia in conversation about the wedding, and Press moved closer to Rev. Browne. "Celia and I would like to be married by you in the chapel. Is that possible, not being on active duty?"

"Don't worry about details, I'd be pleased to officiate. I've been wondering, though—if I could ask—if your experience changed you in a spiritual sense?"

Press pursed his lips and then nodded. "Yes, it has...yes, it has. In a way I'm confused. In another, I'm congealed." He turned and took Celia's hand. They looked at each other in a manner that made Rev. Browne and the ladies smile.

Gloria a té.

GLOSSARY

122 mm rocket   Katyusha rockets were a popular and effective NVA/ VC weapon during the war. They had a maximum range of 20 kilometers but lacked the accuracy of howitzers. Long and narrow, they could be fired singly or in multiple tubes and were highly mobile. With a delay-action fuse, a 122 could easily penetrate a bunker protected by six feet of overburden. The author had the unpleasant experience of working on a fire base near the DMZ, where hundreds of 122 mm rockets fell, some with devastating results.

201 File   Personnel file for members of all military services.

3.2 Beer   Lower alcohol beer available in Vietnam to US servicemen, subject to ration card limits. The author consumed a can or two of 3.2 beer daily, preferring it to sugar-based sodas or potable, but often not palatable, water.

ADM   Atomic demolitions munitions were low-yield, light-weight nuclear land mines of the Cold War era. While in his last weeks of AIT, the author was given the opportunity to guard ADMs in either West Germany or South Korea. The prospect of spending a winter walking in circles outdoors in South Korea dissuaded him.

AFVN   The American Forces Vietnam network, both radio and TV, was the primary source for news and entertainment. TV shows were mainly re-runs from the early 1960s.

Agent Orange   Aerial herbicide sprayed over much of Vietnam from 1965-71. Maps show that it was sprayed in the mountains of the two most northern provinces, but the only evidence of it was a smaller than what-you-would-expect bird population and some defoliated treetops in the second or third canopy. The author drank freely from mountain springs without ill-effect.

AIT   Advanced Individual Training. AIT was an eight-week specialized (MOS) course following basic training.

AK-47   Kalashnikov assault rifle used by NVA/VC forces. Although less accurate than the M-16, it was far more reliable.

AO   Area of operations.

APC   Armored personnel carrier. APC crewman was the occupational specialty with the highest KIA rate in the war. APCs were highly susceptible to RPGs and land mines.

Arty   Short for artillery.

ARVN   Army of the Republic of Vietnam. In the author's opinion, the allies would have prevailed had the *ARVN* come close to matching the discipline and fighting qualities of the NLF(Viet Cong)/NVA.

AVLB   Armored Vehicle Launched Bridge. An AVLB is a folding, 60-foot portable bridge mounted on an M-60 tank chassis.

Azimuth   Used in map reading, it is the angle formed between a reference direction (north) and a line from an observer to a point of interest on the same plane. The author had little difficulty plotting location coordinates, etc., during training. The mountainous jungle of Vietnam was a different matter. At dawn on the first day of a major operation of the war, he displeased his battalion commander by misstating his position by several kilometers.

Bangalore torpedo   Extendable sections of pipe fitted together manually, filled with explosives and used to take out minefields and other obstacles. Combat engineers would push the segments (the first having a nose cone) forward on the minefield ground. The author can attest to this being a nerve-testing procedure, as the accidental setting-off of a mine, even forty feet away, would detonate the entire torpedo.

BCT   Basic Combat Training, the Army's introductory eight-week course. During the winter of 1969-70, the author was the officer-in-charge of a hand grenade range, witnessed the detonations of perhaps 200,000 fragmentation grenades and was amazed that not one exploded prior to its 4.5 seconds fuse-burn time. Not so amazing (having been through BCT during the winter at Fort Dix, N.J.) was how quickly a trainee, bundled-up and sitting on a bleacher in freezing weather, could nod-off.

Beanhead   Many different derogatory terms were used by OCS upperclassmen to berate first-term candidates. Beanhead (a bald head) was the most popular in the author's OCS company.

Blitz cloth   Along with Brasso, the Blitz cloth was used to polish brass, mainly belt buckles.

BOQ   Bachelor Officer Quarters. A married officer traveling single could also stay in a BOQ.

C-130   Four engine turbo-prop transport plane—the aerial workhorse of the war.

C-4   Plastic explosive that could be molded to fit most any shape. It was detonated by inserting (very carefully) a blasting cap, set-off either electrically or by a burning fuse. C-4 was an engineer's constant companion, for in some missions destruction rivaled building. While operating in the field, soldiers used C-4 for making coffee and heating C-rations.

CH-54 Skycrane   Heavy-lift (20,000 lb.) helicopter with a skeletal design. During operation Dewey Canyon II, the CH-54 carried the heavy materials of war to locations along Route 9 and on to Khe Sanh. The author experienced the wash of a CH-54 while releasing a bridge it was carrying—a memory still vivid.

Charlie   A nickname for a VC/NVA soldier, from the phonetic Victor Charlie (VC).

Chinook   The CH-47 Chinook was used both as a transport helicopter and a troop carrier by the Army.

CID   Criminal Investigation Division.

Claymore   Antipersonnel mine shaped in a 60 degree arc. It used C-4 to scatter 700 ball bearings to the front. It could be detonated electrically or by pulling on a cord. The author's platoon set out claymores when making night defensive perimeters, using a battery, a trip wire connected to a plastic spoon, which separated two electrically wired popsicle sticks (one connected to the battery, one to the claymore). If the tripwire was disturbed, the spoon would slip away and current would flow to the detonator. No NVA ever accepted the invitation.

CO   Commanding officer.

Composition B   A high explosive used in fragmentation hand grenades, shape charges, artillery, and various other munitions.

Convergence Theory   Semi-popular during the middle Cold War years (esp. 1960s), the theory predicted the eventual convergence of the political systems of the US and the USSR into a democratic socialism.

CP   Command post.

C-rations   Canned food consumed in the field. "C-rats" were filling rather than tasty and came in a fairly large variety of meals with fruits and dessert, cigarettes, etc. The author feels sorry (40+ years later) for pawing through C-ration cartons in search of ham and "eggs," spaghetti and meat-balls, and pound cake. Unlike infantry, who had to "hump" with a seventy-pound rucksack, engineers could stockpile enough food in their vehicles to feed an army.

CS Grenade   A tear gas grenade.

CYA   Cover your ass. There may be some reader, somewhere, unfamiliar with this term.

Det-cord   C-4 explosive in the form of a rope. Det-cord was used for many purposes, e.g., severing a tree trunk or linking various objects together to be blown-up simultaneously, using one blasting cap.

Deuce-and-a-half   2.5 ton truck used mainly to carry troops and supplies.

Dink   Derogatory name for a Vietnamese.

DMZ   Demilitarized Zone. The DMZ was located at the 17ᵗʰ Parallel in Vietnam, separating the North and the South. The author once took a short "sightseeing" trip to FSB A-4 on the southern edge of the DMZ to view the outsized flag of the Peoples' Republic of North Vietnam.

DMZ-Dustoff   The medevac unit operating in the two northern provinces of South Vietnam.

DOD   Department of Defense.

Dung Lai   The command to "halt" in Vietnamese.

EOD   Explosive Ordnance Division. It had few members but a high casualty rate. The loudest laugh of the author in his year in Vietnam came when an EOD team detonated a 5,000 gal. fuel truck a couple of days after it rolled off of Route 9 during a night convoy, coming to rest forty feet below in the dying cockroach position. The blast sent the rear duals (tires) carriage up in a perfect parabolic arc, landing in the Da Krong river. The fuel failed to ignite.

FEBA   Acronym for Forward Edge of the Battle Area. After OCS the author never gave it another thought.

Fragging   An attempt to kill a member of your own side, normally an officer or NCO, by throwing a fragmentation grenade, usually in or under his billet. The author witnessed an unsuccessful fragging incident aimed at a CID warrant officer.

FSB   Fire support base.

Full bird   Slang for full colonel, derived from the rank insignia (eagle).

Guidon   Military standard that represents and is a symbol of a unit, e.g., a company. The guidon bearer and the commander lead the unit in parades and on marches.

Ho Chi Minh Trail   The area of Laos and Cambodia adjacent to South Vietnam down which the NVA sent troops and materiel.

Hootch Slang for a billet or for distilled spirits, depending on the context.

Huey UH-1, single rotor helicopter. Gunship, medevac, troop assault craft, etc. Hueys were ubiquitous and emblematic of the war. The author only had two short trips on one. The first involved boarding a hovering Huey from the headboard of a five ton truck.

INS Immigration and Naturalization Service.

JP-4 Type of aviation fuel. Ignition was much easier than for diesel fuel, so the author gave a wide berth to trucks carrying JP-4 while traveling in mortar-range areas.

Klick Short for kilometer, .62 of a mile. The military uses the metric system, with some off-hand interspersion of the English system.

KP Kitchen police. In the first of three times pulling KP duty, the author was caught in the middle of a hard roll fight between two cooks in a mess hall and beaned once in the head.

Lifer Derogatory term for a career soldier.

Lock and load The derivation comes from firing ranges, meaning to chamber a round in an assault rifle. Euphemistically, it had various meanings, e.g., an imperative to get ready to move out; to understand an order or some information.

LRP Long range patrol.

LZ Landing zone for helicopters.

M-14 American assault rifle used in Vietnam during the early part of the war. It was gradually replaced by the M-16.

M-16 American assault rifle introduced during the war. It was notorious for jamming in combat conditions.

M4T6 Bridge Easily airlifted bridge frame and components could be assembled in a short time (single span of approximately 23 feet).

M-60 Machine gun issued to practically every platoon in the field. Weighing almost 19 pounds, it was usually carried by one of the biggest members of the platoon.

Medevac Medical evacuation by helicopter, normally a Huey, during the war.

MI Military Intelligence.

Minderbinder Milo Minderbinder is a major character in Joseph Heller's great satirical novel of World War Two, *Catch-22*. A war profiteer without a conscience, Minderbinder is a symbol of the military-industrial complex. The author experienced an event consistent with the "your own side is trying to get you killed" supposition in the novel. A single US artillery round detonated on his jobsite while he was there on a rained-out workday. One of two nearby fire support bases fired the round but claimed not to be at fault because of the "courtesy clearance" given to it by the other fire base. For the remaining eight months of his time in-country, the author heeded Heller's message.

MOS   Military Occupational Specialty, e.g., infantry, artillery, armor, engineer, signal, transportation.

Nash   In 1953, Nash introduced the Airliner model, which featured seats that could be fully reclined into twin beds in 30 seconds. This, coupled with the halcyon years of the drive-in movie theater, augmented the baby boom.

NCO   Non-commissioned officer.

NDP   Night defensive perimeter.

OCS   Officer Candidate School.

OD   Olive drab, the predominant color in the Army, but often used as a euphemism for the Army.

Ops   Operations.

OR   On report.

PIO   Public Information Officer.

Pogey bait   Any unauthorized food in OCS.

Port arms   Carry position of the assault rifle, centered on the chest, normally used while double-timing (running) or during inspections.

Pos   Position/location. Used mainly in radio transmissions, e.g., "What's your pos, over?"

POV   Privately owned vehicle.

PRC-25   Standard issue radio for all allied units in Vietnam. It weighed 20 pounds and was carried by a radio operator (RTO). Every jeep was also equipped with a PRC-25 with a long antenna. Although the range of communication was adequate, operating in valleys surrounded by hills reduced reception.

Profile   Medical release from duty or regulation, e.g., a facial skin rash may result in a release from shaving.

PT   Physical training.

Ranger helicopter   Single rotor helicopter used to ferry field grade officers, mainly battalion commanders.

Respighi   Ottorino Respighi, a 20th Century Italian composer, wrote the *Pines of Rome*, a tone poem with an ever-louder finale evoking a Roman legion marching along the Apian Way into Rome. The author's many references to (and interest in) classical music originated from his dad's many years of playing in the Racine (Wis.) Symphony Orchestra.

Right Guard   A Gillette deodorant popular in the 1960s.

Route 1   The major highway in Vietnam, a coastal route linking major cities, running north-south, paved two-lane.

Route 9   Runs east-west from Dong Ha to Laos. The road was paved west to Vandegrift. By early 1971, the road was overgrown and the bridges destroyed from Vandegrift to the Laotian border.

RPG   Rocket propelled grenade. Fired by a single soldier, it could penetrate light armor; e.g., APCs and Sheridan tanks. RPGs were used effectively by the VC and NVA.

RVN   Republic of Vietnam (South Vietnam).

S-3   Battalion operations. S-1was administration, S-2 intelligence, S-4 equipment.

Satchel Charge   An explosive device in a satchel popular with NVA/VC sappers.

Sheridan Tank   M551 Sheridan was a light, mobile tank with speeds up to 45 mph. It could be dropped by parachute and was amphibious for short distances. It's thin skin was easily breached by rocket propelled grenades and land mines.

Short-timer   Although there is no specific number of days remaining in one's tour to be considered "short," under 30 days would be universally recognized as short during a 12-month tour in a combat zone. In Vietnam, most soldiers would begin to take more safety precautions as they became "short." Some experienced deleterious psychological changes.

Sit-rep   Situation report.

Smack   Slang for heroin.

SOI   Signal operating instructions. A frequently published booklet listing friendly radio frequencies.

SOP   Standard operating procedure.

Spec 4   Specialist four rank (E-4), one grade lower than a sergeant, same as corporal (a seldom used rank).

Spider hole   A hole in the ground just deep and wide enough for a soldier to hide in, usually covered with vegetation. It could be used as a sniper position or a recon.

STRAC   Popular Army acronym in the Vietnam War era: Strategic, Tough, Ready Around the Clock. A *STRAC* soldier had the appearance and demeanor of a first-rate serviceman. In colloquial terms, he had "his shit together."

TDY   Temporary duty.

TO&E   Table of organization and equipment. Every unit in the army had a specific TO&E. You could look up any unit's org chart, manpower requirements, and equipment. At least on paper. The author's platoon in Vietnam was never at full manpower strength.

TOC   Tactical operations center. In the author's experience, the TOC was a well protected underground bunker on a fire support base.

Two-twelve   Refers to the provision of the Uniform Code of Military Justice under which a member can be involuntarily separated from the military. It was not an easy task and most units preferred a transfer to initiating 2-12 procedures. The author, during a stateside training assignment, tried unsuccessfully to two-twelve an incompetent subordinate, a buck sergeant who refused to make car payments on his new Plymouth Fury or provide support for his estranged 16-year-old wife and infant son. The Red Cross would phone the author several times per week to complain. Higher command would not support the author's months-long effort, but instead transferred the miscreant to another unit, which did separate him from service.

VC   Viet Cong were indigenous South Vietnamese members of the National Liberation Front.

Vil   Abbreviation for village.

XO   Executive officer.

Weathermen   Also known as Weather Underground. Domestic anti-war terrorist organization in the US from 1969 to the late '70s.

A Note on Generals: General officers have been at times lampooned or denigrated as "political" in various media. My experience with the few I met generated only respect. Brig. Gen. Preer was the model for the general who visited Press's hand grenade range. Brig. Gen. Sweeney appears in the novel. Brig. Gen. Sidney Berry, traveling in a jeep on a jungle road in Vietnam, stopped to chat at a worksite. After being warned of the dangers of driving to the mountaintop fire base (most senior officers would take helicopters), he waved it off and proceeded. Gen. Raymond Davis (Asst. Commandant of the Marine Corps) attended the dedication of a children's hospital the Marines built and my platoon did the finishing touches on in Quang Tri. He was wearing a bandage on his right hand, and when I idiotically gave it a firm shake, perhaps looking at his Medal of Honor ribbon, no hint of a grimace crossed his face.